C000241656

PIANO ANGEL

Esther Woolfson

TWO RAVENS
PRESS

Published by Two Ravens Press Ltd.
Green Willow Croft
Rhiroy, Lochbroom
Ullapool
Ross-shire IV23 2SF

www.tworavenspress.com

The right of Esther Woolfson to be identified as author of this work has been asserted by her in accordance with the Copyright, Designs and Patent Act, 1988. © Esther Woolfson, 2008.

ISBN: 978-1-906120-34-4

British Library Cataloguing in Publication Data: a CIP record for this book can be obtained from the British Library.

All rights reserved. No part of this publication may be reproduced, stored in a retrieval system, or transmitted in any other form or by any means, electronic, mechanical, photocopying, recording or otherwise without the prior written permission of the publishers. This book may not be lent, hired out, resold or otherwise disposed of by way of trade in any form of binding or cover other than that in which it is published, without the prior consent of the publishers.

Designed and typeset in Sabon by Two Ravens Press.
Cover design by David Knowles and Sharon Blackie.

Printed on Forest Stewardship Council-accredited paper by Biddles Ltd., King's Lynn, Norfolk.

Mixed Sources
Product group from well-managed forests, controlled sources and recycled wood or fiber
www.fsc.org Cert no. TT-COC-002303
© 1996 Forest Stewardship Council
FSC

The publisher gratefully acknowledges subsidy from the Scottish Arts Council towards the publication of this volume.

Scottish
Arts Council

About the Author

Esther Woolfson was born in Glasgow. She studied at Edinburgh and the Hebrew University of Jerusalem, and has a degree in Chinese. Her short stories have been broadcast by the BBC and published in many collections. She has received two writers' bursaries from the Scottish Arts Council. A non-fiction account of living with birds, *Corvus*, was recently published by Granta.

For more information about the author, see
www.tworavenspress.com

Chapter 1

Glasgow, late autumn, 2001

I walk towards the steps of the house and it's with the same anticipation, the same apprehension, as if I'll always do this now, walk towards this house, unlock the door, be forever on the point of calling my brother's name. As I approach, he's still here, fixed in that state beyond time, waiting. I see myself approaching, carrying things in my arms, calling, and I might be in a photograph, one of my own, one of the ones I've taken of places of loss all over the world, on which I've built my life.

For the last weeks, I always knew Mark would be here, waiting. He may not have been waiting but it felt as if he was. It may only have been that I wanted him to be.

I walk in but there's none of the incurious stillness of an empty house. On the contrary, restlessness seems to blink from unseen corners, nothing as prosaic as a presence, perhaps just a space of heightened consciousness, one of the things you experience after a death, indeterminate, not quite the sound of a voice out of earshot, the movement of light on glass, unexplained and inexplicable but there, a sense of lingering, coordinates which lead to a place we cannot know, signs picked by grieving minds from the air, from nothing, from the feeling that it's impossible for all that to be gone.

I close the door. This time I'm not carrying much, only a carrier bag with printer ink and more envelopes for the replies I still have to write to the pile of condolence letters on my desk. I've been trying to reply as soon as they arrive but there are more every day. I have to make myself do them. My natural inclination would be to delay for a while, push them away and all the other tasks I've had to do – paying bills, informing people, all the sundry things no-one can tie up finally before they die, not even my brother, away for another and another day, claiming the exigencies of grief – but this time, I haven't. I haven't because Mark would have expected me to do just that. He didn't say so. He didn't say anything beyond,

'You will see to it, won't you?' and I knew that in this way, he was urging me to be not like me, but like him. A *mensch*. He was. I often

1

find myself using the word without thinking and then I have to explain it, with all its implications of rectitude and dignity. Remarkably few words in Yiddish can be explained by a single corresponding word. 'A person,' I usually say, 'who does the right thing.' Really, he was a *mensch*. I'm pleased, more than grateful to admit this now.

The rooms change with the light, the walls. I walk through the sitting room and watch late afternoon slide from the plaster wings of the angel we brought here, stippling her feathers, darkening the line of her limbs. I see the languid coolness of the way she trails her bare feet, lightly. Another moment of change, of convergence, hanging the angel. Mark directed operations from his chair. I was impressed by how organised I'd been, all the appropriate fixings from the hardware shop laid out, drill, hammers, plumb line. I'd even asked permission from the youth at the estate agent.

'I'll make good any damage to the wall, although I don't think there'll be much,' I said. 'My brother has had a look at it and says the wall's strong enough. I think I said, he's an architect.'

'That shouldn't be a problem, sir,' the boy said, 'as long as it's done properly. It's people putting things up with blu-tack that causes the most damage.'

He'd probably have objected if he hadn't been quite so eager for one or other of us to buy the place when the lease is up. He's amiable enough but I find talking to him slightly depressing. It's the words he uses, stiff and sucked of life: *properties, features, amenities, prestigious*.

It took the best part of the afternoon to hang the angel. She's heavy in her gilded frame. We started to laugh early on and couldn't stop, it felt so ridiculous: Mark giving out orders like a potentate on his throne, my quick assumption of the role of vassal, the way that afterwards we both acknowledged wordlessly that we had slipped a stage further into the intimacy we thought we'd never have.

I still find myself invoking the weight of Mark's head on my arm. Latterly, it felt light although of course it wasn't. Its weight could stop my blood until the ends of my fingers tingled, which happened first, before they began to hurt, before they progressed to numbness and then the shutting-off of all feeling which I'd endure for an hour, an hour and a half at a time, not wanting to disturb him. To this day

I've never lost the sensation of the warmth, the texture of his scar under my fingers that morning at Ellis Island and I'll never lose it now. Both sensations hung on my fingers, never receding so that I still look at my hand as if something communicated itself then, a knowledge which I had to learn and assimilate through his fine sprinkling of hair, through that healing fissure in his skull.

After that day I often thought of Ellis Island, our time there, but now I can hardly bear to go back to it in my mind, knowing how it must have changed, everything I've held in my memory since altered or ruined, lying still under a few week's weight of terrible dust. Such fresh destruction, too much to think of, a labyrinth of grief. I'm glad Mark never knew. At the time, keeping it from him felt wrong, duplicitous, although in the end it was only for a matter of days.

I go into the kitchen and put the coffee machine on. It's one Mark bought, complaining about the instant stuff I always used to drink,

'How can you touch that crap?' he said. He bought the machine and just as I always watched him do in his kitchen in New York, demonstrated the preparation of coffee as ceremony, as sacred rite. He did it here for as long as he could and then I took over. I've begun to do it too, exactly the same, all the measuring out and respectful hovering.

I look out of the window. It's raining. The afternoon's begun to close round. It gets dark early now. The clocks'll go back soon; the official embrace of winter will have begun. I'm glad I'm back here in Glasgow. For years, all the time I was a child, I used to pretend it was somewhere else. I remember how I always used to dread leaving the intense unreality of a cinema, knowing I'd experience the moment of return to everyday life as a painful disappointment, but now I feel an equanimity about it – more than that, something closer to love.

The headlights from the late afternoon traffic have begun to illuminate the drops on the window, spraying them in wide fans of light. I still feel myself growing tense as it darkens, even though I remember that I don't need to any longer, that dark or light, it doesn't matter any more. For a while, it was easier for Mark when it was dark, but the fact of its being so made us both think about how dark it would be soon and because of it, I dreaded the shortening of the days. Every change in the weather – the cold wind in June, a couple of grey days in July – was difficult, another phase passing, a time ending. A function closing down, irreversibly gone. After the summer, the days were eaten up so soon. By then, the light hurt his eyes so that the darkness was almost welcome. Almost. The street lights would come on. He'd light candles in containers of frosted glass as if every moment of light was a celebration. His hand began to shake last May. I pretended until June that I didn't notice.

I take my coffee, sit in the armchair by the window. I'm still here, in this flat. I'm here only because I haven't been able to think without panic and fear about handing it back. I don't want to imagine the moment of locking the door for the last time. I'll consider it all soon. People try to give me advice, truisms, that these things take time, that it's only sensible to wait a little before deciding. Should I leave, I think of the angel and the piano and the company of small ghosts who will assemble in my wake to follow me.

A reviewer said once of an exhibition of mine that I'm a photographer of ghosts. I am, he said, the antithesis of the war photographer. I wait, he said, until there's nothing there but ghosts. I'm still not sure if he meant it as a compliment.

In the last photograph I took of him, Mark has his hand raised to his eyes. He's smiling in the sunshine. That day, at the last moment, he lifted his hand. It looks ordinary enough, that photograph, not the last one that would ever be taken of him. His hand blurs there, a flash of whiteness and it makes him look as if he's gesturing, warding off the blow of light. I didn't take any of him later, although the thought of an exhibition did occur to me. Portraits of an illness. He'd have said,

'Oh fuck it, Dan, some people would try to make a cheap cent out of anything,' and we'd have laughed, but I didn't anyway.

There was never any real doubt, not from the beginning. Although we used the words of reassurance to one other that people use at these times, any hope we held was kept unspoken in the depth of our minds in spite of the fact that we both knew the tumour in his brain was one which would grow and keep on growing. From that first phone call two years ago in November, I knew. In that moment, I knew just as he did, and felt that evening the inescapable substance of it and of what we'd have to say to one another one day; the names we'd have to speak.

I have a sense of regaining the past in a way I can't explain. Past becoming future, ordinary things illumined, lightning flashes from a fathomless sky, as well as the ones people readily call history. What

I do know is that the dead don't just go away. They open doors and whisper names. They loom from their place like sirens on their rocks, beckoning with long, long fingers. But now, I just think of him, of what he told me I must do. I think of the lamp which I haven't got round to switching on yet, and of how he'd laugh at me for sitting here in near-darkness, his voice pinning me with practised accuracy.

'Ah, a temporary flicker in a dark cosmos.' His voice from across an ocean. At this time of day in New York we'd be out, impatient, seeking as he is, was, both of us ambling through the dusk crowds on Fifth Avenue as we loved to do, his hand extending towards my sleeve, gripping it with the perennial, winning excitement of his life.

'Look!' he's saying, indicating something or someone I can't quite see, towards which I turn quickly, holding my breath, in the grip of his hand, and in his voice that urgency which tells me that this is a chance I might miss and if I do, I'll have missed it forever.

'Look!' he's saying, 'Dan, quick, look!'

Chapter 2

New York, November, 1999

Walking up the three terrazzo steps to ground level, Mark Blum reaches an oblique, unremarkable point where darkness and light become indistinguishable, where in combination they catch at him for a moment to stop him from seeing clearly the way he should turn, how the light shines down the corridor, the pale glow of the street, of outside. He turns, looks back down the cavernous split of carpets and doorways, turns again. A broken line of fear pierces him, enters the stream of his blood, interrupts its flow, lies on his skin, cold, then hot.

'Let me out of here,' he says aloud to the empty space. Thin, changed light fills the corridor, a new light, the light which now, he thinks, will always be like this.

The watered white blur of outside makes him breathe more deeply, slowly, as he moves towards it. It leads him, draws him on through a broad doorway into the cool, glazed hall. A tall doorman steps out. He is young, a dark bulk which moves forward, in front of him. He speaks words to Mark as he pulls open then holds the heavy glass door which separates those inside from the unrelenting roar outside. Mark smiles, nods, replies before he walks through the door into the street.

The afternoon is grey, drizzling, hazed with damp and traffic and moving headlights. Hesitating for a moment, he begins to walk down the avenue towards the office. He wraps his scarf more firmly round his neck, draws his coat around himself, wondering if everything is zipped and buttoned and tied as it's meant to be. It must be. He'd feel the cold on his skin if it wasn't. Something would feel loose or fall down. Things would flap, feel uncomfortable, asymmetrical. He can feel Dr Jaegerson's cool hands on his skin.

He isn't sure how long he has spent in there. Half an hour? An hour? Looking at his watch, he notices that the angle of his hands creates a falling image, a slam or a fluttering towards earth. Wings, hands folding, a move unstoppably downwards. Twenty past four. It has a quality. Beauty. It has certainty too, momentary and passing but certain. He has never noticed it before. Mark realises that he will see things altered now. A world changed. A bus sign looms at him: *Lonnigan's buses. The civilized commute.*

From now on, all will be different. It will etch or cut or dazzle. It will leave an imprint and its own particular memory behind. Everything. He will never be blank again, never be unreceptive, free.

As he walks he's aware that it has already happened, that there has been no transition, no slow move towards change and now the cold, the rain, the cloud, the trees on the other side of the avenue drift from all he has felt about them before, or indeed, about anything. They sharpen and concentrate, arrow themselves razor-thin to pierce him as he passes by, under, through their vapour and shadow. Remaining daylight falls in threads towards the sidewalk.

Today is ordinary. An ordinary, chill November day. He stops for a moment, walks on. He feels love for November, for rain haze, chill afternoons, for twenty past four. The sweetness of day, this day, any day, all the strength and power dredged up to him from the gutter water and mailboxes, the slick panels of passing cars, their wet tyres, shiny, spotted windows. The face of the youthful doorman only now becomes clear in his mind, too late, ringed as it was with a pure and matchless innocence. His deep, soft voice is still saying words to him, *good afternoon, goodbye sir, a cold day today, goodbye sir.*

The voice continues in his head. It soothes him, becomes absorbed into the net of his thoughts. He has no memory of going into the building. He must have passed through its smart, unremarkable hall, given his name, waited. He sees distantly in his own writing on a diary page: *Jaegerson, 2.30.*

He thinks about Jaegerson. A dull little prick. Mark smiles at the obvious childishness of his response. Would he have used those words about him had the news been other than it was? Probably. He's a type Mark dislikes, a tight, watchful little – what? German? Austrian? He doesn't know. You can't always tell from names, not here. There is the suggestion of an accent, the careful words of a language learned just too late for perfect fluency. Mark cannot tell and does not know, therefore, exactly where to direct his dislike. He has tried to dispel it but retains his own hierarchy of prejudice. Jaegerson has told him nothing he did not know already. He is not a self-deluder, not a man to mistake the signs, and now he can be almost impressed by his deductive power and diagnostic ability. He wonders if he ever

7

considered, even momentarily, a career in medicine and thinks what he might have thought then, of those intimate dealings with stomachs, urinary tracts and of course, brains. Probably he did, at least once or twice, but dismissed the idea. Just as well. He wouldn't have been good with those aspects of humanity. Walls and heating systems and the ways light shines through space are the things he understands. He thinks of Jaegerson, like a dry-as-dust cleric, Jesuitical, knowing, poised like an intermediary between himself and this hollow place of knowledge, the sight of his own scanned skull, the predictable beauty of outline, slices of bone and space, patches of light blossoming among the black and grey of an indecipherable map of symbols in which he could see, unaccountably, the wings of butterflies and tightly curled roses, thinking only of that as Jaegerson pointed out, explained what, in other words, he already knew.

Mark's placing of his own feet on the familiar pavement seems different. There is a consciousness in his limbs, the joints of his hips, the imperceptible tap of his heels touching down. Do your heels touch down when you walk? He reflects on this, slows his pace, ponders the actions of his heels, resolutely aware now of every movement of his body, the slight weakness and pain in one thigh, the residue of a long-ago skiing accident, the only reason he has ever before been in hospital. He thinks about his insurance, this worst, most expensive of events. It is not an event. It is a – what? Mark cannot think of a word. The voice picks up, carries on, the smile which seemed kind, *good afternoon sir, goodbye sir, take care.* There seemed more in his voice than his words. The boy must know that many of the people who walk through his politely opened door are newly, freshly doomed.

The rest of the day swings suddenly beyond his reach. Morning has moved incomparably far away, evening too distant to see easily. There is only this, lights blazing, breaking against his eyes. You can't do this, he thinks, raising his hand to his eyes for a moment, you can't do this, bastards, shine your headlights straight towards me like this, I'm ill. I have a tumour in my brain. *Sir,* the voice says, soothing. *Sir.* Ill. An idea. Only an idea. Malfunctioning, like some damned computer. He is glad he didn't say as much to Jaegerson. No, no, not at all like a computer, Jaegerson would have said, not at all like a computer, his face crunched into a little whorl of disdain. A computer we take away, open, replace one part with another. Unfortunately, illness is not like that. Mark knows it. He begins to feel the dangerous, softening quality of it, as if he has begun to make excuses for himself.

The city this afternoon is half-disappeared into mist and rain. It is what happens at this time of the year. The top of the city is engulfed into the ether, blanked off, lights glowing phosphorescent, haloed, helpless and drowning behind the mist until they too are engulfed.

He will not go back to work yet. Later, but not yet. He will go to one of the places he often goes at this time of day. Usually, he is meeting someone or preparing to work late. This time, alone, he will sit for a few moments and by so doing, replace himself into the indelible framework of his life. He walks toward the windows and lights of his favourite coffee house and turns in off the street. He finds a seat by the window but hesitates before sitting down. He is bound to see people he knows. He is bound to anywhere, not only here. He sits down. He places the large envelope containing his scans on the chair next to him. He turns it face down so that the words *X-ray film. Please do not bend* cannot be seen. It is a popular place, one where people look in and look out. They gaze from either side of the window, wave, gesticulate silently through the glass. Often, a friend will break off from an intended route and come in, as he does himself, weaving though the closeness of tables and waiters and stands of fancy breads. It is a place where business is done, future promises made, ideas presented, pieces of gossip handed out as prizes. He thinks that he wants to have this time alone but cannot stop himself from looking out of the window. Company might not be so bad. He wonders if he will say anything. It will depend on who is first to appear, which one from among his numerous acquaintance. What will he say? He practises a few words but by so doing, has already removed all possibility of spontaneity. He will say nothing.

About this morning, he has no regrets. There will be no other morning when he was as he was this morning. Knowledge alters time. Confirmation alters time. A tremor of his hand causes the menu card he is holding to waver the columns of words and numbers into a liquid, a moving mirror of printed flow. Coffees and wines and waters toss, meld, blur. He puts the card down. He doesn't need it anyway. He looks up towards the girl already standing waiting by the table. He gives his order, the same one as always, to the girl who leans a little towards him. She knows him. She asks if she can get him anything else. She is tall, thin, dark-haired.

'No, thank you,' he says and she bends her head in accord. Mark sees in the gesture a separation between him and her. It is a separation of expectation, her life still there, carried with her, rich, alluvial. He feels stationary and fixed. He is the silent centre of a world already moving on.

Even thinking of this morning and indeed the preceding days, Mark has a sense of sorrow, unfocused, as if for someone else, a person in the news perhaps, someone he doesn't know but whose situation is universal, poignant, worthy of sympathy. Himself on the last morning of what? Pre-lapsarian bliss? This is not so. He knows it isn't. He recalls the care with which he showered, dressed, how he chose a shirt which would suggest sobriety, taste, but not too much wealth, how he chose socks and underwear and anything else which would be appropriate for the soured gaze of Jaegerson. How he had felt the leaden drag of it.

'Boy, you for it,' he'd said to himself in the mirror. He had known. There never was innocence or shock or disbelief since the first sign, the first indication. He knew. He has never understood the people he hears saying, 'I didn't think it would happen to me,' 'It's the kind of thing that happens to other people.' If not you, then who? he always wants to shout. Why not you? What makes you think you might have been immune? Immune from harm, immune from the world, immune from the blatant act of being human. If at any moment, Mark thinks, you can say, ' I didn't ever think it wouldn't happen to me,' you have fulfilled an important duty towards humanity, that of listing yourself firmly among its members, fallible as they are, vulnerable. Nothing has changed, there is no shock and no surprise.

His coffee, when it appears, tastes more of itself than he could have imagined. It is a taste to be remembered, complex and redeeming. *Goodbye sir, sir, take care*, the words soothe him. They seem to him inexplicably understanding, profound.

Evening next. He has postponed the meeting with the man who requires a remodelling of his apartment to befit a new, improved alteration in status, until tomorrow. He has been organised. He has anticipated. His mind is filled suddenly with new responsibilities, who he must tell, inform, advise and he sees the ripples of his telling spreading outwards on the still surface of water, which will swell to become a tide, one which will end by covering the earth. He catches the eye of the young waitress and by a series of measured nods and smiles, secures her agreement to bring another cup of coffee.

For the moment, he wishes nothing but to sit between indeterminate points of this day. He wishes he were a child again, not for the added years, a hapless winding back, but for the ability to see time, to be aware in that uniquely accepting way that time is slow, endless carpets of it before you, rolled tight. When you were four or five, what did a day mean, a week? An eternity of longing spun out in formless expectation, a delay till evening, a delay in the very processes of the universe. When did it start, the notation, the too-fast click, click, click of the meter? He avoids looking at his watch. He has learned from twenty past four. He wants to avoid the pattern the hands might offer, the inexorability of supplication, the muteness of fixity, the self-abnegation of hands flung wide. He guesses by the rush and stir outside that he has been here for longer than he thought. He could stay, sit, order a glass of wine. Jaegerson said nothing about what he should do or should not do, drink or run or smoke or make love, nothing and he knows that it is because nothing will make any difference, not even Jaegerson's little waiting knife. Still, he can hear Jaegerson's tight, narrow-lipped drone, 'I advise you to abjure all alcohol,' but he hasn't said it and now, Mark has no way of being defiant. He only has ways of carrying on like this, sitting, undecided, knowing that whatever he does, even if he does it slowly, very slowly, the day will catch him, time will catch him, reality will have its way and he will have to go home. He will have to walk the few blocks to where he lives, draw out keys, exchange greetings with another doorman and possibly a few predestined words on some current matter. He will have to press elevator buttons and open doors. He will have to re-enter what has already become an old life. And then, he will have to begin phoning. He will have to tell people, his family, his friends, ex-wives, those whose lives will be changed by the mass of cells dividing wantonly in his brain. He will have to make the thing real, declare it absolute.

The new cup of coffee steams. It appears to him to have been prepared with special care for him. He smiles at the young waitress.

'What a day,' she says mournfully. 'I hate it when you can't see the sky.'

'Have you had classes today?' He remembers that she's studying somewhere nearby.

'Today, no. De Soto's away. No Renaissance or Etruscan for a week. He does both, you know. They're the ones I like best.' She puts on a doleful face.

'I'm sorry your week's spoiled,' he says. She smiles at him, as if she's grateful for his sympathy. 'I'll manage,' she says and walks away. He sees their conversation as the foundations of a wall which has begun to exist between him and other people. It is not that their concerns, her very reasonable, indeed praiseworthy regret at missing her favourite classes for a week, are trivial or without merit or even absurd. It is only that now, their concerns exist in different worlds.

He thinks again of being lost in the corridors of Jaegerson's office. Perhaps the experience should be seen as a metaphor for his being lost, for an unrecognised inability to find his way. The idea seems ridiculous and anyway, he can't allow himself metaphors. Everyone gets lost, takes one or another wrong turning into darkness, into an unmarked corridor which they realise they have never been in before. He has the urge to lay his head on the table, an urge he resists. He knows that time has become alien, and that the earth upon which he is obliged to walk is a place which has sudden edges, abrupt, malign drops unsignalled by the signs reading *Danger!* so beloved of cartoonists and animators, the signs noticed only by their helpless protagonists in the moment when it is too late and they are suspended absurdly for a moment over the infinity of space.

He will have to stand up soon and go. He will have to collect himself, re-order this familiar life. He will have to begin to contact people. How? He has lists of names to choose from. Will they be the same as the ones to whom he sends Christmas and birthday cards? Chanukah cards? Which will he pick this time? The sympathetic? Everyone? Relatives? Only close friends? What does he tell? The truth, or the truth as he knows of it, or partial truth? Whose business is it, after all, the progress of his mortality? Only his children? His children. Noah, Tamar. Dan, of course. His brother Dan and oh Christ, Sarah, their elderly aunt. He thinks of having to visit her to tell her. A phone call to her home for Jewish elderly in New Jersey would be impossible, fraught, laden with opportunities for misunderstanding. Does he need to tell her? In any case, what could he possibly say?

Thoughts fly through his mind, hospitals, operations, how he will be, how he will feel, knowing that it will not be easy, no, none of it will be easy. *Easy.* It is not the word to use. Other words present themselves.

'What will happen?' he seems to remember asking Jaegerson.

'Oh, it's too early to discuss that. First, we need to know a little more than we do. Let's get the surgery behind us before we move on to there.'

Us. Mark doesn't know whether to feel angry at the use of the pronoun but decides he won't. There is no point in it. They each have their predestined role in the matter and he must not attempt to deny Jaegerson his. *Us.* It's neither comforting nor alienating, it is merely a kind of truth.

He will have to tell his children, adults now but to him, still children. Where are the words with which he can soften what he has to tell them, ease them and Dan too, into this intimate knowledge with which he has lived now for weeks? It is different for him. He has woken to it daily, felt the changes in his eyes, the sensation which he cannot describe to himself, which is new, one he has never before experienced and which, despite his hoping in the early days, has not gone away, a sense that he is no longer as he should be, each movement to tell him that it is serious, profound, the words he did not need to hear from Jaegerson. What can he say? He has not been, until now, a person for whom words are elusive, and he wonders if he has ever really thought of them expressed one after the other like this, conveying this particular message and it is another reversal, another way in which he is altered. He lays the money to pay for his coffee on the small tray placed there for the purpose and stands up. He nods away the change and the girl smiles, clearly pleased.

'Good night, Mr Blum,' she says.

He will walk home. He steps from the comforting warmth and noise of the restaurant into the damp cool of softened, fracturing light in the broad avenue of cars and people. What time is it? What time will it be for Dan? Best that he should wait until later to phone so that it is evening for Dan, when it is past evening for him, already into night but when they will both have a possibly consoling drink nearby. When did he last speak to him? He thinks more of their separation in time than distance. Rosh Hashanah probably, it must have been at Rosh Hashanah. He thinks of the phone calls to Dan which he began to make a few years ago. He'd phone specially for the festivals – not all of them – Pesach, Rosh Hashanah, Chanukah. At the beginning Dan often had an air of surprise, as if he didn't know it was Chanukah or Pesach. Why should he? Here, it's inescapable, a city in which one cannot forget these dates. Or perhaps it was because it was him phoning, a trail of past angers hovering between them, unspoken. When was it exactly he began them, and why? He can't recall with any precision but it must have been at a time when he was seeking the consolation of family, after Kirstin left perhaps or when Noah left home. He phones and sings a little of one of the Pesach songs, or *Maotzur* at Chanukah. They have become his own, the festival calls, almost like a gift and after they are ended, in the lonely, heart-dropping hiatus of the moment of hanging up, he always wonders what they mean. Are they to take the place of religion? Is this what he wants to gain or provide through a momentary connection with all that finds singleness of expression in his phone call? Is it acknowledgement of a common past he seeks, a shared but unspoken yearning for the unquestioned ritual of childhood?

He can recall nothing of the last one. It can only have been a few weeks ago, a couple of months but he can't remember exactly. When was it that his symptoms began? Between then and now. The word *why* pierces through the weave of his thoughts but he picks it out entire, a word which must never be allowed, the word he despises if used in this way. There is no answer as there should be no question. Again, he knows that he believes profoundly that there are no reasons.

His feet feel oddly heavy. Is this another symptom, a new one? Will every bodily twinge or flutter be a signal or a false signal from now on? He knows it will be so.

'The brain,' Jaegerson said to him this afternoon, 'is, in many ways, still mysterious to us, Mr Blum.' It was not said in response to any question of Mark's. Did he really imagine Mark doesn't know this? Mark imagines a small checklist of pompous, physicianly phrases, one of which must, at some unimagined cost, be uttered at every consultation.

People move, cross roads, stop to look into shop displays, intent upon pursuing their own pathways and it occurs to him that each is, as he is, an isolate making a heroic journey through the haze of damp mist on Fifth Avenue. He feels a sympathy with them and for a moment, sees that they are there to help fulfil a purpose of his own which is to be able to watch and appreciate the beauty of the scene in front of him, the shapes of forms, of people's bodies, the movement of their clothes under the dark, Hiroshige print-like undulation of their umbrellas. Mark blinks, bends his head forward as the street in front of him shimmers slightly in this way which is becoming familiar. The people are still there unseen and he knows then that they are there for another purpose entirely. They are there to drive through him the knowledge that in known and finite time, they will be here and he will not.

Dr K. L. Jaegerson, Neurosurgeon
Specialties: Neuro-oncology, Endoscopic Neurosurgery
Suite 53, 43 East Reveille Avenue
New York, N.Y.

Dr J Baker, Family Physician
Suite 67, 130 Braklynn Street
New York, N.Y.

November 8th, 1999

Dear Dr Baker,

Mr Mark Blum, 25th May, 1936.

Many thanks for asking me to see your patient, Mr Blum. I saw him this afternoon and agree that he may have a cerebral tumor.

This 63-year-old architect has had no previous serious ill health. He gives a history of recurring episodes of tremor and slight clumsiness in his left hand. These symptoms are preceded by a vague sensation of unease, which lasts only for minutes. Significantly, he describes some intermittent difficulty following plans and diagrams which could reflect a lesion in the right parietal area. The history is of two months duration.

On examination, he is very fit. He has no evidence of vascular disease and I could find no localizing neurological deficit.

I agree that the history is worrying. These episodes are likely to be partial epileptic seizures and I am afraid he will prove to have a tumor in the right hemisphere. I considered the possibility that these were transient cerebral ischemic attacks but think that complex partial seizures are the more likely explanation.

I would like him to have an MRI scan which will be carried out tomorrow. I have ordered some routine blood investigations and an X-ray of the chest. The results of these investigations will be available within three days and I will arrange to review him with the results.

15

Esther Woolfson

I am grateful for your referral,
With kind regards,
K.L. Jaegerson,
Neurosurgeon.

Kelly Street Imaging Centre
MRI Report 9th November, 1999

Mr Mark Blum
d.o.b. 25th May, 1936.

Scan No. 32333

MR Brain: Axial T1 and T2 and CORONAL T1
Axial T2 post gadalinium

The scan demonstrates a lesion in the right parietal lobe. This is relatively well delineated. There is some surrounding edema but minimal mass effect. There are several small areas of cyst formation. After gadalinium there is patchy enhancement of the lesion.

The appearances are those of a primary tumor. This is likely to be an astrocytoma.

Dr O. Steel.
9th November, 1999

Dr K. L. Jaegerson, Neurosurgeon
Specialties: Neuro-oncology, Endoscopic Neurosurgery
Suite 53, 43 East Reveille Avenue
New York, N.Y.

Dr J Baker, Family Physician
Suite 67, 130 Braklynn Street
New York, N.Y.

November 12th, 1999

Dear Dr Baker,

I have the results of Mr Blum's MRI brain scan. As I suspected, he has proved to have a tumor of the right parietal lobe. This has the appearance of a relatively low-grade astrocytoma. His laboratory investigations were

16

all normal.

I have explained the findings to Mr Blum. The first requirement is to treat his seizures. I would recommend that he starts to take Phenytoin, starting at 300mg daily. I will arrange to see him again after two weeks. I believe he will require surgery followed by radiotherapy.

I will discuss the details and the risks and prognosis with him at our next meeting.

With kind regards,
K.L. Jaegerson
Neurosurgeon.

Dr K. L. Jaegerson, Neurosurgeon
Specialties: Neuro-oncology, Endoscopic Neurosurgery
Suite 53, 43 East Reveille Avenue
New York, N.Y.

Dr J Baker, Family Physician
Suite 67, 130 Braklynn Street
New York, N.Y.

November 23rd, 1999

Dear Dr Baker,

I met with your patient Mr Blum today. There have been no further seizures since his last appointment. He has suffered no side effects from Phenytoin.

We discussed the implications of his diagnosis. He is aware that there is no definite cure for this tumor. Radical surgical excision using imaging guidance followed by Radiotherapy provides the best chance of remission but there is a high rate of eventual recurrence. Of course, the prognosis depends to some extent on the histological grading.

Mr Blum and I will meet again in two weeks and I have suggested a date for surgery in three weeks time,

With kind regards,
K.L. Jaegerson
Neurosurgeon.

Chapter 3

Glasgow, late autumn, 2001

We lived here, or rather Mark lived here, from early spring this year. I can't put a time to when I did, because I came to live here in increments, a night at a time, a few books left on the desk he designated mine. The pleasure of that moment stays with me, the day Mark said,

'I've left that article on your desk for you to read' – a confirmation beyond any that once I could have dreamt of.

The piano doesn't belong to us. It was already here when we came. Mark was incredulous when he saw it because I hadn't mentioned the fact that there was one. When he walked into this room and saw it, he turned to me.

'Is that yours?' he said, unable to believe, as I was, that anyone would leave a piano of this quality behind them. Then he asked me if I'd play, his voice eager, a voice which quelled forty – more – years of a certain kind of silence. I was wary at first about playing for him, though I'd prepared myself to do it. After the first couple of times, it didn't feel any longer as if it told too much.

One corner of the stone balustrade outside the window of this room catches the wind when it blows south-west. Wind on stone, a shrill, dry howl. It's almost the sound of a voice, alive, one of the things here which enchants me, an acute reminder of the distinction between inside and out, of how evanescent safety is. I like sandstone, how it weathers and softens and shows it's already begun to revert, melt back into time. Mark liked it too, how it holds warmth, the smoothness under the faint rasp of its surface. Last spring, when he first arrived, we'd wander through the city together admiring architraves and pillars, and he'd talk about the qualities of different types of stone. On sunny days when he'd sit outside on the step, I'd look at him from where I was sitting at the piano and I'd see him stroking the stone as if it were the hand or face of a beloved person.

I've had to become more organised in the past months. I keep lists too now, things to do, things to be done. After he arrived, Mark set himself to initiating me into the art of the list. He kept every kind:

18

paper, electronic, mnemonic, random bleeps from pieces of equipment to startle him into memory.

'See, Dan,' he'd say, peering at his phone or his computer screen, 'how useful it is for reminding you' – although more often in the last few months, he forgot.

'Got the list?' he'd yell from the door before we went out. 'Don't forget the list.'

I have a list of the letters on my desk waiting for a reply, a list of papers to go to Mark's children, Noah and Tamar, the envelope already addressed, a list of documents to go to the bank and to the solicitor although he has most of them already, of bequests to deal with, of generous donations to charity. On one piece of paper I turn up from time to time when I'm trying to keep things in order is the single word *Sarah* – her presence there more symbolic than purposeful because I can't forget about her. Perhaps I should tell her about Mark's death but won't because there's no point now. I did phone the Shoshana Blumstein Home to tell the staff after I had the passing thought that one or other of the residents might see it in the papers and tell her, although from what I understand, she would no longer know who Mark was or why it should matter to her if he is dead or alive. But I thought at least that they should be prepared. Mark told her about his illness but not how serious it was.

'It's nothing, really,' he said and she was only too willing to accept that. She'd apparently forgotten all about it by the time we saw her at Ellis Island.

'Why d'you get your hair cut so short?' she kept saying to Mark, 'I don't like it.'

'Oh, it's fashion, Sarah, all the rage,' Mark replied every time and every time she simpered nervously, uncertain whether she was being humoured or teased.

Drawers, clothes, books, mostly ticked off, mostly done, only the small, stray items still to do. There hasn't been much, a lot less than people usually have to do, clearing houses and so on. Still, it's melancholy, sorting out the effects of the recently dead. I'm even not sure why I use the word *effects*, so dry and bone-ish, as if things die too and stop being what they were, as if socks don't remain essentially sock-ish after their owner's death. It's a word which contains something of the fear of revelation, the fear of the darker recesses of the ordinary. It reminds me of the story of the transvestite's mummy which Mark told me. He'd read it once in a magazine.

'Only in New York!' he said, recounting the bizarre details of the random find made by new owners in a cupboard in their apartment. He loved anything like that, any hint at the eccentricity, the dangers of the place where he'd lived for more than thirty years.

I never found anything remotely weird or interesting when I helped sort through other people's things. I helped our mother clear an elderly cousin's house once, and with friends a couple of times. The family house, too, after our father died, because I was the only one here to do it. There was never anything even mildly revelatory, only the secrets of underwear, secrets of the cough bottle. I found a few passports with their corners removed and details of foreign birthplaces I hadn't known about, ancient strands of hair in brooches or tied with ribbon, hairpins in small wooden boxes, the occasional evidence of feeling in people I'd suspected of never having any, a letter, a garish Valentine.

On the table here beside my cup there's a small, smart bottle of heavy glass. In it still is about an inch of liquid, the remains of Mark's scent. The label is handwritten, thick writing, black-nibbed on cream. Every time I look at the amber bottle and the small ellipse of fluid, I know how soon it will dry, how quickly it will revert and acquire the same dead smell to which all scent returns, the common grave of rose and musk and sandalwood. The last, sensuous aspect of Mark. I probably couldn't even buy any to replace it because it was made specially for him, to his specification, in some clever place in New York. The name's on the label on the bottle but I don't know whether, if I phoned, they'd even agree to make me up a bottle, or if both parties sign a mutually binding contract which prevents the stuff ever falling into the hands of a person for whom it wasn't concocted. What would I say, anyway? Make me up a bottle of the essence of my dead brother? I can't imagine how much it would cost. For years it used to irritate me that he could deny himself nothing, but now I take pleasure in the thought. What would I do with it, even if I could buy it? Wear it? Keep it to sniff secretly in the dead of night to cause myself to suffer? I say that as if I haven't ever done it – kept scarves or hidden pillowcases when I haven't been able to relinquish the scents of hair and body. I've stolen empty scent bottles from waste-paper baskets, and once I depleted a girlfriend's precious bottle trying to decant a few drops to carry her with me after she'd left. Two known components of nostalgia, music and scent; quick, utilitarian methods to summon pain and longing. I know because I'm an expert.

I found a couple of small pieces of jewellery in the pocket of his favourite jacket. They're here too, beside me. I assume that they belonged once to Lee and Kirstin. I wonder why he had them. There aren't any instructions about what to do with them so he probably didn't buy them recently. If he had, there'd have been cards attached to them, as to everything else he sent or left for me to send. They've been very helpful, those cards, thick and white and pierced with dark red ribbon for tying.

'This to Ed, please. I only realised I had it while I was unpacking.' 'This for Noah.' 'For my friend Mid, with love.'

Mark will have known a shop where they sell cards that are hand-made specially for attaching to bequests and posthumous gifts. I suppose they should go to Tamar. When I found them, I took them out of their small containers and held them in my hand and thought of the independent life of objects, an integrity and self-containment, kept secrets and history, and I felt a strange envy of their inanimacy. Why did he have them? Were they tokens returned to him by his ex-wives? Were they thrown back at him in anger? I thought about them striking Mark's face or the wall or the window, those long windows of his New York apartment, impervious, no doubt, to the blows of precious metal. They wouldn't have, though. Kirstin probably isn't much of a thrower, but who knows, you can't ever tell about these things. She wept on the phone, her voice full of a staunchless regret which shocked me. Her piece is in a little white box with the name of a Danish designer on it. It is made of silver, a perfect sliver of distilled chill.

The one I suppose to be Lee's is in a small turquoise pouch, the name *Tiffany* fading away from the *T*, the *& Co* still quite legible. It's a gold bracelet with a tiny diamond heart. I can't stop thinking about them. Did Mark find them after his divorces? Had he taken them to the menders, collected them from the menders? He was always good about that sort of thing. He'd collect their fur coats from storage in October and take them back again in March, rush out in the middle of the afternoon to carry out some minor errand for one or other of them. Always a man who loved women.

Lee said only, 'Oh, Dan, no. Oh no,' when I phoned to tell her. She felt like a sister for a short period, during that youthful time before we all knew what lasted and what didn't. Telling her was worst of all, I don't know why. Kirstin was more a friend, a co-conspirator, someone I giggled with in corners at family occasions.

There are a few books left: his prayer book, the *Psalms* in Scots. He wouldn't, latterly, be without that. That makes him sound as if he was a *frumer*, some black-hatted *ba'al tshuva*, though he wasn't. He was like me, a hedger of bets, a Jew who was happy to lie back against the comforting pillow of genes and acceptance while casting an occasional watchful glance towards the firmament. His tallis, naturally, went with him. It was the same as mine – exactly the same. We'd had them since barmitzvah. We weren't able to celebrate Rosh Hashanah this year. Everything, by then, was symbolic. Everything.

There are a few things which are hard to deal with, ones which were precious to him: the watch, the leather-covered notebook.

Ticked off, listed, the death notice which appeared in all the papers he named: *The Guardian, The New York Times*, one or two odd little publications he supported in one way or another in New York, some of the architect's journals. He drafted it himself. He must have written it quite soon after he came here, because the writing's still recognisably his, the wording perfect, a succinct summation of his life.

'Now all you'll need to do, Dan,' he said, handing me the details, 'will be to fill in the date.'

Chapter 4

London, late autumn, 2001

This morning, she passes the photograph on the wall with a different sense. She stops beside it, looks at it in a new way. It has hung there for three or four years now, clutching into the present a moment that she hasn't thought about for a long, long time. She wouldn't have hung it from choice, not a photograph of herself – herself, in black and white and grey; herself, young and blurred, almost heroic, poised there in the pose of a street fighter or a martyr or a leader of men – but since it was a gift from one of her sons, found in negative, developed, enlarged, framed, presented, there was nothing else to be done. Part of a project for his school photographic club during his last year there, she recalls; it's to that this wayward image is due, this portrait of wildness, hands outflung, head arched back, any useful detail lost in the imperishable fog which apparently surrounds her. She was mutely shocked on seeing it: herself, returned from a place almost forgotten, not entirely another person. Michael's interest on finding it had extended beyond the sliver of negative, seeking, almost romantic, the continuation of years of half-answered questions.

'Where was it taken?'

'Oh, here somewhere. I really don't remember. Look at it! God knows what I can have been doing.'

'Not Hungary?'

'Oh, no. It wasn't there. I didn't bring any photographs from there' – disappointment pinching at his face as she snatched the promise of a strand of past away from him again. About that, she was honest. She'd told him before. She had had no photographs to bring.

'Who took it?'

'Now that I don't remember.'

But she did remember, and this morning she stands beside the photograph, names cascading through her head, the knowledge that this greying image lays bare the truth of the sight of a moment, the eye behind the light.

Names have caused Anci Goldmann to get up quickly from her desk this blowy russet morning and, unsettled, walk through the hall, past the photograph to the kitchen. The newspaper still lies outspread across her desk. She won't concentrate as she should on her work now, so there's no point in going on. There's a testing, a re-evaluating feel to this morning's air. She's still repeating words inside her head. Twenty, she thinks; she can't have been much more than twenty in that photo.

Walking through the house, she still feels other, even these months, these years on. How many is it now? Not years, only one, one year and eight months, but she's not yet used to the almost-silence, the sense of pleasure and ease with which she passes through the house. She has been alone now, a widow, for this short time, but she never feels lonely because even during the hours of night the city outside continues, alive, busily luxuriant, noisy and feral beyond the walls of the garden. She's not even afraid of the burglars and sundry miscreants who patrol the streets of areas like this, breaking in and committing acts of depredation. For immediate defence she keeps to hand a pair of baseball bats the boys used for a couple of seasons, years ago, one downstairs and one up, and thinks she wouldn't hesitate to use them. She imagines it sometimes, a cinema scene of flailing and smashing in which she's the inevitable victor, which makes her smile. Small, still quick, quickened, she believes, by the opportunities provided by having lived through the worst, the most incandescent events of an incandescent century. Nothing else, she knows, makes you properly vigilant, properly afraid: only judging correctly what there is to fear.

The house, hers and István's, now only hers, has become more impressive with the years. The fabric of it has changed only in small ways, but other factors have made it so: the stealthy creep of circumstances and economics which dictate the lives of cities. Decisions they made through poverty and lack of alternatives in the early years, after she and István first came to this country, now give the illusion of far-sightedness. This house should ensure a degree of wealth which will help the boys' future. These things happen with time; it's not any percipience on their part, although István liked to think it was. The truth is that the city has altered imperceptibly around them, changed its topography, with themselves at its patient, waiting centre. The district was a slum when they came here, almost a slum, and on some of the more dismal days of the years she thinks it still is, a small voice from a far-off past inside her talking with elevated scorn for streets like these: narrow, car-filled, dirty, the houses of poorly-built brick, testament only to Victorian haste and greed. All the same, the house is too big for her, and now strangely sited in this new world of wealth. The voice persists, asks the questions she asks of herself. She doesn't forget, and often, the absence of a movable past seems almost more a spur to memory than the weighty accoutrements she sees in other people's houses. How blithely they display their family photos, how easily they incorporate into their daily lives their parent's furniture, cutlery, their mother's favourite vase. There is only the photo of her from the past, no others, no letters, nothing to bring a physical reality to words, objects to be brought out to kindle the nostalgia she's always despised, nostalgia, the property of those who have never experienced true loss or true suffering. It is the pointless investment of objects with arbitrary meaning. There is only time and time is unforgiving. You carry everything with you, she has always told herself, but only in your mind.

Today she's alone here, although for part of the week, István's study, a large room upstairs, is inhabited by the young woman from the university library to which she's donating István's books and papers. At the moment she's still going through everything to see what they want and what they don't. When the girl, Isabella, is there, István's study feels like foreign territory, as in some ways it always did. Anci decided long before to donate everything and not to sell it. She and István discussed the question a few times over the years, at first lightly.

'Don't throw that away,' he'd say, 'some worthy scholar will surely alight upon it. "Ah, the missing link!"', only part-joking and she'd laugh and go about her tidying and perhaps go to him for a moment to kiss him as a reward for his absurdity.

Selling, which István marginally preferred, would have been disgusting.

'I can't insist,' he'd say, 'but I suggest you wait for offers.' She knew he regretted that he wouldn't be around to witness what he liked to think of as the frantic bargaining which would undoubtedly ensue. She had almost wanted there to be none, but there has been, and the fuss being made over his papers is faintly amusing to her. The thought that it was so wafted into her mind when she received the first phone-call on the subject and has developed, become allowable, an idea she would once have dismissed long before it came to any sort of sensible articulation, even in silent, secret dialogue with herself.

István always assumed that he would die first, quite reasonably since he was so many years older, but nonetheless she's surprised to have outlived him. His sturdy determination in all things seemed to her to root him in the earth, alive in an almost immovable way until she almost believed that he would never die.

She's hardly aware now of walking, agitated, from room to room, what István called 'prowling'.

'Why are you prowling?' His voice, barking from upstairs. 'Can't you stop?'

They spoke most of the time in English together. She can't remember when they stopped speaking Hungarian, if it was as soon as they came here, when the children were born, or in a slow process of near-forgetting, over time. István liked using other languages freely too, dropped in to illustrate points, quotations, grand statements, a permanent focus for their sons' imitative powers.

'"*Tu penches, grand Palatane, et tu proposes nu / Blanc come un jeune Scythe…*" as Valery would have said…' 'And who will not think instantly of Goethe!' – whispered, giggled just out of earshot.

This morning she feels an unaccustomed sorrow and excitement, a return of feeling which flows warm again, pulses in her, a return of sensation after numbness. It reminds her of the flush of blood seeping back in mauve and black patterns to the ends of her fingers which chill icy-white in the slightest cold. Her mind too seems suffused, synapses alight, snapping with memory and questions, some of them the questions everyone asks of themselves at a certain point in their lives, the questions to which any sentient being will require an answer, but there are more this morning, other questions to be answered on this morning which has become jagged, split by time. Years flow between the crevices, through the unmendable breaches. There's nothing to be done. She has read what she has read. She forces herself to sit down at the kitchen table and tries to oblige her mind to return to work, or to the notes for István's life, the promised memoir, a short personal history beginning with the Austro-Hungarian Empire of his birth in 1915. *The world into which he was born…* she has written *…is almost unimaginable now…* She focuses on the words, tries to add more to the sentence but her mind's wayward, determined in its refusal to be deflected. There's only one matter on which she can concentrate this morning, the one she read in the announcement column of the newspaper which she left lying on her desk, the announcement that Mark Blum is dead.

Chapter 5

New York, November 1999

Strangeness, a word among many, a word among imponderables, among all the minute examinations of the anatomy and behaviour of the brain that there are – but it's this one that Mark chooses. *Strangeness* is his favourite, the one used to attempt a description of what he feels every few days, a sensation which engulfs him, hoists him, lifts him airily distant, detaching him swiftly and mysteriously from the immediacy of his day, never a sensation of perfect ease. *Strangeness*, the electric moment of destiny when Jaegerson uses to him a word he'd already thought of himself.

'This, Mr Blum, is what we used to call all sorts of things: *aura, déjà-vu, dream-like state, strangeness* … but now we're more precise, because we know more about its causes. Now we call it a *complex partial seizure.*'

But Mark prefers the old description's near-poetry and the fact that in his experience it's superior in describing, in telling, this: his particular story, as it is. He wants to protest the case for his chosen word, but resists. He's dealing, after all, with science. How could he dare argue for the value of his arcane, personal knowledge? Still, he'd like to describe it in detail, show how the word fits, how the drug he begins to take alters the feeling but does not completely remove it, as if the space for it has been created, inhabited now by only the memory of the knowledge, refusing to be forgotten. It's an obligatory acceptance of new words, of ways of explaining new sensations, a tide which continues to remind him that even in his vocabulary all is changed, swept by this undertow of loss and grief for the man who died in Jaegerson's office at 2.30pm on a November afternoon. In his grieving, Mark is able to look back on that man with a kind of fondness: a man, after all, of some benevolence and goodwill; a *mensch*, he hopes; an innocent who, for a very short time only, tried to tell himself that the strange feelings he was experiencing were probably no more than the vague and indeterminate symptoms of age; who fed himself, although only for days, emollient tales, who lied to himself without any true conviction. There was, is, the existence of

28

the other one too, the fearless one who said no, this is serious, cannot be denied: the one who was right. Which was, or is, he? Naturally, he mourns both, the correct and the incorrect, both equal before the future.

It's later, when he has already dealt with the maelstrom of the beginnings of acceptance, if indeed he ever accepts, when he's dealt with the idea, the facts, the surgery, with other people, his family, his friends, the ever-widening ripples of closeness, that he no longer mourns. Passing the United Nations building from time to time, he finds himself gazing up at its wide façade, angry flags tumbling and tossing in the wind, thinking of the business of diplomacy, wondering if anyone striding the labyrinthine corridors, perplexed, might have need of the gentle skill he has acquired which might be adapted for wider use, that of making people feel better about impossible facts. But this will be later, long after the first days, when he has to live holding inside his quivering brain all that he's obliged to consider after seeing Jaegerson; facts which, over time, will grow dilute and fill up the weeks and months; months which quicken one by one, become with each season and each passing more bitter and more precious.

At the beginning, every action seems to delineate his sense of being suddenly apart from all that was familiar, all that was his own. The person who unlocks the door that early evening, who closes it firmly behind him; the person who walks through the rooms and lingers for a time by a window looking down into the deep, wet valley of streets, is himself ... but other than himself. Minutely, subtly other. He knows it, characterises himself, a lens unfocused, a chord ringing out in dissonance, a half-tone wrong.

The feeling is accentuated by each new object he lays his eyes on, evidence which he now realises may no longer be entirely reliable. His surroundings appear the same, the calm colours and furnishings in his apartment deliberately chosen, the shimmer of evening beyond the windows just as it always is, looking on that evening just as it always does on evenings of rain in early winter – his favourite time for the exciting shift a shower can bring to the dry, pure clarity of the city, its effect on the light, the way a wash of water softens it, creates small mysteries from each change or concealment of texture and perspective.

The building as he approaches it is unchanged, the usual clutch of taxis picking up and disgorging people in front of the portico, the purposeful movement of people through the lobby carrying on in its unceasing, varying pattern. The picture-light illuminating the long abstract in reds and purples on the lobby wall throws its spread of brightness as it does every evening as he passes by. Reaching his own door, he recognises yet another change. At an unknown point during his walk home, he must have lost the unexpressed feeling that behind his own door he might return, intact, to the life he's known. The unformed hope must have dissolved itself among the billows of steam from the manhole covers, lifted into the cool and steady drizzle because, by the time he reaches his own door, he knows that he will not.

The quiet and stillness of his apartment at the moment of entering it has always been a moment of savour, a contrast and an escape, the frantic, wonderful noise and movement of the city continuing but now unheard, unseen. He left it in the morning with the knowledge that it would appear the same on his return, and it does. It's quite unaltered and only he is altered, an intruder in a constant world. Objects around him seem – feel – innocent, untouched by the singularity, the precision of illness, and only he does not.

As he stands by the window in the evening light, still he holds the large brown envelope in his hand. He has already decided that he won't be one of those people who display their scans widely across the wall or pinned blithely to a kitchen notice-board as art or evidence of a courageous ability to accept the black and white facts of bodily malfunction. He's seen it done too often for it to seem anything other than an act of despair. The shadowed sheets of film with their mystic markings are images from an unknown world, distant, intriguing but inexplicably far from the prosaic nature of disease and while he understands that they might be fascinating to other people, he doesn't know exactly why. After all, the interstices of brains are common and any change which distinguishes them from their universal commonality is their owners' private affair.

He takes off his damp coat and opens the door of the closet, confronting himself in the mirror. He's thin, too thin. *An aged man is but a paltry thing, A tattered coat upon a stick.* Whose is that? Yeats, he thinks. Of course. He hangs his coat on its usual hanger, puts it in the warm closet to dry before he walks into the kitchen, opens the refrigerator door, only as he does every evening, routinely, a near-reflexive act, but his doing so this evening feels alien. The simple movement is undermined swiftly, shockingly, by an open, quite clear knowledge of the pointlessness of all things, a total retraction of hope and pleasure and the constant small expectations which have led him, and probably everyone else, to live from one day to the next. He feels far away from himself and wonders if it really was he who opened the refrigerator door, and why. Why is he continuing to enact this pale simulacrum of ordinary life? He has to lean for a moment against the wall to steady himself. Whoever he has become, an immaterial question in itself, is the person who must answer. Why? Because he has to, he's the one who has to endure everything which is to follow. Endure. It's a new word for him to turn in his mouth. There will be more. Fear, he feels already. Pain. Beyond these words he doesn't want to think, but there is no other way. The ineffable weight of preordained destiny, a destiny which will have to be seen out, presses close into his chest, extends a cold, unloving embrace around his back. The presence inside his brain is there, a wily, absurdly persistent companion to his every thought and movement and the span and power of it spreads before him and a slow, crushing weariness at the thought of the future, of things which must be done, makes him close his eyes for a moment. They'll have to be done, or rather, he'll have to do them, however pointless. How is he to continue? How is he to eat, to drink? Imperatives before him, daily actions, to shower every morning, to shave, to wash his clothes, buy provisions. He'll have to go to work, see people, friends, colleagues, family, and will have to talk to them and, in some cases, care for them in one way or another. He will, at first, have to explain himself. Every function of life will have to continue while it can, even though he doesn't know for how long any of these things will be possible. No escape, only inevitability, a wall before him, blank.

'What's the point?' he says to himself, aloud. What is the point, and he wishes in that moment that it were closer, nearer, his own death, that Jaegerson had said something even worse, now, tomorrow, only so that he knew, only so that he wouldn't have to live as he's always lived, as if he would never die. He feels foolish for having carried on for so long without this knowledge. It seems nothing more than an anomaly: ordinary, optimistic, unthinking life. He's standing in his kitchen, the open refrigerator door leaking cold but it's not that cold which steals the warmth from his body, from his skin which feels, in spite of the warmth of the apartment, freezing. He's standing, shivering, when the phone rings. He answers.

'Well?' Kirstin's voice says. Her tone is hesitant, frightened and nothing he will say, he knows, will alter that.

Later, this feels like the worst of it, this evening with its phone calls and moments of unavoidable revelation. His conversation with Kirstin lasts for twenty minutes, or a little less, but seems to him an exemplar, a first tentative exploration, his first rehearsal of how he has to explain, the first enunciation of words which will, too soon, become repetitive, his first hesitant wait for a reaction, the first act of consolation which it is he who is obliged to undertake. He knows that after they hang up she'll crouch on the floor, a posture she always adopts when weeping, her forehead pressed against the ground, the praying posture of a religion not her own. For him, there's the faintest relief in the accomplishment of having told at least one person, but after speaking to her entire lists of people remain to be phoned, the lists he drew up tentatively over his coffee earlier that afternoon. Phoning's quite clearly different from being phoned. Noah and Tamar first. He wishes he need never tell them but contrarily, as of right, they have to be first. Later, he often recalls his hesitation, his reluctance to ring Tamar's number, his sense of what this call would end for her too. Why Tamar first? After all, Noah's older. He has to phone her first because it will be the more difficult call. He hopes that she'll answer to allow him to avoid the routine, pleasant conversation he always has with her boyfriend Sam or with one or other of the friends who always seem to be visiting their house in San Francisco. He taps in the number. Tamar answers.

'Darling,' he says first, unsure which tone to adopt. He has already told her about the appointment with Jaegerson, but no more. Her pretend brightness, her brittle, assumed optimism is overwhelmed within moments,

'What did Jaegerson say, Dad?'

He tells her. Her voice, he thinks, sounds like rain beginning, like something breaking. She pretends otherwise. She's kind and encouraging and urges him to be brave. She asks if he's in pain and if she can come to see him immediately while, all the time, her voice cracks and crumbles into pure, liquid distress.

'Sweetheart,' he says, not knowing how to comfort her, using the possibly worthless, possibly deeply philosophic words to which he'll have recourse many times when all other words escape recall to a place beyond his reach – 'it'll be fine' – as he urges her to the kind of optimism that he can't allow himself.

'We'll come for Christmas, Dad. That'll be before you have your surgery, won't it?'

'Yes, darling. That'll be lovely. I'll see if Noah can come too. It'll be good, whatever. Don't worry, sweetheart.'

Don't worry, then silence. Mark goes into the kitchen. He pours himself a large glass of wine. This cheers him more than he expects. This is, after all, a continuing prospect. The world might have changed but it's unlikely to be without at least some of the important consolations.

'Whatever else,' he thinks, wishing himself *le chaim* automatically then smiling, slows himself, his breath, his thoughts, letting the liquid light his blood and veins.

Phoning Noah, he's never sure there'll be an answer. There's no knowing where he'll be, out in some wilderness place where he's studying corvid behaviour, a place phone signals do not reach or where he's turned off his phone for fear of unwarranted disturbance. This evening Mark is lucky and the number rings out. He's been expecting the call.

Noah is immovable, reassuring. He knows what to ask. He knows about biology, about medicine, about bodies and malfunctions and problems, and if what he knows about is the bodies and problems and malfunctions of corvids, he does not remind his father of it at that moment.

'The parietal? What about the histology? When's your surgery?'

He talks in the manner of a strong son and Mark is grateful. He thinks later of Noah's words:

'Dad, you're getting the best of treatment. We're with you. It's not you alone, I want you to know that, it's all of us. Of course I'll come for Christmas. I was planning to anyway. We'll see it through, all of us.'

But it's not all of them: it's him, Mark. Nor does he want it to be Noah or Tamar, particularly not them. Not his children. Another consolation to add to his small collection is that he will not, barring accidents, outlive his children. *This way,* he thinks for no good reason, *it is meet.* Their lives, though, seem a little more fragile now, bounded, almost defined by his and he thinks of genes and what he might have passed on to them through the by-ways of inheritance, deciding that he must look it up or ask Jaegerson or find some other way to reassure his children that this is his disease, not theirs. His death, he thinks, will oblige them to face the vast, echoing coast of unfathered life, the first great emptiness. He's always been relieved when each stage of their lives has passed without mishap to any of them, wanting not only to live long enough for them to be independent, but beyond the point where they might still have been unaware of the extent of his failings. It must, he's always thought, be particularly hard to lose a father still ringed with a child's glow of faith. He thinks of them often and can, just by looking at their photographs on his desk, bring an instant rush of recall, the time since their births passing before him in snatches, drifts of morning, the ordered pattern of life with young children, voices, sounds in shade and sunlight, on car journeys, at celebrations, the years stacking close behind the thoughtful, beautiful faces smiling at him from their frames.

After speaking to Noah, speculatively he tries Tamar's number again, but as he expects, it's busy. He tries Noah's but now it is engaged too and Mark knows they'll be talking, arranging to meet, comforting one another. Not for the first time, he feels a surge of envy. He's touched, too, although it's mere supposition that they're actually talking to each other – but he knows that they'll share his illness in a way in which is almost unknown to him. It's not that he has never been intimate with another being in quite that way, it's simply the quality of their sharing which is, and always has been, beyond his experience, a source of pleasure and wonderment as they grew up, always part of a group of friends, class-mates, college friends. It is, he knows, a difference of culture and expectation, and he thinks briefly of the careful, limited friendships of his own school and university days. And Dan. A difference of place, culture, time.

Time. He's impatient this evening, urging it to pass, for the moment to come when it'll be decent for him to phone Daniel. After he's spoken to Kirstin and to Noah and Tamar, Dan will surely have gone to bed. He calculates yet again the time in Glasgow, the enigma of hours silently lopped from the roll of numbers between one voice and another. He'll have to wait now till Dan wakes up, and knowing this makes everything feel suddenly urgent. With a resolution he doesn't feel, Mark quickly phones a few of his closest friends. In some respects it's easier, because they're mostly of similar age to himself and so there's no-one who hasn't had, at some time or another, close experience of illness and death: widows, widowers, a couple who have recently lost an adult son. Still, with each, he finds himself adapting words, altering emphases, relying on their reactions to find his words until it feels like a process in physics, he thinks, a natural law, balance, gravity. He wants to make it easy. Who is he doing it for? Himself? The person he's speaking to? It doesn't matter. Anything will do to ease the process, any subtle adaptation, even the faintest, most negligible of lies. He knows from these first reactions who will be the ones he'll seek out in future months, the ones who will see him sensibly through whatever's ahead.

There are, in spite of his news, other things to talk about, other people's news, other people's concerns and it's already late when he reaches the name of Lee, his first wife, among the final names on his list. Lee, Noah and Tamar's mother. Tamar asked if she should tell Lee.

'No, sweetheart,' he'd said, though tempted. 'I suppose I'd better.'

Since their divorce twenty or more years before, Lee has seemed more vague acquaintance than ex-wife, but one acquired by chance, accident, one of those people whose names he would not necessarily keep in his phone book but who is there nonetheless. Sometimes he can hardly remember how, and when he thinks about it as he does occasionally, reflecting on an early intimacy, he finds it evaporated beyond even memory.

'Lee?'

'Mark? Oh, hi. How are you?'

'That's what I'm phoning about, Lee. Anyway, listen; first, how are you?'

'I'm fine. How might I be?'

The answer is as he expects. He has prepared himself against the questions she'll ask: who's treating him, how, intricate questions of drug names, chemotherapy, radiotherapy, things he doesn't yet know. Lee, as he knew she would, gives the impression of believing that death and disease may be avoided altogether by those who pay questioning, intelligent attention to the minutiae of available information on hospitals, doctors, current treatments, statistics of outcome, and that illness is no more than the result of a failure to have done the necessary research with sufficient rigour. She's not satisfied with what he tells her.

'Who are you going to for a second opinion?'

'Second opinion? No-one.'

'Oh, now that's sensible. Mark, you know you have to have a second opinion.'

'No. I don't. I trust what Jaegerson's told me.'

'Trust? It's not to do with trust. People make mistakes. Doctors make mistakes. There are new treatments all the time. You need to know. I'll send some names tomorrow.'

'Lee, that's kind, but don't.'

'Mark, don't the children have any rights in this? Don't they deserve to know you've done all you can?'

He feels a sense of panic, a familiar, ancient acquiescence.

'All right then, Lee, send me some names,' he says, knowing that he won't contact any of them and that now, he'll have to find ways to lie to her forever.

The next name is Sarah's but he realises that he wrote it without even intending to phone her, not this evening, or even at all. He'll tell her one day but when he does, it won't be the truth. He'll go one Saturday afternoon to carry out one of his duty visits and then he'll tell her an ameliorated version and when he reassures himself that it's for her benefit as well as his, he has no doubt that he's right.

Darkness, by the time he's accomplished this much, has spread itself beyond the windows of the apartment, across the flat expanses of Queens and Brooklyn, over the Bronx, over every person and creature in a city which transforms itself nightly into a glittering, mystical landscape, which this evening looks more startlingly beautiful than he thinks he has ever seen it. As it grows late, he reclines in his chair by the window, his glass on the low table beside him. The telling has eased a pain within him. I have eased myself by spreading the pain, he thinks. He also understands that he has lost any control he might have had.

He'll have cause often in the next weeks to reflect on this, on how right he was to regret the moment when people other than himself and Jaegerson knew. He'll learn that this is a world without secrets, a world where it's no longer possible to evade a fervid, relentless hail of knowledge. Euphemisms will no longer do, *a long illness, poor health*. He'll wish himself Victorian, his illness a Victorian illness, barely understood by himself and even less so by others, a secret almost kept, all whispers and taboos and words one must not say, a time when you went to the doctor, were diagnosed, possibly correctly, were operated on, fell silent, when afterwards, alone, three times a day you'd swallow liquid from the glass-stoppered jar which probably was killing you more surely than the disease it was meant to cure, when alone, you dealt with the slow disintegration of your very substance. If he'd had recourse to hushed-voiced mystery, he might have been able to avoid the voyeuristic excesses of the many people who, in time, will take an instant interest in the state of his brain. Every day, he'll have to be prepared to check his e-mails, to delete from mind and screen suggestions from Lee, from others, about treatments which might be superior to those he's receiving, inappropriate websites which might offer him hope, alternative therapies, holistic treatment centres in places he'd never, ever want to go. He'll be ready for the words which will shriek from the television, the book-shops which will daily assail him with their piled tables, their dump-bins and posters pressing other people's intimate stories into the questions you're supposed both to ask and to answer, what does it feel like? Tell us. How do you cope? Describe. Tell us, tell us everything.

Going into his office in the late afternoon for the final hour or so of the working day, he said nothing to his colleagues, nothing to the young woman at the front desk, nothing to the boy who is there for a few days to observe the workings of their firm. Everyone treated him as they always did and he knew that he must savour, appreciate, remember this last and final time that he would be entirely and fully regarded as himself. While only he and Jaegerson knew, he had mastery, and now it's gone. He understands why people decide to keep illness to themselves, to allow whatever it is to grow, burgeon, eat away, their own property and their own fate, theirs, inward and secret. The moment others know, the knowledge has escaped, knowledge which fills the world, the skies, the atmosphere, knowledge which changes the tilt of the earth but most of all, the way people will look at you, speak, think, act towards you although you think you are the same. But you are not the same. You are different, and possibly dangerous.

It grows late. He's begun during the evening to think of the unwelcome prospect of sleep but it seems merely another dread, another new experience, one to be put off for as long as possible. His sleep of the past few weeks has been sufficiently perturbed, waking, worrying and now, the prospect of the hours of the night scares him, wakening to the body's lowest ebb, the relentlessness of the mind which can destroy over and over again, between three and four in the morning, every achievement or success, even at the best of moments, the mind which will without reason torture you with every bitter memory, plague you with its callous, unforgotten trail of every hapless mistake. He can't bear to think of how it will be now, his thoughts on waking, if he sleeps at all.

He's looked frequently at his watch during the evening, waiting, calculating what time it'll be in Glasgow and when Daniel might wake up. Four, then five, and six. He'll have to wait. What do you think if you get a call that early? That someone has died. Someone is ill.

He hasn't even told Daniel of the first indications of his disease, but feels this evening a sense of overwhelming relief that he has taken at least some steps toward repairing his relationship with Dan. For so long, it was difficult. He doesn't want to think of it all now, the past, everything which separated them, the days of their youth which feel unreal, half-remembered. Maybe, he thinks, things past should stay that way, undisturbed.

He waits until it's seven in Glasgow. Dan's an early riser and it'll be better to catch him before he leaves the house. Mark hates phoning cell phones to call people whose routines he doesn't know, thinking of the combination of inappropriate circumstance which is the discordant corollary to the ease of the things, bad news dealt out in ridiculous places, the question 'where are you?' before you talk about death to a person buying underwear or sequestered in a shop lavatory, relating tragedy to two people laughing in a taxi, news too terrible to utter through the screeching inebriations of an office party.

He remembers suddenly, vaguely, that Dan has a journey planned. Perhaps he's already left. Perhaps he's somewhere on the far edges of communication, further. His heart beats too fast as his number rings out and it's with a terrible, welcome relief that he hears Daniel's voice.

'Oh, Dan,' he says. 'Oh, Dan.'

Later, during the night, Mark dreams that it's Dan who's ill, that it's he who phones Lee for advice on the matter.

'Tell him he must drink green tea. That's what Dr Shapiro tells me,' she says cheerily in his dream. He dreams of Dan's offer of his immediate presence, a near-replica of their conversation.

'Why don't I come over? I could come straight away.'

'Not yet. I'm not really sure what happens now.'

'Well, when you have to go into hospital. I could come with you. I could take you in.'

'Noah and Tam are coming. Why don't you wait until I come out of hospital and I can face you like a *mensch*?'

'For God's sake, I don't care how much of a *mensch* you will or won't seem.'

'That's nice of you. How about if I let you know?'

'Why don't you come here?'

'What?'

Mark, confused for a moment, thinks of flying, holidays, the impossibility, the foolishness of the suggestion although he doesn't express the thoughts. He answers Dan's questions, thinking only later of the conversation. It's bad enough that Noah and Tamar are planning to be here to suffer the mixture of anxiety and boredom which characterises visits to hospitals, the interminable waiting during operations. It's not that he doesn't want to see them, only that he doesn't want them to see him, not like that, groggy and possibly vomiting and all the other horrible, disgusting things which will almost certainly ensue from surgery. Later, he thinks of what Dan has said to him: 'Why don't you come here?' He was probably half-joking, suggesting that he should go back to Glasgow, mentioning money, that treatment was free there. Mark thinks of it later, dismissing it. It wouldn't be free for him anyway, a non-resident for thirty, forty-odd years, but that isn't the matter which lingers in his mind. It's something else which makes him return to Daniel's suggestion, the mere fact of the suggestion being made at all.

'I'll phone you in a day or so,' Daniel says before they both hang up. Mark is aware that as soon as they do, he's already begun waiting for Dan's return call, looking forward to it although he doesn't quite know why. Daniel's voice has reassured him, his calm which, at times, seems to have its roots in a kind of profundity and at others in phases of passivity, perhaps, ultimately, the same thing. He wonders too, in the moments after they've spoken, if Dan still plays the piano and the thought causes an immediate chill of guilt to flow through him, the thought that he doesn't know, almost as if, by negligence, he has erased part of Dan's life and he realises that this too is new, an interest in what has been, that it can't remain undisturbed, that suddenly, even his previous life has changed.

He is, of course, entirely correct about the prospect of sleep. It's terrible, as terrible as he has anticipated, the first night achingly prolonged, unending, sweating hours of torment, lying in darkness with only his twin companions, Jaegerson's, or more precisely his, diagnosis and that which has caused it, here, living, multiplying inside his head, the exploding mass within his brain. When he thinks of it later, it's to remind himself how far he has come, the measure of both his nights and days. He lies against the pillows, too hot but sweating coldly, his skin and sheets damp, and he touches the bony curve of his skull, as if to communicate with the malevolent living entity beneath it, as if to implore it to desist. He moves his limbs anxiously, testing them, his toes and his fingers, rubbing his nails against the skin of an opposing digit and he gazes through the night air towards the lit numbers of his clock, shutting one eye, staring, and then the other, watching them change and move on through the hours of night. When he does fall briefly asleep, he knows himself too near to consciousness, his mind breaking through the thin, thin fabric of his sleep, words speaking themselves through sleep or dreams, it's impossible to tell which, a shallow, troubled tumble of words in many voices from which there's only such brief escape that awakening seems each time sharper, the stab of regret and fear, of knowing this will never go away. The smallness of himself and his life is made smaller, infinitesimally so, by being in the true heart of such an awesome city, and when he cries on that first night, he sits up and bends over the sheets, grasping them to his nose and mouth, gasping, his voice shrill and interrupted, rocking himself rhythmically against the darkness, wondering who else in the vast mass of people in this city is doing the same, thinking with love and with sorrow of themselves and of every other lone weeper in the night. He goes over, word by word, what Jaegerson has said.

'What you have been experiencing, what you describe as *strangeness* is what we call *complex partial seizures …*' Jaegerson's veined hand points out the landscape of his brain. 'And here, the lobes of the brain, and this, the one we call the parietal...' A voice, practised and dry. 'Mr Blum, I have to tell you that for this, there is no cure. It is one of the conditions which defies our attempts to find one. There will be one day, but unfortunately, as of now, there is none.' 'These are questions I will be in a better position to answer after surgery.' 'I will prescribe a drug for you which should control the seizures...'

He thinks too of his replies, the same ones, he assumes, that everyone uses, every grateful, angry, bewildered person like himself, standing swaying on the very edge of infinity.

'Thank you, Dr Jaegerson, yes, I quite understand, thank you, thank you.'

What else is, was, there to say?

Often he dreams of God and of Jaegerson without knowing, when he wakens, which is which.

Chapter 6

Glasgow, late autumn, 2001

It was November when Mark phoned to tell me. I'll never forget that call, the precise words he used, how my own heart began beating oddly, unevenly staccato and how hard I had to struggle to make my voice sound ordinary and unshocked, although I was utterly, profoundly shocked. I asked questions which seemed sensible at the time although they probably weren't and afterwards when I went over what I'd said, I found a thousand ways in which I might have seemed unfeeling or thoughtless or crass. I even suggested he come here for treatment, I don't know why, because even as I asked, I knew he wouldn't.

'I began getting weakness in my hand and trouble with my eyes. I knew it had to be this,' he said. My intake of breath sounded louder than anything I'd ever previously said to Mark.

'Tell me.'

His account was precise, informed and technical in the odd, pernickety way Americans talk about their health, symptoms, aetiology, prognosis. it was one of the first things I'd noticed which showed his gradual absorption into another culture, the way he began to talk knowingly, almost neurotically, about his health.

'What about treatment? What are they going to do? Will you be able to afford it?'

'Oh yes,' he said, 'the insurance should do it.'

'Look, why don't you come here? It's still free, for the moment, anyway.'

'Thank you, but no,' he said and I heard the hesitation and surprise, the amusement in his voice, 'I think it should all be covered.'

As Mark's familiar voice talked to me of operation sites, scanners, radiology, statistical outcomes, I felt the superstructure of our lives, a shared thing, shared in its bone, its cells, its enzymes, its blood, undermined, shake, crack irrevocably along the veins and fissures of its foundations.

'They won't know any more until the operation. It's not good, though. They'll biopsy it, decide what to do then.'

'Can I come over?'

'Why not? I'd like that. Wait till the worst's past, the operation and some of the treatment and I can face you like a *mensch*.'

Later, when I was on my own, I worried about having asked the question about money but I had to ask something at that moment. My heart was beating too fast, my head peculiarly swathed by a fine nimbus of cold, my legs without power. Even hearing about illness from a casual conversation in a shop or on a bus, the illness of someone I would never see or meet, I would find myself becoming bone-cold, shivering. After I spoke to him I found that I couldn't remember what Mark had said, although the chill stayed around my head, a weight about my chest which woke me early in the morning to make me wonder for a second what it was, till consciousness broke through the thin, outermost layer of memory, an anxious, arrhythmia of my heart.

In the days after, I could feel years slipping away from their ordered places in my mind. Everything certain, past and present, unravelled around me, blew away, was lost into the atmosphere. I think that I understood even then that there would be no hope of restoring them. Mark was ill and his illness was one from which we both knew he wouldn't recover. At the time, I was in the middle of planning a trip, assembling my gear, trying to familiarise myself with the layout of foreign cities from books as I always have to so that when I get there, I don't get lost. I always do, though. I don't have any perceptible sense of direction.

The day after Mark's call I put my plans aside, delayed the bookings and for a few days did very little other than walk. I didn't even know why but there seemed nothing else to do, sliding myself through time into a city of the past, walking, free-falling, dropping from one long-closed episode of memory to another. It felt as if there was one significant moment I had to return to, one moment which might explain every subsequent moment, as if something might be mended. I didn't have any idea which moment, only that finding it might help. Might help what? Even that I didn't know, but I walked out every morning with a half-acknowledged sense of seeking. I walked for all those days to summon demons or to keep demons at bay, I didn't know which. I walked, I suppose, to understand, to accept, to find a way to believe what Mark had told me, which I knew I wouldn't, not that easily. I remember the colour of the streets during those few days, that emphasising greyness which I love, the monochrome which lights all colour, the underpinning of emotion. I'm always aware of the colours I wear and how I might fit into any given frame or mood. The girls laugh at me.

'I think I'll ruin Dad's day and put on my yellow scarf,' they'll say, and while I protest my case, they laugh anyway.

'Such delicacy,' they say, 'just imagine how he suffers!'

During those days I did precisely what I'd decided, without any strong conviction, that I wouldn't do. I retraced streets of the past, that overlying, explanatory map of all I come from. I'd told myself since I came back that it was circumstance, that I simply lived on the other side of the city but now I examined it all, my feelings on seeing the signs directed towards that old district, my knowledge that it was still all there, solid in stone and slate and grass. I wondered whether or not I really could avoid examination of all that was gone. Was it maturity or anxiety which had kept me away? I didn't need to spend very long in answering that. It felt almost like a pilgrimage to a shared past, a seeing in double vision, mortality itself opening my eyes. I make it sound like some grave and grand undertaking, which is ridiculous because it's only a few miles across Glasgow from here to there. Across the river, across the huge bridges. At least one of them hadn't even been built when we lived there in that smaller, grimmer city.

I took my camera, but for once didn't feel confident in what I was seeing, which streets I walked in, which houses surrounded me, who the people were, passing about their ordinary business in front of me. Everything through my lens had changed, buckled decades in the moment of looking, another time, a dissonant miracle of perception, and when I saw the photographs I had the same feeling I would experience a few weeks later in Mark's apartment in New York, seeing work of mine from years before, a piercing sadness, a sense that whatever we think we capture in light and in darkness, it's always more than we can ever imagine.

Time went with me, nagging me at points during the day to calculate how long it was until I could phone Mark again, my only way of believing I might have a small place in this new geography of illness, that there was, however negligibly, something I could do.

I spend more time now in Glasgow than in London. I work more in Scotland. From Scotland. It's much easier to travel from here, both to leave and to come back. London's so terrible. After Tal left, there didn't seem to be very much to keep me there, only a life which felt like the thin imitation of a past life, a house in which I felt out of place, almost invisible.

My flat here is the one I bought for the girls when they were at university. It's nice enough. Nira kept it on after she qualified because it was convenient for her at the beginning. The hours she worked were so long. I am the father of a doctor and a lawyer: Nira and Dalit. It sometimes seems almost incomprehensible that the time should have passed so quickly.

The girls, who are both in London now, see their mother a couple of times a year although they refuse to go Israel to visit her. They meet elsewhere, in Italy or in Greece. When I know they're together, I think of how they must talk about me. I'm sure they're all kindly and affectionate, even Tal, although I may be wrong. I don't think there'll be any rancour. I'll simply take up the position of the harmless and ultimately hopeless man which I've no reason to doubt that I deserve. I think of Mark and I think of Tal and the places to which we feel we must return. I worry every day about Tal. I wait for the news at lunchtime and at six. I waken anxious before the radio spits the news at me. I speak to her often. She seems reluctant to have been pulled back into the language and the ways and everything which she criticised for so long. Even her accent has changed, reverted. She addresses me at first in Hebrew, and I reply,

'*Dani, manish'ma?*'

'*B'seder. Ha col b'seder. Ma shlomech?*' The usual greetings.

When I look at the years, I see that I've lived haphazardly. There's still a house in London. The tiny square of grass at the front grows disgracefully wild with dandelions while I'm away. The window glass is dusty, filtering the light into rooms which are bold and bright. Scattered through it are things which are precious to me, the gaps left by what Tal took with her. As I've mentioned, I'm untidy.

I'll file letters as I get them. Most of what I have so far are from people who have just seen the notices in the papers. I suppose the initial flood will fall off to a thin flutter soon. I think of it as a kind of code, the short message in simple words which produces this material

45

reverberation, a code sought out in particular by the ghoulish or the triumphant. I can just see rows of the old and gloating, as Sarah was when she was sufficiently sentient to gloat, scanning birth-dates, scoring off the fading victories of time, fuelled by the weakening fires of *schadenfreude*, spectral social occasions for those of an age to find the method of gathering the names of friends to whatever avail, all that's left. Already I've noticed that some of the letters have a personal, almost confessional quality, a common desire to express a degree of closeness or understanding more profound than probably really existed. A convention, the way people have of siting themselves in a world of life and death. It may even be a way of dealing with regrets, omissions, chances lost. I think about it every time I hear one of those breathless reports on the radio, the interviews you hear with people who've been close to disaster, the excitement, the desire to find the precise moment of realisation, the long reach of fear extending beyond their voices as if they're try to understand what has changed for them forever.

I confess to keeping my own little obituary collection. I have it stashed it away, just pieces I cut out of newspapers and put away in drawers, all quite random. While I was sorting through my own things before I came here I went through some of them, the lives and deaths of people I don't know, and I thought about throwing them away – but didn't, from sentiment or because I enjoy my role as morbid marriage-broker – post-mortem *shadchan* to the disparate companions who I've united in unlikely conjunction in the drawers of my desk, overflowing into the untidy boxes where I keep the papers I'll probably never look at again, the acclaimed but forgotten actresses who lie in casual disarray with scholars of Chaldean, the once bright-eyed air aces of the Royal Flying Corps or beautiful, tragic young pop stars rubbing their printed images softly against heavy-browed Bulgarian playwrights, be-jowled dictators, fighters of the Spanish Civil War, gypsy poets, Nobel laureates and all the other people whose stories I've detached for no good or apparent reason other than that I fancy their stories or themselves or their pictures. They are, I suppose, examples or warnings, token acts of mourning, a fascination with the pictures of youthful faces carrying with them distant birth-dates, or smiling as if in calm acceptance of fate. I'm always bemused by obituaries of famous people I thought were already long-dead. They make me feel guilty, as if my knowing or not might have made a difference to them. I always think I'd have taken some time to appreciate them in a more concentrated way if I'd known they were still alive. Completely irrational.

It makes me wonder who might have read Mark's name. Which politician or artist or egregious criminal might have scanned it, almost without noticing, before passing on to the crossword or the stock exchange report? And the others, people who knew him, or both of us, in one way or another throughout his life. I can't help thinking about who might be feeling exactly what on knowing that Mark is beyond us all, the person I didn't know who loved him secretly, or hated him, the person who meant for months to phone him but had lost his number. Perhaps someone is, even now, wondering whether or not to write to me – if, for anyone else, his death has been one of those moments of revelation, of realisation of what was or wasn't important, the speed and inexorability of our lives, that when one misses a chance, it may or may not be lost forever.

The festivals were early this year.

'Just as well,' Mark said when I told him. In fact, he asked me, 'I don't suppose you know when Rosh Hashanah is?'

It must have been just after Pesach when he asked. I looked in the American diary he had given me which has the Jewish festivals marked.

'September 18th,' I said.

'I might see it then,' he said.

As it happens, he did.

Mark often said over the summer that he hoped he'd see out the festivals.

'What's with the festivals?' I asked him. 'Such a *frumer* all of a sudden?'

'Oh, just cussedness,' he said. At every step there was something he wanted to do, to come here, to see this film, that exhibition, to read this or that book. For a while, he was almost fixated by it, laughing, saying that he bet God had written him in the book of death last year and that he'd have to try to cheat Him by hanging on.

'What would He do? If He was wrong, I mean? Get that bugger Jaegerson to send me back my money?' I laughed at that too.

I hear a car turning into the drive, then the well-modulated slam of the outer door. I like knowing there are people around me, above, to the side. This house is so well-built that you hear hardly any external sounds – so that, when you do, they're heightened to a level of mystery, the dull blows of a distant hammer, a waft of voices from a window briefly opened. I wonder if anyone hears me play. At first I tried not to play too early or too late, but gradually I stopped worrying about it. Music has become important to me again. I say *again* as if it ever stopped being important. What I mean is that it has resumed the force in my life that it held years ago. I'm calmer about it now, no longer wrestling with the leviathans which I always felt writhing their suboceanic way through my consciousness. I no longer worry about playing. If I drop a note or make something beautiful sound less beautiful than it should be, my personality, my ability and all that I am doesn't hang by it. If I can't play something perfectly, then there are lots of people who can. It simply feels far too late to need to prove anything, one of the profound joys of age. Mark said,

'I feel bad at having forgotten how good you are.'

'Why should you remember?'

'Because. Because it's you. Because.'

Towards late summer I began to wonder about his hearing, about his senses in general, the nature of his perceptions. I noticed other things changing, deteriorating, and wondered if his appreciation of music might be changing too. It horrified me, the thought that he might, at the end of his life, be living in a world leeching itself of beauty – although I would never have asked him and he certainly wouldn't have told me. Not that.

Chapter 7

London, late autumn, 2001.

This morning, there's no settling. It's more than just what she's read, it's an unease of the mind which she can't readily identify and which impels her. Already she's walked up and downstairs three times, once up to the top floor and into the rooms of her sons where all in their absence is neat, ordered. These rooms have the air of small museums, individual histories laid out from the earliest childhood fascination, progressing through each passing, transitory obsession: shelves of dinosaurs, robot toys with elaborate names now forgotten, discarded items of early electronic interest. There are also, surprisingly to her, lines of sports trophies for martial arts and judo, baseball shields, school football team photographs. There are old CDs, chess sets, photographic equipment. The sensation she experiences stepping into these rooms is wistfulness, but not sadness. She's glad they're both away. Michael is in his second year of studying history in Edinburgh. Joe, although still here in London, is in a flat with friends, almost absurdly pleased with his first job as a sound technician with one of the independent television companies. The thought of how ordinary this all is, how normal, delights her and makes her inexpressibly grateful to her sons for being so little aware of her vast pride and relief in their growing up to be as others are. It's probably related to age, this sense of savour, of appreciation. Already over forty when she had them, she'd thought her sons would never be born.

On the middle floor, in István's study, unfamiliar cardboard files lie bound with broad elastic bands, papers are piled in blue plastic trays, yellow Post-It notes inscribed with words written in Isabella's neat hand-writing assign destinations. She's methodical, Isabella. Anci wanders round the room, touching nothing.

'This must be really difficult for you,' Isabella said when Anci led her upstairs for the first time into István's room. Anci had been on the brink of saying, 'No, why?' but had hesitated, instead saying, 'Of course,' bending her head in acknowledgment, graciously. She'd thought of tidying or dusting a little before Isabella was due to arrive, but didn't. A little scholarly dust would do no harm.

'Everything's exactly as it was when he died,' she'd said. 'I've left it all like that for you.'

'Oh, that's so helpful!'

'I'll hand it over to you then, shall I? I'll be downstairs if you need anything,' she'd said and gone back to her own study.

Difficult? Why difficult? A room in which there are papers. Still, it was thoughtful, just to ask. She and Isabella have formed a relationship by now. Mid-morning, one or other of them makes coffee, and they spend twenty minutes or so sitting by the kitchen table chatting. István would have liked Isabella, her long, thick fair hair, which Anci thinks of as very English, her sturdy girlishness.

'Oh, Anci, before you go back to work, can I just ask you…'. Often, Isabella needs her to verify dates and events, moments in the sequence of István's life. She listens and writes them down in her little notebook.

'And you met him, when?'

'Let me see, 1951. 1952. Yes, '52.'

'In Budapest?'

'Yes.'

Isabella is careful in the things she asks pertaining to Anci's own life: sensitive. And so occasionally, as a reward, Anci tells her some small piece of information that she knows Isabella desperately wants to know. About the war, usually; that's what they all want to know. The revolution, too – the ones who know that once there was a revolution.

She hesitates on the landing, looks out of the window toward the autumn garden. This is ridiculous, she thinks, wasting time like this when there's so much work to do. Rigour! she says to herself, sternly. It's her only piece of advice to herself or to anyone else. Rigour, the one thing which doesn't fail you. There's concentration too. That's important, a useful property of the mind. Contrary to common perception, hers hasn't diminished with age. It has grown slightly fickle, refusing itself to her on occasions while at other times presenting itself in an almost fierce intensity which prevents her from resting or leaving her desk at all. It doesn't matter now to anyone else that she stays in this room sometimes until it is two, three in the morning. This morning, she has so much to do. There is the memoir, but more urgent than that, there is her own work, the illustration she has to finish and hand in within the next few days. She walks downstairs and into her study. She sits down at her desk and rearranges her papers and pens.

New York. She wonders why he didn't die there. It was where he'd lived for years. He died in Glasgow. With Dan. She wonders why. New York. She's the same as everyone else in this, the two words clanging in her head newly, ringing in a fresh and awful set of images. The past weeks fall round her shoulders. The difference between herself and other people, she believes, is that she is unsurprised – not about the specifics, but the results. To her, it's only the confirmation of years of dreams, years of nightmares, the immediacy of this vision, walls scored, holed, dust rising, cities falling, the way she's always known that nothing's ever safe. She knows what there is to be lost. The wave of instant judgments and assessments she's heard every day bemuse her, the realisation that people feel confident in believing they can judge events after days and weeks rather than decades or centuries. What she's written is true: the world into which István was born is unimaginable now, the one into which she was born twenty or so years later, a different one even then, equally so. She's always aware of writing from the bastion of the safety of time and is made weary sometimes, appreciating the length of life, or its brevity. She tries to think why that world seems so different, but they're not the reasons people think of, it's that there was a safety then that there isn't now, talking of open, unlocked doors, trust and quiet and car-less cities. The golden-age theorists, whose one noticeable characteristic is their ignorance of fact, are the only ones who imagine it was a better, more innocent world. It wasn't. Might it be because people think that in those years people still believed that the capacity for conflict was finite? Is that why?

Could Mark have died suddenly? On a visit to Dan, perhaps? But the words *a long illness* are mentioned in the announcement. You don't travel if you're in the last stages of a long illness.

She picks up her drawing pen. It might be easier to work on the drawing. It's of a child and a goose, the illustration for a new book of nursery rhymes. She's developed a name for herself over the years but the achievement has been the quietest of affairs: slow, unnoticed by almost everyone except a few specialists in these matters, and of course by those – mainly children she hopes – who like her work. In most ways she's almost invisible, the second, smaller name on the title page, relieved, in general, of the burden of authors, book-signings and readings and the horrors of the public gaze. After years of this quiet, painstaking work, she's now sought-after, the recipient of awards no-one has heard of, acclaimed by others who do very much the same. These affirmations, while appreciated, valued, make her think of the tiny splashes made by the gilded tails of the beautiful fish who swim in one small and perfect pond. She would want it no other way.

The newspaper lies on the corner of her desk. She'll put it away when she gets up to go for lunch.

The illustration is the final one of twelve. The others are safely with the publisher. She's pleased with them, with some more than others. She loves illustrating nursery rhymes, folk tales, anything which gives her the freedom to create entire worlds. They are, as all her work, crowded with colour, with detail, with every small and cunning device to delight a child's eye.

'Ah! My dear, surely the Dulac *de nos jours*!' She puts her pen down.

Blum, Mark. She pulls the paper to her and reads the announcement again, wondering what there is about it that surprises her. Is it his age, that he was too young, in today's ridiculous terms, to die, only on the outer fringes of maturity, merely skirting the notion of old age? The same as she is. Mind you, we see it so differently as we age ourselves, she thinks, recalling István's view, reflected in some of the people he used to invite to dinner, visiting scholars or colleagues she hadn't yet met, his descriptions of them beforehand. 'Such a very bright young lad.' 'Clever little girl, I think you'll like her.' She got used over the years to answering the doorbell to find someone of her own age or even older, most neither young nor little. Concealing her amusement, she'd extend her hands towards them, welcoming them in.

Is she surprised only that Mark died in a place where he didn't live? Or that Daniel is mentioned in the way he is? Both.

Anci takes her scissors from the drawer and cuts round the words of the small announcement. It's a pity it isn't a formal obituary rather than a notice, because then there might have been a photograph. Perhaps there's one in an American paper, most likely *The New York Times*. She'd like to know what Mark looked like latterly. It's not that long since she saw him, a few years, five, perhaps six. And Daniel too, although it's much longer since she last saw him. It would be as it always is. They'd look like themselves. Added years and no surprises. There never are any. She looks at herself in the mirror often, unsurprised. She could have drawn herself as she is now when she was eight. You could always tell with people, even when they were children. You could look at them and know which ones would change and which wouldn't, who'd grow fat or lose their hair or develop catastrophic wrinkles – but even as she's formulating the thought, she stops. What are you talking about? she says to herself. How in God's name would you know? She tries to oblate thoughts which she knows to be neither useful nor productive. She picks up her pen again and begins to work on the area of grass and plants being gracefully trampled underneath the broad, scaled feet of the quizzical goose but the past is like a tide, creeping, creeping. Turn your back and it's round your feet, and rising.

Chapter 8

New York, November – December 1999

The few weeks between seeing Jaegerson and his operation are, against Mark's own expectations, crowded, busy weeks – time which keeps him, to some small extent at least, from himself. Matters which have to be planned surround him and form themselves into further lists to keep him occupied, things to be done, work to be completed, preparations to be made for Christmas and Chanukah, presents to be bought and wrapped and labelled because whatever might befall him or anybody else, the holidays will happen. There's what he'll need for hospital too. What will he need for hospital? Pyjamas and toiletries, he supposes. Books? Will he need books? Up till now he has always needed books, but will he still be able to read, afterwards? Will his eyes still work, will his brain, after the operation, still understand the words of the titles he now reads, occasionally without seeing them, in his local Barnes and Noble, in the small specialist bookshops in which he browses for hours at a time? He has always read constantly, consistently, from need, but will he still be able to afterwards? After this operation, who will he be? Jaegerson has already explained in fanatic detail his dry list of complications, dangers, possible mishaps, the worst of outcomes, dreary statistics to which Mark attempts not to listen while appearing to pay intelligent attention. What difference can it make to him to know the percentage of people who are paralysed after surgery? It's almost, Mark thinks, as if he has a choice.

In the apartment in the evenings he tidies his papers, goes through drawers and files, throwing out the extraneous, of which there isn't much. He didn't bring that much with him when he moved here, not so long ago. He hates keeping things unnecessarily. When he reflects on it, the only warning of Jaegerson's he needs to consider seriously is the possibility that he might die during the operation, and the idea of Noah and Tamar opening drawers, pulling out papers, reading them, having to decide, is unbearable; the thought of their suppressed exasperation, their expressions of frustration at his wilful hoarding of unnecessary items. Everything has to be neat. Everything has to be in order and ready. When there is no more to be tidied, he reads.

During these weeks Lee phones him, often. He blocks her number, decides to answer one in four of her calls.

'I can never get you,' she complains.

'Lee, I'm so busy at the moment,' he says, trying to sound apologetic. He erases her messages and e-mails without listening or reading them and when Tamar asks if he's avoiding her, he denies it.

'Not at all, darling,' he says, 'I just find talking on the phone tiring.' A lie, a manipulative lie, but one he tells anyway, knowing that there's nothing anyone can say to this. He deletes the lists of names of doctors who, he knows, would be more than delighted to provide him with second opinions. He deletes too the recommendations from people he doesn't know, the encouraging messages he assumes to be from friends of Lee.

People, in general, are wonderfully kind to him. Friends phone. They invite him out for drinks, to go to exhibition openings, to see films. Colleagues too, people with whom he's had nothing more than a professional relationship for years suddenly extend themselves into offers of company, help, whatever they can think of to deal with a situation which is as new to them as it is to him. They're kind but he's had to work hard to redress their kindness, to ward it off. Very early, he decides on the limits of what he can accede to and what he can't, who he'll see or won't. He becomes attuned to the cadences of politeness, the mild deceptions, and now he can tell who knows about his illness, but is pretending – either from natural reticence or fear – that they don't. The words 'Hey, how are you?' take on meanings even beyond the ones they already hold, his responses suddenly watched, listened to, unspontaneous words, some true, some not, issuing from his mouth. 'I'm fine,' to someone who already knows he's not, when he has to avoid smiling with wry recognition in the moment of their disconcerted silence, the rebuff of the words both know to be a lie. He becomes careful in his acceptance of invitations, avoiding those which will take him to dinners designed to allow him to talk in sympathetic circumstances about his illness, or with people he hasn't had dinner with before. There are quite a few of these, it being the time of year for parties and dinners, and while it's easier to assume that they're offered out of kindness than curiosity, he doesn't accept. With old friends, he suggests meeting at a restaurant or in a bar, preferring to be in places where he can, at least, leave on the same terms as his companions. He's already learned that leaving someone's apartment alone will always be the moment of stepping back into the solitary reality which now separates him from everyone else. He goes to work, drinks coffee in his favourite restaurant and, occasionally, forgets. It's the penalty of leading an almost unchanged life. He forgets. He'll be walking to work or chatting to a colleague and will forget. It keeps happening. He feels light. He plans, looks forward and then again remembers, having to realise that it will always be like this, the stalker on the sidewalk, the murderer outside the door, an idea, a conceit he becomes accustomed to, almost fond of, the knowledge that the waiting murderer has made him look at his life, has made him calculate the worth of what's about to be lost. The assessment's much the same as the assessments he's always carried out now and again, after a particular momentous event or for no reason at all, or sometimes on waking at four in the morning, the same subjectivities, the same weighted scales – only now, there isn't enough time for the major changes or minor repairs he's tried to cull from the process. Not quite a final summation, although he often feels it is. He says words of simple cheer to himself, that he has made from his life as much as anyone might expect, more, that he has two children of whom he's both fond and proud, that he has enjoyed more of his life than anyone has a right to expect – but these blandishments are only that. They lack the power to delude.

He's begun, too, to read books about the brain, although the impulse to do so surprises him. No, it shocks him. There are plenty of people who collect books on the subject of their specific ailments and he's always laughed secretly at the ones he knows and at the displays on their bookshelves, the A-Zs of *How To Cope With ..., Living With* this or that or the other, as if knowledge in any of these disparate cases might really be power. But with him, he thinks, it's different, trying not to excuse himself too far. Brains are different. They're qualitatively, cosmically different, objectively interesting, vastly far removed, in one way and another, from the day-to-day dullness of joints or bowels or skin. He has begun with the anatomy of the brain, roughly sketched out for him by Jaegerson: lobes – occipital, temporal, frontal, parietal, and sometimes as he reads, he finds himself running a hand over his own head, locating, seeking, lingering over the marked spot, the stain on the scan, fixed now in his geography of names. The brain's interesting – more than that – and he regrets that he didn't think of it before. Has he ever really thought about his brain? How come he didn't? We are our brains, he thinks. They are what we are, in their – and our – entirety; the universe, in fact, because, in all probability, there's nothing else. He adds a small disclaimer, because on this he still has to make up his mind. In any case, if it's an indulgence on his part, so what?

During the week, he goes to work. He's aware of a lesser acuity somehow, a lack of clarity in seeing and interpreting, but now that he knows the cause he tries to find ways to compensate or circumvent, taking time, asking colleagues, checking, re-checking.

On Saturday evenings as usual, Mark takes Kirstin out for dinner. The regret he's nurtured since the end of their marriage, already dissipating under the weight of circumstance, has almost completely disappeared. It feels, simply, like one less matter to be dealt with although the concern he feels for her future increases. The man for whom she left Mark years before has been in a psychiatric hospital since eighteen months after his marriage to Kirstin, and as far as Mark can judge he is unlikely ever to be released. On Saturdays Kirstin spends the afternoon visiting him, and in the evening Mark takes her out for dinner. He can't remember how the habit developed, but it did, and he looks forward to it and relies on it as much as she does. Often, they go back to Mark's apartment and spend the night together, making love as long-time lovers do, with affection and expedience. They hardly talk about Sy now over dinner as they used to, Kirstin saying over and over again, 'Mark, how did I not notice?' because now, there's nothing to be said. They seek out new places and talk about the food and more often in the past few weeks, about themselves, in a way they haven't done for a long time, almost ruminatively, careful expeditions into their frightened hearts.

Making his way through the city is a new experience now, comforting, almost. A day alone can change his view, an infrequent subway journey, the passage between echoing walls when the gaze of every other person, in whatever state of comfort or misery, says to him, with whatever hostility or indifference, *we're all here, in this together*. He's aware of the fact that there are a lot of people who look much, much worse than he does and he gazes at them with equanimity, noticing now pallor, a sparseness of hair, a jauntily-worn head-covering on a pale woman, the quiet signs of illness, manifestations with which all human beings living in cities, certainly this one, are surrounded during every moment of their lives. Hasn't he thought of this before? Of course he has. He has worn his red ribbons as assiduously as anyone throughout the years, and he thinks of the ornament, now smashed, which every year hung on his perfect Christmas tree, the glass globe with its glistening twist of red at its heart, the frail skin of glass enclosing the words *Miracles happen.*

Relentlessly and without regard to him, the stores and streets alter their character for the holidays with the lush promises of Christmas, the lights of Chanukah. The ice-rink in the Rockefeller Centre is installed again, the Christmas tree raised. The sight of both causes a catch in his throat, quick tears which come to his eyes as he strolls as ever he did with sharp, undiminished delight through the crowds, through the scents of chestnuts and honey and smoke. The white lights are draped round the street trees, wired and covered with burlap; extravagant displays are set up in the marbled hallways and atria of banks and apartment buildings, poinsettia mountains, heavily jewelled conifers, shop windows glowing with the beauty of their wares. Walking past flower-shops, the scent of flowers and pine branches makes him close his eyes with the pain of transience, the sweet waft in a darkening street.

Carefully, he prepares the gifts he sends every year to his children, one for each of the days of Chanukah, individually wrapped. Chanukah is early this year, too early for them to visit. They'll be there for Christmas. He goes to the same shops as he does every year to buy the children's treats they still love: small mechanical flying birds from China, bead bracelets and fans and cheap penknives, crazy dreidels made of metal or glass, as well as the larger presents which he takes a long time to choose. He wraps them and packs them into boxes and sends them off. He chooses, with some care, items to send to Sarah at the Shoshana Blumstein Home: expensive bath essences, soaps in boxes, matching, which she'll show off to the nurses and to less fortunate companions as trophies, inviolable proofs of love.

When, later in the month, in the days before Christmas, Noah, Tamar and Sam arrive in New York, they manage with admirable skill to make the time as pleasant as it can be, all of them almost concealing their concern and vigilance, fussing over him just enough to display affection without forcing on him the impression that they're overly worried about him or even aware of any limit of time. They spend time seeing friends, and the ones who come to visit them seem noticeably polite to him, politer than he might have expected from some of those that he's known from infancy. Illness clearly makes him worthy of a respect he wasn't worthy of before. They do what has to be done together: the cooking, the preparing, going out, and after Christmas is over it feels to him as if they've all been taking part in a play, acting out what Christmas should be, and that they've done it tolerably well. Considering everything, it's an achievement, and one for which he's profoundly grateful.

The drugs still control the episodes he refuses to think of as other than 'strangeness', but an afterimage remains, spectral but there. Mark almost regrets their absence for, after all, nothing has changed. The tumour is still there, but now it's quite free to do its work stealthily, without trace. He thinks about its progress, its daily purpose. He is not alone. He has a companion, a deranged, uncontrollable presence, intent on the steady, inexorable destruction of the cells of his brain.

By the time he packs his smart leather rucksack for going to hospital, he's glad, relieved, almost looking forward to what will be, at the very least, a welcome distancing from everyday life. The only experience he can liken it to is going to the gym, that sensation he enjoys – the moment of entering through the door, thereby passing into another territory of sound and activity, the escape from one particular world into the enclosed, specialised embrace of another, and towards the end he realises that what he'll be most pleased to escape is kindness. It has become more than he can bear during these odd weeks, half-frantic, half-becalmed, between seeing Jaegerson and his surgery. Is there, he wonders, anything worse? Having wondered it he feels ungrateful and sour, but perhaps another element is to blame and his is a wilful misinterpretation, and what it is he dislikes is not their kindness but the knowledge of their pity.

On a damp morning in late December, he and his children hail a taxi in front of his apartment building and give the driver the name of the hospital. As they drive through the streets, Mark wonders if he'll see them again and if he does, will they look the same to him? What will change? What will be different? The Metropolitan Museum stands as solid, as packed and weighty as time and people and history, Central Park too with its hidden corners, lakes, meadows, the thriving unseen life within, the spiralling hawks and downy woodpeckers, the flocks of migrators who annually touch down like summer tourists, great green spaces changing one season to the next, but permanent, and only himself, here temporarily, seeing, as if for the last time.

Chapter 9

Glasgow, late autumn, 2001

The piano tuner appeared yesterday. I didn't even have to summon him; he phoned first and then he was at the door, as if conjured from some music-lover's ether. It must be some kind of annual arrangement. After he'd finished with the piano, I made coffee for us and we talked, inevitably I suppose, about the news. There's no escape from it, no respite. Conversations don't feel like conversations, more like colloquia of stunned, mutual shock, each party eager to give voice to images replaying in their minds and, no doubt, the minds of people everywhere, images which I'm sure will be with us for the rest of our lives, repeating themselves in that endless, ineradicable falling, those plumes of dust rising to the sky. I keep thinking how glad I am that I wasn't there at the time, or anywhere near, and that I didn't have to decide either to photograph it or turn away.

The piano tuner insisted on telling me exactly where he was when he heard – every small detail: the house whose piano he was working on, the phone call from his wife, what she said. Fortunately, I didn't have to respond because he turned his attention immediately towards the angel, asking me what she is and where I got her. He assumed she must have come from a church, which she didn't. I told him that she belonged to my parents, and that my mother found her at the back of a junk shop when they were first married. She's Danish, I told him, a plaster cast of a marble original.

'Magic!' he said. 'Mind you, you've some nice things. That's a brilliant piano.'

'Oh, it's not mine. It was here when we moved in.'

'You're kidding! No disrespect, but you wouldn't find me leaving that for a stranger.'

'Me neither.'

'But you play. That's your music, isn't it?'

'Yes.'

'Then I'd stay put if I were you. Do you know what you'd be talking to replace it?'

I didn't tell him that it'll be included if I buy the place, a valuable, almost irresistible addition. I didn't like to mention it because it seems like too much good fortune to flaunt. *To him who hath ...* which I've always known to be painfully true. I don't know why the owner doesn't want it any more. I've asked a few times, but the estate agent either doesn't know or won't say, and I quite like the sense of romance it gives. I think of it every time I sit down to play.

'How odd,' Mark said when I told him. 'Clearly the centrepiece of some great love affair. Or *crime passionel.*' He asked if the neighbours had said anything, but they hadn't – not about that, anyway.

After the tuner left, I tried the piano. He'd made it sound perfect again, the small falls and dissonances tightened and corrected. It reminded me of the car after a service, the brakes quick and taught, the sense that all is well within.

I've spoken to Tal quite a few times in the past couple of weeks. She phoned every day in the last stages of Mark's life. I took the phone out of his room so that it wouldn't disturb him. He wouldn't have noticed anyway, but I still felt slightly guilty doing it, as if I was engaging in a clandestine activity when I spoke to anyone. I felt, too, as if in some way I was betraying him by talking so much, so exclusively, of him. I felt that dying should be more private.

'Dani, aren't you afraid?' Tal said a few days before he died.

'Of what?'

'You know, just...'

I did know, and I was, and I thought of the way she's always been able to say things other people might think but never say, of the days when I'd first known her, the constant experience of faint shock, surprise, exhilaration. She was Israeli in that way until her last day here. She would pull at the covers of a baby's pram in the supermarket, scold the mother for not wrapping it up sufficiently warmly, comment on things she found out of keeping with her idea of what was appropriate or sensible. When we lived in London she had quite a few Israeli friends, expatriates like her. I'd return to the house and open the door to hot gusts of their talk. I know just enough to understand and to converse simply. In the early days, I'd hear her singing the songs of her childhood round the house: *Uri Sheli* and *Emek Tiferet* and the sound brought me inestimable joy, as if I was unable to believe in the fortune which had made everything better than I could ever have expected. Even now, when I flick the switch on the radio and turn to short wave in the evenings, I can still hear those songs and bulletins of news, the political discussion programmes I can't quite understand but which sound like cats fighting in a sack, the dry reports of hellish events followed by dolorous lists of names, then weather forecasts, *me'unan chelkit, ma'alot chom:* partial cloud, degrees of heat.

'I've been thinking more about home recently,' Mark said to me during one phone call. That was around Christmas last year.

'Where?'

'Glasgow,' he said, in that tone of voice, as if I should have known.

'So you still think of it that way?'

'Dan, d'you know, I didn't realise I did until I said it.'

Home.

"Pilgrimage" will always be the way I think of my walks through the city in the days after Mark told me of his illness – but pilgrimage to a time rather than to a place. I did wonder why I felt compelled to do it, but knew it wasn't from nostalgia. Nostalgia longs for the past, while I longed for something else. I was too afraid for nostalgia. I even looked up the word "pilgrimage" in the dictionary. There were two definitions: "one who travels a distance to visit a holy place," and "one journeying as a stranger in this world." I knew which was the more accurate. During those few days I carried with me the same feeling I'd have in New York a couple of months later, after Mark's operation: apprehension, a fear of revelation of some sort – of what sort, I didn't know.

One afternoon while I was in the street where we used to live, a woman came out and addressed me as I was taking photographs of what was once our house. I'd noticed her looking out of the window of the house next door. I could understand her curiosity or concern. It's not a place where you see many people walking or even taking photographs.

'Excuse me, but are you from an estate agent?'

'An estate agent?'

'Yes. Is this house about to be sold?'

'Oh, nothing like that. I'm a photographer. I'm taking photos for an article someone's writing on Glasgow architecture.'

'I see. Where will it be published?'

'It's an American journal. They're very interested in these things.'

'Really?' she said, obviously pleased. 'Well, perhaps you might send me a copy. I live there, number 97.'

She told me her name.

'Yes,' I said vaguely. 'I'll see what I can do.'

I lied because I didn't want to tell her that I'd been brought up there. It would have ensured discussion about when I left and where I'd been and what the district was like then and who had lived in her house. As I said goodbye and walked away I thought of what I might have told her: that it looks very much the same, that districts like this don't change, only the people do, only the details; that the stone's cleaner and the wealth more glaring and obvious but really, nothing else. I thought of that encounter a few months ago when I was looking for this house and read the estate agent's descriptions of our old district, their use of terms so effusive as to be risible, the inappropriate words they used to try to indicate exactly how desirable the place is meant to be, superlatives, words which have more to do with religion than property.

I hadn't decided on a route or an itinerary. I just wandered and as I did, I could feel the past opening to me, sensations I'd forgotten assailing me, odd things, the memory of cold, freezing bathrooms, breath-clouded bedrooms, the smell of coal fires and soot, the knowledge that this was how everybody lived then, a chill equality of winter. People too lay in wait, the aunts and uncles and cousins who'd lived in the district, our father's brothers, our mother's sisters, and I walked deliberately past their houses, those which had been their houses, and they were there, a mystic assemblage which gathered to accompany me on those few days of November, all of us passing together through endless drizzling time, through the afternoons of childhood days, the certain brief luxury of freedom and light before early twilight. And I seemed to glimpse the essence of time as we promenaded, live and dead and far away, through dusks the same as those I now lingered in, while my camera sulkily recorded the leeching of the day's brightness. We did as we'd always done in the clear, unchanging heart of my memory, and even the variegated tonal crunches of the gravel under our feet came back, what I'd always thought of as an overture of arrival and return, a single glow beckoning from a fanlight. History unpeeled itself from the wrappings of time, the reverberation from all things, the glow filling the skies from Clydeside's burning, that up-draught of fire, one of the many that was to roar in the background of our lives. Names danced their way through my head in streets where Suez still bubbled, where the travesty of honour was still about to unfold its disgrace, Anthony Eden's voice still speaking its strangulated syllables to a frustrated nation, Hungary's voices imploring us day after day from the wireless for the succour which never came.

Those houses. The same life, but different. Names: Sarah, Mark. Anci and István. No wonder I was afraid, Anci's voice suddenly wailing to me from long ago:

'How can you not know? Daniel, think! This is how we were, once.' Nothing purer, then or since, than Anci's grief.

Round the district, the same streets, the same routes, ancient habit seeming to impel me to turn corners without thought, towards destinations I couldn't even remember. I walked back home as it got dark, through the traffic and bustle of the centre of the city. My head was crammed, planning, frantic, sad. I passed not far from where our school once was. My God, I'd forgotten since Mark's call to think about Sarah, and in one moment of fierce panic, I wondered what was I going to do about her. Mark, I found myself yelling silently: you can't die. If you do, what will I do about Sarah? In any case, Mark, I said more calmly, as if a calm appeal would be more effective than a hysterical one, addressing myself to three thousand miles of separation: you can't leave me here, alone.

Chapter 10

London, late autumn 2001

Extending her nib towards the edges of the lake she's drawing returns her mind to water and the ever-welcoming margins of the swimming ponds. Swimming is the only activity she can imagine which might absorb some of this displaced energy, these distracted thoughts, pull in the roll of movement which won't let her be still, but Anci has swum already as she does every day in the open air, today in the early grey light of morning. Usually she swims only once in autumn, in the morning, because to get up and go straight from the warmth of her bed lets her blend it into her day, her body accustomed, neither too hot nor too cold. She's adjusted over the years to the seasons of that water which draws her in and inexplicably dissolves her anxieties into its cool, dark depths. The habit of a lifetime. Not, in truth, that one can judge without knowing the length of the life, but a large part of one. She began swimming a couple of years after she and István came to London, once they had a house, were established, after Glasgow, after the times of moving, renting, after István got his first job, his first salary, when they were no longer new and raw, making their way in a country they had never thought they'd live in. Before that too, even before, but it was summer when she discovered these ponds, here, the first summer in this house.

She replaces the tops of her ink bottles, cleans her nib and brushes and stands up. Swimming. It's still the only known remedy. Walking upstairs again to collect her things, she passes the photograph. It seems to beckon to her, the siren on the stairs. She stops, nods towards it as if to indicate to the young woman depicted that soon, together, they will deal with matters outstanding between them. Not now, but soon.

She closes the door and begins to walk quickly up the hill, thinking of how she learned first about the ponds from a woman in a shop queue at whom she must have stared, because the woman turned to her to explain, in an accent which definitely wasn't English, why her hair was wet. Her accent must have been pronounced, Anci thinks, for her to have noticed at all. It took her years to be able to make these subtle differentiations. They conversed for a few moments before the queue woman said, in a way which had left Anci smiling, close to tears,

'You must come one day, join us.' She had gone, newly purchased swimsuit inside a shopping bag, nervous in case she couldn't find the place. She'd been scared by the use of the word 'us' but excited because it had felt like a personal invitation, the first she'd had.

It wasn't, in spite of her fears, difficult to find, following the woman's instructions, *up the lane till you see the railings then the sign*. There weren't the facilities then that there are now, the changing rooms and lavatories, but she'd been thrilled by it all, the privacy, the feeling of being in a place made special by rules she didn't yet understand, by a voice with an accent yelling, 'Hello! Hello! Oh good, you found us!' from the middle of the water.

'Us'. She thinks now of her fear, this one word to encompass the people who were to sustain her life. Is it too much, too exaggerated, over-dramatic to describe them to herself in this way? She scans her mind over the faces, the times since her first visit, the women who surrounded her, hierarchies of their histories, women like her, so many of them with accents, with numbers glimpsed from inside wrists, the signs of ruined circulation, the odd scar, a twisted, wasted arm and herself, the youngest, the last, the baby of them all, for a time at least. It was the lack of need for explanation which had been both balm and weight, her age and her accent telling them everything with no need for more, the wondrous sense that here she was absolved from accounting for herself, that the air itself would fill the spaces. From her first visit they'd closed around her, insisted that she return, taken her home with them, given her somewhere to go, someone to meet. They became friends or didn't, people like her, truncated, people with a past and without, like her, lost in the balance of creating and forgetting.

'Oooh! Twice in a day, darling! That's a first!' Mary the lifeguard emerges from her hut, clutching her mug of tea.

'I can't concentrate this morning, Mary. I thought it'd clear my head, you know.'

'Nothing better. The water's fine today.'

The water is fine every day. The water is always the same, except when a few years ago they drained the ponds and hauled away the years of silt and mud from the bottom. The water doesn't alter although the weather does, days when it spills rain from a billowing grey sky round the swimmers' heads, streams it over their smooth and busy shoulders, their arching, graceful arms; days when ice begins its stealthy formation to float in cloudy islets round their moving limbs. The water is reliable. It is the unvarying recipient of bodies, of water bird and human and insect. It is the bearer of every reflection cast by the progress of the hours and the days. The swimmers all have favourite words to describe the water on any particular day.

At first she came only in summer, slowly extending into autumn, a process which took years, beginning earlier in spring, then finally, as now, throughout the winter. 'You get used to it,' the year-round swimmers used to say to her sceptical gaze. 'Wait! You won't be able to do without it.' Without what? Swimming in freezing water in December, January, February? Hot springs are one thing, as she knows, freezing water entirely another. But now, this is what she does, every morning, as essential as any of the acts we deem essential in our lives, some of which are and some of which are not. It has, she believes, maintained her as she is, as unchanged as she can expect to be for someone of her years. It is responsible too for establishing a reputation for eccentricity among those who know of it, especially her sons' friends, a reputation of which she's almost proud. Swimming means that every morning she wakens with purpose, nothing more important in the moment of waking than this, swimming things assembled every night from habit, swimsuit, towels, jeans, underwear prepared automatically, straight from the dryer, no better moment than walking out into the early darkness, or into fine dawn light, than the moment of water opening to skin. She has long understood her own need and that she's not the only one who swims from necessity, to hold the world together, seeing as she watches the alert heads of the other women who do as she does, swim determinedly, even passionately, through this area of calm which keeps itself, on the whole, such a magnificent, Byzantine secret from the maelstrom of the city.

'*Les baigneuses*,' István called them, inevitably she supposes, herself and her swimming friends, the nymphs, naiads, the water-sprites. Lorelei; Partenope, Ligea, Leucosia,

> *Ich glaube, die Wellen veschlingen*
> *Am Ende Schifer und Kahn,*
> *Und das hat mit ihren Singen,*
> *Die Lorelei getan.*

She'll never stop hearing that in her head as she changes into her swimsuit.

'I hear the faintest voices singing as I pass up the lane,' István liked to say to people, 'and all I can do is steel myself and run.'

As she swims, she tries to order her thoughts. She watches the small white tern who flickers patiently above the water. It's this that she loves, the otherworldliness of it, among moorhens and mallards, among damselflies and waterboatmen who skim the surface as she swims. It took years for her to acknowledge that this wasn't a new pursuit, to allow the memory to return, to realise the continuity of it all, but only, as she recalls, after she had children, when they were of an age to ask about her life as a child, only then was she able to think of it, did she dare remember, to tell them in any way she could manage, meanly, sparingly she knows, of her own childhood, Budapest, streets, schools, hot springs, feeling names unfamiliar in her mouth, Széchenyi, Király. They liked most of all for her to describe bathing outdoors in mid-winter, how steam would rise from the water around the bodies of the bathers and she thought they didn't notice the hesitations, the lapses in her seeking to find words amid her portrayal of the elderly chess-players in corners of clear blue pools and snow lying on Baroque roofs, trees, streets, how they'd march all of them, her family, through snow along the entire length of Andrássy ut. What she remembers and what she's read and reconstructed later is never clear to her. Memory, it appears, doles itself out grudgingly, or it shrinks itself small, in protection, she doesn't quite know which.

'Can we go there, can we go there?' the children would shriek and inside herself, she'd shut and lock.

'One day, my darlings, we'll see,' she'd say, smiling, smiling, talking to them sweetly in a way which even then they knew meant 'no.' This reminds her, Joe and his girlfriend are coming tonight for dinner. In spite of the warm beginnings of mild panic, she will not change the easy pace of her swimming. She'll manage it all. She will go home and draw and write and cook and give the girl on the stairs the answers she deserves. It might not all be today, but it will be done. She will be rigorous.

István's memoir is lagging. There is a limit of time. Before everyone forgets him, she wants to say to the publisher, who will politely demur although both will know it's true. She'll do it. When she gets back, she will carry on, plough through the chapters as easily as she ploughs now through lozenges of colours on the water which break and split and close around her.

Chapter 11

New York, early January, 2000

Later only impressions endure, ideas of days, the limpid imprint of hours, echoes of voices, pain and lights which will last beyond the concept of memory, too indistinct for memory, rooted in stabs of brilliance and in sound, of moments dealt out slowly over days, connected but only incidentally, one single prolonged, passive journey towards an unknown destination. The beginning is fixed clearly enough when the time comes for him to go back, testing, trying to refine the detail day by day and hour by hour, but it becomes impossible very quickly as he moves into lost time, lost days.

Exactly what do I remember? he asks himself as soon as he can, but also, do I want to remember? Piecing together from fragments the altering kaleidoscope of segments of time which will not fit, turning them upside down, over and over, jamming them in, a madman's jigsaw. Days of dreaming, near to dying. Only later, wakening one morning, does he realise that a thousand years have passed in his dreams.

The beginning of his journey remains, delineated clearly enough, the practised rituals of hospitals which take him over instantaneously. What does he know of hospitals? Only from other times and other places, distantly, the quick, green light glancing from walls of polished paint of his father's dying, the slower light of his mother's illness, her small body and small face almost lost into the whiteness of a high, white ward. The births of his children which were, at the time, too frightening and purposeful for reflection, all too womanly, too stern and humorous, with himself as a guest barely tolerated or a creature hatched awkward from its chrysalis, a father, a known irresponsible. There's nothing of those pasts here under this brisk and brilliant lighting, not in the answering of questions, not in the presentation of insurance forms, in the filling and signing, the speed with which he feels grateful for and even touched by the equalising power of pyjamas, the principle of the tallis, he thinks, that all-covering garment designed to conceal outward appearances of material wealth, rendering all men equal in the sight of the Almighty. All men who have insurance. As his forms are taken and checked, simply recalling Dan's words about the NHS makes him wistful, the almost unimaginable state of not having to think of the cost, of being able to concentrate fully on all other pressing matters to do with this, the most urgently, literally pressing of matters. This he will remember, this day, the language of hospitals which is marvellously, terrifyingly strange to him, the routines, clocks on the wall, lavatories, signs on the doors, the lighting, the colour of floors, the complex totality of sounds which voices and feet and wheels weave in corridors.

Noah, Tamar and Sam, after bringing him in, stay just long enough to hand him into the care of the staff. They embrace him, smiling, stroking him, patting him, giving him presents, magazines, books, the tiny stuffed rabbit he finds in his palm after Tam has folded his fingers round it. He watches both Noah and Sam put supporting arms round her as they walk away down the corridor, her face, effortfully cheerful, turning to look back at him, her hand blowing a kiss. After they've gone, he feels a deep stab of envy, knowing that after the initial regret at leaving him there they'll enjoy a guilty freedom which they'll examine and discuss over coffee, then over lunch in one of their favourite places. He wants to be with them, out of this restricting, ordered labyrinth, in his clothes again, free.

'Mr Blum? I'm the intern. I'll be looking after you today.'

The boy looks too young to be qualified for anything but he dutifully answers the questions and submits to the examinations. So quickly, a total submission to others, an abrogation of oneself, a situation in which, invariably, he assumes a manner of ease, joking where he can, smiling. Contrary to other's perception, it's not bravery which makes him do it. It's the opposite. He can remember bidding himself, more than once, some stout farewells, some poignant ones too. He's affectionate towards himself, full of sober, faux-drunken praise. A visit to the lavatory, potentially his last, cheers him. Such bathos, he thinks, realising suddenly the potential of the word in his present surroundings. Bathos! He resolves to remember so that he can elaborate later upon its themes, particularly to Dan. He'll remember as he will only the very beginnings of oblivion, injections, pre-meds, the sensation of fraying or fading which becomes very abruptly the edge of a precipice over nothing, time gone, then he himself, gone.

What happens? What takes place in this interval of unimaginable duration? The mechanics of it he knows, explained in what, inadvertently, he has described to Dan as skull-splitting detail, by Jaegerson. About the incision in the skin, the drawing back of the scalp, the creation of a flap in his skull which will lift to reveal dura and brain, he knows. Then there's the seeking out of his malevolent companion and its brisk excision, the reversal of the processes, of the anaesthetic, the return of himself, with good fortune, unimpaired. He can raise his hand to feel the thickening edges of skin drawing tightly together, covering over the traces of the experience of which there's nothing, only depth, a sense of much time until returning, until one crack opens in the splitting darkness, the first of many returns into still more darkness, into interrupted darkness, into a liminal twilight and then into light which hurts, sounds which he can't immediately interpret, his name, he recognises that, questions which approach and recede. He likes it better when they recede. There are whirlings, turnings of his body in space, moving or being moved, floating perhaps, changes of direction, levitating. Levitation, that's the word, levitation. He likes this too but then it's over without his knowing exactly when it began and when it ended.

'Mr Blum?' Can you open your eyes for me Mr Blum?' More of these annoying voices when he's supposed to be sleeping, his brain shut down, shut away even from himself. Why are they waking him? Whose is the face above him?

'Dad? Can you hear me?'

Need he respond? He can't decide whether or not to pay attention to the voices and faces, the bleepings, squeakings. Mosquitoes, he thinks, satisfied at his clarity of thought. Car alarms too. There is heat, a stifling, sweating heat. It must be summer. How long has he been here? All this, he knows, has nothing to do with him.

'Mr Blum, can you tell me what day this is?'

What day? Why? His head's tight. It's hot, tight. Everything has swelled. Something pushes against the walls of his skull. Sore. It's sore too. Then the name, Jaegerson. Of course. His fault. Bloody Jaegerson.

'Mr Blum?'

Why is she asking? Is it some special day? How is he meant to know the day? What day? Who cares?

In snatches, himself, there, asking. Am I alive? How do you tell?

He thinks he is, but how can he be sure? What are the signs? He tries to move things. Toes. Fingers. He feels pinned, tight. Hot. He tries an eyebrow. Can he believe that he is here, attempting to move his eyebrows to test if he is alive? It must be done. Anything he tries moves. Tentatively. Is this proof enough? Is what he feels sufficient? How does he know what objective proof might be? God, he wishes he wasn't here. But he's glad he is, not here but alive. Or is he? What did his infinitely complicated books say about near death experiences, the sensations of dying, the working of the brain approaching death? But if there's something beyond death, memory, retained consciousness? Beyond every puzzle, a further one and then again, the darkness.

Later, he questions the idea of oblivion. At which moment would it have made no difference had he died under Jaegerson's little knife? Which was the instant of purest dark?

'Dad? Can you hear? Do you know what date it is?'

Surely Tam can find the date if she wants to know it. The words 'look at the newspaper' float over his mind but the effort of transferring them from there to his lips seems too difficult when he considers their banality.

'It's a new year, Dad!'

How long has he been away from the day he remembers? Is it the same day? How can he answer? A new year? Which year? It is not only another year, it is another century, another millennium.

On his own again, days later, for no reason he can think of, he remembers Ecclesiastes: "a thousand years is but a day," and turning his head as far as he can into the pillow, he wonders what the sensation is that he feels as his eyes blur, as a slick of warmth coats his face, raising his hand slowly, clumsily to inexplicable tears.

'Mr Blum, how are you today?' The day when at last he returns from nowhere, from no sleep, no distance, returns from the unfathomable shallows of another place entirely. Now, eagerly, they wish him happy New Year, exchange kisses, wishes, and he feels like the person, whoever it was, who slept for a thousand years. A thousand years is but a day, a thousand and one nights, a thousand and one things to be done. He begins to feel restless. The children bring in books, magazines whose pages he turns carefully, staring in nervous evaluation, the ancient Monopoly board, too, which Noah has found in the apartment. Tam carries in portions of chicken soup made reverentially to the near-sacred recipe belonging to Bubal Maskin, Lee's mother, and in its familiar, celestial taste, the world seems to begin to stir, to restore itself in sight, sound, sensation. He, Tam, Noah and Sam sit together in strange, strange surroundings and laugh, slowly at first from relief and shock, pretending that they're laughing at their memories of the Monopoly board bought on a trip to London and Mark's hopeless, irascible attempts at explaining which place was desirable to buy or wasn't.

When alone, he feels properly alone. The presence with whom he has co-existed for an unknown time has gone. Alone apart from his family, attentive staff and of course, Dr Jaegerson and the words he knew beforehand would be used. Mark wishes he'd laid a bet.

'Mr Blum, it is as we expected…'

Inevitable words. The sum of it is known and what Dr Jaegerson has to tell him is that, although now the presence may be gone, unfortunately, assuredly, it will return. The only unknown, as Jaegerson puts it, is when.

OPERATION RECORD

Surgeon: Dr K.L. Jaegerson; **Anesthetist:** Dr M. S. Park

Preoperative note

The patient presents with focal seizures involving the left upper limb. MRI brain scan shows a tumor of the right parietal lobe. Appearance suggests a low grade astro-cytoma. Patient started on steroids pre-operatively.

Operation

The patient was placed in the supine position. The head was immobilized using the Mayfield head holder. Hair was shaved from the right parietal areas and the proposed incision marked on the skin. The scalp was infiltrated with adrenaline. A bi-coronal scalp incision was made and the skin flap reflected forwards. Using the craniotomy an osteoplastic left frontal craniotomy was fashioned. The dura was incised and the front lobe exposed. The brain was tense and the gyri were compressed. Using image guidance, the margins of the tumor were delineated. The tumor was excised. Frozen section histology indicated that this was a grade 4 astro-cytoma. Haemostasis was completed. The wound was closed in layers and a bandage applied. A suction wound drain was used.

Dr K.L. Jaegerson

Chapter 12

Glasgow, late autumn, 2001

During those few weeks before Mark had his operation, I couldn't go back to what seemed – wrongly, I'm sure – the calm, settled place I'd been before his call, a place where we were more or less as we'd been for years, following parallel, brotherly paths, unhurried, quietly trailing every legacy and burden, shared points of conflict, sharp divergences and heavy secrets as if we had time unlimited, our own slow but civilised progress towards a day when we might or might not lay out our lives and thoughts for examination and repercussion. There might not even be need for that day; perhaps adults lived with the past, accepted and denied in appropriate measures of wisdom and caution. I've never been sure I know precisely what adults do, nor that I know very many people who fit into that particular judgmental catch-all from which I've always felt comprehensively excluded. But now everything was changed, and my only duty was to try to accept the components of change, disease and time. Time was finite now, unpredictable in perpetuity. The realisation travelled with me, a succubus whose small, malign presence was there at all times, making me aware that I was in some way waiting, forever waiting, sometimes even breath-held, as I shopped, conducted my walks through the city, as I re-planned my journey. I tried every day to imagine the fortitude which underpinned Mark's wakening every morning, his getting up, going to work, carrying on his life, all the things he'd been doing which he'd recount, still amusingly, in the quiet hours of the night when the traffic outside had stopped and it felt as if we might be the only people awake and communicating, sending our chosen words out towards one another, across the delicate surface of the planet.

We spoke often in those weeks: more, I think, than we had in the previous three decades. It was inevitably late at night for one or other of us. I phoned him a couple of evenings after he first told me he was ill. I was nervous dialling his number, anxiously aware of each sound, the alien tone of the ringing of his phone, the glassy clatter of sleet against my windows, his voice saying, 'Dan? Hey, it's late for you.'

'Two. I sleep less these days. What about you? D' you sleep?'

'I take things. I'm given things.'

I made myself ask about Sarah, something I've never been able to do easily, without a tremor of reluctance, of remorse even, always in the faint expectation of a reaction I might not entirely welcome,

'Tell me, how is she? She's been on my mind lately.'

'Oh she's fine. A bit frailer. Still a bitch,' Mark said, but his tone was neutral as he told me about her, that she'd been recently robbed of her purse, how she'd offered her watch but they had refused because it wasn't worth their trouble. The robbers, obviously gentlemen, he said, had suggested that she should stay at home, which for a while she did, refusing to go to her charity meetings or out to her friends' houses to play canasta.

'She listened to them!' Mark said. 'Can you believe it?'

'We'll have to talk about her.'

'Indeed.'

'Are you sure I can't I take you into hospital?'

'Sure, but thank you. No. No bedside scenes. Wait till I'm out. I'll let you know when. It'll be round Christmas, just after. I'll get the surgeon to call you.'

'Have you said anything to Sarah?'

'About the tumour? God, no. I'm not going to. It's enough to deal with without her.'

Tal asked me recently about Sarah,

'How is the old so-and-so?' She always uses a particular Hebrew word to refer to her: *clafty*, a word which makes me smile, one which seems to have neatly tucked into its brief syllables the entire world's history of gossip and malintent.

'We can see Sarah together when you're over. Something to look forward to,' Mark said.

The first necessity was for me to re-arrange my trip. Its purpose was to take photographs for an exhibition to be put on first in London by a group of other photographers I sometimes work with, people from many different countries. The theme, suggested by one of my colleagues in France, was *demi-jour*. When I'd first read his e-mail, ages before, I'd laughed because the idea seemed a typical fantasy of romanticism, all idylls in black and white, but I realised soon that it wasn't as it seemed and as always happens to me, as the date for completing the work approached, I found the very words I'd used in criticism germinating, exploding into ideas which burst in on me from nowhere, yelling to me in the quiet of the night until I felt I was wrestling with more possibilities than I could deal with. I began thinking of places with high walls and hidden lives and the ideas made me restless, filling every available space in my mind, until Mark's phone call.

I don't know how I became what I've become – a photographer, that is. Whatever else I've become, and how, is all too clear to me. Chance, that's how, the usual serendipity of circumstance which creates us, moves our lives, shapes them, turns us this way and that while we struggle and question and try to take seriously the notion of free will. I'd never considered photography as a career. I was studying music, although now I can't imagine what I thought I'd do, teach perhaps, be lucky, find the moment of chance which would elevate me a little above what I really could do. I was good, I think, although unconfident, moodily despairing. In those days of youth, I'd believe one day that as a performer I was supreme, the next that I was worthless, with only the slightest under-performance to bring about the catastrophic change. My teachers encouraged me, people I trusted to tell me the truth, but even then there were times when I looked at them and wondered why they were lying and telling me what was patently designed to deceive.

I'd begun learning the piano when I was four, at my own request, more likely at my loud demand, fuelled by whatever motive it might have been, one that's lost now, though I suppose it was the same as it would be today: the desire to create, an instinctive pull towards infinite possibility. While I was on my lone visit to the streets of the past, I stopped for a moment outside the house of Mr Fredrickson, my piano teacher for many years, a wash of metronome and dog-barking, of green corduroy and the russet semi-darkness in which for years I practised scales and played my tentative first pieces, colouring the very shift of time, certain afternoons still marked by that charged atmosphere of expectation and fulfilment. Mr Fredrickson was unusual for a piano teacher, gentle and encouraging, inspiring with restraint my own need to excel. Now, I realise that he was deeply homosexual and that the atmosphere, one of closeted, cloistered maleness was all there was in those dangerous days before acceptance. Not that anything happened, but it makes me sad to think of it now, his suffering and loneliness. He was a man I trusted to the infinite extent of trust and even then, I knew that any doubts I had were mine, any questioning of him was a reflection only of my own uncertainties. If he told me a piece was good, it was. If it wasn't, I had fallen short. He had, he said, the highest hopes for me, that I could do anything I wanted. But I didn't. I didn't. Even though I've begun playing again, I haven't ever, or yet, been able to regain even for a second the person I could find within myself when I was young, a person I became only occasionally, only when I was playing, the transcendent moment when I could forget myself.

My father bought me a camera when I was eighteen. I didn't think at the time about why. He said he'd seen it in a shop, a new model that he couldn't resist and had to buy it for me. Now I'm sure it was a distraction, and though I've tried to bring back a moment three-quarters of a lifetime away to re-examine the circumstance of his giving it to me, whether or not a second's complicity, a glance, an intake of breath was exchanged between my parents, I can't. It was a time when they were concerned about me, I know, but what I don't know is what made them decide on that. It was while Anci was still there. I took a lot of photos of her and when people praised them, I assumed it was the subject they were praising and not the photographer. When I gave up the piano not long after, it was uncharacteristic, an act of anger and denial which could have left me drifting, resentful for years, without the camera. It was startling, particularly for myself. Usually I slide into decision, let events happen or not happen by default but this was different, dramatically, foolishly, entirely decisive in a moment of anger and impulse and love and instead, I clung to that camera as if the genie inside it would speak to me, impel me, tell me what to do. It did. It cancelled out the voice of István Goldmann which, even now, I can allow to haunt the air I breathe.

The photographer of ghosts. It's true, in a way. I've taken photographs in many desolate places, beside dried-up salt lakes, destroyed forests, in places where the unimaginable happened in pits of screaming, pits of silence, places of quiet horror. I've photographed the effects on the earth of human events, chemical disasters, of every kind of ruination. Time, I think, doesn't ameliorate atmosphere. It's the question people ask me most.

'Can you tell from a place what's happened there?'

But I never like to say that I've got no idea, that I believe you can but not how, not why. They forget I'm not an objective observer, I go only to places where I know what's happened. Knowing, it's easy enough, rightly or wrongly, to experience some unobserved reverberations of the past. I know there's more to it than that, that the essence of photography is that connection which can't be broken, the single, immutable move between photographed and photograph, the brevity of the step which makes it real.

My photographs of Anci weren't spectral. On the contrary, when I first looked at them, I felt as if I'd captured her, or at the very least hinted at her story. I was proud of them but surprised too, exhilarated. Later, when she left, they were something of her to keep, the only thing I could.

I was amazed when I arrived in New York to see Mark after his operation, to find the photographs I took of Ellis Island years before, hanging in the hallway of his apartment, expensively mounted and framed. I was almost shocked when I saw them. They felt remote, like a childhood friend I hadn't seen for years. Everything in them looked ragged, the line of docks, the plain devastation of the island but most of all, my own invisible presence, lost, there behind the camera.

It was in my first weeks in New York, all those years ago, that I sought out Ellis Island. I can't even remember now how I heard about it. Ships had long since stopped bringing immigrants there. While Mark was taking his portfolio and degree certificates round architects' offices, I crossed over to the island with some difficulty. There was no regular service running and I had to hang hopefully round the Staten Island ferry cadging lifts from boat-men. I took everything with me, my photographic equipment, food, sleeping-bag in case I was stranded overnight among the eerie, glass strewn rooms and damp, echoing corridors. I never was. Promised lifts always worked out, even the most grudging didn't abandon me. I was disappointed once or twice when I realised that I probably wouldn't see a night through on the island from the limpid river dusk to the beginning light of dawn.

Music and perfume may well be the two known components of nostalgia, but seeing photographs I've taken holds a particular alchemy of recall, one which can restore me completely, willingly or otherwise, to another time. I remembered it all, how carefully I'd carried the films home to develop, knowing exactly how I wanted them to look, grainy, copper-toned, full of the atmosphere of hope and loss that surrounded the place like a mist. I remembered the fear, the exhilaration. In my amateur's darkroom in my flat in Glasgow, I'd watched them emerge from their wet bath of chemicals, dim shapes flowing from fog, wavering, fixing into the still images of that dead and empty place. Immersed in their chemical bath they seemed a world in which I had no place, watery and fuming, unfamiliar as a strange city on a winter day. When I picked them out of the liquid, it was as if I had found a benighted fly in amber, lit on an undiscovered creature embedded in ice. I thought about film speeds, light meters, the acid smell of my developers and fixative. There hasn't been any of that for years now. It's all done by someone else and comes back to me perfect and distant as if I had no hand in its creation.

I took some of the photos I'd taken for the exhibition with me when I went to New York a few weeks later, some I'd taken recently in Glasgow too. I worried beforehand about showing the Glasgow ones to Mark, sure he'd think them in some way sepulchral; childhood, the past, exactly the kind of exercise in hand-wringing he'd loathe, but he didn't. He picked out those ones at once.

'Hey, look at that! I know that one. Such fabulous houses! God, Dan, to think that we took all that for granted. Oh!' He held one towards me and I thought he was commenting on the architecture but then he said,

'I could pick out one of your photos anywhere. They're wonderful! Always a story behind there, waiting to be told.'

'That's kind. People've said it but I'm sure it's only because I choose places they already know and then they tell themselves the stories.'

'Maybe, but that's not quite it. There's always something beyond the obvious. Your people, too. I look at them and feel I have to figure it out.'

'Pure genius. I don't give a voice to the voiceless.'

'God, Dan, I don't know what more you want.'

That was during one of the long blizzard days when we were together, days of fierce snow which tied New York into a knot of frozen time, tightening it into ice-bound catalepsy. Mark and I were like children in a fairy-tale, standing thrilled by the windows together in the kind of innocent excitement we probably hadn't felt for years, staring wide-eyed from the shelter of our ice-tower, down over the helpless, captive city.

He looked, paradoxically, wonderful when I saw him first, that morning at Ellis Island. I'd dreaded it, thinking he might be changed beyond recognition. I imagined it, dreamed it, suffered waking nightmares, telling myself I must prepare myself to recognise the person of my brother beneath the changed exterior but there he was with his fashionable cropped hair and his new specs and a look of a man who knew what he was doing, Mark walking fast towards me in the Registry room, holding out his arms and smiling.

Chapter 13

New York, early January, 2000

Manhattan on this day in January, the first days of the first month of a new millennium, glows with the hazed brightness of coming winter rain. It's mild for the time of year, the air delicious, fume-filled, familiarly exhilarating after the twice, thrice-breathed, stifling air of the hospital which is behind him now, its doors closing on his last few, bewildering days. The street seems to offer Mark the chance to step into altered destiny. It feels slightly like an escape and he half-waits for someone to come running out to haul him back. Another phase, clearly, is beginning, one he'll have to learn, one he'll have to deal with in yet another way and whether it's by acceptance, acquiescence or rebellion, he's not quite ready to find out. Still, this moment is good, not the one he'd dreaded, of facing an expanded world, a world of other people turned treacherous within days, the short time when the internal world of hospitals, involving the closed privacy of his own thoughts and consciousness, had contracted to the immediate, the bodily, a world of sensation and small, tentative responses, unspoken routines underpinned by knowing that in this place of illness he was among brothers, sisters, comrades, a place where he belonged. For days, since his mind began to re-emerge from gases and swelling and the intrusion of other people's knives, newspaper headlines have been warning him of the future, whispering to him of the feral places in which he will, again, be obliged to take his rightful place. But now, with relief, he feels equal to the challenge. True, he feels odd. It's as it was with his feelings of strangeness, he can think of no better word to describe it. Is it a symptom, that he's content to use these weak, under-emphatic words? He feels slightly unsteady too but tries to walk boldly to conceal it. He turns to catch a glimpse of himself in the glass of the doors to see if he looks remarkable but he doesn't. He looks the same.

Packing his things for leaving hospital, he'd felt a pang of fear, wanting to implore someone in authority not to send him away like this, making up excuses, 'I don't think my wound's healing properly,' 'I still feel a little shaky,' knowing them to be risible fabrications, a child's morning stomach-ache. Instead, he'd concentrated on remembering what he'd hated; attention, being summarily touched too often by other people's hands. Noise. Sweat-inducing heat. At the same time, though, he already anticipated missing the company of others, the snatched corridor-chats with fellow inmates, the ironic intimacies of illness, idiotic jokes of rebellion and escape, the brief, piercing affection which he felt unexpectedly for the few people he'll think of afterwards, the silent comforters, the smilers, the worse-off-than-himself. He must now banish the illusion that he's happier among other people in pyjamas.

Kirstin, who knows him sufficiently well to desist, doesn't take his arm as they walk towards the cab. She allows him to hold the door open for her, gets in first, destroying the sense that he's still a patient.

It's over, he thinks as he leans back in his seat, it's over. It is he who gives the destination to the cab driver. Was it as he thought it would be? What was the worst of it? Neither the surgery nor the mysterious return from a tunnel of darkness. That was, at least, interesting and new. It was, if he's to rank the experiences, the sitting-duck, trapped sensation of waiting for unwelcome visitors to arrive, which they did, unaware that it was the fact that they did which made them unwelcome. The people he most wanted to see are the very ones who knew not to come, the ones who sent cards, wrote sensible, loving messages, said, tell me if you want me to come and I will, and knew that when he said I don't, he meant it. They're the ones who understand the vulnerability of being almost unclothed in the presence of the coated, the booted, the scarfed. Lee, naturally enough, arrived the day after his surgery. Clearly under instruction by Noah and Tam about what not to say, she was ponderously careful during her visit, Tam at her elbow with a watchful, jailer's air, the clamorous suggestion of ways in which he was remiss ringing unspoken above her head during the half-hour of unnecessary, banal conversation. He'd still been tired and hadn't said much, just enough to listen to his own voice sounding much as it always did. To fill the gaps and silences, he'd smiled from under his bandages, what he thinks must have been an inane smile which gave out, as he understood from Lee's reaction, the false impression of his having been improved somehow, purified by the experience of suffering. She'd smiled back, taken his hand, held it for too long, too tightly in a positive, emphatic grip.

In his pocket are the postcards Dan sent him, beautiful postcards from foreign cities, Tangier, Marrakech, Damascus, which he has kept propped against his water carafe. Looking at them, he's let the words of the theme of Dan's exhibition remind him of physics and space, of half-life and half-light, words which flicker lightly through his consciousness, liminal, unbidden.

Noah and Tamar have already left to go back to their homes and their jobs, Tam to her class of infants, Noah to his crows. They left with an air of exhaustion and relief, concealing it under genuine love and concern but Mark knew it to be there, and why not? They've done what they can and have been kind and good and anxious. Before going, they talked vaguely about coming for Pesach, which for years now they have not celebrated together. They were, too, appropriately attentive and grateful to Kirstin, who they've never quite forgiven for leaving him, Kirstin who is here to accompany him back to the apartment, who will stay with him, pretending that she's not keeping a vigilant eye on him, during his first days home.

In the days after leaving hospital, his life will seem skewed, as if another person has replaced him in his own lovely apartment, sleeps now in his wonderfully comfortable bed. His fingers will touch every surface, each item of glass, metal, wood, learning anew, a language of sensation. He will wake in the night with pain in his scalp, sharp, tearing pain, with a different pain in his head and he will raise his hand to touch his wound, feeling in terror for a dampness of blood which, to his vast relief, is never there. The wound seals, heals, pales against the skin of his scalp. He'll think of what's no longer there, the presence in his brain. It is gone but has not gone. It has left messages and reminders, the slight clumsiness he feels in his movements, the aftermath of pain. Even its absence resonates. In these new days, post-surgery, he'll find himself subjecting every routine, every feeling and assumption to fresh, searching scrutiny. He'll ask himself time and time again what is truly necessary and what is not, what is real and what is not.

In a couple of weeks he'll begin radio-therapy, but only after he has happily accepted the invitation of his friends Alison and Berndt to stay with them for a time in their house in upstate New York. Dan will visit.

But now, he leans back against the seat of the taxi, watching the driver's amulet swinging from the dashboard, ribbon and beads swinging, swinging to keep the evil of the world under appropriate control, to keep them all safe from harm. The streets have a January feel, weary but hopeful, as if they too have undergone a major event. It's a new century. He is aware of looking out upon the beginning of a new, fresh thousand years. It's a relief beyond anything he'd imagined, to be here, the same. He feels a diffuse, unfocused gratitude, towards whom or what he hasn't yet thought although he knows that Jaegerson has to fall within the margins of its tender benevolence, Jaegerson who, he has to admit, has done his work admirably, with sufficient skill to have ensured that he, Mark, is still here, and thinking.

Shops, intersections, people. The odd string of Christmas lights startles him, connects him with days now almost forgotten, not long ago, making him realise the truth of time.

Chapter 14

London, late autumn 2001

There are things to be bought for this evening. She'll stop on the way down the hill. The morning has quietened out, spread through the city towards noon, thinning its roar to bursts of individual noise. Could there ever be true silence, Anci wonders, in a London street? The sky over the city looks a painterly white, a dry, powdery whiteness, a line of blue deepening towards the horizon. It lacks only the faint craze that time rends in canvasses, the faint sheen of light on paint. The wholeness of cities can be caught in words, and the ones she thinks of this morning are steel and domes. As she hurries, she considers the evening ahead with the lift of anticipation she always feels at the prospect of seeing either of her sons, a pleasure undiminished by time or by their growing-up. The air is cool in her dampened hair, and raising her hand to push it back it from the nape of her neck she glimpses herself momentarily in glass, and there it is, an image of herself as she is and was, a reflection passing, seemingly without end, in the glass of these same shop windows, a scene in perpetuity but ever changing, Joe in his pram, then Michael, she with the two of them toddling then walking; this, the twice-daily route towards their school, the boys growing, grown and now herself, here again, alone. A reflection smiling in these windows, bending to listen, stopping, wiping something, picking something up. The days of the toils of devotion, days which at the time, you don't imagine will ever end.

She stops at a favourite shop, a delicatessen, to buy food for the evening, savouring the word as she pushes open the glass door, *delicatessen*, a lovely word which summons a sense of attention to detail, fragrance, all things fine. As usual, she avoids buying the items the boys used to enjoy in childhood because she hates the idea of persecuting her children with a mother's obdurate refusal to relinquish or forget. They can buy what they like themselves now. She wonders if they still like the horrible things they did, chocolate paste, peanut butter in stars and stripes jars. What she buys now are beautiful purple olives, a fat loaf of sourdough bread, cheeses which are carefully wrapped for her in heavy wax paper, plump, long-stalked capers. She hopes Joe's girlfriend Florence will like the food she's choosing. Anci has met her only once, briefly, when she went to deliver some clothes Joe asked her to bring to his flat. A girl with light green eyes, she recalls, tall.

The moments of conversation with the helpful, smiling boy behind the counter have taken place. The proffered bag is filled with bread and olives and wine. What's she doing here, idling when there's so much work to be done? Ahead, as she walk down the hill, are the evening, the table, the candles, the meal she'll cook. She thinks of what she has to remember to tell Joe, one or two small things relating to money, a reminder of his brother's impending birthday, an account of a conversation with one of his schoolfriends met in a cinema foyer. He'll ask about Isabella. The boys always ask about her and the progress of her work. They both regard her as a source of amusement for some reason: 'the lubricious librarian,' 'the foxy femme of the box-file.' This reminds her that she must show Joe the photographs of Franz Ferdinand she found in a book. They're ones she's never seen before, and everyone she's shown them to so far, including Isabella, seems stopped by history and she senses them afterwards lost in a reverie of chance.

Both boys mourn István still, she knows.

'Something'll come up in a lecture and I find myself thinking, I must ask Dad about that, and then it's awful, I remember that I can't,' Michael said recently, his voice sounding childlike and very distant. 'I know,' was all she could say to him, 'I know.' The slow realisations are worst, the hot frustration that, incontrovertibly, someone is beyond the reach of either asking or telling. What Dan must be feeling now.

Mark was her age. In fact, there were only a few weeks between them. Five. Dan was eighteen months younger. She's surprised at the ease with which she remembers this, and that they discussed age on her first day there like small children trading days and months and years. Tentatively, she begins to probe her memory, finding herself complete, even the skirt she was wearing on that day and the shoes, the coat which she hung up in the empty wardrobe of the bedroom in a house in Glasgow, a city of which she had barely heard. It is 1956 and she flinches momentarily at the notion of time, although truly it's nothing because she's still that girl, not quite twenty, who stands at the window of that room looking out with terrible wonder over the quiet valley of lush gardens, the trees and lawns, the unscarred sandstone walls under whole roofs of cool blue slate. Chimneys send out wavers of coal smoke to the damp air above wrought iron roof finials, slick from recent rain. She stands and looks, unbelieving, and walking here, down this hill, she's the same, the same.

She wonders if she'll mention Mark's death to Joe. Why should she? Why shouldn't she? She tries to remember exactly what she's said about him before, probably only passing reference to her arrival in this country. The boys' complaints about her vagueness have always been justified, beyond dispute.

'Dad tells us too much and you tell us too little.'

What was she meant to say to that? It's true. Only what she has said, many times.

'But darlings, I'm so old that it's all a long time ago now!' 'Oh, you know my memory!' or some other airy phrase to put off a moment which she knows will come. The excuses have been serviceable till now, deferring rather than quelling their interest although they've never failed to point out that their father was considerably older than she. Soon, too soon, there'll be insistence in their questions, a suggestion of urgency, a hint that she can't deny them, that it's their right to know. She's heard notes of it already, because of her age she supposes, because her sons already anticipate the day when she'll no longer be able to tell them anything, or be there to tell them anything. Now that their father's gone. It's as if she sees them assessing their requirements as they approach the days of their own fatherhood, as if they intend to become properly adult upon the bedrock knowledge of their parents' unknown past. They're right, she knows, but what is she to say? Years of the words with which she's soothed herself, ones which tell of the futility of worrying until the moment for it arises, *sufficient unto the day,* feel thin now, any usefulness or ability to comfort eroded into nothing. The moment's already arising and she finds herself anxious, her heart beating a little too fast, calculating whether telling Joe about Mark will hasten it. She wonders if, nonetheless, it might allow her, by the very act of speaking, to understand that what has happened is real. Mark. What has happened? Why does she feel this way, that after years of silence the death of a single person can be the slipping of a cornerstone, a long jolt which opens a penetrating crack in the surface of past? Even if the name itself means nothing to Joe, he'll understand that it means something to her. Is that reason enough? But why? Why does she feel the need to enunciate the words, 'A friend has died'?

Outside a house on the hill, a skip swallows the thin lathe ribs of a demolished wall. Whatever small front garden there was has been stamped into pools of standing mud by the boots of the builders who hurl brick and plaster against the skip's echoing steel walls. The house like a thin, unready shell stands open, vulnerable, but soon she'll pass by and there will be light on new walls. There will be lamps, new people, faces looking out towards the evening air. The garden too will be re-designed and will live again. A young woman will bend to plant green and pink flowered hellebores between pebbles and slate.

The thought of it all lodges over her mind like a small area of darkness, the darkness of what to tell, what to remember, a mere part, or all, a process of breaking the seals, one after the other, to enter the caverns of her memory, a brutal process which will not depend on her, she knows. Someone else will be responsible for wresting them apart, someone else will break them open to gaze and stir and have a hand in the plunder.

The wide view of London sinks below the line of trees and roofs. Cities, steel and domes, other cities, other places, other words to practise and use again, images which will have to be taken out to be displayed under light, the words she might use of the city of her birth, hills, water, bridges, but even this is difficult, her habit of rigour so deep, so practised that she worries sometimes that by now it knows no reversal. She reviews what of her life her sons know and what they don't. Not very much, since she was always able to take refuge behind the abundance of István's telling. She remembers when they began to come to her to ask her more about what István had just told them, as if requiring confirmation. She understood why, although she always felt the need to reproach them slightly, as if they were wrong to appear not to trust their father's word. Everything István told was, or seemed, embellished, mythic, the core of truth swathed in inimitable, elaborated detail. Difficult sometimes to sort through, even for herself, what was and what wasn't, which avenue to follow to which conclusion. She didn't contradict.

'Oh, is that so? Well, it must be. I always thought that there were four of them but I must have been wrong.' 'Is that what he said? He must be right. Your father's memory is so much better than mine…'

And now, there's Isabella. Anci amuses herself sometimes by imagining how Isabella might have dealt with István, the mutual dance of charm which would have initiated journeys to nowhere, false trails, lingering questions. He would have enjoyed it, in the end, more than Isabella. She herself has already told Isabella things which aren't true. It wasn't 1952 when she met István. It was 1954. A lie, small and pointless. Isabella can't check, she thinks, she can't check anything. As far as Anci knows, all known records of their lives drowned. They were bombed too and then blackened by fire and all of them were, no doubt, eventually swept away, just as everything was, history, cleaned up, changed, another history begun then ended. How could anyone know anything? Does it matter? Yes, she supposes it does, but records are only one manifestation of what surrounds you. It's not easy to become another person. Even if you don't carry the memory of your previous self with you, then someone else will. Someone else will carry the weight of you, what you are and what you were.

The silence of the night frightened her during the first days in Glasgow. She'd waken abruptly, heart dancing with fear, mistrustful of the quiet darkness. She'd lie and stare till night was over and there was a steal of light through the curtains, a bird call in the chilly dawn. At that time, she couldn't even cry: 1956, when time went deaf.

She's never really blamed the boys for asking, always knowing it's what children do, demanding repetition, continuation, the ever-seeking, rapacious need for stories. Stories, like the ones she illustrates which are even now waiting for her on her desk, the ones which demand that she step between their words and the children who will read them as interpreter, enchantress. Once she's finished this set of drawings, a new edition of a famous book of fairy tales is waiting to be illustrated. Fairy-tales are complex, the weight of them gathering, growing with the years. Fairy tales absorb meaning, they change their emphasis with everything that happens, ripe for new, fresh interpretations. When she first began drawing, years ago, she read the theory of fairy tales, endless explanations of their origins and ubiquity of themes, stories which bind distant peoples one to another in the sameness of their fears and anxieties. Whence we came, whither we are bound. She has read books on what Freud would have had to say about them, the same things, she thinks, as he did on everything. Freud, called by István, not always privately, 'the charlatan's charlatan', 'the little Viennese fraudster'.

The illustration of fairy tales is the most difficult to do. She reminds herself, as one of her teachers urged her, to keep in her mind the word 'illustrate,' and she tries to as she considers the portrayal of degrees and depths of kindness and of cruelty, ugliness balanced against beauty, picking from the air with careful fingers a portrayal of all things human, joy and disappointment, suffering and love.

When they were small, she and her brothers and sister had lots of books, but the two she remembers best were books of fairy stories in English which their father brought back from a trip abroad, big books with maroon covers, tooled in gold, the pages of thick, rough-edged paper, the illustrations intricate and beautiful. Even before they'd been able to read the text, they'd loved the pictures, princesses and djinns, minarets and woods, lost maidens with wild hair and cold, bare feet, huge birds flying over vast blue seas. Those books, just another thing lost. However she does it, she tries to make her drawings beautiful because they were made beautiful for her. Her eyes were trained by those pictures, drilled in detail and colour, and even when she had no books, she remembered them. Was Freud right? And all the other people who have told her, in their various ways, that fairy tales are a preparation for life in its infinite and unimaginable progression? It may be so, but often when she thinks of it, she wonders which fairy tales instructed her, which fairy tales prepared her for gingerbread houses and witches' ovens.

Chapter 15

Glasgow, late autumn, 2001

Half-light now. It makes my angel look particularly lovely. She's always beautiful, but shadow gives the sedate, upright position of her angel-flight a stately air, serene in near-darkness. My angel is Aurora: Morning. The infant Day rests on her arm. There is, somewhere in the world, her counterpart: Night, with her children Sleep and Death. I know this but haven't tried to re-unite them; it's the kind of pursuit that can lead to madness and bankruptcy, I know. I bought a feather duster specially for Morning after Mark and I installed her. It's the only way to sweep away the dust which settles on her wings. My girls have always loved her. They used, when they were small and she rested on floor against the wall, to stroke her feathers with their mucky little hands, and now they're big they petition me regularly, individually, about who'll inherit her. I'm not in the least offended that they do. It reminds me of when they were three or four and some cheap toy was involved. I love their honesty and appreciation, the openness of their desire in the face of beauty. When I came back here first, I had her brought up with a few other things, but my sense of impermanence prevented me from doing anything as definite as hanging her up. I had her moved in here before Mark arrived and here she was, leaning trustingly against yet another wall when I showed Mark in. He was instantly tearful. 'Dear God, I'm sorry, Dan,' he said, putting his hand on my arm. 'It's pleasure, believe me.'

Tal was always a little suspicious of the angel. I think that secretly, she thought her a bit too Christian. She's not, of course. To be accurate, Aurora is *Eos*, Greek. I did point out to Tal that we have our angels too; it's just our iconography which doesn't.

I was always amused by Mark's attitude to Tal. He liked her, but was wary of her as he claimed he was of all Israelis he encountered. They are, he always said, too rough-hewn for him, too new and certain of being right, and far too rude. Latterly, I'd hand over the phone to him when I was speaking to her and they'd have quite a prolonged conversation. Her directness refreshed him, speech leeched of euphemisms or sympathetic undertones, sadness dealt with as it was. He liked, he said, that there were no evasions with Tal. I remember that he spoke to her one evening not long ago after there had been some horrible incident in Israel, a random bombing, an outbreak of conflict. He told me about their conversation.

'Mark, we are all in a kind of tragedy,' she'd said.

I met Tal at the house of a friend in London during the early sixties. I'd had a few girlfriends by then, no-one significant or particularly memorable, no-one who didn't make me feel wistful or even frankly sad, too aware of my own hopeless thoughts and futile dreams. When I met Tal, she appeared as she turned out to be, vital and bullying and beautiful. She left me no opportunity for doubt and I was amazed by her attention and apparent desire to be with me. As for love, the state of being in love, when we discussed it once a few years ago, shortly before she left, we both wondered if we hadn't mistaken a moment of resolution for both of us, for being in love, the mutual comfort of the promise of security. We loved each other and had, after all, been together for many, many years, but we talked that evening searchingly about what the difference was until Tal, with her usual brisk sense of when enough has been said, ended our retrospections gently, putting her arms round me, saying,

'Dani, what does it matter now?'

She met the dreadful Gadi, a previous boyfriend, when she was back in Israel visiting her mother. I didn't know for a while, and then I did. When I said that she must do as she wished, Tal left. She was furious with me, I discovered afterwards, for not fighting to keep her. I didn't because it seemed *beshert*, meant, somehow. I couldn't fight to keep her from potential happiness. I was glad, as she was, that it had happened when the girls were already grown. Almost sorrowing, she went home to a place which she knew was benighted, one where I'd never wanted to go with her.

I spoke to Mark's surgeon, Dr Jaegerson, on the day of his operation. I was in Morocco at the time and he phoned during the evening. I'd worked well that day, walking, photographing, my mind concentrated fiercely on what I was doing and what was required of me, feeling, for some reason, that this is what Mark would approve of. Towards evening, I went back to the riad where I was staying and waited for Jaegerson's call. When it came, his voice sounded tense, like a spring, precision wound, ready at any moment to uncoil into quick anger. I was scared for a moment but then remembered all the things Mark always said about him, 'uptight little prick' being only one.

'How is he?'

'Doing as well,' he said, from over that great distance, 'as we may expect at this stage.'

He answered the questions I asked curtly, impatiently: 'No, that is not something which normally occurs,' 'Unlikely,' 'That is not usual.' Just before the call ended, I hesitated before saying, 'Dr Jaegerson, do you think he's going to be all right?' and in the very second of saying it, knew the inanity, the open-ended, innocent, ignorant foolishness of what I'd said. I thought he'd respond with withering irritation but instead, there was a weighted silence.

'Mr Blum, nothing is ever certain,' he said.

I arrived in New York towards the end of January last year, after Mark's operation.

It was a significant month, the first of a new millennium. We were to meet at Ellis Island, Mark's idea, a good one as it turned out, one which established us immediately on level ground, avoiding the awkwardness of the fact that I was staying in his apartment and would've had to act as both host and guest, an intruder in a private place. He'd been staying with his friends Alison and Berndt in their house in upstate New York and that morning Alison, who travels into work a couple of times a week somewhere in Tribeca, brought him as far as Battery Park. I hadn't been in New York for a few years, since Sarah's eighty-fifth birthday party a few years before, an occasion of unlikely, mellow cheer.

It always takes days for me to adjust to the theft of hours and I woke ridiculously early on my first morning there, still dark, just before dawn. I looked out at the fine silver lights draped round the ornamental trees on a concourse far below, the sinister rise of steam from manhole covers. The day as it began was balmy, the air a damp, pale haze over the city. By breakfast time, the rain was falling in a steady deluge.

Mark phoned at nine, his voice close and welcome without the hum of distance.

'Have you been up for hours?'

'Of course.'

'That damned curve in the earth! What are you doing today?'

'Oh, wandering about. The shops. Up to the Frick, perhaps. See what's on at the Met. What about you? Are you going for a walk?'

'No, I won't if it's still raining.'

'Are you worse today?'

'No, it's just a bit wet.'

I was disappointed. I'd wanted to think of Mark walking under trees, breathing fresh, restorative air.

Mark's huge umbrella held the rain away from me that morning, turned the steady downpour into a silver, hissing steel curtain falling in grilles, in bars around the margins of green cloth. Walking up Fifth Avenue, I saw wet birds perching among the branches in Central Park, lonely, possibly dangerous figures sitting on benches or disappearing into the byways of the park.

I phoned Sarah in the afternoon. Mark and I had agreed to say nothing more about his illness, only that I was coming for a visit.

'Why aren't you coming to see me?'

'I'm seeing you on Thursday, Sarah. Abe and Matty are bringing you across to Ellis for the day.'

'So they are. I like to see the city. I don't get much chance, you know.'

'Mark'll be there too.'

'Oh, good. Daniel, did you remember my stockings?'

She had told me exactly where to go when I phoned her before I left Glasgow, one of the fragrant department stores of the past where fragile gilt chairs perched beside bright, warm counters. I didn't tell her, nor would I, that they had all closed down.

Sarah is our late mother's sister. She was born here in Glasgow, unlike both our parents who were brought as children from Eastern Europe. She was nine years younger than our mother. I realise that I've never known much about her, only that I believe she, like our mother, trained as a teacher and that she was married once, briefly, to a plump, bearded man who still lives somewhere in the very distant vision of my childhood memory. He was, I remember our mother telling us, a traveller in prayer books and phylacteries, although at the time she told us I had no idea what that meant. Mark and I, when we discussed him not so long ago, couldn't remember much more than that although we were delighted to recall the same single moment of his handing each of us, with some solemnity, a large nut chocolate in a silver paper wrapper. We had no reason to doubt what we were told, which was that he'd died, until later when we began to wonder. It seemed odd that his name was never mentioned, that he hadn't taken on the status that the dead invariably did, being spoken of in terms of quite unrealistic perfection, and when we overheard our father, after an argument with Sarah, muttering about it being no wonder poor Harry hadn't been able to stand it, we understood. Still, Sarah took on the role and status of widow, playing bridge with other widows, meeting groups of them in town for coffee in the mornings. Looking back on it now, I realise that she must have been very young when Harry left, not that one would have thought it. That generation always looked old, not, I think, just to the eyes of children. I look at photos now and wonder at young faces in elderly guise, a blight on an entire generation, as if a pair of wars had, between them, stolen a portion of their lives, plunging them straight from maturity to old age, the ugly clothes, the punishing hairstyles. I've never thought of her as anything but omnipresent, so that her longevity fails to surprise me. Sarah always favoured Mark. I can hear her now:

'Such enthusiasm, *kayn ahora!*'

God, that expression! How long is it since I've let those words enter my mind? *Kayn ahora!* That Yiddish incantation against the evil eye without which our mother and Sarah would never speak of anyone, anyone they loved. They never praised or expressed hope for the future without invoking its protective power.

'*Kayn ahora!*'

'Mark will do well, *kayn ahora!*' as if you might speak no word of joy or expectation without provoking the vengeance of the Almighty. It's part of an inheritance of fear, appeasement. It goes along with superstitions about salt and knives and shoes, alien, illogical governances which I've had to struggle against over the years, beat down. The very words make the years seem far away.

Our father didn't believe in any of those things, incantations, sops to Fate. He was in the army during the Great War, and though he didn't ever say it, I imagine that the experience wouldn't leave you with much expectation of the benefits of appeasing all, or any gods. He was a medical student then, with two years more to complete when he enlisted. He spoke of it to us with measured concealment, about coming out of the army where he'd served as a medical officer in France and returning to the life of a student. After he qualified, he became a GP. In the days before the establishment of the NHS., here in Glasgow, going up and down tenement stairs, delivering babies, treating TB, witness to the poverty which made him from the 1930s a quiet but committed communist. He was never, I think, a member of the party, only one of the people who thought that there must be a way of changing the world for the better, believing that to be it. He'd wanted to fight in Spain but was too old, recently married and in doubt as to whether he could do more there or at home. He thought about it for so long that Mark had been born, and by then, that particular war was almost over and Franco victorious. He always regretted not having gone.

Our parents married late and died within a few years of each other while Mark and I were at university: our father first, from a heart attack. I remember the phone call, the mean stripes of brown paint tracing the line of the stairwell in my hall of residence.

We've always felt, Mark and I, that disappointment played its part in our father's death, the aftermath of Suez and Hungary which we'd all followed with a horrified, fascinated interest, a time of fatal disappointment which seemed to lead to an irreversible lowness in spirit from which he never really recovered. I feel a shiver of remembrance and recognition now, hyper-aware suddenly of my fear of the sinister undertow which moves below the surface of events. Dark knowledge, *acidie*, that true look into the heart of the affairs of men, the existential gaze which, when you think of it too much, leads you to believe that, truly, most of us most of the time live in a state of blind and quite inexplicable optimism.

1956, the year which blew apart a fragile, fatal dream. The Soviet Union crushed more than Hungary. The last embers of believers' faith flamed for a terrible moment into their blinded eyes, then went out. We saw it in our father as the wireless re-played distant voices appealing for help which nobody would give. I can still hear it – 'Help Hungary! Help Hungary!' The world turned to stone and ice.

It was the desire to make a small act of redress which made our parents offer a home to Anci and István Goldmann. As far as I remember, someone my father knew who was in contact with István, asked if they would. Anci arrived first. She must have been twenty then, the same age as Mark. She was with us for a few months, in our house. Then István joined her and not long after that, they moved to London and I never spoke to her again. I didn't know until this summer if Mark ever did. I do know that until our mother died a few years later, the two of them corresponded regularly.

Our mother's death was slower than our father's, from the late effects of a disease, probably rheumatic fever, which she'd had as a child in some God-awful village in Lithuania. It's strange to me now that I don't even know where for sure. The girls ask and are frustrated by my ignorance and what they assume to be my lack of curiosity. I tell them that it's the very proximity of events which dictates these things, history, fashion possibly and that their generation has the distance to be fascinated. They will, I've no doubt, ferret out the details and the facts. I've never been able to explain properly to them that our parent's generation left behind a life which they had no desire either to continue or recall and that subsequent events in Europe only confirmed their belief that the places they had left were best left. Occasionally I wondered about it, the day they arrived at Glasgow or Leith, I'm not even sure which, but it became even more irrelevant to me after I travelled in Eastern Europe myself, in Poland and Lithuania and the Ukraine. After that, knowing of the tidal wave which engulfed us all, individual stories seemed to lose their piquancy and point. Our father used to say that the family was heading for America but were so sea-sick on the crossing from Riga that they had staggered off the ship at the first port of call. It's the story everybody tells to explain why they're here and not in America. It must be, I'm sure, the only existing Jewish sea-faring myth. I'm a terrible sailor, so perhaps in our case it's true. If they'd carried on, they'd have arrived at Ellis Island. It's odd to think about it, as I did the morning I went to meet Mark.

That day is fixed in my mind for many reasons, not least of them for the memory of cold. It was, I think, the coldest day I've ever experienced anywhere, worse even than some of the cold-blasted Central European cities when, even in an urban street, you wonder if you'll make it to the next warm place. The air that day felt like the razor I'd used for shaving: fierce, flaying, bone-paring. The weather forecasters said that there would be an hour of snow which would begin at eight, the fine edges of the snowstorm which would fall a little before turning to hurl itself out over the sea. It began at eight, covering the city with thin, white blowing powder.

That morning, I was the only person sitting upstairs on the open deck of the Ellis Island ferry. I kept thinking that if I hadn't put on layers of clothes, woollen underwear, tee-shirts, sweaters under my coat, I could have died up there on that bench. I'd have been found sitting upright, held up by my wall of clothes, my frozen, crystalline blood crackling inside my soft blue skin while light-hearted, chattering people trailed out from the warm saloon below to climb up into the dim insides of the Statue of Liberty, the ferry's first stop. Most people got off there and the ferry moved slowly away from Liberty Island. My throat felt dry, flayed by cold. I was apprehensive, aware of a butterfly in the gut, a deep grab of fear beneath my coat. People must have felt those feelings before on that particular stretch of water, I knew that. They were travelling in the other direction though, a new life ahead, a similar but essentially different set of anxieties. Manhattan behind me was like a natural rock formation, an icy mountain range waiting to be climbed. As we moved though the bay, Liberty gave her eternal, verdigris salute to my left side.

The bay looked grey, a dull, quotidian swell. I'd gone deliberately early while morning was still settling on the city. The scattering of light January snow stopped as they'd said it would, at nine. I was far too early for my meeting with Mark. The promised, or threatened one with Sarah was to take place there too. Mark had arranged for her to be brought over in the early afternoon by her friends, the valiant Schlonskys.

Walking out that morning to find a taxi, I'd had to brace myself against the cold. A gust up Fifth Avenue blew unknown people into each other's arms in a frozen embrace, whirled them in a cold dance, mink against mink across the broad, empty area of Grand Army Plaza. What the homeless did was almost beyond thinking about, all over a vast country, or over the areas of it marked blue or white on the weather map at least, rag-stained huddles clutching skinny dogs under blankets, their handwritten begging cards scudding under cars. The endless patrols of the sad and lonely must have given up fingers and toes that day. When I'd commented conversationally about the weather to one of the staff at Mark's gym early that morning, she'd looked at me almost pityingly. 'If you think this is cold, go to Chicago,' she said. Her tone and look made me feel chastised. I felt spoiled and temperate, effetely European.

I hailed a taxi and the driver, whose thuggish, heavy-browed face glared out from his identity badge on the dashboard, turned out to be Egyptian. We talked all the way downtown about poetry and music and the writing of Mahfouz. He exclaimed with unusual, touching delight over the qualities of the very ordinary peppermint he took from the packet I offered him. I was glad of his company because so far, people had seemed to me to be even more closed in than ever, locked hermetically into the seal of ear-muffs and woollen hats, behind the keep-off facade of fur and wool, inside their leather boots, in behind their cold, blue-lipped faces.

Mark would be there by mid-morning. I hadn't discussed it with him, but planned to be there first. I wondered if he might think of doing that, but decided he wouldn't. Still, I half-expected to bump into him in Battery Park while I was waiting for the boat. I walked for a little while under the trees, fascinated by the meticulous run, stop, freeze of grey squirrels over hard, grey ground.

The wind that morning blasted round the ferry like dry ice hurled at speed. I looked down into the ruffled depth of the bay, opaque with industry and usage and thought, as I always do when I look into a body of water, about falling in. That day was so cold, you wouldn't even have felt it. A few moments of horror, panic, regret, then numbness and oblivion. I watched Liberty as the ferry moved away, followed the upturned line of her raised arm. She had been cunningly placed in the narrows at the mouth of the bay so that only at a certain, dramatic moment of turning towards land was the pale, exhausted immigrant, leaning on some sea-washed rail, lifted from the slough of a squalid, extended crossing to soar, however briefly, into the wide, bright world of hope and possibility. The island across the bay looked as I remembered but brighter, neater now as if someone had taken a giant vacuum cleaner to it. I'm not a natural emigrant, I know it. If I'd been a typical representative of humanity, America would probably never have been discovered. I wondered how many people had crossed that narrow stretch of water. I didn't know, only that it was millions, many millions.

I remember telling myself that I wasn't much more than a teenager the last time I saw Ellis Island, almost a child, thinking of how obliquely time deals with life, makes bridges, cuts out, eradicates huge sections of what once seemed like a seamless transition. I can see myself sitting there, in late middle-age, locked like a piece in a jigsaw to myself as a resentful, bewildered youth. It was an excuse to use words like 'child' and 'teenager'. I acknowledged that, even as I thought it, wondering why I was still trying excuses, as if the words themselves had the power to absolve. We weren't children then, Mark and I. We were in our early twenties, educated, not poor, with all the promise for our lives and careers whole, unspent in front of us. I thought of the things from which we'd moved away, things grown more than distant, ones which had become, during intervening decades, unbelievable, as if they'd never existed, although we knew they had, the husks and hulls lying scattered between us, the air in which they were preserved, controlled and silent.

We'd always been close, Mark and I, with the closeness found perhaps only among the children of elderly parents, a mutual defence system, not required against our parents but against an unpredictable universe, one which contained all manner of perversity, one which contained Sarah. We became, as we grew older, adept at turning her partialities to comedy, her approval as undesirable as her disapproval.

'Well done! Clearly a coup!' I'd echo Sarah's unjudgemental praise, countered by Mark's 'Falling short of the gold standard there!' 'Well, there's no arguing with that!' and we'd raise our eyes to heaven and between us, balance out the pain. The fluency of our barmitzvah readings, our talents, our characters, our ambitions, hopes, intentions, the way we looked and spoke and walked, everything fell into the ambit of an aggrieved and bitter soul.

Never religious, not truly so, we'd done what was required of us, going to cheder for religious instruction, walking en famille to shul for the major festivals, sometimes on Shabbas too, on our own if the mood took us, but it had been eating, the rigours of the dietary laws which provided us with entertainment, transformed to a game, those few years of covering tracks, of constant vigilance. We went to the same school, a high, aging structure of stairwells and partitions, now turned into flats, and learned never to accept food from anyone in case the other was observing silently from a staircase or a balcony, standing by the long window over the school playground and garden, watching with the eyes of a raptor the lunchtime swapping of sandwiches, the offering of a bag of sweets, the easy way a person could forget and dip a hand in and find some kind of undreamed-of perdition.

'You took a bite out of that sandwich. I saw you.'

'Don't be daft, I never.'

'You did. You know you did.' Sweets reputedly tainted with gelatine, ice-cream said, most likely wrongly, to be made with pork fat, all of it under our scrutinising eyes, with Yom Kippur the serious challenge, the annual test, rigorous, fanatic when, for the twenty-four hours of the fast, we watched each other with the iron cruelty of zealots.

'You swallowed when you cleaned your teeth!'

'I did not!'

'You did. I saw your throat move. You've broken the fast!'

'I have not!'

We both almost missed the sweet fire of competition when, not very long after, we stopped observing Yom Kippur.

I didn't speak to Anci again after she left Glasgow. István died in the first winter of Mark's illness. I cut out a few of the obituaries to put in my collection. There were pages of them in the broadsheets with huge photos of him, broodingly pensive under thunderous Hungarian eyebrows, and long, wordy assessments of his life and achievements. In a bookshop a few months after he died, I saw that they'd re-issued some of his books with smart new covers. It was an unexpected feeling, cutting out the obituaries and shutting them away in a drawer. Satisfying. What the Americans, appropriately enough in the circumstances, call 'closure.'

In all, Mark lived in New York for almost twice as long as he lived in Glasgow. In some inner part of my mind, I'd continued to feel for all those years, that he belonged in Glasgow, as if his life in America was a holiday and that one day it would be over and he'd come home. He'd been a few times for visits or celebrations. He came for Tal's and my wedding but was quite silent on that occasion, almost depressed and I assumed that it was because of the comparative failings of Glasgow, its smallness perhaps or the fact that it hadn't changed. When he brought Tamar and Noah just after they graduated from high school, our almost grown-up children were absurdly wary of each other, constrained by the occasion or separated by mutually recognised though otherwise indiscernible tribal barriers. At one dinner out, I recall Mark addressing them all.

'Cousins!' he said, portentous and good-humoured, trying to play the part of a mythic Jewish paterfamilias, trying to forge them into the family I thought they'd never become. They did, but it took Mark's own illness to accomplish it.

No-one even thinks of Suez now. It's a name dropped into the bubbling vat of history, fished out from time to time for cursory inspection, for brief mention of Anthony Eden, usually in connection with political ineptitude or failed gall bladder operations. About the Hungarian Uprising, silence. I think of the words 'loss of innocence', a concept all the greater in the absence of a belief in original sin. Which particular innocence? People born before me have different betrayals, different losses of innocence, Munich, Czechoslovakia, Austria, the ones born after me too, Vietnam, Laos, Cambodia. And now, Palestine, what's just happened in New York. I wonder sometimes if people growing up now can be anything but cynical.

Time invades my mind. It did that day on the ferry, every spectre of love and guilt clawing at my brain, the question of why Mark decided to go, the obvious reasons presenting themselves, that Glasgow was an easy place to leave in the late fifties, grim, seeming irrecoverably cheerless. I used to describe it to the children, the war, remembered with the unreliable memory of a small child, most of it from re-telling, the bombing of the Clyde, rationing, air-raid sirens and I knew it would take decades for them to understand. My favourite, recurring image of the city as it was when I was growing up, was of fireplaces hanging storeys up, rooms bared to view, layers of wallpaper and ripped floors, half-tenements sliced and falling. I never scrimped on my descriptions of the Glasgow fogs, graphic, poetic accounts of pale lights wavering through impenetrable murk, panic feelings of isolation and misery. It was all true, reason enough, our parents no longer there to make us feel we couldn't leave.

I remember the conversation, the pure, chill shock of it.

'What would you say to coming to the States with me?'

'What for? Where?'

'To live, Dan. New York, where else?'

He was always the one who was courageous, the enthusiast. They always said that Mark would do the unforeseeable and exciting. Sarah particularly. He had to persuade me.

'Come for six months, a year, see what it's like.'

'I might.'

'If we go, we'll have to ask Sarah if she'd like to come.'

'Will we?'

'Of course. We can't leave her here alone.'

When our mother died, she had became ours, as if she'd been left to us, like the codicil to a will or an awkward piece of furniture.

'Perhaps she won't want to.'

We asked Sarah and of course, she agreed.

That morning, echoes of ancient conversation whispered at me in the wind, from the lap of river water,

'Mark I never said I would ...'

'But Dan, you did, you did,' bringing the slow, cold creep of ancient feelings, ones I'd already felt just by staying in Mark's apartment, a set of responses I'd thought dormant, siblings responses, a congenital irritation, a wide, enduring amazement at how inseparable and maddening were the threads of familiarity and distance. Actually being there, in the rooms themselves, Mark's possessions in their careful, even beautiful, order had seemed to put me vividly, terribly in touch with the way I once was, making me look too closely at my own place in life's slow, laconic stir.

I was always certain that I was right over the matter of what I'd said to Mark about staying in America. I've told myself often enough that I'm not a person who would fail to leave open clear lines of retreat. My proviso got lost but I reassured myself, wrongly as it happens, that it hadn't been my fault. I wondered often where it had got lost, in whose memory, whose imagination.

'Mark, I only said I might.'

'That's not true.'

'I don't really want to stay. Anyway, I never said I would.'

'But Dan, it's what I thought. It's what you said.'

'You were wrong, then. I'm sorry.'

'What about Sarah?'

'I'll always share my responsibility for her.'

Now of course, I see the full enormity of it and though I'd like to be able to blame Sarah for what happened, I can't. Reasons delineate themselves and will not leave me, only some of them worthy, only some of them able to bear the weight of examination. I can explain to myself why but can't find the way to make it seem other that it was, an abrogation, fuelled desire to separate my life from Mark's, the suspicion I couldn't dispel which made me wonder if, when he asked me to go with him, he'd wanted to get me away from here. I thought of Anci, and of István, and wanted nothing more than to live my life without the sense that I would forever live in the shadow of my brother.

I came back here and felt free. Miserable and lonely, too. I was oppressed for years by the guilt I felt about Sarah, and tried to make myself feel better by preventing myself from forgetting her cruelties to my younger self, her crimes of omission and commission, although by now even I've almost outlived my resentment of her. That day on the ferry, too, knowing I was going to see her later, I thought about them but they seemed to shrink in my mind to infinitesimal pin-holes, blinks of light before they disappeared into a vastness of insignificance. I'd held words there, ready to be summoned up, undimmed for three-quarters of a lifetime but I didn't summon them, not at that moment when I knew that, across in the hazy chill of New Jersey, she would be beginning the long preparation of the elderly for a day out.

The island was on my left as the ferry approached the quay at Ellis Island. Its copper domes glowing across the bay even on that dull morning. The ferry turned, rocked, moored. Standing, moving out from between the seats, walking were all awkward, ridiculously constrained by the impossible layers of clothing. I made my way down the steps. The party of Koreans I had seen in the ferry queue clutching their bags with their travel labels from a Seoul travel agency, were ahead of me, some of them wearing the mock spectacles they had bought on the ferry, hideous things with Liberty's crown executed in brilliant green plastic. Even some of the neat, beautifully elegant women were wearing them. I shuffled slowly behind them off the boat.

As I walked along the quayside in front of the building in the freezing air, it seemed an entirely different place, a place renewed, and I felt a faint, possessive jealousy of its new accessibility. The sun began to glow over the bay. It was odd to think that I knew the temperature for every day of the rest of the week. The forecasting in the States always seems so accurate, so authoritative. In Britain, one never knows, and I often wonder if that's the way I prefer it, a balance of possibilities, walking out not knowing if there would be rain, the future hovering, oscillating in a state of undecided equipoise.

I have here with me the books I carried that day: Mark's childhood prayer book with his name in our father's hand on the flyleaf, and a copy of one I bought for him, the Psalms in Scots with which he fell inexplicably, passionately in love. The copy is worn now, pages detach themselves and fall out and when I pick them up to try to replace them in order, I hear his voice exclaiming, declaiming and my voice too, blurry with three-in-the-morning sleeplessness, lines in barely waking sequence in a room and no-one there but us.

Chapter 16

New York, early winter, 2000

Dr K. L. Jaegerson, Neurosurgeon.
Specialties: Neuro-oncology, Endoscopic Neurosurgery.
Suite 53,
43, East Reveille Avenue,
New York

Dr D.Rocca,
Department of Radiotherapy,
Mount Shalom Medical Center,
New York.

25th January, 2000.

Dear Dr Rocca,

Mr Mark Blum: 25th May, 1936.

This patient presented with a 6-week history of partial seizures. He was found to have a tumor in the right parietal lobe with some mass effect and surrounding edema. He was started on anti-convulsants and dexamethasone. I carried out a craniotomy on December 28th and he has made a good recovery with no new neurological deficit.

This was a subtotal resection. The histology has proved to be a glioblastoma. I have explained the significance of the pathology to him and recommended radiotherapy.

I would be grateful if you would see him and advise about radiotherapy,

Yours sincerely,
K.L.Jaegerson,
Neurosurgeon.

He's slow in the mornings these days, staying late in bed in the guest room of his friend's house in upstate New York, not sleeping but lying in the warmth, retracing time, trying to recover the stilled momentum of his life. He listens to the sounds of the house around him, the sounds of phones, kitchen clattering, the barking of the dog. All is domestic, timeless around his peaceful wakening every morning to a sense of absence, of wondering what's gone, lifting his fingers to his head.

The few days he spends there seem even at the time, a dream, one of quiet rain, of deep green waves of trees outside the tall windows he sits beside during the afternoons in the part of his friends' house he himself designed. He can't congratulate himself excessively on its beauty because it was the least he could have done, given a felicitous site, level, perched above an interesting, well-tended garden, within sight of a loop of fast water, somewhere between stream and river. His design in use is as easy as it should be, and as appropriate.

For once, carrying his things into the comfortable room where he's stayed many times before, Mark has felt willing to succumb to the offer of care and over the days he spends there, behaves in a way he'd once never even have considered, sitting idly, watching other people cooking, lounging after dinner with his feet raised on a footstool, allowing other people to replenish his wine glass, in obedience to Alison's constant instruction to relax. This is all alien to him, both the slowness and the acquiescence. On every other visit to Alison and Berndt, he's always been first up, walking or running in the morning air, preparing breakfast for them, baking muffins, smiling, the perfect, cheering guest, but now, it's different and he has no choice but to accept. The guilt of it never entirely vanishes and often, he dislikes the tacit agreement to this leisure, feeling at his back both conscience and the need to act in reciprocation. He needs to make something, do something, chop the wood or prune back the hedge although it's not the season for pruning back the hedge

Every morning when he does get up, he examines the appearance of his scar under the excoriating lights in his bathroom, tilting his head towards the magnifying mirror which shows it still to be fading back nicely into the tones of the skin of his scalp. Every morning in his pyjamas he carries out a small ritual dance, testing for function, movement, sensation, flexing feet and hands and knees, stroking the length of his fingers one by one, turning his head, lowering his chin, raising it, testing his eyes by picking out a detail on the horizon, checking to see how much of the newspaper headline he can read before putting on his glasses. Tentatively, he bends forwards, the pull of his spine making him feel hopeful, measuring the distance between fingertips and floor.

He must, he realises, act as if recovery is a purpose in itself, but it's too weak a proposition for him to approach with any great enthusiasm. It's an abrogation, but of what, he doesn't know. He must, he tells himself, be careful, but he doesn't know the consequences of being otherwise. His obligation is to effect a re-entry into the atmosphere of earth. Circumstance has removed him from its air and its necessities but now, like a spacecraft or meteor, he has to crash through a barrier to accept the harsh inevitability of falling. He has to do it, to re-enter the atmosphere of his own life again, but the thought scares him, of what he has to do, of the day which will come when everyone else is gone and he's alone.

His friends are peaceably busy people and although Berndt is recently retired from his job as an economist with one of the large banks, he's still working, writing the book he's been planning for two or three years now about Third World debt. Alison, who works part-time as a physical therapist, has a share in a small shop in Tribeca, a shop which sells the work of craftsmen, some jewellery, the odd antique item which catches her eye or that of her diminutive partner Lizzie who runs the shop.

Mark and Berndt eat lunch together every day. Mark is amused, watching Berndt newly domestic, fussing with plates and recipes. After lunch, Berndt returns to the catastrophic, long-imploded economies of Zaire and Sudan while Mark takes his books and laptop and sits in the afternoons in the summer house he designed, watching the trees shifting in the wind, the broken turmoil of light on the surface of the stream now tumbling with winter rain. He draws, still testing his hands, eyes, brain. In the mid-afternoon he goes back to bed for a couple of hours, sleeping more profoundly than he does at night, waking every time to the same image of destiny presenting itself to him as a series of rooms through which he must pass, whose doors close perfectly, silently behind him. He rises, slightly, pleasantly disorientated, to the imminent prospect of Alison's early evening call:

'Mark? Bernie? Ready for drinks?'

He begins to compile a list. It's his first list since his operation and a list, he knows, is comprehensively affirmative. Elaborating upon it as he sits in the afternoon, he begins with the idea of restoring his body. He's no longer too thin. The steroids have altered that and now he's scared of becoming fat, of losing the fitness gained over years. He has to be fit, sharing the obsession of his peers, the maintenance of the body as both competition and reward. And practical necessity in this land of vultures. He'll go back to running, he thinks, but then re-considers. It might be better to start with swimming. What is this, he wonders, this mad paradox, the feeling that he has to be fit in order to face the likelihood of further illness? A paradox, or good sense, the unavoidable consequence of the way he lives. So, swimming first for a week or so, then walking. Build up the speed on walking, then running again. Call the gym. It's probably wise to enquire about their policy towards the newly operated-upon. Or not. He deletes this item. If he drops dead on their Italian marble floor, so be it. If he merely collapses, they'll have him removed. They already have the name of his physician and will, no doubt, contact him without a second's delay. Then, returning to work. A couple of hours on the first day, see how it goes. Build up slowly. There is also the radiotherapy. This one is imponderable. Having written the two words, there's nothing more to say.

New spectacles. He's been meaning to do that for a while, even before Jaegerson suggested it, and a haircut, a way-station on the road to likely baldness, before radiotherapy makes it all fall out.

Another thing he must do is to get rid of his collection of books on the brain. Now, they seem to signal only unhealthy preoccupation, his buying them a lapse of the sort he overcame in order to buy them. He'll take them to one of the second-hand shops where they sell medical books. Better that a student should have them than him. Give books away.

Writing his list gives Mark energy of sorts, suggests to him that soon he'll grow tired of lassitude, the limbo in which he seems to be living, the limbo which might, if he's not careful, overwhelm him and suck him in until he comes to enjoy it and to expect nothing further. But this is time for recovery. For God's sake, he says to himself, listen to someone else for once! Listen to what Ali's saying. Relax!

The word, annoyingly enough, recurs with predictable frequency.

'I hope you're relaxing, Dad!'

'Don't do too much, Dad, I know what you're like. You have to relax. It'll make recovering all the quicker if you do.'

Why does he hate the word so much? Because it's too like the word 'lax', or even 'lacks', because there's something of opening, gushing about it, something uncontrolled implicit, a sense that he mistrusts.

Mark uses his time to be in contact with his children, exchanging frequent e-mails about nothing in the feckless, self-limiting way the medium demands. It's not a way to express anything important, one too easy, he finds, in which to be flippant, or to say too much. Far too easy. Tam describes her days with the five- and six-year-olds she teaches, sending the odd drawing or poem, works of charm which, nonetheless, make him appreciate the awesome difficulty of spending entire days with little children. Tam is a language graduate, but now teaches with a fervour and enthusiasm which both frighten and fascinates him. From the first, he loved the process of his own children's acquisition of knowledge, the brutal, living challenge of it when they faced him throughout their childhoods with facts and observations he'd neither known nor considered, the catalogues of avian taxonomy dealt out by Noah over years from the leafy alleyways of Central Park. Now, he sends sonograph recordings he's making of corvid calls, patterns of wavery blue stripes on a background of black, impossible to interpret but oddly touching. Obeying the instructions to click on the image, he's able to hear the same sounds Noah does, the ones he's studying with minute attention, small, disembodied crow voices which call to him from forests far away.

Contact Sarah. This, he must do urgently because Dan'll have to see her when he's here. Thinking about it, he wonders why Dan has to see her, but long-extended gestures towards duty and politeness apparently prevail against all sense or justice, and he knows that there would be a lingering hint of something neglected if he didn't. He e-mails Tamar.

I'm busy making lists. One of the things I have to do while I'm here is to get in touch with Sarah and Abe and Matty and arrange something for your uncle Dan's visit.

When exactly is Dan coming? she replies, *and by the way, will Sarah be ninety or ninety-one, this year? I can't remember.*

He smiles when he sees it.

Ninety-one. God, Tam, think of it! She's ancient, so ancient I can't even grasp the idea of her age. It's beyond decency. It's frankly disgusting. It's selfish. It's monstrous to carry on living for so long.

Having tapped in the sentences, Mark quickly deletes them again. Tam would not approve. She'd send the message on to Noah and both would reply, conveying, in one way or another, that he's unredeemed, irredeemable. He has never expected understanding from his children. He's always thought, hoped, that it might be something which would develop in time but he no longer knows how much time. They all seem old enough now, himself included. It may, though, be differences in generations, differences in emphasis which lead him to the feeling that often he's disapproved of, not sufficiently serious. Had he sent the e-mail, the one he got back in return would have been unforgiving but instructive. They both love to instruct. His children deny him the luxury of flippancy about things like this, about anything. He remembers the air of disapproval which seemed to ring, to buzz in the air when they still lived at home or spent time with him after he and Lee split up, when they'd strike as one, arguing him into the silence of oblivion, but now they're more likely to exchange glances, mention the matter individually later, 'It's really not funny, Dad…' He used to feel a certain small resentment at their unity of mind. Supportive, the word they use of one another, of their friends, an estimation of their deepest worth. A word he didn't know for the first thirty-five years at least. Is it retrospective guilt that makes him feel like this, thinking of Dan?

'Your great aunt is ninety,' he writes instead, 'and will be ninety-one on the 24th of June, but of course you remember the date. She tells me every year when you and Noah send her cards. She tells me triumphantly, as if the fact of her receiving a card means that someone else hasn't, that you, and indeed I, and Dan and anyone else who remembers, have favoured her over someone else. She probably takes each card she gets round every lonely, ancient virgin in the Shoshana Blumstein Home to remind them of the dry, salty taste of their aloneness. I remember the occasion as I do the date with consternation and foreboding because we always had to have a tea-party for her when Dan and I were small, and she insisted every year that we dress up and treat her like the queen. I always thought of it as one of the minor festivals, one on which we remembered a great tearing down, or the after-effects of another small, sad tribal war. She said apocalyptic things, even then: 'Another year gone!' 'I wonder how many more I'll see out.' That, bear in mind, was when she was younger than I am now. It was during the brief, few warm weeks of Scottish summer when people talked of 70 degrees in tones of awe and warning and Dan and I wanted to be out on our bikes or messing around in the stream in Pollok Estate, not paying obligatory court to Sarah. We knew, though, the value of seeing that the formalities were performed (the result, no doubt, of long training.) They consisted of – first at our house – a coloured iced sponge cake with candles and then, a few days later, among Sarah's little tables and scratchy sofas and cut-glass dishes in the shapes of baskets, an array of delights probably thought of fondly only by near-centenarians or antique collectors: Empire biscuits (!) fairy cakes and tough pink meringues glued together with oozing yellow cream. There was always some Greenbaum's cheesecake too, and apple strudel, a small consolation indeed.

In a way I'm fascinated by Sarah's longevity. I hope that it means that her genetic inheritance will fall to you (and not my apparently lesser sort) and see you both out as ancients and sages. That, at least, will be the difference. You'll be the repository of every earthly and unearthly piece of knowledge on the corvid. Library shelves will groan and even call out for mercy and you'll have cast a beam of light which will illuminate a piece of the universe forever. Tam too, wizened and feisty, toppling under the weight of her pedagogic knowledge and enlightenment.

Sarah has never learned anything in her life. Not how to deal with people, not even the simple fact that people will respond to you if you're nice or even pretend to be nice. Or that, if you do pretend to be nice, it's in your own best interests to maintain the pretence for as long as possible. Canasta, that's about it. Crowned canasta queen of a Jewish retirement home in New Jersey, no small achievement in itself, I acknowledge, although it doesn't seem much for an entire lifetime (and a half). (That, and malicious gossip, deliciously called in the scriptures, *lashon ra*, evil tongue!) I don't want to be unfair to her; I know that women didn't have the opportunities and she was left on her own early and so on, but what has she done with all that time? Your grandmother, her own sister after all, had the same education as Sarah but became a woman of learning and independence, and widows, even self-styled ones, can learn things, grow, expand their minds. All those years and no philosophy, no understanding, none of the wisdom which you almost can't help picking up along the way, the stuff that's due to younger generation, to yourself, to your suffering family. And then I say to myself, who cares, what's this about groaning shelves and venerability? Who cares. Clearly now, she'll outlast me.'

Re-reading it, Mark deletes everything but the first sentence. He adds some small bits of news about Ali and Berndt, a message Ali wants him to pass on to her about something she might like in the shop, a description of the garden. Having done this, he clicks 'send'.

Abe Schlonsky is phoned. Affable as always, as willing as ever to be helpful, an arrangement is made for Sarah's transportation. Abe's wife Matty is one of Sarah's friends and canasta partners, a few years younger than Sarah and still vigorous. He decides he won't tell them about his illness. Why burden them? The Schlonskys are kind and willing to the point where Mark wonders, often, why.

'Hey,' Abe says, 'it'll be good to see you.'

'You too, Abe, you too.'

Then Sarah. His conversation with her is as always, or not as always but almost so, a small degree further along a line of retreat from lucidity, a point on the continuum of the irreversible processes of age.

'I mentioned it last time I spoke to you, Dan's coming over next week.'

'Oh. Why? Has he got something to do here?'

'Just seeing us.'

'He's usually got something else too, hasn't he?'

'Has he?'

'Oh yes. He does. He always does. I asked him to bring those things.'

'What things?'

'For my legs. The things for my legs.'

'Stockings?'

'Yes, that's right. I hope he brings them. He forgets a lot.'

'Does he? Anyway, Sarah, are you well?'

'He's always forgotten things. Me? I've still got that, you know, when I walk about. The doctor was here but he never spends enough time. I was hoping he'd examine me properly this time but he didn't. They all say that, the people here. He doesn't do it properly. He's always in a hurry to get away.'

'That's Thursday then, Sarah. Abe'll collect you at twelve. Do you want me to phone Mrs Spellman to tell her and she'll remind you?'

'No, you needn't. I'm perfectly capable of remembering.'

He will get, he knows, half a dozen calls from her over the next few days to check the details, which day, what time, where is it they're to meet, messages left on his phone, a querulous voice saying, 'Who is that?' before the call's abruptly ended. How many people does he know, looking after elderly parents, who say it: when I get like that, shoot me. He's said it himself to Tam and Noah. Shoot me. He always wonders what happens when the moment arrives. Does anyone ever say, 'You're like that now. Bang!' He'll give an account of the call to Dan later and they'll both laugh ruefully and will feel guilty without quite knowing why.

There's a quality to afternoon, the feeling of a section of the day adrift which leads him to reflection, a pursuit which in ordinary circumstances he avoids as the pastime of the self-destructive, the morbidly self-obsessed. This, though, feels timely, a slow, lyric trail from now, far back to an indeterminate then, the prospect of his imminent meeting with Dan obliging him to this small pain, this small luxury, the re-examination of old angers and bludgeoning of elderly ghosts from their long-accustomed niches. The most accustomed of these is the mutual assumption that Dan's decision not to stay here still lies as an invisible barrier between them. In truth, he hasn't minded for a long time that Sarah stayed and Dan didn't. On the contrary, it has been the memory of the details of Dan's going which has proved stubbornly indelible, in particular his refusal even to take Dan to the airport. Dreadful, how one moment of petulance, one wrong decision can live in you for ever. Now, from this cool and planetary distance, he's able to see it as it was, now that there's no anger left, none of the righteous judgement which infiltrated those moments when he wasn't engaged in the frenetic pursuit of his own life. How long it takes to understand anything, clarity expanding like an ink drop flowering in a pool of years. It may of course have been that he simply lacked perception, but now, suddenly, it's easy to see himself and Dan as they were when young, all armour and spears about everything vital, tongue-tied, all angular, awkward love. He thinks of the years of Dan's tentative transatlantic phone calls; how, with an actor's timing, he'd deliberately hesitate on answering the phone in order to disconcert Dan. Did he derive pleasure from it? Was it from anger? He can't even remember. What he does remember is the day when the earth and ocean shifted, when suddenly he was unaccustomedly alone, when he realised one evening, sitting by himself, that he needed Dan.

In most cases, he thinks, decision is illusory. We can act only in the way we do. He was right and Dan was right, although at the time there could have been no accepting such an obvious idea.

Less accustomed is a cryptic ghost, one long undisturbed, by him at least. Even recalling the time ploughs his mind back to what feels like a land before the invention of colour, a land encased tightly in a sobriety of black and white and grey, Hungary, 1956. Anci, István, Dan. Everything he thinks of is stark and sparse, even the words he remembers being exchanged. Hopelessly, pointlessly, he reflects that, had he and Dan been able to exchange more of them, all might have been other than it was. But, if they had, they wouldn't have been the people that they were. A long time ago, he says to himself, trying by means of a feeble banality to bring a conclusion to these particular thoughts, but one lodges, disconcertingly, persistently in his mind. He tries various ways to dispel it but it will not go away. Until now, he's been quite proud of his perspicacity in having considered every possible aspect and angle of the repercussions of his illness, but now a new, unexpected one has occurred. What, short of bearing them with him in perpetuity to whatever his unknown destination, is he to do with other people's secrets?

Often, in the midst of the quotidian business of living, Mark has considered coincidence, the threads which seem to underlie the small, quick snap of events, the reading of a name the day after you hear it mentioned, mysterious forces which tie one thing in this opaque and cross-webbed universe imperceptibly to another. There is, among Berndt and Ali's considerable collection of books, one by István Goldmann. This may be less coincidence than literary or academic fashion, but it feels like coincidence, eerie chance, a confluence of moment and thought, and one evening after dinner he lifts the book from its shelf.

'Bernie, have you read this?'

'In bits.'

'What do you think of it?'

'Oh, you know, as if I'm being addressed by God. Yeah, I suppose he has some good things to say. He just makes it difficult to find them.'

Old habit flares in him. Which good things might István possibly have to say? For a few years after he and Anci went to live in London, István's name was neither seen nor heard, although Mark knew that he was making his living by teaching and writing. Slowly, his work began to appear, a well-reviewed book followed by articles which, as a matter of scrupulous principle, Mark never read. Then István's voice too began, like some exotic new bird, to be heard. The first time, on a broadcast about the Bay of Pigs, Mark failed to recognise who the speaker was, another well-known Eastern European he assumed, another refugee from the iron lands, and he'd listened with irritation, annoyed by the man's manner and opinions, the pomposity of his delivery until suddenly, by a remark, by his use of words, he realised who it was and a feeling of warmth, of validation flooded through him because then he knew that in his profoundest feelings about István, he was entirely right. That was just the beginning. Soon, István began to appear on television too, giving his opinion on everything, the fall of the Berlin Wall, food, women, culture. It was impossible to watch.

Mark can't remember how long István spent in Glasgow, a few weeks at the most before he gathered Anci up and took her off to London where he already seemed to have contacts who, he seemed confidently certain, would find him a suitable university job. Anci was so different, arriving among them as a knowing child, dead Europe alive in her, frightening and furious. He remembers being scared when he knew she was coming to stay, correctly concerned about everything she'd bring with her, everything he suspected but did not clearly know, a past hazier then than now for being, as it was at the time, almost wordlessly subsumed under the busy enterprise of rebuilding and forgetting. She looked much younger than she was. Discovering they were only a few weeks apart in age seemed to have given them instant recourse to a kind of unity. Not only that, of course, not only that.

He was at university at the time. Dan was still planning to study music. For a moment, he finds the words 'if only' hovering on the margins of his mind. For God's sake! he says to himself, frustrated, hating the nugatory, bloody nature of the past, the fact that there's nothing you can do about it. He's quite right about this being the dogged pastime of the self-obsessed. Everything he thinks is abstract, abstracted. Enough, he says to himself. All will be dealt with. He'll write the letter to Anci that he's owed her for months. There's enough to think about without retrospection and he has to concentrate on other things, plans, because Dan will be here soon. The words have a comfort in themselves: Dan will be here soon.

Chapter 17

Glasgow, late autumn, 2001

Mark and I brought photographs to this house. They're all around me now, on the wall in frames, on our desks. Mine are mostly studies I did of Tal and the girls over the years, Mark's are of Tam and Noah – Lee too, from the early years. There are quite a few of Kirstin with her family, Kirstin with Mark, smiling, entwined, all of them taken in Sweden at Bohuslan where Kirstin's parents had a summer house. They look like early experiments in photography although they're lovely, just slightly out of focus, scenes and people caught in mist and amber northern light.

Tal gazes at me unflinchingly from the wall. Every day, she makes me reflect on how unlike her I am. Had I been like her, I'd have stopped her from going. Also, I'd have asked sharper questions of Jaegerson. I'd have asked pertinent ones to do with time, not the idiot question which expressed, or rather revealed, only my pathetic hope for reassurance, my wish not to be told what I didn't want to hear. In New York in the days before Mark came back from Ali and Berndt's to meet me, I thought of nothing but time, trying to understand what might be the nature of the life ahead. Every morning early I went for a swim in the pool of the hotel nearby where Mark had a subscription, finding my way in silent elevators up to the top of the building, through small, perfect gymnasia, past elderly bankers on rowing machines, along marble inlaid floors to the pool, bright in the flickering, cold blue light falling through the domed glass roof. The day before I met Mark it was already growing cold, and looking down on the frost-silvered trees of Central Park, I felt the cold assume its own aggressive life and try to invade the storm-resistant glass. Standing there, more or less naked, I held my hands along the edges of the windows, absorbing its thin, determined force, almost ice against my fingers. It was strange and wonderful to swim without effort through the tepid blue water of that unnatural place, balanced high above the monstrous city, swimming, floating among brilliant, grey-edged clouds, through towering icebergs of buildings, spindrift of aerials, glints of windows. I swam endlessly towards the light, the snow-bearing clouds, into the sky itself.

I made plans as I swam for going over again in autumn, after the worst heat of the summer, in the winter, the following spring. There would be, surely, a number of springs. I'd arrange my work around it. I could always take an apartment somewhere near Mark's. For Pesach next spring, make a little Seder just for the two of us. If Noah and Tamar could come, so much the better, but if they couldn't, Mark and I would manage together. I'd be able to buy everything I needed: matzo, the ingredients for haroseth, walnuts and apples, the shankbone of a lamb, a root of horseradish, the ritual items. It's New York, after all, I said to myself, a Jewish city. The food our mother used to cook for the festival: the eggs in salt water, beetroot jam with almonds. I'd find things easily. I could ask. Someone would be able to tell me where to go. I could always stop one of the hurrying men in black coats and hats you see about the streets and say, I wonder if you'd mind. I'm a stranger here. For Pesach. They'd direct me somewhere on the Upper West Side; give me names, locations, recommendations.

I'd noticed that there was a complete set of festival prayer books in Mark's apartment. At Rosh Hashanah, I could go to shul with Mark. We could walk in Central Park, the zoo, the ice-rink, the pond. We could spend money; we both enjoyed that, and what the hell, we could spend it on the beautiful and transient, on presents for each other and for our children. We could eat out, some of the gorgeous flash places with wonderful food, or in the brick-walled, noisy warehouses full of loud music and dazzling people. The past would resolve, melt invisibly, easily, leaving only the faint, diminishing trail of something we would be moving away from, fast. We would go to museums, to places we always said we wanted to go, to special exhibitions, really special ones, the once in a lifetime chances. I would watch the listings in the *New Yorker* and not miss anything – even the little places on Madison Avenue. You never knew where you'd find something marvellous, something to light you up for a week. I thought about the distant future, the progress of the disease. I supposed it might eventually affect Mark's sight. What might happen? He'd probably reach awkwardly for his glass, in time. He might knock it over on occasions, but there would be no difficulty. I would be there to create a discreet, smooth elision. Quietly I'd say, I'm so sorry, may my brother have another glass please? Mark might fail one evening to see it placed on the right side of his plate. I would reach over, move it carefully to the left, within Mark's field of vision. I'd have to remember to do it automatically, even before we sat down. Move the glass. The cutlery. Walk on his left side. Sit on his left. Always. Probably, he'd eat less in time. Grow thinner. I'm sorry, my brother isn't hungry. No, nothing more. Might he lose words? I didn't know, but I'd be there to know them even before Mark tried to say them. I'd go to the hospital with him. I knew that the pressure inside his head might increase with time, but that they'd control it. What was it they did? He'd told me a little on the phone but I'd have to talk face to face with Jaegerson. I'd sit among the machines and lights in the hushed, muffled strangeness of these places then take Mark home. Until Mark found walking difficult. Until he began to stumble, to miss steps, fall. Eventually a wheelchair. Perhaps. Would that be necessary? If it was, it would be a good one, electric, the best. I would begin to notice ramps, door widths. I'd check lifts. But this would be in the future, a distant prospect. I've no idea how long I'd been swimming when I heard the young attendant calling out, addressing me, saying, 'Are you enjoying your swim, sir?' – the wary note in his voice indicating that it wasn't his habit to address the swimmers. I can only assume that something made him enquire, something about my face perhaps, something careful, automatic in the way I must have been swimming.

'Please do not enter the pool' a notice on the wall said 'under the influence of drugs or alcohol, or if you are bleeding or exuding from any part of the body, wound, sore or abrasion.'

I shouted back to him from the water to say I was fine. A display high on a building opposite indicated the time, the day, the temperature. I got out then, to the boy's obvious relief, and stood for another moment to look down at the brightening arteries of the city, now beginning to be busy with traffic. No sound could have reached me from such a distance behind the thickness of glass, cladding and brick. In that place where rich people paid minute attention to the state of their hearts and limbs, I was protected. Momentarily, yes, unclothed, but nonetheless protected from the world outside. I looked down on the snow beginning to fall on small, small people on the pavements below, on pigeons flying distantly below, glinting flashes of white light from their busy wings.

I watched television briefly the following morning before setting off for Ellis Island, one of those news programmes which dealt out endless vacuous information, adverts, weather-checks, gossip but no news. A sad-faced man with the downturned look of an over-large cartoon dog was sitting in the mock-up kitchen of the studio, talking about the experience of unemployment and what it meant to him and to the small, thin child sitting fidgeting beside him. She was a plain child of about eight, ill-favoured, ordinary, inarticulate. The man talked again and again about his good fortune in the nature of his abilities, his dazzling qualifications, the temporary nature of the set-back in his life. The child kept fidgeting, answering her diet of questions with a small, nasal whisper:

'We get less things to eat. My mommy cries sometimes.' They were so uneasy in the three-sided kitchen set, both seeming without hope. 'I'm very fortunate to be as well-qualified as I am. Not everyone is as fortunate.'

When I left the seductive heat of Mark's building, I felt concerned about what a cold day it was for Sarah to be travelling. The car would be well-heated, though. Her friends the Schlonskys always drive cars which remind me of single-decker buses, nearly as wide and as long, with pale-coloured upholstery. On the ferry, she could sit inside the smoky saloon and look out. The Schlonskys would buy her coffee and biscuits. She would enjoy it, although she would complain. I knew Mark would be travelling in with Ali. I wondered if he'd be feeling anxious at the prospect of seeing me and couldn't help thinking about the early years after he went to New York, when I was still trying mend fences with him, and I used to phone, as if casually, to test the atmosphere. It wasn't easy then to phone as we do now, which made it almost impossible to sound casual with the intervention of operators and long spells of waiting. Often, I phoned from a loneliness I had never anticipated, a profound, familiar loneliness, a sense that whoever else I might encounter in my life, my family were the only ones who would endure, accept, tolerate. I don't know why I thought it, because even then I realised that there was no particular reason for Mark to do any of that. Often, I regretted what I had done. Equally often, Mark claimed to be busy when I phoned. He was sometimes short with me, abrupt and almost rude and I was forced to realise that the possibility of intimacy did not exist, at least not outside my own vestigial, childlike longings or my own imagination. I learned to make the calls purposeful, to keep any hint of wistfulness from my voice, any hint of wanting something I wouldn't get which Mark might wilfully deny me. In later years, when it became a little easier, we talked about money orders for Sarah and payments for the Jewish old people's home in New Jersey she had moved to, or about one of the rambling letters I had received from her claiming that the care attendants were stealing her things, her magazines, her post, her lipsticks. Mark would investigate and phone back to say that her belongings were all safe, including the brilliant pink lipsticks Sarah still painted thickly over her whiskery little lips. 'She's coming to us for Seder,' Mark would say, 'we'll take her to temple with us in the morning.'

I was always bemused when Mark used the word 'temple' instead of *shul*. It's common in America, I know, but the word itself always seems both daring and very holy, something I'll never get used to. It seems to have about it an ominous savour of destruction, messianic, prophetic, the last thing with which I'd ever want to tempt fate.

I think of it now, the way our differences receded to a place at the back, still there but altering over the years by everything else which happened, relationships between brothers subsumed naturally by lovers, wives, children. It was years before the loneliness for family returned, after my own family had grown and dissolved. Like a tide, when I reflect on it, alone again, families taking on the powers of great movements of moon and water, surging, ebbing, casting, inevitably, some lone item up onto the dark beach. We subsisted for more years than I like to think about on the day-to day fare of dollar transfers and magazine subscriptions. The huge events passed by at the end like afterwords or appendices, the births of children, divorces, deaths, disappointments, successes added in the dying falls at the end of phone calls.

I don't remember exactly when it was that Mark began what I still think of as his festival phone calls. He'd phone suddenly out of the vaporous, evanescent blue. I'd know it was him instantly by the odd background hum of near silence in the second before Mark would begin to sing, *Maotzur* before Chanukah, a verse or two of *Chad Gadya* or *El B'nai* at Pesach. Mark always had a handsome, cantorial voice which wasn't thinned or reduced by being relayed along the mysterious ways of the phone line. He sang the renditions we used to sing round the festive table as children, forty, more, years ago, when we were still all there, Sarah, our parents, Mark and me, all caught in the unaltering frame of memory, relaxing amidst the turmoil of linen napkins, crumbled matzo, crystal decanters, wineglasses, candles.

When I heard Mark sing, we were at the table again, swaying, singing, all apparently happy, just a bit more than a little drunk. Sometimes, I'd join in till the end of the verse: '*El b'nai, el b'nai, b'nai beit-cha b'KAROV!*'

He'd phone before the major festivals, Rosh Hashanah, Yom Kippur, sometimes on the eve of a festival as it began at dusk. By then, we were both living alone. Often, I had to check a tendency towards disappointment when the first evening of a festival was over and Mark hadn't phoned. I didn't want to phone him in case he thought I was usurping his idea. Once to my surprise, Mark's call came as darkness fell on Yom Kippur, the end of the most sombre day of the year's calendar. It must have been about lunchtime in New York and I could hear the chirrup and mutter of voices from the studio behind him.

'Just to find out how you fasted,' Mark said. There are no songs that I know of to be sung for Yom Kippur, only the mourner's *Kaddish* and no-one, not even Mark would sing that long distance.

'I meant to send you one of those cards, you know: "Wishing you well over the Fast," but I didn't get round to it. Pressure of things.'

'Oh don't worry, I didn't fast this year anyway. I haven't for years.'

'No, neither did I.'

A stop, a silence abrupt as a circuit break cracked into the transatlantic gulf between us. Neither of us observed very much though Mark still went to his reform shul from time to time. I still hesitate in restaurants occasionally, experience a dropping sensation of fear of being observed when I eat pork, order mussels, lobster, crab.

After Mark's calls, I often wondered what it was which made Mark phone as he did. Interest? Warmth? Love? Often, I suspected that I smelt the bitter, ferrous tang of conscience. I imagined it, a stern unyielding roster, tradition, family, duty in their bleak line, a blunt tally of obligation.

It was still early when I arrived at the island. I was glad to have time by myself to walk round the rooms before Mark came, trying to elide past with present, this renewed, shining monument to the origins of a dream with the way it had been, abandoned, more than abandoned, lost, a place the world had turned its back on, the weight of its history forgotten but alive there in its strewn halls and smashed refectories, its rufous, crumbling infirmaries. I didn't really hear voices there, but somewhere in the broken emptiness I felt the silent cadences of experience which had accrued in every corner of the building and grounds. Even the sight of the grey jetty roused in me a kind of germination, a new understanding of gain and loss, hope and fear, a feeling which pervaded my life for a long time after that, making me look anew at people, ordinary people, people in the streets, the same feeling that made me feel faithless, a betrayer when I left to come back here. That morning, reluctantly, I thought about Mark's making an excuse, all those years before, not to have to take me to the airport. I got a taxi, and on the flight back, stared down into the flitting, misty darkness below the plane's wing, hoping to find the island in the darkness. Of course I knew I wouldn't see it. Dense night, the swiftness of eastward movement, my own disorientation over unfamiliar landscape, meant that I could never have identified from among that sea of gold and silver swirls, ropes, diamond rivers of light, the unlit deadness of an unused immigrant station.

The place still felt familiar, in some way mine, mine by virtue of old knowledge and observation, the window embrasure where once I'd found a trapped bat flapping, the corner where I discovered an unattended ember fire, once quiet rooms where long before my time, endless lines of people queued, muttering their prayers, *please let me be allowed to stay*, where doctors looked for disease, tested for insanity; where officials sought out the unworthy or threatening. Now, restored, anxious eyes watched me from the photo montages on the walls.

The photos I took of Ellis Island were my first published work, accepted almost at once, eventually appearing in a broad, glorious spread in a picture magazine of the time, then in one of the geographical journals. It was the beginning of my career. I was unable to erase from my mind the feeling that it had happened because Mark was no longer there.

At eleven, I walked downstairs. The day already seemed long, half over, extended by early rising, by the change in time. Since I'd known about our meeting, I thought I'd be on the quayside to watch Mark walk down the gangway but now, I hesitated for a moment before deciding to stay inside the building to wait. Standing across the broad distance of the Registry room in the cloister at the far side, I watched as a few people came in from the ferry, looked round, gained their bearings, moved off. In moments, they had all dispersed through the quiet building. There weren't many on this fierce and freezing day. Mark, I knew, would be scanning the facade, noting the restored towers, the cleaned stonework, the renewed sandstone eagles. I looked again into the bag of books I had brought, then saw him come through the glass door. He looked round, up at the vaulted tile ceiling, at the fluttering row of American flags, down the length of the huge room. Then he saw me. A smile lit up his face. He walked in his usual way, fast towards me.

He looked thin. He was wearing a large, grey tweed coat, smiling, pale, his hair a scattering of even silver over his fine skull. He looked impressive, bold, his hair as if it had been specially cut to look like that. He was wearing new spectacles with gold wire frames.

'You look like a Polish film director.'

'Oh, that's nice. Other people have said I look like a Nazi doctor.'

Laughing, we stood together. I could feel the frost of outside on Mark's coat as we put our arms round each other, Mark a fraction taller than me. I breathed in from his shoulder the exotic, urban odour of wool, subways, cologne.

'Dan.' Mark took my hand, led my fingers to his head. 'Feel this.' He drew them from above his ear through his soft, new, short hair, across the thin, raised line which curved back over his head.

'There it is,' Mark said.

The warmth of his head lingered on my fingers. He took my arm and we began to walk round the rooms. It was, we agreed, a good time to be there, a freakishly cold day in January, few enough tourists, the atmosphere untroubled by heat or noise or crowds. I watched Mark and he watched everything else, delighted, excited by what he was seeing, pulling me towards glass cases, pointing things out to me, exclaiming with joy at the sight of the disparate things people had brought with them to their new lives, wedding veils, first shoes, icons, thumb pianos, bread boards. Precious, useful things turned to relics. As we walked, I handed Mark the books I'd brought and he took them out, opening them one by one.

'My God, look at this, Pa's writing! Where did you find it?'

He began to riffle through the pages as we walked through the medical room, past pictures of a doctor turning back a young man's eyelids with a button hook to check for trachoma hung from the ceiling. Mark began to compare the texts of the psalms in his own child's prayer book with the psalms from the book in Scots.

'Dan, stop a minute. Listen to this: *As for man, his days are like grass, as the flower of the field, so he flourisheth.* Now look, the same one: *Man, as he stan's, his days are like gerss, like a flowir o' the field, he growes, Forwin' it wins owre him, an' gane is he, the neuk whar he stude, sal ken nought o' him mair.* Isn't that wonderful? Dan? Isn't it beautiful? The Hebrew too. Have you read them?'

I had but could only shake my head.

'A voice! The best barmitzvah I've ever heard, *kayn ahora!*'

I looked at Mark. I felt a strange, sweeping unease, a fearful tie of brotherhood, a familiarity so strong that it seemed to overwhelm part of myself, altering it so that it belonged irredeemably beyond what I might regard as my own life, beyond anger, far, far beyond anything I knew I might think of as my own in the world.

We carried on walking along the balcony, leaning over to look at the few people crossing the broad, brick floor below.

'Look Mark, down there.' I pointed out a man in a parka standing by himself.

'The dark one?'

'Yes. How peculiar. I saw him on television this morning on a news programme, talking about being unemployed. That's really weird, seeing him here. I mean, in a city this size. I felt so sorry for the poor bugger.'

'I didn't see it.'

'He's got a little girl. She was with him. She must be about somewhere.'

A thin, watered sun began to light the hallways. Sarah would be well into her journey. Slowly, we walked to the first floor window on the river side where we would be able to see the ferry arriving from New Jersey. The sun threw cold, pale light but the sky was clouding, greying over, the translucent brightness being swallowed slowly into the dullness of early afternoon.

'Dan,' Mark said. He leant his arm against the window frame, his forehead against his sleeve. His face was towards me.

'Jaegerson says it'll recur. Almost definitely. He can't say when. Nine months. Six. A little longer. A couple of years at the most.' He turned to look out of the window again.

'Look. D'you see the colour of the sky? The forecasts say the snowstorm's going to miss us but they're wrong. There's going to be snow again tonight.'

'What did you say?'

'Look at the sky. What a colour! It'll snow again tonight.'

I looked out. Snow clouds were turning the sky tarnished, leaden. Grey water moved sluggishly against the jetty. The land, I knew, would soon be white. It would be covered over, unfamiliar and I realised that it would have become a place I would no longer recognise.

The rest of the day was as I had expected it would be, Sarah too, spirit, such as it is or was, undiminished, unmellowed by the years. Physically, she was more shrunken, drawn in like a small, malevolent bird. She turned her flinty eyes upon me once or twice but apart from asking me where her stockings were, didn't really seem to notice me. It didn't matter. I no longer cared what she said or didn't because that afternoon, my mind was far away.

Chapter 18

London, late autumn 2001

Evening begins with the moment of a key turning, the creak of the opening front door, a sequence which brings with it the past, seven o'clock, his voice sounding through the empty hall, calling her, scents of meat and cinnamon flying warmly around her through the flung-open kitchen door, through the darkly shelved corridor to expand into the hall where Joe is helping Florence with the fluster of arrival.

Anci is ready. Afternoon has been accomplished. The drawing is finished and will have to wait now until tomorrow when she'll take it to deliver by hand, the final one of this long sequence. She's even tidied a chapter of the memoir, writing with what accuracy she can of István's family, none of whom she ever knew. The meal too is ready, a leg of lamb pierced by darts of garlic, rubbed with olive oil and cumin, an apple pie baking, salad and wine and bread all where they should be, the table set, awaiting wine pouring and candle-lighting.

All afternoon as she's worked, her brother József has stood at the edge of her mind. She traces his presence to the recollections of their books, Hans Anderson, *The Arabian Nights*, the swirl of illicit purple crayon which one or other of them, the youngest of the children, had scrawled down the margins of one page standing clear, a memory of guilt. Which one of them was responsible for the transgression, she can't recall. She thinks of him, Józsi, at five, at ten, at twenty. She thinks of him too because of Mark. Grief, she's discovered, is not linear. Grief is not gradual, the preface to another ordinary ending. It's an infestation, a malarial parasite. Once present in the blood, it can't be removed. Lurking there dormant, it's curled in every cell. It flares without warning from its sleep of years, freshly virulent. It waits, as today everything has waited, her work, her duties, the evening, the girl on the stair.

And now Joe stands under the photograph and she can see, as she hasn't before, a similarity in the faces, the pointed chin, the angle of the jaw. Anci loves to see her sons like this after brief absence, to be surprised again by their beauty and by the strange, almost alien reality of young men, a solidity and sweetness nothing could ever have prepared her for remembering. József too was like this, the same diffident grace, the same wide, sagacious eyes. She marvels yet again as she kisses Joe, that this person is, in whichever loose way one wants to interpret the words, *hers*.

The girl, who she does not yet know, Florence, bears in her arms gifts they've brought, flowers and chocolates and a recently published history book which Joe thinks may help his mother's work. Anci watches Florence look around her and she tries to see the house through the girl's pale green eyes, with a newness of seeing. This is the moment of judgement, of making assumptions about them, quite reasonable ones she supposes, because you can't deny what's there in the most material of terms.

As the key sounded, she'd been tipping olives from their container into a terracotta dish, wondering if she could remember when it was she last spoke to Mark. It has been this way all afternoon, moments of reference, moments to be traced to their source, a tidying of the mind but her mind's not tidy as their conversations overlap with questions and answers in the hurrying, enthusiastic way at the beginning of an evening's company. There are pieces of news which have to be expressed first in a set hierarchy of importance or lack of importance, specially the minor things which must be said quickly before they're forgotten. Joe and Florence seem efficient together, adult, knowing what to do, Joe's lighting of the candles, Florence's deft way with the corkscrew, dealing with the flowers, picking a vase from a shelf, saying, 'Shall I use this one Anci?' Why should this surprise and impress her? They're adult, after all, but not as she was at their age. She's never been like them. It's not the small acts in themselves but the manner of their being done which affects her. Even the things they've brought, exquisite chocolates, flowers swathed in paper so lovely she'd like to smooth it out and keep it, the ribbon too and flowers, unusual ones, pink and dark red, tied round their even stems by strands of raffia. There's nothing of the anonymous, half-embarrassed offerings of the past, the cheap wine, dusty boxes of chocolates in cellophane which used to be the medium of exchange.

As they settle round the table, Joe says, as she knew he would:

'And how's the lovely Isabella?' He mocks her accent very slightly.

'Whose Isabella?'

127

'She's doing my dad's books.'

'That doesn't tell Florence very much, sweetheart,' Anci says. 'You make her sound like an accountant,' and she explains. 'Joe and his brother are very rude about her, I can't imagine why. She's a nice girl.'

'Good sort,' Joe says. Florence laughs.

Florence is, she tells Anci, from Belfast. Catholic, Anci thinks, picking her conclusion from no obvious source, no mention of it, no particular name. Just something in her manner which suggests it. Why? She could formulate a theory about the air of oppression clinging, pervading an individual's entire persona, but she won't. There have, after all, been careers built on this sort of thing, but she acknowledges that she's wrong too often to rely on brief impression.

Florence is in her final year of medicine and as you'd hope in the circumstances, appears to be sensible, in this way and others, different from Joe's previous girlfriends, mostly airy, arty girls of astonishing vacuity, girls he was at school with, then university, ones she still meets in the street and in shops, sometimes behind the counter, with whom she engages in warm, interested conversation. She was fond of most of them at the time, sorry to lose their company at the end of those youthful, volatile relationships, after she'd become used to them, one or other of them always somewhere around the house, in the kitchen, sunbathing on the terrace in the summer, standing pink-eyed on the doorstep handing over sundry items belonging to Joe, the tangible aftermath of an acute but temporary pain.

'We must keep in touch,' she and these girls would say to one another, full of mutual female sympathy but of course, they didn't, lacking the context, bowing to the graceful forward movement of life which pulls everyone apart. Florence gives a more lasting sense but Anci knows not to trust it either. It may be in the way she uses words, carefully, names too, addressing her more than once as 'Anci', which strikes her as unusual in someone of her generation.

'What do you want to do when you qualify?'

'Obs and gynae. I've loved doing that.'

'Will you stay here?'

'I don't know. Maybe. I'd like to go away somewhere for a bit, China maybe, south east Asia, see what it's like in the rest of the world.'

'Different, I imagine.'

'Right.'

'I hope you like lamb.'

'Love it. It smells wonderful. Thank you, Anci.'

Lifting the roasting tray from the oven, Anci wonders what was the last thing she said to Mark. What did they usually say? She scrapes the glossy, dark pieces of onion and aubergine from the tin onto the serving dish. After dinner, she'll tell Joe and Florence about Mark's death. It will be a testing of herself.

Only when the meal's cleared does she have an opportunity to look properly at the book Joe has brought.

'It's got stuff about some of the places Dad lived. I thought it might be useful.'

'Darling, thank you. It looks splendid. That reminds me, there's something I must show you.'

She goes to her study and brings the book with the photographs of the Archduke Franz Ferdinand, black and white photographs, the kind you might simply glance towards and pass on until you read the captions and it becomes clear what you're looking at. History trapped, still and dead. In this case, very still and very dead. Hapless, hopeless Franz Ferdinand minutes before the end. Minutes!

'God, weird!' Joe says, turning the pages. 'Look, Flor…'

'That's so scary. God, a few minutes later and the guy was dead!'

She's stared countless times with pointless frustration at the figure in the silly feathered helmet descending the steps of Sarajevo City Hall, smiling wife beside him, and though she's found herself begging the image silently, earnestly to turn back, to delay, to alter his plans, he will not. He will forever descend those steps, forever be sitting in the back of the open-topped car with Count Harrach on the running board, be there waiting for the engine to be cranked, be waiting to set off to the world's doom. There is another photograph, of Gavrilo Princip and two friends sitting on a bench in a Belgrade park. They are wearing wrinkly suits and the image is enigmatic as they are. She has tried to say to them, Don't! but they are as unyielding as Franz Ferdinand, more so, for they have a purpose in mind. So vain, this fluttering against glass, the moment, against the consequences we know, which they did not.

'Imperialism, my dear, would have had its way,' is what István would have said, and he'd have been right, but it's impossible not to wonder.

She refills their coffee cups. Joe begins to roll one of his miserable little cigarettes, a teenage habit he refuses to relinquish.

'Disgusting!' Florence says. 'In your mum's house too, Joe!'

This is, she realises, the moment when, if she doesn't say something about Mark, the chance will be lost. She obliges herself to enunciate the words.

'I heard today that someone I knew a long time ago has died.'

'Oh, who?'

'Someone called Mark Blum.'

'Who's he? Never heard of him.'

'You have, I think, darling. The people I stayed with when I left Hungary.'

'Oh yes, I remember. How did you hear?'

'It was in the papers.'

'Can I see?'

'Of course, here.'

'Now that's interesting. New York. If it didn't say 'after a long illness,' you'd think he'd had a heart attack on holiday, wouldn't you?'

'*Looked after with devotion.* That's nice, don't you think? They sound unusual people, Anci.'

'I suppose they are, were. So long ago now, it's hard to remember. They were certainly kind. Mark, and his brother. Daniel. Their parents took me in.'

'Why didn't you keep in touch?'

'Oh, you know, time, all that. I did, with Mark anyway. He went to live in America years ago.'

'And Daniel?'

'He stayed here. He's the photographer.'

'Oh, yes, of course, him. I didn't know you knew him, Ma. We went to that exhibition Flor, d'you remember?'

'Of course. The one with the bats. Were they his? No, they were by a woman. I was really impressed by it all. Anci, did you see it? Which were his?'

'Ma, why don't you get in touch? A letter of condolence or something?'

'No. I don't think that would be the right thing, not after such a long time, don't you think?'

'Why not? He'd be pleased.'

He and Florence begin talking about Dan and the exhibition. They're interesting, informed in their criticism and praise. Anci listens, transfixed. She must hear everything they say, every word of praise, every word of admiration. She opens the box of chocolates, eased in this moment of wondering but the conversation has moved on, moved away and she's lighter now, thinking only of Dan, the words enunciated, past, until Florence raises her head and gazes towards her with those surprising grape-green eyes.

'Anci, why did you leave Hungary?' she says.

They are an enthusiastic generation but in so many ways ignorant. And free. Free, Anci always thinks, of the burden of knowing too much about history. It is as they all are now. Florence, if she knows nothing, will not be alone. Even her own sons' ignorance often shocks her and she thinks of István's fury, gathering momentum, increasing over time.

'People who cannot even read!' he'd shriek, 'that is what they send me!' Nothing new, he'd been saying it for years, decades, long before what he called more recently, this dismaying flight into new barbarism. She doesn't think it barbaric, only interesting. She doesn't believe any more in that neat dictum about remembering history because if we don't, we're doomed to repeat it. We're doomed to repeat it anyway. That, if anything, is what history has to teach. Ironic. They're nice with their ignorance, she thinks, the ones she knows anyway, full of good intentions, groping but ambitious, untainted by the worst of knowledge. Perhaps it's best this way; she doesn't know.

'I left in 1956. A lot of people did at the time.'

The candles glow in their glass spheres, the wine with which she fills their glasses is the colour of the ink she's used recently for velvet and rubies.

'There was a revolution,' Joe says, frowning, relighting the recalcitrant cigarette, 'something to do with Russia. Isn't that right, Ma?'

'Yes,' she says, 'yes, that's right darling, that's quite right.'

It is a week night and so not late when Joe says,

'Come on Flor, we'd better go.'

'Let me get you a taxi.'

'No, don't worry, we'll get the tube.'

Stooping slightly to hug her as she says goodbye, tall Florence says,

'My God, Anci, you're the size of a tuppenny rabbit!'

She's preparing to be irritated as she always is by comments on her size when Florence puts a hand to her mouth and says,

'Oh God, I'm so sorry. I can't believe I said that!' and they both laugh. Suddenly, she hopes she'll see this girl again. Waving from the step, she watches them put their arms around one another as they walk down the path, their moment of pleasure after being in the presence of another person.

English, she thinks, is a wonderful language, noncommittal without evasion. 'You', it's possible to say without condemning oneself to what might be wounding decision, male or female, singular or plural. 'See you soon!' she can call after them, without the weight of expectation falling on either Joe or Florence. It's up to them to decide if she was using singular or plural. She knows that it annoys both boys when she appears to make unwarranted assumptions. She'll see Florence again only if Joe decides.

Closing the door, she wonders what Florence's impressions of Joe's family are. Obvious ones, no doubt: well-to-do, bookish, typical of what she herself feels distant from, a rootedness undermined by a foreign knowledge, the dissonance which informed her parent's generation to take nothing, *nothing,* for granted. As she begins to clear away the detritus of the evening, she wonders what her sons know of it. After all, she and István were already established by the time they were born. *Established.* What does she mean by that? A word with overtones, thrumming dully with ideas of buildings, solidity, permanence, money, all things she knows to be evanescent, illusion and dust. She could have told them more, but is it knowledge or an unease of the heart passed on subtly, a habit of mind, being forever on tip-toe, feeling for the first ominous tremor of earth beneath the feet? Impossible to tell. She doesn't even know what she and József understood of it. If one ever does understand. All the things which, in Glasgow, once she knew them a bit, she accused Mark and Dan of not knowing. How annoying she must have been.

'Would you rather we'd suffered too?' she remembers Mark asking her.

'Yes,' she'd replied, 'then at least you'd understand!'

Nibbling as she clears, she picks the roasting tin of its delicious scraps, toffee-coloured garlic cloves, slivers of deep red onion oily again the blue-black surface of the enamel. She wraps the meat in foil and lines the dishes neatly in the dish-washer.

They did understand, as much as anyone can, and even seemed to forgive her anger. When was it that she last spoke to Mark? She can't remember. It must have been, as always, with promises of keeping in touch, as if you had to say these things to the people with whom you most wanted to keep in touch, knowing they were and are, inexplicably, the people you're most likely to allow to flow beneath the inexorable, too fast surface of the passing days. Three or four years, anyway. Before István died. She'd wondered if she'd hear from him afterwards, but didn't. That, she can quite understand.

It's almost a relief after a time of company and talking, even a time she enjoyed as much as she did this evening, to be alone again in the quiet house, everything tidied, ordered, the dish-washer sloshing and humming its inimitable rhythm. She sits down at the table. On the noticeboard is an invitation to a lecture to be given by one of István's protegés. There are people who still phone her, still ask her to receptions, university events, almost as if she's István's representative on earth. She's learned not to give opinions publicly, because István's opinions are wanted, not hers. Asked what he thought on a particular subject, she's as likely to say,

'What a pity you didn't have a chance to ask him,' with an overlay of politeness and faint regret. She's seen people wondering afterwards exactly what she meant. She could say 'Read his books', but that would seem too frankly impolite.

'Goldmann?' they say, 'Are you related to…?' as if some of his intellectual standing might rub off, the gilt which they seem to imagine coats her, which, although she's never noticed it, must shine faintly from her. They ask and then they turn away. She wants to laugh when she hears women complain of being known as the wife of some famous man. What is there to complain about? It appears to her to be the most complete cover available, the unrestricted freedom to be almost invisible. As a way of deflecting curiosity or interest, it is without parallel. Goldmann. It's her name and always was.

She picks up the piece cut from the newspaper and again, reads the few lines. Mark must have written them himself. His style is still recognisable. His voice rings clearly below the near-formulaic surface of the notice. With the words, the years, decades of their knowing one another close around her with the pressure of depth-tuned gravity.

There's no past tense implicit in the idea of knowing. Knowing is a continuum. Who you know, you know, and you can't un-know them, unfortunately, in many cases. She thinks of the ways people's traces cross and cross again, the imprints they leave, how, once they're met, known, they're indelibly there, even in forgetting. In Mark's words, himself as he was, Mark who urged her gently, persistently from the places of the past, cajoled her from the habits of sorrow. He's dead and now his death overwhelms her. She needs urgently to speak to him again. *The closest friend*, she thinks, pinning him with words because only in this way can she measure the dimension of loss, a sonar-sounding to an unknown depth. From this depth, too, echoes back the knowledge that too often this is the result, contrary, bitter, a counter-weight and acknowledgement of failure, a result of laziness or prevarication, whichever it might be, the ways in which we are unable to allow ourselves to act as we might or as we want, our inability to demonstrate love or need. She's angry with herself. Surely the events of her own life should have taught her to honour the tension between transience and constancy. Why didn't she anticipate that he might die? Why didn't she simply phone to hear his voice, to thank him for his friendship? For the same reasons that we are irrational in some things, for the reasons which, invariably, leave us with regret. It is the universal law of those who survive. Survive. Only as she and Jozsi did for those few years, continuing to live, waging constant battle with the weight of living. Then the years when she was alone.

Tomorrow she has obligations, places where she must be at particular times, meetings. She has first to take in the drawing, and afterwards she's to have lunch with a publisher to discuss the next piece of work she's to do, the book of fairy tales. It's an Isabella day too. She must remember to leave a note for her in case she doesn't see her. She'll suggest that Isabella might like to have some of the food left from tonight's meal for lunch, drawing particular attention to the apple-pie and to the chocolates left in the box.

Anci prepares the house for night, snuffs the candles, checks the door locks. Her swimming things are in their bag by the front door. The lamps on their time-switches will turn themselves off, one by one.

On the stairs, she'll have to stop to confront the girl. It's not herself she has wanted to evade, who she was or who she has become. Her reluctance has been in knowing where the girl will take her, to places almost lost. As she reaches the photograph in its frame, she puts her fingers against her image under glass and together, she and the girl hold the names between them, József, Mark, Dan. She told her son that she didn't remember where it was taken but she did. It was taken by Dan in a park in Glasgow. She was alone, Józsi a few weeks dead. She hears Joe's words. *There was a revolution. Something to do with Russia.* The same. The eye behind the light.

There have, she knows, been days over the past years, unimaginable numbers of years, when she hasn't thought of Dan. Months, even, when she hasn't but he's been there nonetheless, beyond the immediacy of thought, waiting for the unanticipated snatches of return which tie her to the day they last saw one another, the day she left Glasgow to come here. Over the years Mark has talked about him, not often, not much, just enough for her to know of Dan's marriage, the births of children, his work, the return of his wife to Israel. He must have told her that the last time they spoke. She looks at the girl. Her head is back, chin raised, her arms flung wide. She must have been braver than she thought, that girl, enduring. It's possible to see it on her face. In his photograph, Dan told it all, and now it's like seeing silence.

She knows of the exhibition Joe and Florence were discussing. She went to it several times during the months it was on. Banners hung from the portico of the grand building where it was being shown, his name fluttering above her on the breeze. She liked the name they gave to the exhibition. *Demi-jours.*

The light clicks off in the hall below her. Mark is dead. What she needs to know, has to know, is why.

Chapter 19

New York, winter, 2000

D an visits. The morning when they're to meet is itself startling.
'My God, Mark, it's arctic,' Ali says, gasping in the harshness
of the air as they leave the house to walk out together towards the
car on this day of exceptional, frozen greyness. 'Are you quite sure
you feel up to sitting on a ferry on a day like this?'

Even the car, when she turns the key, seems to have to persuade
itself into life, its cold engine whirring briefly in a small mechanical
rebellion.

'It's heated. It'll be fine.'

'Whatever you think. Put on some music. You choose.'

He chooses from among Ali's CDs: Schubert, Bruce Springsteen,
Hildegard of Bingen, John Lee Hooker, and Jan Garbarek, which
he takes out. The saxophone feels right for this morning, the music
suitable, appropriate for occupying the empty space where talk might
be required. Not that he minds talking to Ali but music will allow
them the quiet pleasure of thinking. He likes to be driven. It's just
as well, because now he probably wouldn't be allowed to drive. It's
years since he owned a car. A car in the city's too much trouble, the
parking and the traffic, all needless anxiety and expense. Instead he
takes taxis, walks, uses the subway. Being driven is pleasant. Ali hums
a little occasionally, makes the odd remark about the traffic or the
weather, but apart from that the journey to the city is swaddled in a
sound which isolates them more completely than anything else could
from the day outside. A saxophone is all soul, he thinks, all sorrow.
On the sidewalks, people's faces look stiff, expressionless from the
cold, and he feels he's witnessing near-pain in those who have so
obviously been taken by surprise by the nature of this day. He stares
into cars which pass, cars beside them waiting at junctions, and he
thinks of them converging, Dan, Sarah, himself, closing in, and he's
not sure if they feel to him more like opposing armies or colliding
stars. Why does he think this? He wants to see Dan, has been waiting
to see Dan. It is, he knows, the unusual fact of it, of their all being
together again after years of separation, as by celestial plan, a mapped-

out trajectory of past and future. He's scared now, unable to forget why these images of grandeur allow him to elevate a family reunion to cosmic status, and wishes for Dan's sake that there was another reason, that he wasn't carrying with him this invisible, invidious gift. Clearly, Ali knows something of this, because when eventually she draws up at the point nearest the ferry terminal at Battery Park, she takes his hand.

'Is this going to be difficult for you?'

He thinks about it briefly. 'No, I don't think so,' he says, 'not for me.' Before getting out of the car he embraces her, expresses his gratitude for hers and Berndt's considerable kindness. He must remember to arrange for flowers to be sent, a gift of some sort. Dan can help him choose.

Ali drives off. Later today, she's to drop his bag off at his apartment with the groceries they spent the previous afternoon buying, pushing trolleys companionably, amicably through the aisles and lanes of the shops at the local mall. He has always thought that there's a lot to be learned from the observation of couples shopping for food. He and Ali giggled their way around, pointing out to one another the late middle-aged men, probably recently retired, shopping with their wives, displaying their waning power by questioning and wrangling and nit-picking over cost, the women by their sides expressing on bewildered faces an awful, quiet despair. Men, they'd agreed, can be such bastards. All the same, he'd felt wistful, realising that one of the things he missed from his previous lives, from his marriages, was the easy companionship of conducting ordinary life with a woman, the first excitement of it, corollary to the privacy and closed intimacies of love. As he walks over to the kiosk to buy a ticket, he realises that it's an intimacy he won't experience again, the rich suggestion of the life that surrounds a man and a woman together. He breathes in from the impact of the cold and a small noise like a sob emerges from his throat. He hands over the fare money and takes his ticket.

The journey across to the island is strangely exciting, as if he's travelling to a far destination, not just to the middle of the bay. He walks up to the top deck for a few moments but it's absurdly, almost laughably cold. Even under his cashmere cap, his head with the new smart haircut acquired on yesterday's shopping trip stings slightly. To stay outside voluntarily on a morning like this, he thinks, would be the act of a serial self-mortifier, a lunatic. He goes down to the warm saloon and buys a coffee. The city beyond the water rocks gently on foundations of ice.

When later he thinks of the days of Dan's visit, he returns first to the point of unaccountable, childlike nervousness he'd felt on walking into the Registry Room at Ellis Island, seeing, with relief and an inward, collapsing pleasure, Dan standing waiting for him across an expanse of floor. He remembers trying consciously to capture the halo flashes of first impression, the instant before true recognition. He'd tried to observe as a stranger might, trapping the ghosts of seeing as you trap a moth between two cupped hands, the words *interesting, an interesting looking man, a fine face, humorous, kind*, almost at the same moment as they were together, hugging, an embrace which merges into the days which follow, and afterwards the weeks, which becomes too speedily the heavy embrace of parting in the chilly departure hall of JFK. There, they extended to one another a mutual exchange of unspoken hope in the promises they gave, *next spring, next summer,* as too quickly the implacable details of the evening flights rolled onto the relentless, existential time-shift of the departures board. Then the moment of separating, a beginning of distance between them as Dan was swallowed into the gulf of doors and x-ray machines, leaving him to the lost, cold interval of turning away, walking through the wintry airport towards the cab rank, towards the journey alone back home. Alone, with all to begin and all to end.

Radiotherapy begins. The date is marked on the calendar from the week after Dan goes home. It's to continue for the next six weeks, a daily visit. At least, he'll have weekends off. He is anxious at first, self-protective, prepared to dislike both process and staff, but he's wrong, misguided in his instincts. This one further intrusion into his yielding brain, he discovers, is miraculously simple and the greatest intrusion, truly a cellular massacre, appears to be the least. After some initial work and fuss and calculation to get him and his skull and underneath it, his wayward parietal lobe, into correct alignment for the attentions of the peering, burning monster which is to send out its wicked, murderous rays towards him, the thing's done in a single blink. The monster approaches, contemplates his problem, closes its giant eye and is gone.

'That's all?' he says to the young radiographer on his first morning.

'Sorry to disappoint.'

'Far from it.'

'Tomorrow, then. Same time?'

He resists the urge to complete the phrase. There'll be enough time for the jokes to build, for the little web of relationships which, no doubt, will leave him nostalgic again when they're ended six weeks later. He'll see at least some of the same people every day, the ones who will pass in corridors, their presence glancing from one to another with the airiest of touches. The words they'll exchange in the waiting area will be weightless, without guile or future. Their names will be spoken daily, each known to the other, each called to his or her own account. It will be, he knows, a roll-call of the chosen, theirs a secret society, the society of the balding, the old and balding, the young and balding, this company of united strangers, this company of ghosts who daily, trustingly, expose to the giant's eye their cells and bones. Even through his own two eyes, they have, each one of them, a temporary, spectral air. Unreasonable, he knows. Some of them will be cured. Some of them will lead long and ordinary lives but already they're changed by their experience, people who have become skilled now with words, with greetings, people who sidestep questions, who never ask the ones which have no answers.

After the first day, the names of his clinic companions begin to run through his head. They are names to accompany him now in perpetuity. François Duval will always be with him, Cynthia DeWitt too, Ellen Steinberg, Charles McColl, Art Williams, Fred Chun. The way they look will be too, the way they are, all will stay with him, François, a Giacometti bronze, slow, his skin too thin, silvering over clavicle and forehead; Cynthia's rush and fluster, the words on her first day which he'll always remember,

'My little boy thinks I'm coming to Radio City!' as he will, her perfect blonde hair which, over the course of the weeks, thins to the point where he can see the curved pink outline of her head glinting beneath what's left.

His own hair, as he expects, begins to pepper the shower floor, lines of iron-filings swirling in the turning of the water towards the drain. People he knows notice but do not comment. Other people assume, entirely reasonably, that he's just bald. Kirstin, though, says, 'Oh, it looks so nice,' and means it. But soon his scalp develops a scaled, itchy circle where the beams of killing rays pass through. At first he worries that his scaly skin will make other people think he has a terrible disease, but since he has, his concern seems, though vain, pleasingly elliptical.

The routine of treatment, after the first few days of novelty, becomes dull. At first he walks, setting off briskly on this daily imperative, but after a few days he's tired and hails a cab. He hails another afterwards to take him to work. In spite of his lethargy and a new, recurring headache, he works on. There's never a shortage of work, never a shortage of structures and consultations and site visits, never a shortage of demand for the walls which will enclose other people's lives, the windows which will allow the light to illuminate their every action. These are what he loves, the meticulous processes of planning boundaries in air. He can see no reason to relinquish them before he has to.

Every day on his way to and from the clinic, he passes places where he went with Dan, restaurants, shops, the big synagogue that so shocked his brother. He smiles thinking of it, Dan's whisper during the one service they attended together:

'Closest I've ever been to the Golden Calf!' He was, Mark thinks, only half-joking.

Sarah phones a few times, always when he's out. The disjointed, dysphasic messages she leaves annoy him more than usual because he hasn't forgiven her for the way she behaved at Ellis Island. He can't foresee a time when he ever will. He'll defer a visit to her for as long as he can but knows he'll have to go sometime, her invitations changing tone from demanding to needy, the commensurate increase in his feeling of guilt. In spring. Pesach. Just before Pesach. He'll set aside an entire afternoon to spend at the Shoshana Blumstein Home. Kirstin usually drives him there, Kirstin who has long been designated by Sarah as the *shikse*, a word he hates, redolent of a narrow past. He thinks of Kirstin's family, her venerable, bearded father, a professor of linguistics, some years dead, her statuesque, jolly mother and his own feeling of treading gingerly into another, but strangely welcoming, world. The family summer home in Bohuslan made him joyously aware of it, the gracious enthusiasm, the feeling that, without explanation, he'd been blown into another dimension of time, to Yashnaya Polyana perhaps to be in the company of Tolstoys, to one of the beach resorts of the Courland Spit during the becalmed years of northern Europe before revolution and war.

Kirstin, while he's sequestered among Sarah's fellow-residents, goes for a walk, has a coffee, reads a book in the car. She's long been maddeningly uncritical of Sarah, suggesting that to behave as she does she must have been very unhappy in her life. This view has always seemed to him annoyingly charitable. Hearing her express it first made him realise that marrying a Christian might involve these unfamiliar virtues: forgiveness, the turning of the other cheek.

He's had a couple of calls from Matty Schlonsky too, recently: uneasy, dual-purpose calls during which she's expressed in the gentlest of ways both a hesitant concern for him and a general unhappiness with the outcome of the day with Sarah. She doesn't express any of it in quite such straightforward terms.

'You're well, are you, Mark?'

'Yes, fine, Matty.'

'Oh. Good. I hope you don't mind me phoning; I'm just slightly worried about Sarah…'

Her worries turn out either to be trivial or ones about which nothing can be done, inevitable adjuncts of age, and as he reassures her, he regrets that it's Matty who seems to have suffered most from the recent encounter, poor Matty with her over-extended sense of responsibility, who has assumed everyone else's burden. He realises that she can't ever have witnessed Sarah as she was that day, reverting in habitual mode to the behaviour of the past. He'd watched her attempts to compensate, her embarrassed attempts to cover over, to make some redress for Sarah's first attention to Dan, the moment when she'd cast him a glance and said,

'Oh, you're here too.'

'Matty, don't worry. Dan doesn't care any more,' he wants to say to her, but won't, because although he's sure it's true, it's not what she wants to hear. She doesn't want to hear anything. She wishes only that the day hadn't left her with a sense of failure. All that afternoon, he'd watched Matty try to engage Dan in conversation as she might the lone child left out of a party game, asking him about work, the girls and their careers, what he was planning to do in New York, conversation interrupted only once by Sarah over cakes and coffee at the cafeteria table:

'Did you bring what I asked you to?'

'Your stockings? Indeed I did. Here they are. I hope they're the right ones.' He'd handed her a small bag with cord handles, obviously from a smart shop.

'But I told you to go to Daly's.'

'I couldn't, I'm afraid, Sarah; it's not there any more.'

'What?'

'It closed down.'

'What! When?'

'Quite a while ago. Years.'

'No! How could it?' Sarah said, her face displaying only triumph at the confirmation of old doubts. 'Such a lovely shop! Your mother and I used to go there for everything.'

He and Dan talked about Sarah afterwards on the ferry back, in the taxi home. They laughed and he'd been aware of the new tone of their conversation.

'In some ways it's a relief she hasn't changed,' Dan said. 'It's reassuring to know there's one constant in the universe.'

In any case, Dan had been quiet that afternoon. He'd wandered off for a little while with Abe, who'd wanted to have a look upstairs. It was, he knows, because of what he'd told Dan before Sarah arrived, the news from Jaegerson. Before he said it he needed to desperately, but after he did he wondered why. Because Dan had to know, that's why. Because he had to place this knowledge in someone else's calm, accepting hands.

In spite of the forecaster's assurances, a blizzard began the night they got back from Ellis Island. They'd gone out for dinner in tacit celebration of having endured the day, the afternoon, Sarah. Being in the city together again seemed to delight and animate them both, and that evening he'd felt optimistic, as if the city itself would cure him. The snow began while they were in the restaurant, and by the time they left it was blowing horizontally towards them, fast and hard. He'd felt a few moments of panic as they'd made their way home and suspected that Dan did too. They'd had to link arms and, giggling, they'd found their way blindly through the dense, white streets.

It was the worst blizzard for years. That night, until late, they watched from above as the city filled with snow. Like children, they'd imagined it never stopping, the level of it rising, rising.

It might have been the effects of their forced seclusion, but being with Dan made him feel content, as if that was the way it should be, himself and Dan, chatting and pottering, reading companionably, denied the choice of where to go and what to do. They stayed in for the days of the worst snow, tip-toeing out tentatively one morning to sniff the air with the unwarranted feeling of having endured, survived. Now he treasures the time, forgetting, as one does, the moments of irritation, points of frustration flashed into being by familiarity, the ingrown habits of age and of those who live alone. During Dan's stay he'd woken most mornings with a sense of relief, almost peace, knowing that Dan was here with him, a sense of having reached a place he'd thought he'd never see again after a dangerous, turbulent journey. He'd noted the small ways in which everything was familiar, habits of mind and body, their reading as they'd done together as children, in their youth, interrupting the mutual quiet by sudden enthusiasm, sudden desires to share, reading snatches aloud to one another, Dan saying, 'God, Mark, listen to this!', reading out descriptions from his book about Russia in the Second World War, all portraits of horror, tallies of numbers beyond imagining, names, Zhukov and Stalin, the random place-names of campaign and slaughter. He'd replied with his own different enthusiasms, delights, lines from the copy of the Psalms in Scots Dan had brought:

'Dan, how about this:

"My folly, O God, ye ken weel yerlane; an' fauts o' my
ain are no frappit frae ye..."'

This book has become indispensable to him, the one he always has near him on the table, the top of any pile of books he's reading. It's the honesty of the words which moves him, words of love and veneration, the words of passionate flawed David rendered in the language of those unused to speaking of love. He can smell earth as he reads them. He can see a man poised between soil and sky. They make him envy the straightforward, unquestioning belief of the past.

As he makes his way through the streets on his way to and from the clinic, he passes the shul where they went on the one Shabbas of Dan's visit for the barmitzvah of the grandson of one of his friends. It's huge and imposing, a reform shul, the kind of shul and the kind of building he could never have imagined before he came to New York. He can hardly remember his own surprise at everything new when he first arrived, but as they'd walked there Dan said,

'I suppose I'm just not used to it but I'm always amazed at being in a place where there are so many Jews.'

'And you think it's a good thing?'

They'd laughed at that, the things Jews can say to one another which other people can't. It takes the presence of someone from another country to make him aware of this aspect of the city again, an aspect which amazed him too when he first came here, the men with their beards and *payyot* and fancy hats, the sight of what, oddly enough, are his brethren going about in every one of their odd forms and manifestations. He reflects on it again the spring morning when he crosses Madison Avenue with an elderly Chassid, not precisely 'with', because the elderly man concerned doesn't realise that someone has attached himself to his road-crossing endeavour as he shuffles out into the deranged currents of traffic. Mark walks a small way behind him feeling, rightly or wrongly, that the rebbe will protect him, which of course in one way he does, because no-one in the city would choose the kind of hell that would be let loose if he ran over an elderly Chassid. He feels safe too because of the man's learning, his wisdom, his knowledge of Torah. The notion's crazed but at the same time, he feels a gratitude for this man who gives him the feeling that at the very least, if he isn't doing it all, everything the Shulchan Orach instructs him to do, the davening, the study, the observance, all of it, someone else is and for a reason he doesn't understand, it seems important.

Dan had expressed real shock at the sight of the shul.

'This isn't a shul. It's a cathedral!'

'You're just a primitive European *shtibl*-hopper.'

'Mark. Look, the rabbi's not even wearing a tallis!'

Dan's horrified reactions had amused him.

'What are you talking about? It's not as if you observe anything.'

'I know I don't, but at least what I don't observe is Orthodox.'

He'd sat there looking round him like a child, nudging, whispering, 'Look, Mark, he's reading from the English!' Staring at the people around him, at the women with their lifted faces and skinny legs, hissing, 'My God, don't look yet, the one just sitting down. What planet is she from?'

'The one where time doesn't exist.'

Afterwards, after the service, the congratulations to the barmitzvah boy, the conversations in the hall on the way out, Dan had said to him as they left the majestic facade behind,

'I'm glad to be out of there. I kept looking at the ceiling to catch the moment when the thunderbolt from the Almighty would come crashing through.'

He'd teased Dan about being superstitious but, in a way, felt that he was right – about the women's faces too. He's always thought that what they do to themselves is unnecessary and often horrible, something to which his vision, or mind, has become accustomed, accepting, but after Dan's visit, whenever he passes a woman with a face like that, all he sees are razored bones and needy, altered eyes.

Everything seems different after Dan's visit, the way he sees, the way he feels. There's an innocence in Dan, perhaps not quite innocence but a quality of simplicity which for so long he's thought a weakness or a lack, but which now he knows is not. He thinks back to the early days of anger. How could it have seemed to matter to him the way it did? The word 'forgiveness' comes to his mind but he's unable to decide to which of them the word might possibly apply.

During his first week of radiotherapy, in obedience to the list he made at Berndt and Ali's, he begins going to the gym in the early evenings after work. He decides to ease himself into a routine by swimming a few lengths each time, which he does with caution before getting out and lying for a while on a sun-lounger wrapped in his towelling robe, regaining energy for the short walk home. He enjoys these few minutes, the incongruity of sun-loungers in winter, watching through the huge glass walls as the city lights itself for night.

Another item on his list is to deal with his books on the brain. Gathering them into a pile to prepare them for their journey to the second-hand shop, he makes the mistake of hesitating, of looking through them one last time, as if in farewell or apology to unread chapters, but as he does, words fly out at him from the pages to land blows in his eye and on his head: *consciousness, visual reality, conscious awareness.* The words themselves demand that he stop this obsessive gathering and piling. Before surgery, he realises, he'd been pulled in by the brute mechanics of it, a traveller's necessity of names and places, practical approaches to a sojourn in a foreign land, but now he's there. He has arrived on this alien plateau and the nature of what he has to know is different. He has to be able to find his way, to anticipate the pitfalls of the road. One by one, he takes the books and replaces them on the shelves. While he's doing it, he glances up to the top shelf where he keeps the children's books Anci has illustrated. She sends him the ones she likes best. He stares at them, wondering if they're out of their usual alignment. It's not that he catalogues his books or arranges them alphabetically or any of the other fanatical things people do, but he's used to seeing them in a particular order, the colours of their covers, a vague arrangement by size or subject. He looks and though they seem slightly different, he can't be sure if they've been taken down, looked at, moved. The only person to have been looking at them would have been Dan. If he had, he'd have seen the inscriptions, the letters Anci wrote to accompany them which he keeps inside each one. Mark remembers his reassurances to himself before Dan came. *All will be dealt with*. A moment's anxiety pinches at him. When? he wonders. How?

The first book she sent him was unheralded and unexpected, a small treasure of beauty and surprise. He'd phoned her immediately, or as immediately as one could in those days, and yelled, 'I'm so proud of you!' down the crackling, hissing, now-here, now-gone phone line, and from faraway heard the sound of her beginning tears. He opens the book of Russian fairy tales. Babi Yaga and her chicken-legged house, Vasilisa and the Golden Cockerel dance in gorgeous colour and detail across pages framed by intricate friezes of snowdrops, hearts, dragonflies and stars.

It's the same feeling, wishing, needing to speak immediately to Anci which he experiences during the latter days of his radiotherapy when, reading the *New York Times* one morning, he reads of István Goldmann's death. This time, he stops himself. If he phones, she'll ask him how he is. If he doesn't admit, she'll know anyway. 'Mark, why do I think you're lying?' and she does not require, at this particular moment, to know about his illness. He considers sending her a card, a note, *thinking of you*, or some such platitude – but he hesitates, reluctant to seem as if he's reminding her, as if he's raising spirits not yet settled in the place where spirits settle. He'll wait for a few weeks and phone her then. He wonders if Dan has seen the obituaries in the papers. He's certain to have done. The British papers will be even more packed with lavish obituaries and articles, assessments of his life and work. There'll be memorial services, a rush to acquire his books and papers. Mark reads the obituary carefully, realising that other people will too, other people who certainly will believe every word it says. He won't mention it. He won't say anything to Dan about it yet.

As the weeks progress, he becomes weary. It's only what he's been warned will happen. The battery indicator of his phone seems to measure itself against him, taunting him with its three-barred power. He's down to one, flicking on and off. Movement drains what's left, forces himself with unwieldy will to every step, raising himself to the upright in the morning, only the first effort in a day of sitting, walking, lifting his weakened arm to hail a cab. He tries to look as seldom as he may at his own face which, each time he does, peers balefully at him in reflection from under a hairless, flaking scalp, a steroid-bloated, alien moon.

On the final day of radiotherapy, Mark goes into his favourite flower shop and buys flowers for the staff at the clinic. He chooses sweet-smelling jonquils, double petalled narcissi, miniature irises, hyacinths of vivid blue. He is clutching the heavy glass vase in which they've been arranged, manoeuvring it through the outer clinic door as Cynthia is coming out. 'Oh,' she says, 'it's your last day too. I took in some cake.'

He steps back outside, and awkwardly they stand for a moment on the sunlit sidewalk looking at one another before Cynthia leans gently over the flower heads to kiss him on the cheek. Helplessly he stands, hands, arms engaged in holding tightly to glass and flowers while slowly Cynthia moves away from him, closing her lips as she does, folding them decisively in, like the pink edges of a sea-shell, beginning to walk backwards at first, half-turning, raising her hand to give him a small, bent-fingered wave.

The weather has lightened over the weeks of his treatment. The days of his and Dan's magical imprisonment in snow disappear into late winter and one day, walking slowly in Central Park, he notices that sparrows, jays and starlings are swooping, bustling in the still, chill air, chasing one another, turned to flashes of purposeful, feathered brightness and he realises that it's almost spring.

Esther Woolfson

Department of Radiotherapy,
Mount Shalom Medical Cente,
New York, N.Y.

Dr J. Baker
Family Physician
Suite 67
130, Braklynn Street
New York, N.Y.
28th February, 2000.

Dear Dr Baker,

Mr Mark Blum
d.o.b. 25th May, 1936

I saw Mr Blum for review today. He has completed three weeks of a six week course of radio-therapy for his glioblastoma. He complains of tiredness and local scalp irritation. He is free from seizures and has a slight degree of clumsiness of his left upper limb. There is some erythema of the scalp and some hair loss.

I have advised him to reduce his steroids. He will be reviewed after completion of his course of treatment,

Yours sincerely,
Dianna Rocco, Radiotherapist.

Department of Radiotherapy,
Mount Shalom Medical Center,
New York, N.Y.

Dr J. Baker
Family Physician
Suite 67
130, Braklynn Street
New York, N.Y.
20th March 2000.

Dear Dr Baker,

Mr Mark Blum
d.o.b. 25th May, 1936

I saw Mr Blum again today. He has now completed his course of radiotherapy. There are no new neurological symptoms or signs but he complains of tiredness and headache. He has substantial hair loss and is somewhat

148

Cushingoid.

I have suggested a reduction in steroids with a view to complete cessation in 2 weeks time. I will see him again in 3 weeks.

Yours sincerely,
Dianna Rocco
Radiologist.

Dr K. L. Jaegerson, Neurosurgeon.
Specialties: Neuro-oncology,Endoscopic Neurosurgery.
Suite 53,
43, East Reveille Avenue,
New York

Dr J. Baker
Family Physician
Suite 67
130, Braklynn Street
New York, N.Y.
4th April, 2000.

Dear Dr Baker

Mr Mark Blum
d.o.b. 25th May, 1936

I saw Mr Blum today after completion of his course of radiotherapy. He is remarkably well apart from steroid side-effects and the loss of hair. There are no new neurological features and he has had no seizures. He has begun to reduce his steroids and should soon be able to stop them totally.

We discussed his prognosis. He accepts the likelihood of recurrence. I have indicated that in some cases, this period may be relatively prolonged. I have advised him that he may return to all former activities and habits, except driving. He informed me that he has not driven for some years but I took the precaution of advising him that, should he decide to alter this course, he should gain the consent of the NY DMC.

I will see him again in one month's time.

Yours sincerely,
L.K. Jaegerson, Neurosurgeon.

Chapter 20

Glasgow, late autumn 2001

L eaving New York was difficult, or more accurately, leaving Mark
was difficult. The evening before did, I spoke to Noah and Tamar,
as I had done a few times while I was there. I couldn't say much to
them because Mark was in the room with me. I said only, 'Keep in
touch', to which they both replied that they would. I assumed they
knew what I meant. There wasn't any reason why there should have
been a sense of finality about the call because, after all, we could
speak any time we liked, but the feeling I had was of being almost
excluded from the tense, knowing circle of a family dealing with
illness. It was disturbing, more than that, and when I examined it, I
realised that it was because I felt that I might, by returning home, be
missing something. What?

While in New York, I hadn't even considered staying longer but
on the plane back, wondered if I should have done. I wondered too
if I should have been more definite in my plans for visiting again. At
the same time, I told myself that it would have been intrusive to have
stayed longer and anyway, we both had things to do, lives to lead.
Our lives are separate, I thought, but even as I did, I accepted that
they weren't. Not any more. They had been until Jaegerson's words
fused them to a single point.

On the journey, I slept in the same way as I always do on planes,
with the memory of illness, waking febrile, not sure if I was more
afraid of the length of the night or its brevity. Each time I woke, I
looked down at the long, pale, meaningless blur, all deep and terrible
ocean below the small square of plastic which first was filled by
land then by half water, half land, then only water, scuds of drops
flitting across the salt-blasted surface. The Atlantic is forever night
or forever an interminable stretch of half-lit afternoon, a median
state, without time and only a mythic destination. In my half-sleep,
I made myself remember how chill and drab plane travel used to be,
brazenly metallic, ringing with the fierce, continuous roar of engines.
It's quieter these days, more luxurious. I buy the comfort which allows
me to remember why I do.

Coming back was difficult but also a relief, a release, a temporary one, an illusion of escape. I came back thinking that I'd resume my life as it had been but I didn't. My life before my visit felt safe but changed. I began to work on the exhibition the morning I got back and for a day and a half, managed to persuade myself that soon I'd regain my former perspective, be able to look at the future again in the way I did before I went to see Mark. On the second morning I woke in panic, thinking of Mark, with no memory of a dream. I saw him stumbling in a subway, too near the track, having a fit alone in a crowded street. In that moment, I felt the rush of measured time, the presence of the future, the same presence which was there that late afternoon on the ferry back from Ellis Island. Three of us had crossed back to Manhattan, myself and Mark and the echo of Jaegerson's words. Snow was beginning to fall again, the first few flakes whirling darkly against the dun, ochre sky, melting into the water of the bay.

That evening in New York we were right, Mark and I. It was the forecasters who were wrong. They said that the approaching shadow of snow would turn and spin out, dissipate itself over the ocean, but it didn't. The few flakes in early evening were just the beginning. The storm began properly later, the worst blizzard for years and once it began, it snowed for days. On the news every evening, satellite pictures swirled a maelstrom palette of colours across the screen. The map of the United States amazed me yet again, the vastness of the place, gradations of temperature in coloured segments across the map, the knowledge that in the same country at that moment, people were basking in terrific heat. The forecasters wrung their hands and tried to explain why they had been so wrong. Outside the windows, far below us, the city banked with snow, black and white and grey.

That afternoon at Ellis Island, time had turned fragile. On the journey back, we used the reliably engaging topic of Sarah to take our minds from it. I noticed how much easier it was to share our thoughts about her than it had ever been before. There was a time when even mentioning her name brought a whole army of past grievances to dance at our backs but now, we could laugh.

'Incredible! Do you notice that she still can't find a good word to say about anyone? And how many times she mentioned my hair?'

'Were you there when she was complaining about Mrs Spellman?'

'Please, don't remind me. I live in fear of the day when even the good Blumstein ladies can't put up with her any more.'

'Oh, don't worry, I'm sure even she's not the hottest star in their particular sky.'

'D'you think?

'Of course not. They've got the big league there. Professionals.'

'I suppose you're right. At least there's a certain calculated restraint to her modus operandi.'

I don't know if that's how I'd have described it but there is, or was. That afternoon, Sarah had been characteristically offhand with me. I would say 'rude' but I don't apply the same benchmarks of behaviour to someone of Sarah's previous character as to anyone else. Age, I'm sure, has very little to do with it in her case. She was no better or no worse than she's always been.

'Oh, you're here too,' she said, casting me a glance. All her conversation was addressed to Mark, the remarks about his hair, her recounting of episodes from the Shoshana Blumstein Home. Mark was less patient than usual. I saw the subtle signs of it though she didn't. She would never have noticed. He drew attention once or twice to the fact that I was there.

'Are you telling this to me or to me and Dan?' he said, quite sharply.

'What?' she said, oblivious, and I saw the years of our restraint growing brittle in her presence. I gave her the stockings I'd bought for her but she wouldn't believe me when I told her that the shop she'd asked me to go to wasn't there any more. It closed so long ago that I could hardly even remember when it did but clearly, Sarah thought I'd deliberately gone somewhere else to spite her. Longevity, in Sarah's case at least, seemed a firefly existence, all intermittent moments of light and fading. Neither Mark nor I could help seeing the sadness of it too, seeing how small she was, how many words were lost before she said them. Because I hadn't seen her for longer, I noticed how much her hearing and sight had deteriorated since the last time we were together.

'What is that?' she said, pressing her nose to the glass display case full of the ordinary, heart-wrenching objects people had brought with them to the New World, 'What are all those things?'

Matty Schlonsky, a kind woman, kept trying to make up for Sarah's behaviour, or to conceal it. She engaged me in loud conversation to cover awkward moments and made me go to the café counter with her to carry everyone's orders of coffee and cake. Towards the end of the afternoon, just before she and Abe were leaving to take Sarah back, she put her hand on my arm.

'Don't mind her, Daniel. She's old.'

'I don't, Matty. I'm used to it,' I said, but I could tell she didn't believe me.

When we got back to Mark's apartment, Ali had already been in to leave Mark's bags and shopping. She'd brought a couple of Zabar's carriers for us with a note to welcome Mark home. The two of us went through the bags, pulling out the wonderful food she'd chosen for us, coffee and bread, herrings, lox, huge slices of different kinds of cake, whooping like five-year-olds. Both the gesture and our response to it seemed to set a note of cheer, almost celebration. We decided that we should go out for dinner that evening, neither of us needing to express the simple relief we both felt at having got the day over and our meeting, and Sarah. We had to make an occasion of being together, of being in New York, and though I wouldn't have said so to Mark, I wanted to celebrate his being there, his still being so much the way he'd always been. The pavements were slippery as we left Mark's building, glassy and spangled underfoot. I noticed how he walked almost carefully, slowly, looking around him and knew that it wasn't just because of the snow or his recent surgery. I could see him savouring the experience of being back. I felt it too, but in a different way, that lovely, rarefied excitement you always feel in a foreign city. I've always loved New York.

The staff at the restaurant, a small place near where he lived, knew Mark and welcomed him warmly, although I don't think they knew he'd been in hospital.

'Wine?' Mark asked me when he was handed the wine list.

'Are you allowed it?'

He laughed. 'I'm not giving it up, so it comes to the same. No-one's said anything about it and believe me, I didn't raise the subject.'

I suggested he choose, which he did, and we settled into the comfortable moments of waiting for the wine and discussing what we were going to eat. Mark began to talk about the hospital and the operation and though the mood of our conversation was light, the topics weren't. He tried to explain the intricacies of American medical insurance which I understood no better after his explanations than before. It didn't take very long for him to lose me in deductibles, co-payments and co-insurance, under an avalanche of names.

'Jesus, I can't believe it's this complicated. I've still got no idea of how it actually works.'

'Don't worry, neither have I, really. I don't think I want to have. It's all too cruel.'

We'd ordered our food by then.

'The entire point is who pays. If you have proof that you have, you're more or less okay. If you don't, you're screwed. I haven't been able to think of what happens to you if you have this if you're poor.' He pointed to his head.

'What does happen?'

'God alone knows. I'm serious. I don't want to think about it.'

All the time we were talking, I was watching the other people in the restaurant, wondering about their lives and houses and jobs as we talked about what it would take to change America's health system. Mark said that it seemed an impossibility, that there was too much money involved, too much power.

'After all, look what happened to poor Hillary. It's quite incredible. People talked as if they'd have to hand their souls in to Beelzebub in return for a decent health system. You know, it's an American's right to bear arms and to be poor and ill without state interference.'

'It's not just here. There are people at home now who rumble on about the NHS being obsolete and how it would be better if we had some kind of insurance scheme.'

'Well, they're utterly deranged.'

We were quiet for a little, enjoying the surroundings, the chirrup of talk around us interrupted by laughter or a single loud voice. It felt as if we had reached one wide ledge at least, a low one, the first of what might be a sequence, invisible from this distance, lost in cloud. The evening might have been normal, like any other evening I'd spent with Mark in pleasant surroundings in New York or elsewhere, but it wasn't. It's difficult to say how it was different, which elements were, how we both were or were not, but we knew, both of us, that nothing was the same. Apart from anything else, Mark was perpetually hungry.

'Those fucking steroids,' he'd say, reaching for the bread.

On the way home we tried to carry on talking, bent against the blizzard, snow piling up on our heads and shoulders. We linked arms, blinking the snow from our eyes. At the time, I was reading a book about the Eastern Front.

'Imagine,' I had to shout over the sound of the wind, 'what it must have been like to face the whole of the German army and fight a war in this!'

'I will,' Mark shouted back, 'I will.'

I can't say that everything was altered, that the things that irritated each of us about the other no longer existed, but what changes had happened were significant, specific landmarks in our new terrain. In the next few days, Mark wasn't fiercely proprietorial about every aspect of his apartment. He let me cook. I was trying to look after him without seeming as if I was doing it, asking if I might prepare meals as if it was what I truly wanted to do. In fact, it was what I truly wanted to do. I enjoyed opening the fridge to reveal the exciting, unfamiliar food, things which made me feel that this was the best, the finest the earth had to offer, the most carefully chosen, the most aesthetically wrapped. Mark even let me use his computer and his coffee-machine, a magnificent beast of chrome which reminded me of a Harley Davidson. Before he'd let me touch it, though, he gave me a tutorial so that I'd know what all the black knobs and handles and winking lights were for. I tried to make a point of not deferring in the routine way I had always done, although sometimes it was hard not to.

The few days when we couldn't go out at all were oddly thrilling, sequestered there, high above a city of snow. We sat around, looked at my photographs, listened to music, read. I read about sieges and battles and insane cruelty while Mark read the Psalms in Scots minutely, exclaiming from time to time over a word, a line.

'God, fantastic! Listen to this!' he'd say. The words delighted him: *yerlane* and *ill-deedie* and *stouthrief*.

At the same time, I practised words in between Panzer divisions and Red Army generals, words which remained unsaid. There were books I'd seen in Mark's bookcase during the days when I was alone there which I recognised as ones which Anci had illustrated. I'd wanted to take them down, look to see if they were inscribed and what the inscriptions said, but didn't. I felt ridiculous hesitating like that, realising what my hesitation meant. I knew it meant that time has no power, no meaning, suddenly swept by everything I'd felt then, an age ago, everything I felt now, looking at my brother.

In the high, pure light of Mark's apartment he looked pale but then so did I. I watched him so that I could file each of his movements, which hand he used to reach for his cup, right or left, how he walked, how he would not always be. He was to begin his course of radiotherapy the week after I came back.

Tam and Noah phoned every day to ask about the snow. Lee phoned too a few times. I noticed that Mark avoided most of her calls. When he did answer, his voice sounded quick, detached. It was a voice I recognised, one which I was glad he no longer used to me.

'How is Lee?'

'Oh, Lee is fine.'

'Should I see her?'

'Why?'

'Because she was family.'

'Was, Dan. Was.'

I didn't tell him that Lee and I still exchanged birthday cards, ones in which invariably, we enclosed small, affectionate notes. It would have been impossible to explain to him. He had ended a relationship but I hadn't. She was a sister still, of a sort. I knew I'd have to have at least some dealings with her in the future and decided it was best to say nothing more.

I did see Kirstin. We all went out one evening for dinner. It was a considerable pleasure to see her. As well as being charming and funny, she's a beautiful woman, one grown no less beautiful with age. I didn't know what I felt, pleasure or pain, when I saw how affectionate she and Mark were to one another, recognising the undertow of love and regret which flowed between them although whether it was for the past or future, I couldn't tell.

The snow abated, began to melt. The colours of the city changed, reverted back from purity and light and became first drab after the snow, patches of sidewalk visible again, then suddenly it was bright, full of late winter colour.

On the one the Shabbas we were together, a couple of days before I was due to come home, we went to synagogue for the barmitzvah of the grandson of a friend of Mark's.

'You don't mind, do you? They asked if you'd come.'

'Not in the least. I like a bit of shul-going in proper moderation.'

The shul we were to go to wasn't where he usually went, or rather where he went to when the mood took him which, he said, wasn't very often. This one was a giant of a place, a vast, imposing building more like a cathedral than a shul. Lines of snow were still banked along the sidewalks as we walked there.

Inside the shul was even grander that outside. I was shocked. It felt pagan to me, the very building, the absence of a women's gallery, the service in English, a rabbi who wore no tallis. Even the lights, modern chandeliers, felt wrong. As I sat for the first time in my life in a mixed congregation where women sat with men, I remembered the one we had gone to in childhood, one with the feel of the *shtibl*, the feel of Eastern Europe, although naturally, I didn't appreciate that at the time. It has only become clear to me over years of travelling, photographing in those places, Lithuania, Poland, the Ukraine, photographing gap sites, buildings built on ruins, gravestones, photographing loss and execration. As I sat there, I recalled what Anci had tried to tell me, what then I hadn't understood. For the first time, I felt as if I should be praying.

During the service, I whispered to Mark that I wondered if we'd get herring and pickled cucumber in the basement afterwards and we had to stifle our laughter, both of us seeing the bar-windowed basement of our childhood shul where the men went for a small celebration after the Shabbas service, a phenomenon unknown, clearly, to this particular congregation with their clothes and demeanour hinting at the kind of wealth which leaves a resonance, images of grand apartments and walls of Picassos, wealth which seems to alter people's very fabric. Even the women's faces resembled a new and different sort of human. I hardly even heard the barmitzvah boy's warbling rendition of *Maftir* and *Haftorah*, I was so busy staring round me at faces which made their owners look more like insects, boggle-eyed, pulled up, pulled back, tightened, tight skin dragging over bone, at skin-thin legs protruding from short skirts, stick wrists supporting gold watches, diamond bracelets, a self-consciousness in the easy way they swung their apparently youthful, long, honey-coloured hair as they turned to look around them, noses emphatically gouged, every stamp of racial characteristic knifed from their bones, at their aged hands and sharpened profiles. I noticed that some of the men they were with were Mark's and my age, older too, shaggy, elderly Jewish men who looked the way our father and our uncles had done, the way we looked now. The worst of it was that the women didn't even look young. They looked different but not young and later, shaking hands and chatting in the gold and marble hallway, I watched the unease in their eyes, the horrors of their smiling.

I was childishly eager to talk about it to Mark on the way home. I was cautious in case he'd stopped noticing, or worse, approved.

'It's appalling, isn't it?' he said, 'You never know what to say to people when you bump into them afterwards. You know what you're meant to say, but it's another thing to bring yourself to say it.'

We walked on a bit.

'D'you know, now, I can't even imagine what anyone's thinking of, undergoing surgery for no good reason,' he said.

'At least the old boys look the same.'

'Like us, you mean?'

'Exactly so.'

I'd watched Mark mingling with the other members of the congregation, quite a few of whom he knew. He introduced me and discussed with one or two how he was and the operation and I was struck again by his assurance, his control. It threw me, yet again, into the role of the indecisive younger brother, tagging along, knowing no-one. I couldn't believe it in myself, this vein of insecurity, at my age. I wondered then, as I do now, when, if, one ever grows up.

We managed well enough for the few days we were together, but I'm used to being on my own and so was Mark. I could sense a tentative eagerness beginning in both of us to be alone again, the need for us both to resume our lives. Part of it was from fear, a fear of the ease we had created which might make the inevitability of a return to the day-to-day even more difficult. I knew that Mark's resumption would be rather different from mine which would be straightforward by comparison. He had decided to go back to work more or less at the time he began his radiotherapy.

Our parting, when it came at JFK, was hesitant, painful. It felt like a rehearsal. I held back words and warnings, swallowed down the meaningless advice I wanted to give him about taking care of himself, to cover the fact that there was nothing I could say. We discussed when we'd see each other again, using words which didn't seem to attach themselves to any time, spring, summer, autumn.

For the rest of the winter, I worked on preparations for the exhibition. Most of the photographs I'd taken in Morocco and Syria weren't developed yet and I was glad to have the discipline of a date to work towards. Late in the winter, February, the slough of the year, I heard on the radio news that István Goldmann had died. I knew that Mark would have seen or heard about it too, and though we spoke often, neither of us mentioned it. I kept thinking that I would, testing the words I'd use.

'Mark, did you know that István had died?' 'Did you see the

obituaries for István Goldmann a few weeks ago?'

I practised them but they sounded false in whatever way I thought of saying them. Time elapsed and the moment when it wouldn't have seemed out of place was gone.

It turned out that, of course, he knew.

'Dan, you know that István died?'

'Yes. You couldn't miss it. I heard it on the news first, then there were obituaries everywhere. How did you find out?'

'Oh, the *New York Times*, then the *New York Review of Books* was full of it. I wondered if I should say anything to you but I was sure you'd have heard. And Dan, I don't know if you know, Anci's still alive. She lives in London.'

But that was later, over a year later, when it was easier to say.

Sarah began to deteriorate quite soon after we all met. I'm sure that the deterioration had nothing to do with the exertions of her day at Ellis Island. Already then, that day, we had intimations of it, more than the first signs. She had seemed to both of us on the point of lapsing from a state near to ordinary into that extraordinary world of misplaced words, not dementia but the point where the brain seems to wear out, the synapses collapsing into themselves and each other. Her use of language, always singular, grew more opaque, requiring more and more rapid interpretation, filling in of gaps, following the processes of her thought to do it.

She phoned me a few times.

'When did I see you?'

'January, Sarah.'

'Oh yes. What is it now?'

'March.'

'Is it? No. I don't think you're right.'

'I am, Sarah.'

'Are you sure?'

'Yes, I'm sure.'

'Oh. He phoned. Yesterday. Was it? He's coming to see me. For that. You know.'

'Mark?'

'Yes, Mark.'

'He's coming to see you for Pesach?'

'That's right. For Pesach.'

Chapter 21

London, late autumn, 2001

It's evening when time escapes. It has threatened to all day. Even early she'd felt it, as if she'd dreamt. All day it was with her, like the figure glanced on the periphery of vision, an instant out of sight. There was, all day, a hint of falling, of the fragility of the boundary between one time and another. She's always kept the heft of memory this way, as a power sternly closed away while knowing that it's there, waiting for the flaw in the wall to break through to reclaim her. It is Mark who has done this. It is Mark who, by dying, has rent a hole in the seal of time.

Only the preordained pattern of the day, the appointments she must keep and places where she must be, has kept it contained, from the first of the morning's brightness which, even by seven, was breaking through the grey. Seeing wet light shining across the city as she walked up the hill, she'd remembered suddenly the sound of rain in the night, the low drumming which woke her to the deepest darkness. She'd been certain she wouldn't sleep again, her mind flooding instantly with Mark, but she did almost at once, still thinking that she wouldn't.

The paths were muddy as she walked to the pond but the water had settled chill and starkly clear. A few women were already swimming when she got there and as she prepared others began to arrive, people she knew or at least recognised, a hardy, hardened lot the early morning swimmers, exchanging greetings with robust cheer as they always do, beginning the communal ordering of their forthcoming day. Helga was there this morning, head immediately identifiable above the water as she swam in her jerky, determined way. This morning, Anci did not count the years of their friendship. She waved from the side before plunging in and Helga called from the middle of the pond,

'Okay for Friday?'

'Yes, fine.'

It's their habit of years to meet on Fridays in the late afternoon for coffee, a point of welcome conclusion to the work of the week. They initiated these meetings not long after they met here when Helga, who in those days came swimming with her mother, was still a student. Now, she's a professor of English. There were a few years when other things interrupted, their children mainly, and they met at other times, at one or other of their houses to share afternoons of chaos and noise and the hasty tidying away of toys before six, but in the past few years they've resumed their Friday habit. They often discuss the significance of the timing, more than just that, the sense of both conclusion and preparation they both feel on late Friday afternoons, a legacy, they decided long ago, of a Jewish upbringing, the sense of a week's moving inexorably towards the culmination which is the Sabbath. Neither of them is particularly religiously observant, although Anci always lights candles for Friday night.

'It's a replacement of ritual,' Helga says about their meetings with all the certainty of her profession. She's not pedantic with it, though; she's wry, saying, 'It's all nonsense in a way, of course, don't you think? We're just looking for significance where we can. Everyone probably has this feeling on Fridays.'

Helga's family came here from Germany in the middle years of the thirties, a prescient bunch, as she describes them, bohemian, atheist parents who nonetheless felt obliged to educate their children in the ways of the religion for which they'd had to flee. Her childhood was what Helga always describes as 'passingly religious'.

'The atmosphere of the imperative just wasn't there, and that's what matters really, isn't it?'

It is. She thinks of it now, the atmosphere of the imperative which pervades her memory, lies within the substance of her bones.

There wasn't much time this morning. She swam especially vigorously to make up, pulling herself up the steps and out of the water after only ten minutes.

'Going already?'

'I've got to be at a meeting at nine.'

'Oh God, me too. I'll have to drag myself out in a minute.'

She dressed quickly in the old jeans she wears for walking to and from the pond. There are changing cubicles now. In the first years at the pool there was only a rudimentary cabin, wire baskets to put your clothes in which cost a sixpence, payment handed in to the lifeguards who, on cold mornings, prepared mugs of Bovril and tea. They organised parties in the cabin, too, and it was at one of those, a Christmas party, when she'd begun properly to talk to Helga and her mother, Dolly. There was an invitation from Helga to a New Year dinner. A beginning. Thinking of it is like stepping through into the other world of a child's fantasy story, the recurring, indelible dream in which, panicking, you catch the wrong train only to arrive in a place both utterly familiar and utterly unknown.

This morning, words loomed at her from the water as then they did all day, from the stone of the streets, from the crowds surging round her as she walked. They were the words she carried with her to this country, the words with which, first to Mark and Daniel, she told the story of her life. Helga, too, asked her early in their friendship, with open curiosity, but by then the words had become easier. She'd felt them smoother, becoming rounded with the telling. Today, twenty thousand days have flicked past her as the pages of a chaotic album of recollection which places people wilfully, makes them approach or recede without reason, scatters them easily through inexplicable dimensions of non-linear time.

Isabella hasn't yet gone when she gets back. She calls down from István's study,

'Hi, Anci! I'm still here, I'm afraid.'

Isabella comes down and accepts the offer of a glass of wine. She's appreciative of the left-over apple pie which Anci's note had suggested she might have with her lunch.

'It was yummy,' she says endearingly, 'thank you.'

'And how's your day been?'

'Fine, I think. There's one thing I've got to ask you, just about a quotation.'

'Which?'

'This. I hope it's, you know, nothing too personal.'

Anci takes the book from her, a nice edition of the Metaphysical Poets she bought a long time ago for István. It must have been for a birthday, she sees from the date. It is the inscription which interests Isabella, a few lines in Hungarian in her hand, written years ago. She reads them.

'It's from a poem called *Autumn Breakfast,* something like that, by Dezsö Kosztolányi. He was one of Hungary's great poets. I'll write out a translation if you like. It's just a description of autumn. It's lovely. I can't remember why I chose it. István liked him. That must have been why.'

They talk a little about Hungarian writers, about Attila József and Sándor Márai and then about the language, how odd it looks, how impenetrable its origins and grammar.

'I've wondered if I should try to learn a little,' Isabella says.

'Very brave of you even to consider it,' she says, knowing that she won't.

'I'd better go. Look how dark it is already. Of course, the clocks go back this weekend, don't they?'

'Oh, that's right. Good. I love winter.'

'Oh no! Anci, how can you?'

Later in the evening, she'll think of this again. Winter. She's eight. Snow is falling, covering everything. This is the one winter she can recall with clarity. Others surrounding it have melted in the fire of this winter, the ones before, many after. Winter, with everything else, had burned.

All day she's kept it at bay, but by evening it's beyond her power to stop. She'd planned to begin making notes and sketches for the new book as soon as she came home because it would give her the sense, however spurious, of having embarked on a task which must be finished. Today she was asked the usual question, the one that's always asked when she's introduced to a new editor or member of staff. They all ask it: 'How did you begin?'

Reviewing the business of the day, she feels that it has been conducted felicitously from the first, when she'd been ready quickly after she got back from her swim, dressed in smart clothes, organised, drawings already in her portfolio case on the table, note written for Isabella who would arrive shortly after she left. The morning traffic had been as London morning traffic is. It took a couple of circuits to find a meter but she did. She was five minutes early for her first meeting. The new person there this morning was an earnest, very young man who, after he'd said hello and commented on her drawings, asked the inevitable question. She didn't mind. It's a reasonable enough first question. How did she begin? She has an answer ready now, easy and succinct.

She sees Isabella to the door.

'I'll be back again tomorrow. Is that all right?'

'Of course. I'll be working here all day.'

After Isabella has gone, Anci takes the text of the new book with her sketch pad and charcoal and sits cross-legged in the large armchair by the French window in her study. The garden's dark. The set of low lights which they put in to illuminate the path when István's sight began quite suddenly to fail, glows upwards, casting from the undersides of desiccating leaves, a curving trail of copper and of gold. The first line of Kosztolányi's poem sounds repeatedly in her mind:

Look what autumn has brought us…

Outside, the trees she planted have grown to their full height. In the garden, with its settled look of having always existed, is the history of her life in this country. She has no record of how it was, no photographs of the rubble heap which was there when they bought the house, the wreck of a once-red car perched aloft on broken bricks, the remains of a scrubby lawn dying under mud and stones. Over the first months, she'd found a set of child's rusted metal gardening tools buried among the bricks and stones. There were days, many days, many weeks and months and years when she'd dug in the garden because there was nothing else to do, purpose self-created from the tyranny of will. Someone else took the hulk of the car away but the rest she did herself, carrying bricks to pile in the back lane, digging, planting, laying out the paths and terrace. Anything can rise from rubble, can be destroyed again. The leaves in the garden tremble a little, as if there'll be rain.

Autumn. Memory, she knows, is only movement of the light. It's bars of music stopped in the air, words overheard and never forgotten. It's rooms lit by colour, lit again by fire, castles filling with blood and darkness. Memory can shift, re-figuring the past, melting what's remembered ineluctably into what's been learned. She's tried but has never been able to separate her first memories from the knowledge of war.

In the book on her desk, Archduke Ferdinand is still alive. He's still walking towards his death in Sarajevo where it all began, towards the gorgeous palaces of French nobility's final, dazzling, egregious days where it ended, the future of Europe written into shadow at Versailles and Trianon. These are names she grew up with, Trianon, Versailles, the winner's punishment for taking the wrong side. *Hungary, a country without a coast ruled by an admiral.* That much was true, when she was born at least, Horthy the admiral, the coast Hungary once had, the port of Fiume, taken away at Trianon with two-thirds of Hungary's land and half her people. Trianon, a country doled out, divided, an empire lost. István, who remembered it, wrote about both treaties: *the blind morality of the victor, the seeds of death.* Hungary closed in grief, he said, on the day in June 1920 when the treaty was signed. Shops closed and schools. Newspapers were printed with black borders. The national flag flew, as it did from then on, at half-mast. Written everywhere, '*Nem! Nem! Soha!*' 'No! No ! Never!' *This is why, years later, Hungary will be obliged to barter for her soul.*

She still wonders why no-one saw what the consequences would be.

There's only one time she can return to, when she allows herself to remember. Autumn, 1944, Budapest. She was eight, the last clear picture. The air, thinning towards winter, after that spring, that summer, felt as if it was throwing off a burden of heat and war. Autumn. She was with her parents still, with her brothers and her sister. Together still, balanced, as birds balance on a wire. For years, every wind threatened them. Her first memories are the years of war. She doesn't know if she thought them difficult then or only later, the early years, before she knew what was difficult and what was not. The war was hard for everyone but worse for them, because for Jews, it was. But then, in this sharpening air of autumn 1944, the war was ending. Germany was about to founder in the hell of its own creation. The Red Army was already in Hungary, at Debrecen and Szeged. This, she remembers.

It's to this time she returns because it's where everything begins and everything ends. Autumn, 1944. Budapest. Budapest is many cities. Images replay from darkness to light and back again in her topography of dreams. One of the cities she remembers is the view from a window, another, the night-lit river, boats moving under bridges, black and gold. There is a singular child's city, too, one of paradoxes and enigmas, the domes of parliament which are both, because from nearby they look huge but from far away tiny, two-in-one in the puzzle of perspective, a perplexity of space. There are later cities too, one of earthly, solid beauty, another unreachable, ethereal, a city which, when you look towards it, floods in a moment in mist and snow and fire. There is a city ruined, again and again. Visions overlap, a flickerbook of time.

Before her or behind her, the sum of her life. She's eight and her parents are still with her. Her sister Ágnes, her brothers, Miklós, Jószef. In 1944, Ágnes is fifteen. Miklós sixteen, József, Józsi, is just a year and a half older than she. He's nine. She's eight and her mother is an artist.

Balanced. As birds on a wire. 1944. A spring, a summer of loss and death. Survival was miracle or accident or the fruits of patience. Chance, no more than that but they had, till then. 1944 and the news of summer brought a fresh feeling to the air and streets, the news of British landing forces on the soil of France, the liberation of Paris. June, August, 1944. The Red Army was approaching, and soon they would be liberated too.

Not only them, Hungary too was balancing on its wire. It had balanced that way for years, terrified, evasive, strung between desire and fear. *Who would have the enemies Hungary does, the neighbours?* Names sound to her in the tones of the past, her parents' voices, radio frequencies tuned to the cadences of distant time. There are those she remembers, those she can't forget. *Horthy, Teleki.* Even thinking of them sparks the clarity of recall, a row of named pegs, under them, a wooden nursery bench, a patch of flowered carpet, a line of shoes.

Regent Miklós Horthy, admiral, regent for life. Count Pál Teleki, Prime Minister, geographer and cartographer from whose mind, it seems, maps couldn't be erased. Now, it seems more brave than foolish that they imagined they could steer Hungary through the war neither provoking the Allies nor defying Hitler. Horthy always had more sympathy with Britain and the West than with Hitler but Hitler offered Hungary the prospect of the return of lost land. The price of it was beyond imagining. For Teleki at least, his life.

In her memory, places, names, numbers. *Adolf Hitler,* into the sound of whose name she seems to have been born, *Bárdossy, Kállay, Szótjay, Lakatos.* How does she remember them all so clearly after so many years? Prime ministers all, to Horthy's regent. Some were anti-semites, Horthy and Teleki among them, not much different from the rest of their class and type in that country, at that particular time. Old-fashioned, traditional anti-semites.

Gentlemen anti-semites, aristocrats who were content to maintain the hatred of centuries while gaining benefit from the economic and social influence of Jews, gentlemen who were prepared to enact anti-Jewish laws but, at the same time, wished to have no legacy of blood on their hands…

Hungary wasn't much different from other countries across the span of a wide and poisoned continent. Horthy and Teleki despised the new, brash sort of anti-semitism with its vicious aims, although the new sort had, after all, merely flowered from the permission of the old.

It is, she's always thought, a remorseless story, one with no winners, no triumphs, only the results of misplaced courage or misplaced weakness, of wrong decisions, the wrong enemies. Teleki killed himself in 1941 rather than see Hungary forced by Hitler to dishonour its treat with Yugoslavia. Horthy acted both for and against the Jews. He tried to make peace with the Allies, but failed. If he hadn't, perhaps history would have been different. Perhaps then, her life would have been different. But what's the point of thinking that?

She's always recognised the immediate truth of Helga's term *the atmosphere of the imperative…* It is, she thinks, what Judaism is. It's what must be done, the sense of urgency, the sense of weight behind our lives. As a child it was all she knew, all she ate, all she thought. It was the progress of the days towards Shabbas, the marking of the year, Rosh Hashanah, Yom Kippur, Chanukah, the imperative of her life and other people's lives, implicit in every place and action, dictating the nature of time. In the places where her family lived too, in Budapest, in Cluj, Szeged. It was in the huge shul in Dohányi Street whose size and height stole your breath, in the smaller ones too where they went sometimes for Purim or Succoth. Imperative, as it was for her grandparents, for her aunts and uncles, cousins, friends. Telling Mark and Daniel, they'd urged from her each name, each relationship, *Whose son was that? Was that your mother's sister?* her voice sounding even to her like an incantation, their names an elegy, the only one they'd have.

Places, numbers, names. Is there any other way to remember, or to understand history? Which is history and which is simply the course of her life? *We live history, only sometimes aware of the fact we do.* Not, she knows, that she'll ever understand. What she remembers tangles with what she knows, that at the beginning of the war there were 750,000 Jews in Hungary. At the end, nearly three-quarters were dead. Names too, *Kamenets Podolsk, Novi Sa'ad, Voronezh.* Places of death and murder, rivers of ice, battlefields swamped in blood and snow. Voronezh, where Hungary's second army was destroyed, winter, 1943, *destroyed*, 100,000 Hungarian troops, 25,000 Jewish forced labourers. Now the name Voronezh turns on her, her brother's scorn.

'Miki, why's it called the second army?'

'Don't tell me you don't even know that!'

The prime minister who sent the second army to be slaughtered was Bardossy, and after him there was Kallay. *Bárdossy, Kállay, Szótjay, Lakatos.* How easily Horthy seemed to have dispensed with his prime ministers. 'He is not a gentleman!' he's supposed to have said of them, 'He is not a true Hungarian!' Kállay was the one with whom they were safest. He refused to be forced by the Germans to impose the yellow star on the Jews. Neither would he agree to the deportation of Jews in the absence of assurances about where they were being sent. Since 1942, Kállay had been trying to negotiate secretly with the West, secret negotiations about which German intelligence already knew.

Words trail her through the years, a child's half-understanding, tones of radio grief:

We regret to announce the death of Count Pál Teleki
Today, Regent Miklós Horthy travelled to Germany to meet Chancellor Hitler at Schloss Klessheim…

1944, March 15th, Regent Horthy was summoned to Schloss Klessheim for discussions with Hitler, detained there while German forces moved into Hungary.

Today, German forces crossed Hungary's borders…

March 19th, 1944. The German operation to occupy Hungary was called Operation Margarete. Now, she thinks of the words of a poem by Paul Celan: his writing of the hair of two girls, one golden and one ashen, Margarete and Shulamit; his description of death, so chilling, so accurate, as a master from Germany.

March 21st 1944, when Eichmann arrives in Budapest. He's head of the Judenkommando, *Reichsicherheitshauptampt Sondereinsatzkommando 1V/B/4.* It's the way he likes to think of himself, 'the master', Eichmann, who has spent the years of the war turning murder into industry, Eichmann who will stand one day in the dock in Jerusalem, killer of millions, Eichmann, during whose trial she will stare nightly as they play and replay old wartime newsreels on television, realising that only now, she knows. He establishes himself in Rózsadom, in Apostol utca, in a fine villa stolen from a Jewish family.

It's April when the Americans and British begin to bomb, industrial sites on the outskirts of the city first, but inside it too, bombs fall. Names, numbers, skewered through their hearts. *By May 6th, six weeks after Klessheim, 200,000 Jews from the provinces had already been deported from Hungary, by May 15th, 320,000. By July, 500,000 had already died. Only the Jews of Budapest were left alive.*

In 1944, they didn't know the name of Auschwitz, nor why, one day, it would be known. Only the people who ran it knew, only the people who were taken there, only the silent people who stood and watched the trains pass by.

Helga's parents were percipient, leaving Germany when they did, but towards the people from the past she feels no anger, no desire to question. How were they to know? Hungary was different. In Hungary, they should have survived. From what trick of atmosphere might they have eavesdropped on Eichmann's words?

My arms are long and I can reach the Jews of Budapest…

But still, autumn, winter, 1944, they're waiting as they've waited during all the years of war, every month, every year, for it all to end. Balancing. *Regent Horthy today ordered the German High Command to withdraw officers of its special forces from Hungary…* They do. The Germans recall Eichmann and his henchman to Germany, but only to regroup, to prepare.

It's what she's had, over years, to find the words to tell. *Paris was already liberated, D-day had happened!*

She has no photographs, only pictures in her head. Autumn, 1944, an hour, a minute, fallen on the wing, snatched from the progress of the speed of light. She's sitting at a table. Afternoon. Since early summer they've lived in a new house, in fact an old house, with too many people in it, but one day they'll go back to their own house. In that one, her mother's pictures hang on the walls. Her mother is an artist. She is an admirer of the work of Rippl-Rónai and Tivadar Csontváry Kosztka, both fellow Hungarians, of Cézanne too, Matisse and Vuillard and of the Russian artist, Ivan Bilibin. Although for the time being they can't, when they still could they often went to the

Esther Woolfson

National Gallery of Art to look at the paintings. Her favourite is Rippl-Rónai's painting of the woman holding a cage with a bird in it. She peers at the cage but can't tell what kind of bird it is. She and József like to imitate the expressions of suffering and ecstasy on the faces of saints in the corridor where the religious paintings and states are. They particularly like St Eliza and the beggar, and the Bishop of Vac. Her mother paints pictures which are beautiful. She paints people and rooms and streets of buildings, streets which look as if a light mist is covering the canvas. She and her brothers and sisters all draw too, although she and Józsi are the best. Józsi draws only engines, neat, perfect engines, every detail of them. There's unusual beauty in his engines, although she takes care never to tell him that. Their father can't draw a line. He does, but only to amuse them. He's a lawyer, so doesn't need to draw. In that other house, the one where she has always lived, the room in which her mother paints is a permanent space in her head, an instant of colour-blasted time.

Because there are no other images to replace them, they're as they were, smiling, her mother, Agnes, her father, Miklós. Looking back towards the past, towards them all, she wonders how can she can face them? How can she address them? How can she tell them what will happen next?

October 15th, 1944. Everyone listening, shocked or rejoicing or angry, to Horthy's broadcast:

It is my intention to sue for peace. I request that Hungary's army lay down its arms and withdraw all opposition to the forces of the USSR.

The act is bold but fails. The army won't obey and Hitler won't believe that the war is lost. Blackmail and the threat of murder force Horthy to what comes next. The Germans kidnap his son to oblige him to appoint a new prime minister. October 1944. He does. The new prime minister is Ferenc Szálasi, Fascist, nationalist, messianist, who dreams crazy dreams of a country called 'The United Ancestral Lands of Hungaria', leader of the Arrow Cross. There is panic, utter, indissoluble fear. Szálasi is prime minister. By October 18th, Eichmann has returned.

Look at what autumn has brought us.

Outside the rain has begun, shining gold over the leaves beside the door. Buried under the foundations of the garden are the layers of years, buried, then buried again. A word is buried out there too, one which, for long enough, rang hard against her spade like the stone which rises to the surface to present itself again and again to the digging edge. *Troubled*. The word she overheard Eve Blum, Mark and Dan's mother, use of her on the phone to a friend.

'A troubled girl. You wouldn't really expect anything else, would you?'

She didn't know the word. She had to ask Dan.

'Dan, what does "troubled" mean?'

He'd thought for a moment.

'To have *tsorres*,' he'd replied. Sorrows.

This is where she approaches the edges of remembering, a precipice where time slips and falls. Winter. She's eight. Snow is falling, covering everything. The months before have gone, slid into a depths beyond recall, beyond time itself. 1944. October, November, December, months fallen among words, fallen into darkness. In November, a ghetto's established in Pest. The Red army is moving towards the city. On December 4th, 1944, Soviet forces cross the Danube at Erci, approaching Budapest. Their losses during the operation to cross the river are huge.

From the darkness, names, Ferenc Szálasi, *Nemzetvezetö, Führer, Nyilas-keresztes Párt*, The Arrow Cross Party.

The Arrow Cross were perhaps the most ferocious killers of a murderous time. Feral in their instincts, appreciating the limitations of time for their particular grisly purpose, they slaughtered wildly and without mercy in homes, synagogues, hospitals, in the streets of Budapest and on the banks of the river which flowed red with the blood of their victims...

Places, numbers, names: *60, Andrássy ut*. 60, Andrássy Street, The House of Loyalty, *Hüség Háza*, the headquarters of the Arrow Cross. The address is one which will stay in her mind for a long time. Months collapse into the names of the killers and the dead.

The picture she keeps is at variance with what she knows. The room can't have been as she sees it now, they can't all have been there but nonetheless, they are, and smiling. Does she remember when their smiles changed? If they stop smiling, it's not failure of memory which prevents her from identifying the moment when they do. The picture is wrong, she knows. It's not from a sunlit room they're taken. It's from a grim room in a 'yellow star' building in Pest. It's November at the least, she knows this now, her father and Miklós already gone, taken days before, they don't know where. This is the last time she'll see her mother and Ágnes. Of that, she's sure.

She and Józsi are overlooked, or saved by an act of kindness, she'll never know which, they could never decide, if they really feel a hand poking at the bed quilts where they've run to hide, where they lie together, as still as the already-dead, if a voice does shout, 'That's the lot!', with no clear memory after that, a residue of noises, voices talking, screaming, moving off, away from where they lie for hours until darkness, until day. One patch of uncertainty yields to another, where they went after that and what they did. They are alone. She is eight, Józsi nine.

Eichmann is right. His arms are long. By October, he doesn't have much time left. He still needs slave labour, the German war-effort still needs Jews to work on fortifications, in factories, slave labour battalions. They're rounded up in the city, thousands sent on foot to dig fortifications against the approaching enemy, towards Germany, marched starving through the freezing winter. October, November.

It's on these forced marches, in the forced labour camps that the finest of Hungary's Jewish writers and scholars will die, Antal Szerb, György Sárközi, János Honti, Gábor Halász, Géza Havas, all of them ground into the frozen earth by Eichmann's will. Inside the city, the Arrow Cross murders on. Bodies are heaped in Városliget Park, in the streets, on the river banks, in the grounds of the synagogue in Dohányi Street, even as the Soviet army approaches, creeping nearer to the city. General Rodion Yakolevich Malinkovsky, General Feodor Ivanovich Tolbukhin, veterans of Stalingrad both, command this army which soon, will extend around the city, encircling it.

In November, Hitler directs that the city must be held regardless of the cost to life or property. The entire German army leadership knows that Budapest will fall.

Festung Budapest! Fortress Budapest. Why did Hitler refuse to allow his army to surrender or withdraw? At this last moment, why? To ask that, she knows, is the most pointless of all. Because he was deranged, because he refused to accept the war was lost, because he still believed it could be won.

Morning. She and József put on their coats. József carries a penknife and his birthday book. They take nothing else although they know they won't return. The streets are quiet. The day exists in patches, their walk to the house of their mother's friend, Ilka Neni, Aunt Ilka, her alarm and displeasure at seeing them, the haste of the breakfast she gives them, walking through the streets to another house, up a long flight of steps. Doors of metal and glass. The building may be a house or a school, she doesn't know. It may even be December because there is a Christmas tree, but it may be another day she remembers, time eliding, memory playing false.

Christmas Eve, 1944, the Soviet Army surrounds Budapest. It locks its two hands, closes its fingers, squeezes them around the city inside. The German campaign to lead the defence of Budapest is conducted from the network of tunnels under the Castle. It's led by SS Obergruppenführer Karl Pfeffer Wildenbruch, who although not a party member, will obey Hitler until the end, who will sacrifice the lives of thousands, his own troops, the people of the city, his enemies too because he refuses to surrender to the Red Army until the final opportunity, until the moment when he has to give the order to his troops to try to escape from their garrisons, when he does, to save his own life.

Eichmann, too. On Christmas Eve, before the Russians surround the city completely, Eichmann leaves Budapest, scuttles back to Germany. Szálasi is no exception. He refuses to respond to pleas that he should call on his troops to lay down arms. When the moment comes, he runs, Szálasi, *Nemzetvezető*, Führer of Hungary, would-be ruler of the 'United Ancestral Lands of Hungaria', escapes to the hills.

The circle's closed. They're trapped now, in a siege within a siege. She knows now, as she didn't then, that there were people trying to help, trying to save them, trying to get them out of the country, out of the reach of the Arrow Cross, to hide them, to feed them, to save them from the maelstrom, diplomats and churchmen, Zionists from Palestine, ordinary people who did what they could in the face of this tide of murder. Raoul Wallenberg too, sent by the Swedish government, who saved thousands and in the end, disappeared himself, swallowed into the vast, consuming jaws of Soviet intelligence. There's a Hungarian resistance too, brave people, communists and social democrats and students, people who hate Fascism and fight the Germans and the Arrow Cross, who are captured and tortured and die at the hands of the Germans and of their countrymen. In Debrecen, a Hungarian Provisional Government is formed under a man who had been a general in Horthy's command, General Béla Miklós, the first premier of liberated Hungary.

December, January, February. The Red Army bombards the city. The sound of voices is drowned by guns, by shelling. She and Józsi are in the building where they've been taken. They clutch one another, will not be separated. There are other children there, although she's still not certain what this place is, nor who the adults are who bar the doors, watch from the windows and hurry them all down to the cellars when the shelling starts. Throughout the city, those who can hide in shelters, cellars, the inner rooms of apartments. There are no food supplies coming into the city. She doesn't remember what they ate or didn't but she does remember long hours of trying to sit still in darkness, sucking her sleeve, the dabs of silence between the noise, an uneven music of dripping. Ceilings drip, drip, drip, with breath and fear and hunger. They must, she knows now, have been there for weeks. She and Józsi play games in the darkness. They write messages with their fingertips on the palms of each other's hand. They count the sounds of explosions and guns and the person who scratches out 20 first, wins. Her tooth is loose, a back tooth. During the hours and days, she undermines it, creaks it back and forth in its socket. Her mind is concentrated on the pain, which she likes, on the movement of her tooth.

Snow covers everything, the besieged city, the Castle, the troops who man the guns and tanks, who shell, night and day. The river turns to ice. Budapest starves and freezes. They melt snow to drink. Szálasi, knowing that the people of the city have no food, refuses aid from the International Red Cross because it will be given only if it's distributed to the ghetto too. Budapest dies, person by person in apartments and streets and cellars. There's no food. People eat the horses the armies have abandoned. They eat the flesh of horses already days dead.

None of this stops the Arrow Cross. Not even when the Russians reach Uj-lipotvaros. The siege doesn't deter Father András Kun, holy murderer, Minorite friar who, in soutane and cross, directs the Arrow Cross mobs, leads the killing with his cry of *Fire, in the name of Holy*

Christ! It doesn't stop Mrs Vilmos Salzer who tortures and mutilates Jewish girls before she kills them in the cellars of the Arrow Cross headquarters at 60, Andrássy ut. Nothing stops any of them in the weeks of January, February, not the appeals of the Papal Nuncio Angelo Rotto, nor of the international community, nothing stops them. It's as if they have to complete an awful task, as if they'll do anything to succeed. They kill in Pest as the Russians approach, and when on 18th January the Russians take Pest, they continue on the other side of the river in Buda, at the Jewish hospital in Maros Street, in Jewish almshouse in Alma Street. They murder patients and staff in the hospital in Városmajor Street. By the time they're finished, 105,450 Jews of Budapest are dead. They've done all that between October 1944 and February 1945 and nothing stops them until February 12th, when the Russians break through in Buda too.

On 11th February 1945 the Germans make an attempt to escape from Budapest, but by then it's too late. Pfeffer-Wildenbruch has delayed for too long. He has refused to negotiate the surrender the Russians would have welcomed weeks before. In doing so, he has sacrificed the lives of tens of thousands. By the time he gives the orders, the opportunity for escape has gone. His forces emerge into Soviet fire, they squeeze themselves through culverts and sewers, to be shot as they appear. The streets that night are crowded with the injured screaming for help, with panicking soldiers, running, trying to flee the city. Most are mown down by Soviet artillery. The dead lie everywhere, in heaps, squashed under the tracks of Soviet tanks. The Castle district is lit by fire. Under the castle, the German military hospital is abandoned with its patients still in it. Their conditions are already terrible after weeks of siege but now they're left to die, the wounded lie in filth, in their own excrement, waiting for the end. The generator is taken by the Russians. There's no water, no light, no sanitation. Fires break out, or are started, in the underground tunnels where the wounded lie. Hundreds are incinerated.

February 12th, 1944 and it's over. The Germans are gone, captured, dead. Thousands of them have died. She can't care. Nor can Józsi.

Now, the Russians are in Budapest, wild and strange and angry. They are, everyone will discover, unpredictable people, feral or kindly, childlike or vicious, there's no knowing which sort will arrive at your door, will climb your steps, will come into your house to treat you as ally or enemy. They might embrace you, then steal everything you have. They plunder and they rape. It's odd, Anci thinks, that now everyone knows about the rape of the women of Berlin but not of the rape of the women of Budapest, how the Russians stalked and followed and picked their prey, lurked outside houses waiting for the night, how, indiscriminately, they killed husbands, sons, brothers who tried to stop them. Woman hid, disguised themselves, made themselves look old but there was no escape. Hundreds of thousands of women, destroyed by the inexplicable lust which is the lust for vanquishment, for revenge, by men who, somewhere, had mothers, wives, daughters. Inexplicable. Women killed themselves before, rather than endure it. They killed themselves after, rather than continue with the memory. There was also the disease, the lack of medicines, the children who would be born, that world of horror hidden in whisper and euphemism, the head turned away, the words, 'We all suffered…'

She's fortunate. At eight, she's a child who looks younger even than she is, skinny and small and white with blotch-skinned legs and a face wizened to a point like a pinched triangle. The Russians are kind to children. Terrified recall brings back the experience of being swooped up in a frightful, sick-making arc into the dizzying grasp of huge Red Army soldiers, of being held in a foetid embrace, gazing down to the earth far below, gasping and smiling, too scared not to smile.

Budapest, when they extend their heads out into the icy air of February, is a ruined city. Under the perfect, concealing snow, it's broken, shelled, walls fallen to stone and dust. Domes have burned against the sky. They're shattered. Light pierces copper, winter sun strikes haphazardly through cracks in glass. It's a city covered in death. Corpses sprawl open in the streets. The dead huddle unseen in apartments, are heaped together, in mass graves, locked, tangled, they're fused and charred underneath the castle. Streets and walls and rooms are polluted with blood and death. The bridges across the river have gone and now, only limbs, trunks stand in the brown river. Spans sag, arms of metal wave hopelessly from the water, broken to the wind. All the bridges, the Margit Bridge, the Chain Bridge, the Erszcébet, Ferenc József and Miklós Horthy bridges, all destroyed. When at last, she sees them, the river's the only thing that's the same. The river and the sky.

The Russians are here, in Budapest. Of course, they're not just

Russians. They're Ukrainian and Kirghizians and Uzbeks. They wear padded uniforms and hats with flaps. They look so strange that a child can't help but stare. The Russians are here. It's an argument which will continue for a long time, whether Hungary is liberated or occupied. What is true is that decades will pass, turbulent, unquiet ones, before Hungary controls its own destiny again.

She used to wonder why it was that people knew about Stalingrad and Leningrad, about Warsaw, the uprising, the ghetto uprising but not about Budapest. Now, they still know about the same things but not about 1956. They know the name of Stalin but not of Rákosi. She used to wonder, but not now. She understands better now how events move, change significance, fade, how time deals with all.

That day in 1956, she recited names to Mark and Dan. The only reason she could remember them was because József had his birthday book. From the moment he was given it when he was about seven, he'd insisted on recording the names of every person in the family. He'd pestered their mother, who had to write or phone everyone to ask their birthdays so that he could put it in his book. When she was thirteen, he bought her a book the same as his for her birthday, and in it he'd written all the same names and birthdays, of the living and the dead.

She told Mark and Dan what she could, but with most of them she still doesn't know what happened. She doesn't know if they died at Auschwitz or Mathausen. It might have been in the hellish subterranean rocket factories of Dora Mittlebau which appalled even Albert Speer, Plenipotentiary for Labour Procurement, the man who said he never knew about the mass murder of Jews. It might have been at Bergen Belsen, on one of the treacherous death marches. She's never known.

When she tries to pin the moment, she realises that there never was a single time of grief; instead, a slow hollowing out of her hope, her expectation, a child's persistent knowledge of loss. For years, when she allowed them to, people seemed to cry from the locked areas of her brain, from her bloodstream, in case she might forget but then they stopped, knowing that she wouldn't. Without graves, without rites, there's no rest, no forgetting. They stay, she knows, forever like that, the dead in air, never ending.

It's how she has to see the past, as a room, a painting. She's eight and her mother is an artist. When anyone asks her how she began drawing, that's what she tells them: that her mother was an artist.

When her own sons were eight, she'd watch them playing on the grass. Reading to them or tucking them into bed at night, she'd look round their rooms. Walking through the terraces at the zoo, she'd watch them and all the time, she'd be wondering what they would remember. Would they remember a moment of playing? Their room? The snakes and the condor, the soft-shelled turtle pressing his snout urgently against the glass? Would they remember her? István? Each moment, each day, she'd wonder if this was one they'd carry to the future from their lives so far. Would they remember one another, if one of them was gone?

The rest of the years of her childhood, she remembers fitfully from that day, the house where Ilka Neni rushed them in that early morning at the end of 1944, the one with the flight of steps, the dripping cellars. It'll be their home for a long time, what's still called, in deference to the icy eye of truth, an orphanage. It's filled with children like her and József, children, some of whom will be friends and others who will not, children who'll sleep in the same long rows, who'll drag out their nightly dreams in a commonality of broken sounds, ones who'll laugh to cover silence, ones who, later, will fail to find a place for themselves in the world, ones who will conquer everything, ones who will, in the fullness of extended time, walk into rivers, throw themselves from bridges, down stairwells, ones like her who will simply continue to live, wondering only sometimes why they do when others didn't.

The years, nine, ten, eleven when she'd woken wishing that she hadn't, the effort of a day more than any pleasure in having lived it. She'd waken in the dormitory with thirty other beds, thirty other girls, just like herself. They all seemed the same to her, all of them floating without wires, without the weights and anchors which tie human beings to the solidity of earth. She was lucky. She still had a brother. There was her and there was Józsi . No-one else was left.

The text of the book lies in her lap. The prospect of working on it frightens and delights her, the utmost challenge of illustrating fairy tales. The ones have been newly re-told by well-known writers, all authors she admires who write for adults. She's read most of them at one time or another. These new versions have been written for both children and adults, and now that she thinks of it, she's anxious. The telling will be robust, she knows, the darkest stories interpreted darkly or with humour, embellished or pared to the finest of bones. Each of these she'll have to consider, each with its duality of its purpose. The thought occurs to her, painfully, that Mark won't see it. Each piece of work she's done before has been with Mark as her first, most important observer and critic, since the days when they used to go to draw in the art gallery in Glasgow, then later when she first sent off a drawing to show him, wanting only to elicit his good opinion, approbation, or reluctantly, his possible criticism. His judgement has propelled, impelled her every stroke of pen or brush, and now she's beginning a book he won't see. Dan might, she supposes. She's often wondered, over the years, if Dan has ever seen her work, if Mark showed him, or if in a moment of chance he picked a book up in a bookshop, happened on one in some other way. What did he think if he did? Would he even remember her, ever think of her? My God, she thinks, how sly time really is. How hapless we are, accepting so readily that years change us, make us progress and forget when in reality, all we do is grow a carapace to surround and protect the delicate fibre of ourselves, the time-capsule of our lives.

She opens the folder and begins to leaf through the pages. Some titles are familiar, favourites: *The Ice Maiden, The Marsh King's Daughter, The Emperor's New Clothes*; others are not. Terror and enchantment lie in her lap, the mythic fears of mankind. In these pages, men are turned to ravens and back again, severed limbs are re-connected, people remain silent for years in fulfilment of a vow, time moves formlessly from then to now. Stories for children are easy. Children know that everything's possible. It's adults who are stubborn, adults who won't believe that the world is as it is.

Chapter 22

New York, spring, 2000

It's during the warm, heady spring, after radiotherapy ends, that Mark is miraculously able to resume his former ways, a life without fatigue, one without daily obeisance to the giant eye. These are the weeks when he begins the process of restoring himself, as far as he may, to how he was before. It has been what he's hated most, the external transformation. The internal one, the unseen process he shares only with Jaegerson, is bearable because it's contained invisibly, within his gift of disclosure. He despises the bald, fat, caricature of himself who has mocked him so remorselessly many times a day from every reflective surface, who has winked conspiratorially at him from the chrome facets of his coffee machine. He doesn't need to question why it so disturbs him to be taunted by this face, this distended body. All his life he has tried to maintain an outer structure which reflects the inner one, as pleasing to himself and others as possible, as ordered and aesthetic, as tasteful as he can achieve with the given material. That it has been the peculiar workings of his architect's mind is one explanation he allows himself for the way he thinks about it. The other, more likely one, is because he's absurdly vain.

Slowly, his hair begins to grow back. The infant fuzz which one morning he feels under his palm, pushing gently, imperceptibly through his scalp, grows within days to a lanugo haze which picks up the light to form a crazy aureole around his head.

Every morning he goes to the gym before work and paces easily on a treadmill, increasing his speed gradually until the joyous day in mid-April when he allows himself to break into a cautiously measured run. After work, he returns to swim and lift a few weights. Afterwards, he drinks fruit juice with a couple of his gym friends in the health bar overlooking the park. As in conversation with everybody else, he weighs the words which tell of his illness, tense the steely edifice upon which expectation and hope raise their ambivalent, ambiguous partitions. Does he have, or did he have a disease? Which word conveys more completely the truth of the unknown?

Over the months Lee, with her habitual resistance to acceptance of the way things are, continues to e-mail him addresses, names, suggestions, research papers, statistics which he deletes without reading. Why, he often wonders as he erases yet another message, did he marry her? Time demystifies, provides, in the place of questions, the very explanations he'd have rejected with fury at the time: insecurity, the desire for love, sex, foolishness, youth, or all of them together. He met Lee in his first few months in New York and her family had seemed, unbelievably now, an exotic entity, drawing him toward its mythic warmth, a total, embracing unfamiliarity. Lee's mother, Bubah Maskin, was a kind of Jew he'd never encountered before, one of the shocks of his new life, one of many shocks which masqueraded as surprises. Although she'd lived in New York for years, she spoke only sufficient English to deal with tight, daily commerce, with buying or hectoring, shouting down the phone, addressing her daughters in a different language from the one in which they replied. He'd been pleased to be swamped by it all for a time, losing himself in the idea of a family to replace his own, now dead or estranged, until he knew better, with the first stirrings of panic, and fully realised the mistake he'd made. He thinks of Bubah Maskin's superstitions, the fierce exercise of her control. He often wondered what diverse steps of social evolution had produced her and his neat, precise, grammarian mother in the same generation.

This, he thinks, clicking again on 'delete', is the positive aspect of electronics, the absence of lingering evidence, or at least the absence of the kind which lies around to induce guilt, no papers which demand to be dealt with, no documents to be decided upon or filed away until later. The aspect he regrets, though, is the one which ensures there will be in the future a desolating absence of written records for coming generations, no hand-written letters, love letters, letters of anger or revenge. Electronics are effacing histories, obliterating the history of love. The love letters he wrote once were a matter of care and some pride, good letters he'd thought at the time, full of passion and *tendresse*. He wonders if he'd think the same now. There were other letters, too: the ordinary ones to electricity companies, the ones to friends, the letters one wrote at a time, now almost obliterated from collective memory, when writing letters was what one did, almost more easily than phoning. Hand-writing in itself used to be a pleasure to him. He and Anci for years exchanged frequent letters whose appearance was as important as their content, both of them in the tacit competition which has always been an unspoken vital force in their relationship. The habit has withered in the past few years, for the usual reason, the inexcusable one: time. Mark thinks of the odd characteristic of time, the way it can seem both in too short a supply but inexhaustible too. The thought of it makes him decide that he will write. In preparation, he goes to his favourite paper shop, a place he loves, stocked with dazzling papers and pens, journals bound in leather, organisers and blotters, Noguchi lampshades of delicate opacity, all things he covets which make him almost dizzy entering the place, overcome with the desire to buy everything, to clear the shelves and the glass cabinets of every single, lovely, desirable item. He spends a long time choosing paper he thinks she'll like, deciding finally on thick, handmade Italian paper of the palest cream. He buys fresh sheets of blotting paper, a new bottle of ink and a few things for Noah and Tam, pens and coloured pencils and bright stickers for Tam to give to the children in her class as inducements or rewards.

Beginning his letter, he sits at his desk and writes.

My dearest Anci,

I'm more sorry that I can say that I didn't contact you as soon as I heard of István's death ...

But this is all he writes. He is unable to write the words he should, words of regret and loss. *I'm sorry that István is dead.* He can't write those words, nor the ones which will tell her that soon he will be too. The page, when he rips it, tears thickly into many soft pieces which scatter into his wastebasket with the slow fall of confetti.

Shortly before Pesach, in early April, he does as he has planned and visits Sarah. He phones first to arrange the timing with Mrs Spellman. He doesn't want to turn up in the middle of gymnastics or mahjong or Sarah's weekly visit to the beauty room.

Kirstin, as he knew she would, drives him there. She has her book and some magazines in the back of the car.

'Send Sarah my love,' she says, and means it.

Sarah is standing on the front path waiting for him when he arrives. His phone already has six messages on it which later he'll listen to and delete.

'Hello. Hello? Mark? Is it? Are you there? Have you left yet? It's Sarah. Hello?'

'What's happened? I was expecting you at one. No, at two. I

thought you might have been here. Please give me a call.'

'Hello? Hello? Hello?'

'Eh, hello, thank you. Yes. Hello?'

And then a few completely silent reproaches for his uncommitted sin.

'You got here,' she says in greeting.

The afternoon is as he expects, one which lasts for decades, so that, walking back down the path after it, through the trees to the road and the car and Kirstin, his adulthood has gone and in its place there's a thorn of petulant childhood lodged within, an age-spotted, shrivelled remnant of his former self.

The place is busy during his visit. Many relatives appear, as he is, to be carrying out their before-Pesach duty visits. Families are sitting in the sitting-rooms and in the garden, paying dutiful court. Throngs of young girls are decorating the rooms for Pesach, hanging decorated Stars of David from the ceiling of the dining-room, giggling from ladders.

He and Sarah sit in the glassed-in café in sunshine. This part is not difficult. He has no need to speak. Sarah has always talked wilfully about herself, but the tendency is even more marked now, lacking even the cursory few seconds she used to spend listening to other people's news, and while she talks he reflects on how manners become blown away by age. Not just Sarah but other people's elderly female relatives, the very ones who imposed regimes of unspeakable restriction on any available children, all in the name of politeness, suddenly lose inhibition, make appalling comments. 'What an ugly creature!', 'Look at the size of that backside!', 'Smells like cabbage water!', 'I don't like that. You can take it back!' asking unashamedly for other people's things, throwing tantrums, stamping their feet. Perhaps they feel a demonic freedom to do these things. Perhaps they sail out into clear water, out past the point where the hand of psychological conditioning can reach, where they can stop and gaze shorewards, shouting out the frothing head of abuse they've saved up all their life towards those unable to reach them, heading towards a place where, all at once, no-one matters but themselves, the sole and only time in a state of sentience, or near-sentience, they may enjoy the freedom to say what they like, a sphincter loosening, a valve giving, the girdle of self-restraining steel which held it all together, society, decency, manners, sagging, giving, no longer able to hold in the things they once had done.

Around him, as demanding centrepieces of family clusters, are people much like Sarah, nimble people, determined and enduring, some whose families seem genuinely at ease, happy on this sunlit afternoon. The ones he doesn't see occupy his mind equally, the bed-bound, the long-demented whose lives are conducted and end in rooms upstairs, lines of them opening off long, lilac-painted corridors on the two top storeys of the building. Their presence isn't confined there. Ever time he visits he seems to receive their aerial messages, their promises and threats. He can't help but sense them everywhere, in the curtains blown by the spring wind from open windows, in a faint but irrepressible scent which no synthetic spray can cover. The care wing, it's called. It is there, he thinks, to remind us all.

Sarah is the one who admits first to having tired of company. He's glad. He's won the petty war of who'll be first to curtail a visit. He never likes to be the one to concede victory. When she says, 'You'd better be getting back now,' he assents, as if reluctantly. She comes with him to the front door and waves to him as he walks down the path. By the time he reaches the car, she is out of sight. It takes him hours to recover from the numbness he feels. On the journey home, he wishes he could still drive for the simple experience of regaining control, a freedom to drive too fast and put distance between himself and the atmosphere of age, its stifling stasis and woeful accoutrements. He looks for a radio station which plays the kind of music he's not expected to enjoy, the music of the young which always helps blow away the slight depression he feels on these occasions. All the way back to Manhattan he moans to Kirstin about what she already knows, but even speaking of it doesn't dispel the gloom completely. For hours his mind totters, reels off-centre, spinning back into the disjointed conversations and unfathomable gossip which tangle themselves with intermittent complaint into a maze without exits. He has visited, briefly, a world inhabited by people he doesn't know, of whom he's never heard before, phantoms who have loomed briefly out of a tumble of randomness as players in partial stories, bizarre episodes which have been abruptly, summarily curtailed, all without explanation. He doesn't know who Leslie is, of whom he has heard much, if it's he who has recently been indicted for fraud or if the culprit is Adrian and if he's really the son of the elderly woman who had waved with such friendliness to them from her chair on the lawn. He leaves with names clattering in his head.

It takes until evening for him to dispel the oppression of the disembodied Leslie and Adrian, their doomed aspect, their perpetual wandering in a dreadful limbo.

There is strange consolation, though, in the aftermath of his visit which occurs to him over the next few days. He will never be like them. He will never sit on a high-backed chair nodding and vacant, or if he does, it will not be for time without clear end. He will not live in one room, relinquishing the freedoms and treasures of a lifetime. He will deteriorate, but it won't be like this. It'll be quick, horrible, and over. His children will never have to drive too fast, listening to loud but deadening music, never have to scream their lungs out on a freeway to dispel the misery of their witness of the effects of the cycle of age.

It is Pesach. For Seder, Mark invites Kirstin and Berndt and Ali. Noah manages to take time to come too, though Tamar, with apologies, tells him that this year she feels obliged to go to Sam's parents in Los Angeles, but that she'll visit during the summer. Noah invites his friend from high school, Lisa, a singer who has recently ended a long relationship, and together the six of them crowd round Mark's table, a disparate congregation who, for this night only, will forget about Mark's illness and fulfil their duty of telling and remembering. Setting the table, Mark adds the customary place for the one who cannot be present. This, like everything else he does for Pesach, is his personal tie to memory and the teachings of the past, what he buys for the festival, his careful arrangement of the objects on the Seder plate. His mother's frantic preparations seem near to deranged now, the changing of plates and cutlery and pans and cruet sets, cleaning and scouring in apparent terror of the single errant crumb of *chometz,* weeks of work which, it's said, causes women to faint in shul from exhaustion on the first day of the Yomtov. Do they really, or is that folk myth? He has no idea. No-one that he's seen has ever fainted in any shul he's been to.

It's a pleasant evening. Untraditionally, they take turns to read from the Haggadah, agreeing that none of the men feels quite patriarchal enough to assume the leader's role.

'Your father's and my days of tyranny are over and yours haven't

Esther Woolfson

yet begun,' Berndt says to Noah.

There's a quality to Pesach that Mark forgets from year to year but begins to love again as the festival approaches. There are the moments he anticipates, the spilling of the drops of wine, words which move him, 'this is the bread of affliction…', the incantatory recitation of the word '*dayenu*!' He and Berndt both read Hebrew with the ease of the long-ago cheder-educated. Noah does too, but with a little less facility. Lisa, marginally younger than Noah, reads the four questions, but in English. When they come to the point in the evening where they discuss the nature of oppression, it occurs to Mark that perhaps there's some progress towards hope and resolution, because over the years of his life the names of the oppressed, invoked annually at his Seder table, have at least changed from time to time. The question of why there's never a shortage of names, candidates for the role of the oppressed, feels too contentious for him on this particular evening.

They eat the food of Pesach, carefully bought and prepared. Eggs in salt water, *matzot* and bitter herbs. All has been done as it should. The meal is delicious, chicken roasted with tarragon, chocolate roulade with wild strawberries. Elijah is ushered in, sips and leaves.

Lisa has prepared song sheets for them all, *zemirim*, the songs of all their past, their parents' pasts, and she makes them all sing, even with their different tunes, and drunkenly they sing and laugh, and on this night Mark feels – if not exactly *one* with all those designated as his people, then almost one, almost prepared to think himself one, even with those of them of whom he disapproves, those of them who are difficult and contentious and quite obviously wrong, the ones who annoy or offend him daily in an ascending chorus, from local to cosmic. Tonight, he feels benign. He will think of them on this occasion, acting as they do at this season as one, with one purpose, that of conducting the Seder, wherever in the world they are. This thought makes him feel an unusual, momentary benevolence. After they've sung together, Lisa sings alone and the beauty of her voice singing the songs of Pesach makes him and Berndt and Ali tearful, appreciating in this moment, that they've each attained more than one person has a right to expect or to desire, concentrated this evening to a piercing point, tradition and parenthood and their lives of fortune.

The evening moves towards its end. Lisa and Noah tussle and shriek in the hall in their search for the Afikoman. Lisa finds it but

186

Mark has small gifts prepared for both of them. When they all say the words, 'Next year in Jerusalem,' he thinks of Tal, and of Dan who he'll phone later. There will be another Pesach, he thinks, probably. One more. The thought of doing this again here is more than he can bear.

After Pesach there is a change, an alteration in gear, one Mark can't explain to himself with any precision. It's to do with the way he thinks, how he plans. He doesn't know if it's the annual brush with history which has set him in another context, that of a larger time dwarfing his own, and in truth, everyone else's, necessarily limited hours and days, but he decides that he'll enjoy the spring and summer by walking at the weekends in the park, exploring corners and back-waters he has either never been to before or ones where he hasn't been to for years, at least since the children were young, when their weekend excursions had to include at least one afternoon studying wildlife with Noah. He'll go to all the museums, the odd, small places, the buildings he's always meant to visit but hasn't, as anyone will do in any of the great cities in which they coexist with the daily assumption that they will, one day, accomplish all they meant to, given opportunity and time. That these may be gestures of parting occurs to him, only for him to dismiss the thought summarily. There's time for that yet, he thinks, but still, having thought it at all gives new, determined force to everything he does.

Spring light shines cleanly through the windows of the apartment. It picks out the soft edges of dust on surfaces, a slight haze coating glass. He means to leave a note for the serious young men from the cleaning company who arrive once a week to attack every corner with frightening resolve, but he forgets. The following week, after their visit, he sees that it's all been scoured, polished. There's something that pleases him about its all being done in spite of his having forgotten to mention it. It means that other people too think about these things. It means, in some way he can't explain, that he is properly dispensable. Spring has been dealt with, as it always will be, everything to its appropriate occasion.

The presence of the reprieved books on the brain and mind, all clean and dusted in a row, reminds him of what he has decided is to be his duty to read and understand them. This self-imposed task feels like something he's obliged to do, the preparation for an exam. He has to know and consider all this while he still can. This thought, the words *while he still can* are new, though inevitable. They chill the air around him, inject a slow-building urgency to what he remembers, what he must do, what he has to say to whom. Some of it he'll write down, a list of things he always meant to say, a list of secrets.

On the day when he takes the books down from the bookcase and lays them out on his desk, he experiences the old feeling of pointlessness, wondering why he's going to bother tormenting himself with a subject he probably won't understand when his time is limited, but he knows this feeling is the enemy of any future he might have and so he chooses the book which looks the most straightforward, the most easily understood, and he begins.

Consciousness is... which is about as far as he gets without knowing that he's wading voluntarily into too-deep water, reading on, working his way, often uncomprehendingly, though the chapters, it seems to him as if the entire subject itself is like one of the enigmatic riddles which ask, 'what is both there and not there', 'what is felt but never seen?'

Consciousness, as he understands it, demonstrably exists, or at least he thinks it does, and now he's aware of the state of being aware, everything around him, in him, everything he's thinking, considering, worrying about, planning, it's all there now, his looking at the pages which contain concepts he's barely able to understand. That, he supposes, is consciousness: the fact that he's sitting here, thinking with the mass inside his skull, of thinking of the mass inside his skull, thinking. The question that he ponders, and once he's made a brave attempt at some of the books he understands that other people seem to ponder too, is how.

He takes down some books on brain anatomy, looks again at the structures of the brain, the lobes and cerebellum, the cerebral cortex, hippocampus, brain stem, all of it, this mass folded, curled away inside neat container of the skull. Inside these structures we are: 30 billion neurons, a million billion synapses, dendrites, axons, cranial nerves, all with their pathways and connections, numbers and ideas beyond anyone's imagining, a mad whole, functioning into consciousness, perhaps the activity of 40-hertz oscillations firing in the brain, all of it illustrated by diagrams which whirl lines round and round, lines which seem inevitably, all to meet at the same point.

It's impossible to understand. He gets up, walks round the room for a while to clear the very structures he's considering, to shake down the clogging, muddy complexity weighing his thoughts, hoping he might understand how it can all depend on the minute functioning of this or that part of his brain, on a speed of firing. He wonders what in him will go first, which of the strands of his being which make up his awareness of himself and the universe in which he occupies his tiny, conscious place will unravel first, will fail to fire, will stop, refuse to communicate, will fade and fall and go. Will he know? Will there be a gradual diminution of himself as himself, step by step, so that he's no longer who he once was, quite literally, the physical material of his brain encroached upon, eaten, digested by the presence which, after all, is part of himself too? When will he lose what he sees, hears, feels, smells, touches, all of which is him, his pulsing, winking, thinking, cruel or kind or random brain, the brain which makes him discern and draw and know that this is more beautiful than that, this more desirable than that. What places him in space and time, makes him remember, anticipate, and fear?

One paragraph he happens on in the midst of this terrifying welter of brains and numbers reverberates through his mind for days. He goes back to the book, to read the article from which it comes more thoroughly. It is on the subject of awareness, the relation of the functioning of the brain to perceptions of reality. It describes our ability to trace through every complicated, subtle, minute, invisible structure of the brain, the path through vision, what is described as the scheme of energy, that which leads through the eye to the perception of the world, of the sky, a star. This we can prove, this we know, can see, can demonstrate by this clever means and another, as the book points out to him, but all that we cannot find is the method by which we can prove how the star came into being. The words the book uses instill in him quietude, a wonder, an unlooked-for sense of what he thinks is hope.

At this point, it says, *the scheme puts its finger to its lips and is silent.*

By the beginning of summer, when he looks at himself in the mirrors in the gym, he's not entirely displeased by what he sees. He looks fit, well-preserved, that hideous phrase hinting at un-wrapped mummies or things in jars. He does as he has planned, walks, sometimes with friends or with Kirstin but often alone, tracing the gridwork of the city, seeking byways, feeling that he might never be in this or that place again.

At moments of repose he wonders if, by concentration, he might be able to feel the little fingers of nuisance stirring in his brain.

In summer, Dan sends the catalogue from his new exhibition. They discuss once or twice the idea that Mark should go to London for the opening, but he decides he won't. He's too busy, but there's an additional, submerged reason which prevents him, although he's not certain what it is. It's not to do with work or obligations or invitations he has already accepted. He feels that it's not the moment to go, but he doesn't examine the feeling too closely. It just isn't the right time. He looks with admiration at the catalogue, at the photographs and what's been written about Dan, words which delight him, ones which talk unrestrainedly of talent, ability, fame, and he feels the keen pulse of a new pleasure, one he denied himself for years, that of appreciating his brother. He wonders now how he managed for so long to fail to pay him the dues he so clearly owed, wondering if it was from habit, or jealousy or simply his own dogged failure to forgive. It's regret, the sense of the irrecoverability of passing time which makes him, one warm, restless evening in summer, resume the attempt to write to Anci. Again, he lays out the lovely paper he's bought, the fine-nibbed pen, but on this occasion he writes everything he wants to say, every word of apology and love. He puts the letter away into the front of his diary in its envelope. It is a letter without time, one with no urgency. He wonders what she might think on reading it. Anger and frustration no doubt, but amusement too. She'll laugh at what he says, some of it anyway, and in the end she'll understand. Anci is a woman who likes to know everything and he has, in this regard, done what he can. He applauds himself for wiliness but, at the same time, knows his effort to be less wily than hopeful, less cunning than wistful. Sad bastard, he says to himself, self-deluder, latter-day *shadchan*, broker of dreams, even if they're his own pathetic dreams, his attempt to be too clever, to repair the past, to leave promise and the posthumous prospect of redemption or of joy behind him even as he consoles himself on the self-evident lack of subtlety of the gesture.

In July Tam visits. This time, she's alone. Mark can't remember when they last spent time like this, alone together. He's always felt it a privilege to have his children's time, without the cluster of friends, boyfriends, girlfriends, who seemed to surround them in growing frequency from early childhood. During the week they spend together they talk about families, his own, Lee's, and he understands that she's seeking details which will outlast him, things otherwise he might take with him which she'll carry to the future. She asks about Sarah with some curiosity. Why did he have those feelings of duty? It's odd to explain to her that, at some point or another, their mother had said to him and Dan, with, he thinks, no sense that her death would be as soon as it was: 'You will always look after Sarah, won't you, boys?' and he and Dan had said they would. What else were they to say?

As happens every year, the cards and baubles and tat of Christmas appear disgracefully early. In late September, October, he begins to see the cards, departments being cleared for Christmas displays. Christmas, another Christmas. He feels as he did at Pesach, as he did again at Rosh Hashanah. It's not his illness which has made him feel like this: age has, the nature of years, the cycles of seasons, the annual sensations of time moving faster, spinning the year round and round to place him again at the same point, Christmas, Chanukah, the things to be done, observed, organised, acknowledged, with no escape and no remorse, things to be done and bought and cooked and prepared for the next one and put away after the last one. And he, he reflects, is a man who loves celebration, looks forward to every opportunity to rejoice in the random events which elevate life from the mundane to the extraordinary. It is only, he decides, that one tires, grows wisely weary with one's place in the world. It is the appropriate reaction to diminishing years. It's something he always thinks when he's with Sarah. How can you go on?

It's November, almost a year after his first meeting with Jaegerson, when he notices a mildly unfamiliar sensation in his hand, a weakness of grasp in the line of his fingers, a failing. Closing his eyes, he raises his two hands parallel to the floor to feel one of them drifting slowly downwards, and with this he knows that it is back. It's almost with relief that he accepts it. He has been waiting, every day, waiting, and now the waiting is complete. The seasons have passed, almost a year. A year of living with the knowledge of the inevitability of its return. It has been, he realises, the evasion of a shadow. There's no shock, no surprise. He feels anxiety, but no fear. He accepts. It is back because it is his, and now it will be with him always.

Almost a year, the certainty that this will happen. Afterwards, when it does, he tells himself that it was all pretence, his feeling of well-being, his favoured life of mundane routine, the comfort of the familiar, the chosen: all pretence. He tells himself that all the time, he knew. It's impossible afterwards to discern the un-thought, the perhaps-felt, the almost-sensed. It's the way he thinks of the failed love affair, the pursuit of relationships which, *ab initio*, he knew had no foundation, saying afterwards, I knew, I think I knew, I was sure it was always there, this feeling of doubt, this retrospective wisdom, the pretence of love where it refused to exist. Later he thinks it, that he has lived as he did before, while all the time knowing it has been pretence, the pretence of happiness when one knows that one is sad.

Now, he feels as if he has been given permission to admit to all that he has kept, more or less successfully, below the surface of his conscious fear, worries towards which he has nodded briefly, practical ones to do with memory, to do with getting lost, having fits, waking speechless, having people think him drunk or drugged, avoiding him or abusing him, stealing from him or doing him violence, of finding himself in a public hospital unable to elaborate upon his identity or his condition. There's no remedy. He's vulnerable to the humiliations his body might lay upon him, sudden falling in the street, incontinence, the losses of self and dignity he dreads. He thinks of the forms a fit might take, sudden silence or some other strange, inexplicable behaviour, running into traffic, falling in a place where no-one will find him. He thinks of the hospital's frantic phone-calls to his children, of lying helpless, speechless but aware in a hospital bed being visited daily by Lee.

By the end of the year, he's weary. This life that he lives will no longer do. It's not the same life any more. He's grown far from it all, far from all he once loved. He has waited and it seems as if he has kept others waiting too. Acknowledgement is the most difficult of all but the feeling has grown and he can no longer pretend as everyone else pretends. Death is between them. It breathes its name over his shoulder, over the shoulders of others, is there even while they pretend that it's not. It becomes more than he can bear. He wants it for an acknowledged companion. Dan knows. Dan doesn't pretend. He wants be a person who does not pretend in the company of other people who do not pretend.

There's no sense of decision. All in his mind has been stealthy but certain. In this, it reminds him of the process of designing and creating, when often, he's allowed an idea to develop in darkness, forced it away from immediate thought to grow until the moment when he's ready to approach it on equal terms, to find it ready, developed, better than he'd hoped. At the same time as he has been quietly deluding himself, he has, clearly, been equally quietly planning, because he knows exactly what he must do.

He sees Jaegerson in the afternoon and in the evening, begins to sort through his clothes, write lists, plan. His mind races, leaps, a hot, palpitatory rush towards his purpose, but he slows himself and his thoughts. He has to take considerable care over the handling of what he is to do. There's no decision to be made. It has, at an undistinguished moment lost in all the other moments of the past months, already been made. He will leave New York. He will go back to die in Glasgow.

Dr K. L. Jaegerson, Neurosurgeon
Specialties: Neuro-oncology,Endoscopic Neurosurgery
Suite 53
43, East Reveille Avenue
New York, N.Y.

Dr J. Baker
Family Physician
Suite 67
130, Braklynn Street
New York, N.Y.
November 14th, 2000.

Mr Mark Blum, 25th May, 1936

Dear Dr Baker,

As requested, I saw Mr Blum today and agree that his symptoms may be early signs of recurrence of his tumor. I have arranged further scans for him and will contact you when I have the results,

With kind regards,
K.L. Jaegerson,
Neurosurgeon.

Esther Woolfson

Kelly Street Imaging Centre
MRI Report, 15th November, 2000.

Mr Mark Blum
d.o.b. 25th May, 1936.

Scan No. 32957

MR Brain: Axial T1 and T2 and CORONAL T1
Axial T2 post gadalinium

The scan demonstrates recurrence of tumor growth in the area of the right parietal lobe. There is some surrounding oedema.

Dr O. Steel.
15th November, 2000.

Dr K. L. Jaegerson, Neurosurgeon.
Specialties: Neuro-oncology, Endoscopic Neurosurgery.
Suite 53
43, East Reveille Avenue
New York, N.Y.

Dr J. Baker
Family Physician
Suite 67
130, Braklynn Street
New York, N.Y.

Mr Mark Blum 25th May, 1936

November 29th, 2000.

Dear Dr Baker,

I saw Mr Blum today and discussed the results of his scan. He is unwilling to accept my suggestion that further surgery would be the best course of action but he has agreed to a course of CCNU. I have explained the possible side effects and will see him again in two weeks time.

With kind regards,
K.L Jaegerson,
Neurosurgeon.

Piano Angel

Dr K. L. Jaegerson, Neurosurgeon
Specialties: Neuro-oncology, Endoscopic Neurosurgery.
Suite 53
43, East Reveille Avenue
New York, N.Y.

Dr J. Baker
Family Physician
Suite 67
130, Braklynn Street
New York, N.Y.

Mr Mark Blum 25th May, 1936

December 14th, 2000.

Dear Dr Baker,

I saw Mr Blum today. He complains of nausea and a feeling of general debilitation. I have suggested that he discontinue his course of CCNU.

During our meeting, Mr Blum informed me of his decision to travel to Scotland to live. I pointed out to him that the existing health system there may not be able to provide him with the level of treatment which he may expect here but he assures me that this is a situation he is willing to accept. I have promised to give him copies of his medical records to take to his physicians in Scotland,

With kind regards,
K.L. Jaegerson,
Neurosurgeon

Chapter 23

Glasgow, late autumn, 2001

Mark phoned me early in the morning of the second day of Pesach last year, his last in New York. He wanted to tell me about his Seder. He'd been excited, almost childlike in his planning for it, but now his voice sounded flat and tired. For him, it was late at night.

'*Chag Sameach*! Good *Yomtov*! How was it?'

'It was great. Lovely. What about you, Dan? What did you do?'

'Nothing. Thought about you all. Watched a video.'

'I meant Seder-wise.'

'That's what I did. I watched a video. Then I opened the door and waited for half a minute and then said a *bracha* and shared a glass with Elijah.' Mark laughed.

Friends had asked me to join them at their Seder but I refused. I hate being at other people's Seders, people who aren't family. It's like Christmas, the sole dissociated invitee almost paralysed by his status, beyond appreciating kindness, in the midst of one of the loneliest experiences on earth. What I said was true, though. I did open the door for Elijah.

Mark asked what the girls were doing for Pesach and how they were and we chatted about them for a while. I'd talked to Tal too, earlier the previous evening. She'd just finished her Seder. She sounded wistful, or perhaps that's what I wanted to think. She asked me if I'd be speaking to Mark and to send her love, which I did. Love was acceptable but I'd learned to take care in the way I said things. Asking about his health, in particular. While I was in New York, he'd said that there's nothing worse than the question asked in meaningful tones, 'And how are you?' and so I never asked. There was always another way of finding out. Waiting for him to tell me was one.

'What did you cook?'

'Oh, nice things. The usual. Funny, isn't it, you'd never dream of eating an egg in salt water at any other time, would you? The *charoseth* was particularly fine, though. Then I did chicken with tarragon, and a salad and I made a chocolate roulade. I'll have to make one for you next time you're here, it's good. I'm quite tired now, to be honest. It's an effort, a Seder. I always look forward to it but I'm glad when it's over. Lisa made us all sing, but afterwards she sang for us too. She's got a fantastic voice. You should have heard her *El B'nai.*'

'Where's Noah?'

'Taking Lisa home. They were going to stop in for a drink somewhere. Tell me, how's the work going?'

Talking about work gave me the opportunity to complain about my French colleague Luc, who was fussy and demanding and becoming a problem. He was bombarding me with e-mails full of questions and requests which took hours to answer and to deal with, preventing me from working on my own preparations for the exhibition.

'There's always one troublesome bugger, isn't there?'

'He's a good man really, he just gets nervous before these things. I'm looking forward to it, as long as he leaves me alone to get everything done.'

'I'd wish I could be there.'

'Why don't you come over?'

'Oh, I'll see. You know, there's so much…'

I did know, or could imagine. I didn't pursue it.

'We'll see each other soon though, won't we?'

'Yes, of course.'

I said that, but didn't quite know when. Perhaps after the exhibition, October, November. I could always go to see him straight from London. As I thought about it, I realised that I felt differently about London. I no longer dreaded the idea of having to be there. Everything had changed.

During that winter and spring, after I heard of István's death, Anci returned to me. She did so slowly, a very small wraith emerging from the gloom of time, until one day she was there, as clearly brilliant as when I first knew her, as she was then, alone. The process felt the same as developing an old film found by chance, one you can't remember having shot, the shock of the reappearance of a moment of the past, the feeling that you've calling days into being which you can't even recall having lived. I tried to make the proper adjustments for the passage of the years, but knew so little of her life, only that she has sons. I assume they'll have left home by now and that she must live alone. I wondered how she was. It was the same after Mark and I had our talk this summer. How could it have been anything else? I didn't have the freedom to think much about it then, because at the time I was so involved with looking after Mark. I did, in odd moments, allow myself reflect on the fact that, since she left Glasgow, I've never seen Anci again. I'd never even heard her name until this summer when Mark spoke it to me again. Since Mark died, I've had all the time I've wanted to think of her again.

István didn't go away last winter either, in spite of my having shut him in a drawer. That had felt at the time like an act of finality, and in one way it was, but he was there nonetheless, in some form or another, over the months following his death. Lately, I've realised that my feelings towards him have changed. The triumph, some of the anger, have evaporated and I even feel a certain guilt at ever having felt them, a reaction, I suppose, against low, mean sentiment. I felt it with Sarah too, the law of nature, mine anyway, that the more disreputable the feelings, the sadder and more diminished they make me feel.

Not that I forget. For a few years after István and Anci went to live in London I was determined to make them part of a past life, an episode, but after far too few years István re-appeared. He had miraculously transformed into a political soothsayer, vendor of opinions, the piece of heavy intellectual artillery to be rolled out at intervals to fire starbursts of enlightenment towards what he, no doubt, thought of as an eager but dullard populace. The tone of his voice still maddened me, the obscure quotations from German or Greek, even his accent which, just by existing, appeared to validate without further question the truth of every doubtful opinion. I hated the mildly weary tone of the man, as if only he were capable of recognising the burdensome nature of simply knowing so much. It felt like a peculiar punishment, an ever-recurring reminder of things I didn't want to be reminded about. I like to think that I knew what István was when I was eighteen, and nothing I heard over the years encouraged me to alter my view. I know, because even after years, his words still lay inside me as an abandoned cluster bomb, the potential to explode undiminished. Until very recently I was still able to use the terrible damaging force of their first impact to wound myself.

At the beginning, after István began becoming famous, my daydream was of opening a newspaper to see Anci gazing from its pages with all the smudged ambiguity of newspaper photographs, an interview with the wife of a rising star. I wasn't sure where they had decided to live and imagined her making her life in London or Paris or wherever it was István had chosen. Not always, not even often, I'd create lives for her, think of how they'd be, what house she would live in, seeing the light of northern cities, luminous mornings, Anci, as she was in my photos, but smiling.

One evening, in my early years in London, I happened to hear István on Radio 3 discussing a new book and *en passant* he mentioned that he lived in north London. For days after, I walked around with a sense of animation, looking, searching at faces in crowds. I needn't have worried. I never did see her again. It could have been a disastrous indulgence, feeling that, if I didn't restrain myself, I'd always look back, but not long after that I met Tal and the feeling, for a while, went away.

For years, I didn't even look her name up in the phone book. István's name, rather. It would have been István's name. I wanted to believe I had progressed, and searching the pages of a telephone book would have felt like an act of betrayal, infidelity of a certain kind. Years later, when I did look, István's name wasn't even there.

Anci's voice, too, returned to me during this winter. I'd thought in that shul in New York about what she must have felt, remembering for the first time in years the sound of her small, high howl the morning we took her to shul, the first Shabbas she was with us. I don't know why it didn't occur to any of us that it might be difficult for her. It was the first time I'd seen our life that way, realised what it was, an outpost, the surviving image of the once timeless life which had been erased from the countries of Europe, countries so near, only on the other side of the North Sea. In that quiet suburb where we lived in Glasgow, we still lived that life and it was only then, hearing Anci's voice, that I saw it suddenly as a remnant or a sanctuary, saved, preserved in the face of destruction.

She told us, over the months that she was there, everything I'd dreaded hearing. I'd been frightened before she came and then, when she was there, knew that I was right to have been. I was never in any doubt about being in the presence of a person from another world. She talked about the war and later, about the events she had just lived through, the revolution, 1956. I can hear her voice, full of incomprehension, even years later.

'Paris was already liberated! It was autumn 1944. The Russian were at Debrecen. We thought it was going to end.'

Her drowning voice. She used to tell us in snatches. She'd sit with hair clutched in her hands, pulling it across her eyes, her face, crying as if she could never stop. One day, Mark and I made her tell us the names of her family, cousins, aunts, everyone. We made her remember. She did, a recitation which seemed to take a long time.

She could be happy too, though; often, specially after she'd been with us for a few months. I began then to see the nature of the human soul, or if not the soul, the character, and I knew that her life would always be for me a benchmark, the paradigm of what's possible in this unfathomable world.

I've told myself on more occasions than I can remember that feelings are perishable, elusive, false, that memory is illusion, that the emotion of youth is profound but fickle. I doubt the truth of all that. I never knew, after Anci left, if she and Mark kept in contact. When her sons were born I happened to see the notices in the papers, and I knew she'd begun illustrating only by chance, when I bought one of her books for the girls. The beauty of the cover attracted me before I even saw her name. The girls loved it immediately, and I had to read it to them every evening until we all knew every word of the text by heart. Dalit was still small enough to enjoy picking out tiny details from the illustrations, pointing eagerly to minute rabbits or ladybirds or bees, naming them with pride, whispering, 'Scary!' to herself, sucking her thumb rhythmically with startled delight at the sight of witches and saw-toothed giants.

While I was alone in his apartment, before Mark came back from Berndt and Ali's, I noticed the same book in one of Mark's bookcases in a row of books Anci had illustrated and quite clearly sent to him. I took one of them out. There was a letter folded into it, as there was in each of the others when I took them down, each still in its envelope. From cowardice, from fear, I didn't read them. I was shocked, amazed to find a wave of old jealousy lighting me with its peculiar, inimitable fire. Since I first heard of Mark's illness, I thought often about Lee and Kirstin. And Anci. I've already described Mark as a man who loved women. I might as easily describe him as a man who was loved by women. Both are, were, true.

I continued working through this spring and summer, for as long as I could. The only thing I couldn't do was travel. I had to turn down quite a few invitations and offers of work. The exhibition seems to have generated a lot of interest. I postponed a series of lectures I was to give, although when I had the chance I tried to work on them in the evenings. Instead of travelling, I photographed here. It was good for me. It imposed useful limits of place and time. If he was feeling well enough, Mark would sit in a café or on a bench nearby watching me, apparently content although actually, even towards the end of the summer, preparing to spring surprises by challenging me or being anxious to discuss the intricacies of photography or the meaning of image in his usual unrelenting way. I was glad of it, because it became more important over the months for me to think of all Mark had been, all he still was, not to do what he'd come here to escape, to make of him a man reduced to a collection of cells, defined only by an illness.

For the rest of that winter and spring after I came back from New York, I heard intermittently from Noah and Tamar, once or twice from Lee.

'Can't you speak to him, Dan?'

'About what?'

'His health. His doctors. About getting some further opinions.'

'Lee, why?'

'Because there's just so much more he could be doing.'

I didn't argue. Out of sheer cowardice and the desire not to have an argument, I said I would, but of course I didn't.

In early summer just over a year ago I moved back to London for the opening of the exhibition. I was right in the way I'd thought about it. It was easier to be there than it had been for a long time. Remembering how I'd felt about it before, I think of a tendency to migraine, pain behind the eyes.

When I got back to London, Nira, an organised girl, had arranged for people to come and clean the house and tidy the garden. She and Dalit and their boyfriends and friends of theirs and of mine came to the house and we cooked and sat in the garden with the sounds of the city reaching over the walls, spilling from windows and streets and planes overhead, and there was, if only for brief moments, the illusion that our lives were not fractured by time and change, and that we'd been like this always.

To my relief and delight, the exhibition went well. More than that, it was wonderful. Vitally, we all felt it, every one of the contributors whose disparate work seemed immediately to cohere into one strong voice, one message expressed in different ways. Once it was set up, the experience of being there, being part of it, felt transcendent. The critics and reviewers appear to have agreed, because what they wrote and said made us all, if only for a moment, believe them. Our surprise was because we've come, individually and collectively, to expect less from a set of hard-faced people who, for reasons of their own, can't ever be relied upon to notice quality where it strikes. Their enthusiasm meant that other people, the ones who weren't paid to go, went in large numbers, and better still appeared to like and to appreciate what we'd done.

The thought of it gave me comfort over the next few months. I'd I go back to it in my mind, replay it from beginning to end. I don't always like the exhibitions I contribute to, and I've often left a gallery after a private view wondering why I did, feeling disappointed, or worse, compromised. This one, though, felt special from the first. We're an odd lot, the eight of us: men, women, with a five-decade age-span, no two from the same country, all with a certain reputation, brought together by our work and on that occasion by our shared appreciation of what we'd achieved together. The mood was generous, thrilled, praise passing from hand to hand. We were united, for some time at least; conspirators who have in secret wrought a kind of magic. We congratulated each other and ourselves and kissed and hugged and were for an evening in love with one another and with the potent knowledge of our ability to conjure ideas and beauty and challenge from light and considerable quantities of other-world technology.

My walled cities and their inhabitants, the images I'd photographed in Morocco and Syria, suddenly said more than I thought they could ever say about the nature of closed societies – in this case about fear and history, the lives of men and women, how days are divided between them. They said that presence may be loss, a story told by the figure disappearing veiled behind a doorway, a face looking with clear terror towards the camera, wondering if this is the opening chapter of their own dark, imagined tale. They seemed a metaphor for all our lives, what we never know of other people, how we imagine things to be other than how they are, that the muted voices rising from hidden courtyards in quiet streets may be speaking quotidian words or passionate ones, but passing in a moment, we'll never know.

The evening of the private view, the gallery was crowded. I

wandered round to listen to what people were saying, to look at the work, now open to the scrutiny and attention we all crave but fear. My friend Anne from Belgium, who travels the world photographing bats, was there smiling and serene, her head swathed in an astonishing turban of acid-green silk, explaining the death-defying, terrifying ways she'd photographed vertiginous roosts in flooded caves or above trees in night-time forests to produce the infinitely strange and marvellous images she had of night skies clouded by bats: bats black against canopies of pale, silvered leaves, individual portraits of the maligned little beasts, their squashed faces quizzical and intelligent through her lens.

'This is a ghost bat… This one a serotine… They are, I always think, like dark angels…'

Dorcas from Canada had taken portraits of jail visitors. Luc, who by then had recovered from his anxiety and nit-picking and was again loud and enthusiastic and delightful, had taken interiors and workers at a car factory. Mart, a large, gentle man from New York, had created a wonderfully sinister installation, an arachnid-fest, shot in Prague from the slit windows of one of the lit towers on the Charles Bridge, out onto an arachnid universe. It was mesmerising. In the light, looped, netted over stone lintels, webs centuries in the making, their owners and creators, the descendants of their creators, stout, muscular spiders prowling among the sparkling, dry remains of victims, wings and body-cases dark in the floodlights' sodium glare, in human terms, an ossuary, a history in parallel, and over it the sounds of the voices of tourists, German, Polish, French, English, chatting, twittering, exchanging banalities, exclaiming, arguing, moving off into silence against a background of eerie, atonal music. I watched and listened for a long time, picking up a single voice from the track, a woman's voice, Israeli, calling, '*Aryeh! tistakel, Aryeh! Aryeh!*' her voice urging appreciation of the view, '*Aryeh* – look!', on a loop, repeating and repeating.

I'd asked Mark once more if he'd come over but again, he'd said he was too busy. Instead, I sent him the catalogue and some small prints I prepared specially for him. He was generous, even effusive in his praise. His suggestion that he was too busy to come over stopped me from thinking, as I had done, about going to see him while I was still in London. I decided that I'd wait a few weeks and then discuss going for Christmas or New Year or some time in January.

I did think about staying longer in London, but after a couple of weeks felt anxious that I might fall back into the routines of single life which had so depressed and lowered me after Tal left. I was pleased to come back here, to look from a distance onto the experience of the exhibition in its entirety, as if I was looking from a mountain towards a landscape of infinite charm and beauty. I was soon occupied again with preparing plates for a book and making plans to visit Luc and his wife in the south of France, as I'd promised when I'd seen them in London.

When Mark phoned in November, I experienced one of those moments one feels momentarily to be prescient, almost mystical but isn't. I knew that I'd been waiting for it, even as he had.

'Dan, I saw Jaegerson again today. It's come back.'

It was easier to know what to say the second time. I knew what to ask. I'd learned, as he had, the language of his particular disease.

'What does Dr Jaegerson suggest, Mark? More surgery?'

'What Jaegerson suggests and what's going to happen aren't one and the same, believe me. He's offered me chemotherapy, which I'll consider, but I've refused more surgery. There's no point. I'd rather be wrecked by time than by bloody Jaegerson.'

'Have you spoken to Noah and Tam yet?'

'No. There are things I want to think out before I do.'

'I won't mention it if they phone.'

That was only a few months ago, although it seems lifetimes, time zones, worlds away now. It was a few weeks later, just before Christmas, when he said that he'd been thinking about home more recently. When I asked him where he meant, he said, 'Glasgow,' as if it was obvious. I was surprised that he still thought of it that way and told him so. He seemed surprised too, in a way, and said that he hadn't really realised he did until he'd used the word. I thought about it a great deal after he phoned and so it was no surprise when, a few nights later, he phoned again. Half-telling and half-asking, he told me that he'd made a decision, that he wanted to come back, to come here, home.

Chapter 24

London, late autumn, 2001

The night has been a child's night, one prised apart by giants, watched by witches hiding in the dark. All night, Anci has dreamt or floated towards consciousness with black trees and gaseous marshlands of mossy sage, wide, pale landscapes of ice and infinite skies flowing through her almost-sleeping brain. All night, the Aurora Borealis has shimmered pink and green canopies across her sleep, lighting with sparks of colour the shaggy white feathers of kingly storks, gilding the blue-black wings of the ravens who call warning from the night. Rivers, tumbling glaciers of ice have skimmed cobalt and turquoise in her dreams, pale mountains made of marble, rose and cream and primrose. Vesper bells have rung dolorously over the cries of wild geese. Swan feathers have drifted their down over her, making her turn her head in irritation. Each time she wakens, or thinks she does, she instructs herself to remember in the morning so that she can draw the images she's dreamt, the colours, cinnabar, jade, aquamarine, terre verte. She'll make quick notes, record the words which best capture the thought. Just before six, she's in her study, scribbling, checking her colours, her paints, inks, brushes.

In the daylight, on her walk to the pond, the streets and the trees have already been changed by what she has to do, the textures of lichens and of roots, the twist of ivy leaves around a trunk presenting themselves, reminding her. Ripples created by the movement of a body in water move, turn smoothly from light into darkness, overwhelming, distorting the long reflections of watermint and iris leaves.

This stage is the most exciting, although she knows that she thinks that about every stage, about beginning, about working, completing drawings one by one, making a whole out of them, each her favourite as it occurs. It's only finishing a piece of work that she dislikes, the desolating moment when she has to relinquish the closeness she's had with what she's created. She believes every time that it's a pleasure she'll never experience again, or worse, that no-one will offer her the opportunity again. She's certain of it every time, although up till now, she's always been wrong. All the way back from the pond, she's organising the stories in her mind: which she'll begin with, which is the easiest, which the most difficult. *The Marsh King's Daughter* is the one she looks forward to most. Will it be first or last? She'll go to the V & A one afternoon and browse among the collections of illustrations and drawings.

As she returns home, the phone is ringing inside the house. She hears it from the gate, quickly dropping her swimming things, beginning to unlock the door, which always takes ridiculously longer in haste or panic. Fortunately, the phone rings on. It's Michael.

'Ma!'

'Darling! Is everything all right?'

'Yes, why?'

'It's early, that's all.'

'I get up early. Why are you so surprised?'

'I'm not surprised at all, sweetheart.'

'Yes, you are. I've already been running in Holyrood Park, I'll have you know.'

'You are so good! Was it nice?'

'It was okay. Have you been swimming?'

'I'm just this second back. Anyway, how are you?'

'Fine. Listen, you didn't chuck away my roller boots, did you?'

'I don't think so. I didn't throw anything of yours away.'

'You didn't let Joe nick them?'

'No. He certainly didn't say anything to me about taking them.'

'I'll kill him if he did. Can you have a look?'

'What, now?'

'Yes.'

Still talking, she walks upstairs to his room.

'Where are they exactly? Hang on, I'll look. Yes, here they are. Shall I send them?'

'Would you?'

'Of course. Is there anything else while I'm here?'

'Actually yes, a few things. Can you send my Philip K. Dick books, and my Gap top, the one with the hood? I forgot it and it's getting cold. And my video of *Pi*.'

'Darling, do you need some sweaters? Can I get you some?'

'No, honestly Ma, I'm fine. I'll buy them here if I need any.'

'Are you okay for money?'

'Yes, fine. Have you found everything?'

'Yes, let's see, I think that's it all. I'll shove them in a box.'

'Thanks, Ma. I was just scared Joe had carried out a raid.'

'Oh honestly, why would he?'

'Well, you know him. How is he, anyway?'

'He's fine. He and Florence were here a couple of nights ago for dinner.'

'What's she like? Another Lizzie Siddall?'

'No, in fact not at all. She's a doctor, or almost. She's delightful. Very sensible.'

'Ain't possible, Ma. The two things don't go together. Not in my experience.'

She gathers his things into her arms, holding the phone between her ear and shoulder. Now, she'll have to find a box and pack it and add a few treats and wrap it and tie it and carry it to the post office where she'll wait for a long time in a queue. She wonders if he appreciates that she has work to do too, but as always her pleasure in having him to send parcels to overrides any anger or impatience she feels. It's the least she can do.

'How's the work? Have you begun the new stuff yet?'

'I only got it yesterday. I'm just about to start.'

'What is it?'

'Fairy tales this time.'

'Which?'

'Grim ones.'

'Oh, very amusing.'

'No, really. Hans Christian rather than Grimm. Very disturbing, some of them.'

'*The bitter waves of Acheron, natural haunt of the northern soul*?'

Her sons' memories astound her. They remember odd snippets from years before with amazing accuracy. Their ear for absurdity, their mockery and casual irreverence amuse her.

'Exactly that. Darling, how do you remember these things? Tell me, what've you got to do today?'

'Oh, don't. Renaissance history.'

'You're so lucky!'

'You really think so?'

She knows he's dissembling. He's thrilled by what he's doing. As they say goodbye, she heaps his boots and books onto the chair in the hall. She'll send them later today, after work. It's wonderful to think of him engaged, absorbed in studying. He's remarkably like István in some respects but like Józsi too, the same concentration, the same certainties of purpose. Józsi wanted to be an engineer, nothing else, ever. She goes into her study and sits down at her drawing board. Today, she'll make preliminary sketches. She won't plan too much, she'll just draw, fill pages with the images, snippets, pin down the ideas, large and small, which are crowding into her mind.

For Józsi at least, the years after the war were a wonderful time to be growing up, surrounded by construction sites and machinery, by buildings, railways, bridges being re-built as everything had to be re-built, repaired, made whole again. Few buildings in Budapest had been left undamaged, the whole country desolated, the economy ruined, even agriculture in that most fruitful, fertile country, almost destroyed by years of war. A tenth of Hungary's people had died. The country was poor, its currency worthless, flaring hyperinflation, reparations to be paid to Russia as part of the claims against Germany. The currency lost its value. People had to trade what they had or what they produced, coal, potatoes, meat. There were food shortages in the first years, 1945, 1946, the winters terrible. People froze and starved and still the Russians were there, hundreds of thousands of them, still eating, still looting. It was the strangest liberation, one which wasn't truly a liberation, one which didn't end.

After the end of the fighting, justice, or vengeance, began. Public executions were carried out after trials, some fair, some not in that atmosphere of fury and hatred. Bárdossy, Szótjay, Szálasi and Father Kun were hanged. There's a photo she's seen of Szálasi's face staring from the small window of a prison cell in his former headquarters in Andrássy ut, another of him kissing the crucifix which is being held up to him by a priest in the moments before his hanging.

First, even before the building could begin, the city had to be cleared of tumbled masonry, of refuse, destroyed tanks, flattened armoured cars, the hideous detritus of war. The dead had to be picked from the ruins. Remnants of human beings were scraped from the burned cellars under the Castle which in time, would rise again on its hill above the city. During the first spring and summer, 1945, the new, fresh warmth raised the smell of death from the interstices of fallen buildings. It stirred into mass graves too shallowly dug and when you walked, you smelt the smell which hung in the heat, livid and sickening. Everywhere, flies swarming in a black, pointillist haze. The river water, even after months, still dragged the dead through its fast, grey undertow.

But then, after months, it was done, cleared, cleaned. The building began with a feeling of renewal, images and odours of construction, dust carried on the wind, the inimitable whine of stone cutters, the sounds of drilling and hammers filling the ears and nose and eyes. The bridges across the river were repaired, the railways bridges, the dome of Parliament.

Other things were happening in the country too, ones unseen, more momentous even than the raising of walls. With liberation, Hungarian communists who had been learning their trade in Moscow, returned to the land of their birth. They were ready to do what was necessary in order to hand Hungary to Stalin, step by step. They were stealthy as the Russians had been stealthy. Even in setting up the government in exile in Debrecen in 1944, the Russians were careful, appointing Béla Miklós, who had been a general with Horthy and so clearly, not a communist, as Prime Minister. They didn't want it to appear as if they were appointing place-men, as if they were anything other than a liberation force. The 'time of liberation' which they talked about later wasn't a time of liberation. It was a time of preparation, of planning and the steady creep towards taking power, of planning how to collectivise and control, how to keep Hungary in Russia's grip. Russia had given its blood for Hungary and wasn't going to let go now.

She and Józsi and all the other children began school again. They'd had to try to remember all they'd forgotten. Some of it was still there, stored away, waiting. Mostly, they were glad to be back, although she was bewildered on the first days at their new school, sitting at a little desk again, reading letters and numbers, all of them unexpectedly, exactly as they had been before, their sequences, shapes, forms, all the same. The streets too were the same, the apartment building where they'd lived, the one from which Ilka Neni had rushed them with such anxiety and haste, but at least on the way to and from school, on every corner, there was something for Józsi to watch and linger over, to indulge his fascination with girders and structures and the huge steam locomotives borrowed from America, the ones they called 'Truman engines'. She'd stand and wait for him until they both had to run to catch up with the others. At first, she and Jószi refused to be separated. Even later, when they were older, they'd had to know where the other was, taking their bearings from that point only, where in the house, the school, the street. She tries to think of the details of their lives, what they ate, what they did after school, evenings, Saturdays. She remembers eating bread, but can't remember much else. She remembers them all sitting at the big tables where they had their meals, to do their homework. She remembers sewing lessons, mending, taking turns to help with household chores. She remembers the bookshelves in the big hallway, the books she read and re-read, the box of toys the girls played with, a heap of old dolls in tatty clothes.

As she draws, she hears the sound of a key in the front door.
    'Hi, Isabella!'
    'Oh, hi, Anci. How are you today?'
    'I'm fine. Having coffee before you begin?'
    'No, I think I'll just make a start.'
    'See you at eleven, then?'
    'Lovely!'
    She hears Isabella's tread on the stairs, the sound of the door of István's study closing.

Hungary had lost the war. The Allied Control Commission which administered the country was dominated by Soviet generals. What else were they going to do but further Stalin's aims? They moved slowly. It took four years for Hungary's democratic hopes to be destroyed, four years of manoeuvring, from the free elections of 1945 until 1949, when it was over. Four years of political intrigue, plots, threats, rigged elections, the destruction of parties and of people. The Smallholders Party, the Social Democrats, the National Peasant Party, all of them destroyed, their leaders fled, or imprisoned, exiled, sent to the gulags in Siberia.

    By the election of 1949, there were no choices, no other parties, only the Hungarian Worker's Party. In the previous free elections, they'd won 17% of the vote. This time, they received 96%. Hungary was a one-party state. It would be forty years before there would be free elections again.

Gábor Péter, Mátyás Rákosi, Ernö Gerö, József Révai, Mihály Farkas,

László Rajk, the men who did this, the men who ran Hungary, who ran the organisations of terror, the government, the men who made Hungary a place where people lived in fear.

The Arrow Cross hadn't gone away, either. Szálasi was dead but his followers and sympathisers were still there. All they'd had to do was to admit to their membership of the Arrow Cross, agree that it had been a regrettable error, and then they simply changed their uniforms and became members of the Political Security Department, which was set up in 1945 to search out war-criminals. In 1946 it became the State Security Department, the AVO. The previous members of the Arrow Cross didn't even need to change headquarters. 60, Andrássy Ut., Szálasi's headquarters, *The House of Loyalty, Hüség Háza*, became the headquarters of the AVO. Everything that was needed was already there waiting: the cells, the torture chambers, everything. The records of Arrow Cross membership too, useful for blackmailers, for reminding those who might, peradventure, have been reluctant to do some of the more shocking deeds required of them. In 1948, the State Security Authority was set up, the ÁVH, answering directly to the party leadership, ready to instigate every form of brutality and murder, every method of spying, listening, watching, reporting on and torturing the populace.

By 1949, Hungary was a People's Democracy, a Stalinist state. Mátyás Rákosi was in power. Mátyás Rákosi.The name still holds the memory of fear; after decades, she still feels the chill the two words bring. Secretly, in trusted company, people called him 'Arsehead' or 'Old Baldie,' but they feared him terribly. Looking at his picture now, it's still impossible to imagine that this small, fat, bald man with the almost comic face, almost sweet and cheerful face could do what he did. The stories whispered, passed from one to the other, were unbelievable although you knew them to be true. He had all the qualities required, the usual ones – ruthlessness and charm and brilliance – but more, too: a relentless ability to adhere to doctrine, imagination unfortunately coupled with unstoppable sadistic fervour. More important than any of them, he was close to Stalin, the ultimate weapon and shield, the power of the Soviet army at his back. For years, as children, they were obliged to shout, 'Long live Comrade Mátyás Rákosi!' while in the cellars under 60, Andrássy ut, those chosen by him arbitrarily for punishment languished, freezing, naked, wet, in filth and misery, facing interminable pain and death.

The judicial system was destroyed. Judges who might possibly have been impartial were removed, party men put in their place to carry out trials, show trials, summary justice. Before any political trial, Rákosi would send a note to the judge to instruct him what the sentence was to be. Nobody was safe, not even the party's most faithful adherents, the men who themselves had helped design and bring about this infamous system. László Rajk himself, once the hated, feared Minister of the Interior, Rajk, responsible for murders and torture in his destruction of democratically-inclined political parties, was put on trial in 1949, on the charge of being a 'Tito-ist', the *crime-du-jour*. Tito wasn't sufficiently subservient to the Soviet Union, not respectful enough to the odious Stalin, prepared to take Yugoslavia on an independent road. Rajk believed his trial and sentence were another absurd formality, as was his ludicrous confession, but they weren't. He was executed. The cruelty of it was horrible. Rajk's wife was arrested at the same time, their still-nursing baby snatched from her. In the same prison, she was put into a cell with a high window from which she couldn't look out. Without being able to see, she had to listen to her husband's execution. No-one had any doubt that Rákosi had arranged it. Rajk may well have deserved his fate, but not in those circumstances, not under the cloak of posturing and lies.

1951 and 1952 were the worst: years of deportations, AVO vans cruising their black and ominous way through the streets, every Monday, Wednesday, Friday night, seeking people out, arriving at their doors to take them away. Why? For what reasons? False ones, trumped-up, nonsense reasons, because they were 'class enemies' or 'collaborators'; or real reasons which were almost more dreadful, because someone in a high place wanted their apartment or because of a minor grievance, a personal quarrel. Everyone was terrified, watching from behind curtains, lying silent in the dark. She'll never understand why it should have happened, thousands, tens of thousands, taken to the copper mines of Recks, the camps in Kistarcsa, Tiszalok, Kazincbarcika, moved to Alföld to work as agricultural labourers.

This was the way they grew up, in falsity and fear. At school, they had lessons in Marxist-Leninist theory, on being good citizens of the People's Republic, builders of socialism. Teachers taught this, while in the streets black vans patrolled, and in a beautiful house in one of Budapest's most elegant streets prisoners were being interrogated, being led blindfold from torture chamber to cell. All this under the aegis of 'Our father and great master, Stalin's greatest Hungarian pupil,' Rákosi. His friends were no better: Gábor Péter, head of political police; Mihály Farkas, Minister for Defence. The stories still resonate in her mind, what was done to people, the beatings and hangings, Rákosi's entertaining of guests to dinner when he'd already arranged for them to be taken away the following day, of people being thrown alive into acid baths.

The church too was ground down, persecuted, its powers, its influence stripped away. The head of the Catholic Church, József Mindszenty, Archbishop of Esztergom was arrested in 1948, as he had been 1944 for demanding that Szálasi should desist from his activities. He was tortured, later tried and sentenced to life imprisonment. There were rumours that he'd been drugged to make a startling confession at his entirely spurious trial. Old religion was stamped out of schools to make way for the new religion, the religion of Stalin, of Rákosi.

No-one was safe. Not the peasants who were forced to produce in order to feed both the country and the Soviet troops, forced to pay overwhelming taxes while their land, newly gained after the reforms of 1945, was taken from them and collectivised. Always a target of communist hatred, the peasants' traditional ways of life and production had to be destroyed, changed, new methods of agriculture imposed, ones which, inevitably, failed. Workers in industry too, subject to every ridiculous, impractical, implausible doctrine of Stalin's mad vision of ever-increasing productivity, forced to work as no human being could work, to increase targets, to turn Hungary to 'a country of iron and steel', to fulfil the Five Year Plan, to 'promote Stakhanovism', to carry out the instructions of people who were party functionaries, not experts in engineering or mining or industrial production which led, naturally, to disastrous losses, stupifyingly foolish mistakes, reversing all the economic gains of the post-war years.

Nothing was untouched, the universities, schools, libraries, books. Any work considered inimical to ideas of the state were removed, destroyed, passages blacked out, history revised. Unable to express themselves freely, writers, artists, musicians, film directors left the country. Sándor Márai, grieving, knowing he'd be allowed neither to write what he chose nor to remain silent, left to live in America. He never came back.

They lived, the entire leadership, these maniacs, these torturers, as no-one else in the country lived, in beautiful villas in Rózsadomb, the suburb in the hills above the city where Eichmann, not so long before, had lived in his stolen house. Surrounded by barbed wire, protected by armed guards and dogs, they lived their protected lives, swimming in their private swimming pools, buying in their special shops, being driven in their Zil limousines swiftly through the streets where people lived in trembling fear of every day.

Rákosi, Gerö, Gábor Péter, Mihály Farkas, József Révai. Jews, all of them but so what? What if they'd all been Lutherans, or Catholics, what would anyone have made of that? She understands why Jews became communists: because of centuries of mistreatment, because of centuries of hate and prejudice, because of the Nazis, the fate of their families, a hundred reasons, because clearly they were the only people who identifiably had not collaborated with the Nazis. All this, she understands. The question of why they stayed loyal to Stalin when it became clear what Stalin was, is the same question you'd ask of anyone, with the same answers: because people do unaccountable things, Jews or not, because they're cruel or sadistic or blind or self-interested, or all of them together. She wishes that they hadn't but they were seduced by the same single ideology as people who undermined them with ambition and greed and anti-Semitism. Not that it did them or anyone else any good. They were, after all, the dupes of Stalin, a collection of puppets, used as cynically, as ruthlessly as they were prepared to use others. How could they have allowed themselves to do it? Didn't they ever think of what kind of society they had created?

She thinks of Stalin's terms, the language which talked of the behaviour of the Red Army as 'regrettable excesses,' the same denigrations, lies, loaded words, 'provocation', 'confession', 'mistake', 'personality cult', the tedious slogans, 'Long live Mátyás Rákosi, Wise Leader of the Working People', 'For Better Work to Fulfil the Five Year Plan and Ensure the Happy Future of Our Country!'

In school they were obliged to listen and repeat what they were meant to say, praising Rákosi out loud, but even as they did, they remembered. It wasn't long enough ago for anyone to have forgotten the winter and spring of 1945. Nothing could erase from the memory the way the Red Army had behaved, that soldiers who had for thirty years been raised and nurtured by Stalin's perfect society were the same people who raped twelve-year-old girls and stole from the dying. Throughout the country, schoolchildren sat and listened and repeated what was taught. She did as they all did, waved flags and called slogans, but she remembered, and in 1956 it became clear that everyone else did too.

The children in her school all joined the Hungarian Pioneers' Association, herself included, although she has no recollection of being asked or consulted. In fact, she'd loved the things they did, hiking and swimming and going to the Great Pioneer camp at Csillebérc, which, to Joszi's delight, had a narrow gauge railway. '*Elöre!*' was the movement's motto, 'Forward!' and she'd even been proud of the little red scarves they all had to wear round their necks. You can look back on uncritical times uncritically. She still thinks of these things with pleasure, almost nostalgia. She was happy, sometimes, in that space in her memory where the wider life of politics, the country, the atmosphere of threat becomes eclipsed by the small life of a child. She and József together, for years, grew beyond childhood with the realisation that their lives would always be tilted in the moment of happiness towards memory and sorrow, only as others' lives are, she knows now, creatures of the shaded territory in which we exist, longing for the quick moments of sunlight.

They'd had to learn Russian, but she learned some English too from a girl called Krisztina who worked in the orphanage and spoke it well. A few of them learned until they all became afraid and stopped. It was Krisztina who used to bring in copies of a magazine called *Nök Lapja*, and after supper all the girls would crowd round to admire the dim, fuzzy-edged pictures of women wearing fashionable clothes.

When she arrived in Glasgow, things forgotten crept from her memory to live again. She hadn't imagined what she'd find there; how could she, she barely knew where it was, only as soon as she went with the Blums to their shul on the first Shabbas she was there, the moment of recognition, of being in the midst of the utterly known, looking from the gallery over the *ner tamid, bimah, Aaron Kodesh*, above, the women's gallery, below, the turning, rustling, pale and upward-looking faces of the men of the congregation in that moment, that day, when, in the universal space of the shul, her involuntary wail had opened out to cartwheel over the edge of the balcony in horrifying, unstoppable lament for a realm of ghosts.

Almost forgotten, even living in a house with a family, even that had felt alien, the memory of the experience distant, the reality one in which she couldn't find her way, a maze of mysteries, her institutional questions about bath-days and what days there was hot water and when was the outer door locked, what time she had to get up, which times were mealtimes. The Blums were startled but kind. They didn't let her know how odd they must have found it. It was years before she realised quite how strange or funny they must have thought her. Even handing over her clothes for washing was awkward. She hadn't wanted to give her clothes to Eve, to reveal the poverty of everything she wore, the faded, fraying revelation of hardship and scarcity, even then, when no-one, even here, had very much that was nice. At first, she didn't know that Eve had a machine for doing it and when Eve asked, she refused, saying, 'I've always done my own,' persuaded only by the presence of the machine, a steaming, rocking, shaking miracle, sturdy cream casing and little window which she liked to watch in its busy, foaming revolutions, like a child of two. There was a glass washboard in the room Eve called the scullery, a device for wringing water from clothes called a mangle. Always done her own. Was that true? It's among details lost. All the children had two of each garment, one for weekdays, one for good. During the siege, they'd worn the same clothes for weeks, more like months, nothing to change into, nobody to change them. No water, no fuel. She remembers being conscious of the smell of herself, a child's horrible humiliation.

Eve helped her with English, sitting at the dining-room table with jotters and pencils. She talked about the war in Britain, about air raids and rationing,

'It was very difficult. Everything was scarce. We had rationing here until a couple of years ago,' Eve said and Anci looked at her, wondering if it was explanation or excuse. Of course, there were reminders all around that they'd fought a war, bomb sites, words, songs, memories, most of which revealed themselves to her only with the years when, at last, she understood subtlety of reference and language, the magnitude of this country's war. She thinks now of her disregard, how, secretly and not so secretly, she'd thought it a lesser hardship to do without butter and sugar and eggs for a few years. Deaths, bombing, the consequences of possible failure with which everyone lived, she'd thought lesser too, on a scale unworthy of her consideration. She has thought about it since then, her ignorance and her arrogance. The sufferings of war are only one individual suffering written again and again, a million times, ten million times, multiplied to the infinity of madness. There was bombing here, a lot. Conscription, deaths. The boys told her about the bombing on the Clyde, the destruction of Clydebank, described waiting for the bombers, seeing the glow across the sky.

Glasgow. A funny place to find herself. She'd never thought much about other places, particularly when, after the war, the walls closed in. She knew about the Soviet Union, Poland, Yugoslavia, the DDR. Any world she'd been aware of before melted into nothing, fused into enemy or threat.

After her first days in Glasgow she began to notice an ease in the place. She asked naive questions about the government, the police, who ran the radio stations. It took her years not to be suspicious, always wondering who knew what, who would tell what to whom, what the consequences might be, the pang of self-reproach and fear after you'd spoken, wondering if you'd said too much. She's never been able to defeat the inner belief that when you tell people things, you may be lending them your soul.

When she first came to this country, she heard the voice of Radio Free Budapest still calling its plaintive, ignored plea in her ears, 'For the sake of God and freedom, help Hungary!'

She thinks of Joe's words, 'something to do with Russia.' Under her pen icebergs form, droplets cascading frozen from a waterfall of ice, a bone-littered nest, the spiky yellow feathers on the head of a fledgling eagle.

On the fifth of March 1953 Stalin died. Rákosi's protector and mentor was gone. It was one of those days you'll always remember, the delight behind closed doors, an explosion of rejoicing. As early as June, East Germany rose against its regime and Soviet occupation. The rising was put down in a couple of days, but clearly it worried Moscow, who knew that next it would be Poland, or Hungary. Rákosi had to be replaced. When someone brave, and probably foolhardy, appeared to be prepared to challenge Rakosi, Moscow encouraged him. The brave man was Imre Nagy. The only reason Rákosi didn't have him arrested for daring to criticise was because Russia's new Prime Minister, Georgi Malenkov, supported him.

Rákosi stayed Party head when in 1953, Imre Nagy became Premier. Nagy was an unlikely figure to find among the grim-faced, humourless functionaries of Rákosi's regime, a professor of agriculture, a big man with a walrus moustache and round spectacles, a long-standing communist but a reformist too. Far from being remote and terrifying, Nagy could be seen strolling around the streets of Budapest, drinking coffee in Gerbeaud's with his grandchildren, or gossiping about sport and politics with his friends, following the progress of Hungary's football team. She can only feel sad thinking about Nagy, a man of honourable intention.

The years of Nagy's government were so different. His first speech told it all, his condemnation of what had gone before, his intention to make things better. He spoke out against the cruelties, the arbitrary arrests, deportations. He gave people the right to live where they chose and to return from exile. Nagy did as he said he would. He made life better, easier, but his most profound mistake was one Rákosi wouldn't have made. He didn't destroy the enemies who were still there, waiting for the inevitable moment when Malenkov fell and was replaced by Khrushchev who wanted Rákosi back. People tried to persuade Khrushchev against it, in particular Tito, who loathed Rákosi, but Khrushchev refused to listen, believing that without Rákosi Hungary would collapse. 1955 and back he came as premier, to replace Nagy: Rákosi, the murderer. Khrushchev hadn't understood.

Józsi had been a student for two years by then. In 1953, when he was eighteen, he began studying at the Technical University, moved his few things into a student dormitory, the first time they'd been apart. He'd grown by then to a kind of sturdy confidence, extended beyond his single childhood fascination, become a runner, a swimmer. He'd even had a few articles on sport published in the newspapers.

It was dislocating at first to be without him, knowing when she went to sleep that he was nowhere in the house, but she grew used to it, aware that she herself wouldn't be there much longer. She was excited for him as well as for herself. They stood at the beginning of a new life. Everything was changing.

The year after Józsi, in 1954, she moved too, to another university dormitory, and began to study philosophy. An extraordinary time. Menace and promise both hovering at the edge of thought, private and public mood swaying between anticipation and the anxiety of knowing nothing could continue as it was, that something must happen, though neither she nor anyone else, knew what. It was extraordinary for her too, studying, beginning her independent life. She'd known István for a few months by then.

Why did she choose philosophy? Even now, she doesn't know. It may have been the word itself drawing her towards its gravitas, what she thought were its secret messages of seeking and finding. She had no real idea of what philosophy was and it was probably misguided to study it at a time when there was no freedom of the ideas. It's how she met István. He was one of the teachers in the philosophy department, the same department where the great philosopher György Lukács taught. István was twenty years older than she was and showed an interest in her from the first day. The other girls in her class envied her, one of the less worthy reasons why she allowed herself to be invited for coffee after lectures. It felt exciting to inspire envy. When she thinks of it now, she knows that there was pleasure in having the attention of someone confident and worldly. She'd listen to him raptly, feeling young and ignorant but indubitably chosen. István had a tiny apartment at the top of one of the steep streets in Buda, where he seduced her slowly and with elegance. The circumstances enchanted her, his apartment, the feeling of secrecy, running up the steps at the Fisherman's Bastion, the lights of the city behind her. She didn't know what she felt because she was unused to feeling. It seemed an exciting way to begin her life as an adult, the wild disregard inside her impelling her do everything because life was unpredictable, and brief. She wasn't in love with István. She was in love with feeling and with possibility.

From the first, Józsi was wary of István. She'd been forced to introduce them after they met one day in the street. He'd spoken to her afterwards.

'What is there between you two?'

'Nothing. I don't know.'

'For God's sake, Anc, he's too old. You don't know anything about him.'

'I do.'

'You don't. You haven't been able to tell me one coherent fact. Listen, you have your whole life ahead. Just be careful.'

She had her whole life ahead. He was right. She didn't, after all, know much about him, although he talked about himself a great deal. He was Jewish. His family were, she thought, from the Carpathians, some from Bukovina. He'd been at university in Budapest and then had gone to Vienna, but when Józsi questioned her she realised she wasn't sure about any of it; there were many stories, many layers to each. He'd spent the war in Moscow, she thought, but there were other accounts too, of his fighting with Jewish partisans in Ruthenia, of captures and escapes. She didn't question him, not knowing how to. There were discrepancies, she knew. His first words to her had been, 'We have the same name …' although her name wasn't the one he used. She knew that people changed their names, used other ones. She didn't think it would be important.

Above her, she hears the sound of Isabella's phone ring. The warty toad on her page doesn't look sympathetic enough to be the other, the kindly face of the angry daughter of the marsh king. Next to him, she draws another. This time he's looking upwards, with a face of supplication.

1956. Rákosi was back as premier but now, he seemed almost irrelevant, to be endured rather than obeyed. Writers who'd written as they chose under Nagy's rule, refused to curb themselves again. Articles bitterly critical of Rákosi and his government began to appear and though the brave editors who published them were censored or sacked, it was too late. Nothing could stop what was happening. The journal *Literary Gazette, Irodalmi Újság,* began to publish articles which astonished everyone with the frankness of their criticisms of the regime. In spite of its price soaring people rushed to buy it, thrilled, amazed by what was being written. They were amazed too by what was being said freely at the Petöfi circle, a discussion club named after the poet Sándor Petöfi who died in the anti-Austrian revolution of 1884. It was at one of their meetings that László Rajk's widow, Julia, stood to condemn the regime which had killed her husband and imprisoned her.

'Murderers should not be criticised. They should be punished. I shall never rest until those who have ruined the country, corrupted the Party, destroyed tens of thousands and driven millions to despair, receive their just punishment.'

She'll never forget those words, carried in her head through the heat of that summer, carried with the news of the workers' uprising in Poznan in Poland, swiftly dealt with by Russian tanks which surrounded the city, never forget what Gyula Háy wrote in *Irodalmi Újság:*

'*It should be the writer's prerogative to tell the truth. To criticise anybody and anything. To be sad. To be in love. To think of death. Not to ponder whether light or shadow are in balance in his work. To believe in the omnipotence of God. To deny the existence of God. To doubt certain figures in the Five Year Plan...*'

August. The Writer's Congress swept party candidates from their posts on the executive, voted in new people, independent voices. A revolution begun by writers, a very Hungarian revolution.

Rákosi was in Moscow at the time and rushed home, a trail of fretting Soviet officials at his back. His reaction was the one you'd expect of him, arrest, punish, crush; anything to suppress the possible outbreak of freedom. By now, even Khrushchev had to accept that Rákosi must go and in July he did, as both prime minister and member of the Politburo. One splendid day shortly after that, he was whisked off in a private plane to Russia, never to return. Old Baldie, Arsehead, had gone. The only element to dispel the joy, was that he was replaced by Ernö Gerö. Why didn't they replace him with Nagy? She has no idea, but instead of the one man everyone would have chosen, they got the miserable Gerö, Rákosi's Stalinist henchman.

As his wife wanted, László Rajk was re-buried on October 6th in Kerepesi cemetery, the burial place of notable Hungarians. Thousands were there for the ceremony. The speeches which condemned his killers felt like a rallying call.

On October 19th, Khrushchev flew to Warsaw to try to prevent Gomulka, a reformist like Nagy, from being appointed to power. The Poznan riots had given the Polish reformists heart. When the old guard asked for Russian help, Soviet tanks moved into Warsaw. Students and workers mobilised, the air was sparking, ready to ignite. Gomulka became first secretary, in spite of the Soviet presence, and he announced that Poland would pursue its own way to socialism. When Khrushchev agreed reluctantly to the changes the Polish government wanted to make, withdrawing as graciously as he could from Warsaw, the acquiescence seemed to Hungary like a message of encouragement.

October, 1956: a moment of fusion, when all blended, eased into the certainty of itself, flashed its hot desire for liberty into the waiting sky. The days of revolution are before her, days of revolution, begun in hope. At the Technical University, Józsi's university, on that Monday, October 22nd, the students held a meeting, tempestuous, loud, threatened by communist officials trying to silence them, but nonetheless they were bold and they spoke, called for change. It was happening everywhere, in colleges, universities, students, lecturers, professors were drawing up lists of demands. Now, when she thinks of what it was they were demanding, it breaks her heart. It was only what was their right, the withdrawal of Soviet troops, elections, secret ballots, a multi-party system, freedom of speech. Józsi showed her the statement from the Technical University:

'Students of Budapest! The following resolution was born on 22nd October, 1956, at the dawn of a new period in Hungarian history...'

At her own university, too, Eötvös Lóránd, there were meetings, demands for students to march with peasants, for factories to be visited, workers included in this new and astonishing call for freedom.

A Monday evening. They were to march the next day to the statue of General Bem on the banks of the river. She spoke to Józsi that evening, as she always did on a Monday evening when she'd phone him at his friend Péter's house where they went for dinner after a late lecture. As always, she had a brief chat with Péter's fussy mother.

'...they're just telling me all about it. Really, it's quite worrying. I just hope you're all going to be careful...' Then the breathless voice of Józsi, almost speechless with excitement, 'You wouldn't believe it!' Almost gibbering, his voice too fast to be coherent, recounting what had happened, what had been said, but she doesn't remember telling him to be careful. Who could be careful? They were twenty and about to be free. Also that Monday evening, very late, she phoned István as she'd promised to do, but there was no reply.

October 23rd. Permission for the demonstration was given, then withdrawn. It went ahead anyway. By then nothing could have stopped it, not all the Ernö Gerös in the world, nothing could have stopped the crowds who marched that day, surged through the streets of the city to the statues of Hungary's heroes bearing flags, Polish, Hungarian, the banners of universities, of the Petöfi Military Academy too and the Communist Youth Organisation, students, workers, soldiers in uniform, surrounding Petöfi's statue, the crowd singing, an actor, Imre Sinkovits, reciting Petöfi's poem, 'Arise Hungary!' all of them moving in a flowing sea of people, along the banks of the river, across the bridges, surrounding the Bem statue already garlanded with flowers and laurel wreaths, hundreds of thousands of people singing the

National Anthem, climbing the statue to hoist the Hungarian flag to the wind, dipping into quiet to hear the voice of Péter Veres from the Writer's Union shout;

'We have arrived at a historic turning point...'

She walked behind the banner of the university with her friends, glancing, as everyone was, towards the barracks which overlooked the statue and the soldiers who watched from the windows as the crowd sang and called for change. There was unease. No-one was entirely certain how the army might respond. She remembers hearing the voice which yelled, 'Long Live the Hungarian Army!' the moment before the barracks' windows opened, the shower of red stars which drifted like autumn butterflies as the Soviet emblems torn from soldiers' caps fell, a rain of red stars falling onto the unturned, watching faces. She remembers seeing the first flag with the hammer and sickle torn from its heart waft its message of freedom and defiance. She remembers it, every second, the sense of greatness and grace of this crowd moving through the dusk, across the river bridges, Széchenyi, Erszébet, Margit, a cross-current, moving as one, as starlings move at dusk in a concert of smooth and sky-skimming ease, the press of people, shoulders and arms against hers, the rhythm of their walking as they marched to Parliament Square, the profound stillness as they stood, thousands, tens of thousands, silent as suddenly, the lights went out, as people began setting light to pamphlets and copies of *Szabad Nép*, the official party newspaper, silence and darkness lit by flares of burning, chemical light.

That evening, Tuesday, as they gathered there, Gerö's radio speech was broadcast. Entirely predictably, he insulted them, called them traitors and reactionaries and Fascists, referring to the demonstrators as 'enemies of the people.' As they heard his voice from open windows, groups began to split, moving away from Parliament Square, to Sándor Bródy ut, the headquarters of Radio Kossuth, to insist that the peoples' demands be broadcast, to Heroes Square, to remove the huge statue of Stalin from its plinth. The statue, made from the bronze from melted-down statues of Hungarian heroes, was immovable. Tugging at it with ropes wouldn't overturn it, only oxyacetlylene welders melting Stalin's knees could, only then did he buckle, sway, fall. Roped behind lorries, he was dragged to the centre of town and within hours was gone, smashed, bits of him hammered away to be kept as reminders of oppression and of freedom. His head was abandoned at a road junction. Only his giant feet were left standing on the towering plinth.

The first shots were fired that evening. When people were killed at the radio station, a peaceful revolution became armed uprising. As far as she knows now, an army officer who'd tried to get into the building to find out what had happened to the student delegation who'd been let in earlier, was shot dead at the door and as the crowd pushed towards the building, they were fired at from above by the AVO. AVO reinforcements arrived in ambulances, pretending to be medical staff, rushing out to fire on the crowd. She still doesn't know how many people died there, a hundred, more. That at least, was what was said at the time. The beginning of it all. Workers from an armaments factory in Csepel brought weapons to Sándor Bródy ut to distribute among the people. By that evening, demonstrators had been turned from unarmed protesters into freedom fighters.

No-one knew that night that Gero, in an attempt at concession, had re-appointed Imre Nagy Prime Minister. It wasn't announced. The next day, the radio referred to him as prime minister, that was all. Nor did they know that Gerö had already called for Soviet help. Next morning, when Soviet tanks were in Budapest, no-one knew who had called them in, Gerö or Nagy.

She went home that evening after the crowd began to disperse, still with her group of friends. They ate late, talking, shouting, elated, their hearts staccato with the newness of hope and they went to bed, still dazed, drunk with the day, none of them knowing about the bloodshed which had begun. By morning, there were tanks in the streets.

No-one knew that it wasn't Nagy who had called the Russians in, and moreover, that the Russians were forcibly preventing Nagy from denying it. When he was allowed to broadcast, the nation didn't know that it was with Russian guns at his back. All that people understood from what he said, was that he had failed them. A curfew was announced, martial law imposed. Suslov and Mikoyan, who arrived from Moscow, removed Gerö as Party Secretary and put in his place the lacklustre János Kádár, duplicitous, dull Kádár, once deputy police chief, who, even having been a victim of Rákosi's torture himself, couldn't relinquish his subservience to Moscow, couldn't stop himself from turning on the revolution, Kádár who, in the end, would be rewarded for his disloyalty and treachery with the leadership of

Hungary.

Thursday 25th October was the day when huge numbers of protesters gathered in Parliament Square. Still, no-one knows who opened fire, the Russians from tanks around the square or the AVO, from positions on the roofs above the square. A hundred unarmed protesters were killed, hundreds wounded. Anger surged through the crowds, through the streets.

The Russians brought no infantry, only tanks. Perhaps they thought they'd quell the uprising just by being there, but by then the population was armed, had already formed itself into groups of workers, students, whoever wanted to fight and could get hold of guns and, however inexpertly, use them. Nothing was organised. Fighting was spontaneous, passionate, with impromptu leaders and little strategy. Russian tank crews, on the other hand, were scared, clearly unenthusiastic. They were vulnerable too to a population who'd been forced for years to learn Russian, who could shout in Russian, 'You can't fire on fellow-workers!' Sometimes, they didn't. Often, they did. Fighting seemed to explode all over the city at the same time, in Buda in Széna Square, in the Castle District, everywhere. In Széna Square, the fighting was led throughout the revolution by an old soldier, János Szabó, known as 'Uncle Szabó,' who gathered bands of youths together and led them in attacking and destroying Soviet tanks. Oil was poured onto the cobbled streets, barricades of beer barrels and coaches dragged across the streets as barricades. The building of *Szabad Nép*, the party newspaper, was taken over, part of the building set alight, destroyed. The Szikra publishing house too and the Horizont bookshops, the purveyors of Soviet propaganda.

Because the fighting was with tanks, it was possible to be at one moment in a peaceful street, and in the next dodging into doorways, hiding from fire, returning fire. Again, the bodies of the dead lay in the streets of Budapest.

'I don't feel ready for this,' she remembers Józsi saying to her on the first or second day. 'It doesn't feel long enough since the last time...' She heard a lot of people saying it. It didn't stop them from fighting but it was true. The city was being ruined again. All over, paving was torn up to be used as weapons and barricades, buildings were torn apart by tank shells. The beautiful museum was destroyed, its cupola like black lace over a pale autumn sky.

The murder which had taken place in parliament square, it seemed, was the signal for the AVO to be sought out for vengeance. It was horrible. When AVO men were found they were grabbed, hung upside down from lamposts, beaten to death. She understands now as she did then why it happened, but still hates the thought as she hated the sights, heads smashed in, faces of pulp and blood, unrecognisable, bloody bodies swaying upside down. Because they'd joined the AVO for money, these Arrow Cross remnants, these criminals, because for money, they'd tortured and spied and lied and murdered, when they were caught, their pockets were emptied, 100-forint notes stuffed into their mouths and set alight. Their money was pinned to their clothes as they hung dead and dying, but no-one touched it. No-one would.

During the days of the uprising there was no theft, no looting. Smashed shops were untouched, goods left where they were. It was a matter of utmost pride. In a people's uprising, people didn't steal from themselves. Empty ammunition boxes lay open in the street as collection boxes, money piling into heaps for the families of the dead. Only flowers were taken from smashed flower shop windows to be laid across corpses in the streets. It didn't prevent Radio Kossuth, the state radio station, from broadcasting lies, talking about robbing and plundering, blaming the people who were fighting for their freedom.

There was no anti-semitism either, not in Budapest, anyway. It was odd, notable, considering history. A lot of young Jews took part in the revolution, marched and fought and hoped, as one with everyone else. A different generation perhaps, a different mood. Perhaps, on this one occasion, people had learned from history. Who knows?

Throughout the days of the uprising, Radio Kossuth broadcast lies as it always had done, but this time people could see the falsehoods for themselves. They knew they weren't Fascist insurgents or counter-revolutionaries. They knew they weren't armed hooligans but even when, on Wednesday 25th, the building was attacked and occupied, Radio Kossuth's transmitters moved and carried on pumping out its poisonous, traitorous messages.

The government was unprepared for these dastardly, unprovoked attacks and has applied for help from Soviet formations stationed in Hungary under the terms of the Warsaw Treaty...

Everyone knew it to be nonsense. The Warsaw Treaty would have justified Soviet intervention only if there had been foreign aggression against Hungary. There was, but it was by the Soviet Union.

Nagy, a virtual prisoner of the Russians, called for 'calm and order' while children of twelve, thirteen dropped Molotov cocktails down the petrol caps of Russian tanks. They weren't just children having adventures, unaware of risk, everyone knew that. It was more. They were fighting against the past, parents deported or shamed, against the lies they'd been brought up with, fighting for a future they couldn't even imagine. The indoctrination of the past years, the slogans and obligatory praise for Mátyás Rákosi hadn't worked.

The Hungarian army, almost in its entirety, joined the freedom fighters, tore the red stars from their uniforms. When Pál Maléter, an army colonel, was sent to take back control of the Kilián Barracks, he went over to the side of the revolution, led soldiers and cadets in fighting alongside the revolutionaries where the heaviest fighting was, at the Kilián Barracks on Ülloi ut, one of the main roads into Budapest, and outside the barracks at Corvin Alley and the Corvin Cinema. The fighters there became legends, heroes of the revolution for the ferocity with which they beat the Russians back, destroying seven Russians tanks on the first day of fighting. When the Russians used anti-aircraft guns, they were knocked out by Maléter and his men. Bottles of nitroglycerine sent from a chemical plant to the fighters at Corvin alley were used against the tanks, turning them to flaming torches. There was spontaneous firing at the Russians from every strategic point, from high windows, corners, anywhere a quick and mobile fighter could fire and run. Molotov cocktails were dropped onto passing tanks from windows, small children ran up to tanks, snatched the soldiers' weapons, unscrewed the petrol caps and dropped in their burning bottles.

The police and army in other towns joined the revolution which spread, broke out, exploded all over the country, Szeged, Pécs, Debrecen, Magyaróvár, everywhere. In Magyaróvár on the 26th October, eighty-seven unarmed protesters were killed by the AVO. She has seen photographs, lines of dead lying on the floor of a church, in the foreground two young girls, pale, as if they're sleeping. She'll always see their blood-smeared skin, their bare feet, the circle of weeping relatives and foreign press men crowding round them. After those killings, the crowd turned on the AVO to take their revenge. AVO men were lynched, chased, killed. After burial, their bodies were disinterred and thrown over the graveyard wall.

Revolutionary Workers Councils were set up all over the country in preparation for the future, a model for socialist democracy. The council in Győr, the most powerful voice in the country, took over the radio station and Radio Free Győr broadcast calls for Russian troops to leave Hungary, Radio Free Miskolc too, both broadcasting their demands for freedom.

Farmers brought food into the city. Everyone did what he or she could. A group of farmers handed a barrel in to one of the hospitals, saying,

'We sterilized our knives and washed the barrel out first with sulphur!' The barrel contained a collection of their donated blood.

She and her friends joined the university revolutionary committee and were given sub-machine guns. They wrote and printed the leaflets demanding to know of Imre Nagy exactly who it was who had called in the Russians. They manned telephones, set up road blocks, fought when they needed to. Her sons, she knows, would be amused to think of her with a machine gun. 'You? You wouldn't know which end to use,' she can hear them saying, but she did. She's never told them much about it. Nor István.

Józsi was with his university friends, Péter, Imre, a few others. They managed to keep in contact, phoning and meeting once or twice during the fighting. They were, she knew, gathered at the apartment of someone's parents, a strategic corner, Jószi said. She did, she think, say, 'Be careful,' but only as everyone did to loved ones, only as Jószi said to her. In any case, would it have made any difference?

On the 25th October, President Eisenhower declared that the USA 'deplored the intervention of Soviet forces in Hungary.' 'The heart of America goes out to the people of Hungary...' he said, but the heart of America didn't help them very much.

Gerö fled, or was swiftly removed by the Russians as the fighting continued on those terrifying, hopeful days, the days when Nagy must have realised he had to make a decision, to allow the Russians to crush the revolution or to agree to revolutionary demands. He chose the latter, formed a new government but filled it with the old guard, old Stalinists and only one or two people from other parties to give the impression of being a multi-party government. It wasn't enough. One person he did appoint was her professor, the philosopher György

Lukács, as Minister of Culture.

Nagy announced too that he was beginning negotiations with the Soviet Union for the withdrawal of all troops from Hungarian soil. He offered an amnesty to fighters and abolished the AVH, agreed that the revolutionary committees would be recognised, their demands incorporated into the new formation of the state. March 15th was to be a national holiday again, the Kossuth arms reinstated as the national insignia. There were to be new economic policies.

On the 29th, Soviet troops began to withdraw from Budapest. Hundreds of buildings had been destroyed or damaged, hundreds of people killed, but the revolution had been won. The next day, a National Guard was formed to try to control the activities of the disparate groups of fighters to avoid anyone taking any action which might jeopardise the withdrawal of the Russians.

Nagy made further appointments to his government, to include representatives from a wider spectrum of parties, including the redoubtable Anna Kethly of the Social Democrats. The hero of the Kilián barracks, Pál Maléter was made defence minister to ensure the support of the army. On October 30th, as the Russians began to withdraw their forces, the new cabinet abolished the one party system. Almost a thousand prisoners were set free from the notorious prison at Vác. Cardinal Mindszenty was set free and stepped back into his role as head of the church.

And then, there was Suez. Would it had been different if Suez hadn't happened? At the time, she thought so. Now she doesn't. It would have been exactly the same. After Nasser nationalised the Suez Canal in July, everyone knew that Britain and France would take action to restore their access to it. Why did Israel attack Egypt just when it did, on the 29th, just at the height of Hungary's uprising? The USSR, formerly Egypt's backers, withdrew their advisors and support, from Egypt. Having made it easy for the West, it didn't expect the West to interfere in Hungary. It didn't. Dulles handed a document to his Soviet counterpart, saying, 'The USA has no military allies in Eastern Europe', which in the language normal people use meant please, feel free, do as you like.

That day, the Politburo held a meeting. It seems that it was then they decided to crush the Hungarian revolution. Nagy's promise of free elections probably decided them. They might have agreed to a more independent Hungary, but not one in which free elections would see the humiliation or destruction of the communist party. They took the decision they did knowing that Suez was taking world attention from Hungary, with the confidence that they'd been given *carte blanche* by America to do as they wished.

How innocent their rejoicing seems now, how exciting those few days. On October 31st, Soviet tanks left Budapest. The next day, the cabinet decided that Hungary would withdraw from the Warsaw pact and declare itself neutral. Nagy told the Soviet ambassador, Andropov, and sent a telegram to Voroshilov, the President of the Praesidium of the USSR to inform him too. Then he addressed the nation:

'The Hungarian people, on the basis of independence and equality and in accordance with the spirit of the UN charter, wishes to live in true friendship with its neighbours, the Soviet Union and all the peoples of the world...'

As he spoke, he already knew that huge Soviet troops formations had reached central Hungary. He'd asked Andropov about the troops but Andropov denied it was happening. Andropov wasn't the only liar. The Soviet delegate to the UN, too, announced to the world that reports of Soviet troop build-ups were 'utterly unfounded'.

That broadcast was the signal for Kádár to be whisked away to the Russian Embassy to wait for the moment when he'd return to the Parliament building six days later as Russia's choice for head of state.

On November 3rd, the delegation which had been sent to negotiate with the UN and the Russians for the withdrawal of Soviet forces from Hungarian soil,was seized by the Russian secret police, the NKVD. The Hungarian delegates were arrested, including Pál Maléter, the one man who could have led both army and people in the days to come.

She knows now that the night of the 3rd November was the last night of hope. She didn't then. Some people knew, of course; some people may have guessed, but she and her friends didn't. They thought the revolution had been won. She, and at least some of the rest of Hungary, slept well that night, not knowing.

The Soviet attack began at 4 am the next day. Operation Whirlwind, they called it, 15 armoured divisions, 200,000 troops, 2,500 armoured vehicles invaded Hungary. Shells fell on Budapest. MIG fighters shrieked low over Budapest and Györ. Nagy broadcast to the world:

'*This is Imre Nagy speaking, President of the Council of Ministers of the Hungarian People's Republic. Today at daybreak, Soviet troops started an attack against our capital, obviously with the intention to overthrow the legal Hungarian government. Our troops are fighting! I notify the people of our country and the entire world of this fact.*'

Fighting broke out again, near the Royal Place in Buda, in Széna Square, in the working class districts, Csepel, Dunapentele, Ujpest, Köbánya. When the Russians reached Parliament, Nagy had already fled to the Yugoslav embassy. At 8 am, the Soviets occupied Parliament and the Russian commander issued an ultimatum that Budapest would be bombed from the air if fighting didn't stop. It didn't stop, but Budapest wasn't bombed.

The free radio stations sent out their messages of desperation:

'*Since early morning, Russian troops are attacking Budapest ... please tell the world of the treacherous attack against our struggle for liberty. Help, help, help!*'

'*Keep fighting! Keep fighting! Do not surrender your arms!*'

'*Urgent! This is Hungarian army radio. We are breaking off. We are in imminent danger. We ask urgently for help!*'

Why did no-one help? Not only because they were busy with Suez, they were scared of Soviet power, scared of war, unwilling to risk such a possibility because, simply, Hungary didn't matter. In Glasgow, Dr Blum talked earnestly to her about his horror, his disappointment, about how people had already left the British communist party in droves. He talked about the awful feeling people there had, that there was nothing anyone could do. She ha forced herself to be rational, to remember the atmosphere, the fear of the Cold War. She knows no-one would have risked nuclear war for Hungary, but she's still angry. *Realpolitik.* How she hates the term and the idea.

She spoke to Jószi that afternoon. The last time they'd met, they'd been rejoicing, hugging, congratulating themselves and each other for a revolution won. This time, they were in despair.

'Anci, I can't believe they'd do this,' Jószi said, almost weeping. 'I didn't think even they were capable of this!'

They arranged to meet the next day.

'By the way, have you seen István?'

'Not for a few days. Why?'

'I just wondered. There's something I wanted to tell you about him. Just be careful...'

'Jos, what is it?'

'I'll tell you tomorrow when I see you.'

The Russian troops who arrived this time weren't the same as the ones who came the first time, Russian-speaking, with an unfortunate propensity to sympathise with the population. This time they were Central Asians, people who didn't speak Russian to prevent the fraternisation which had hindered the straightforward pursuit of murder. They didn't know where they were. They thought that the Duna was the Suez canal. They behaved very much as the Red Army did in 1945, raping, stealing, smashing in the fronts of wine-shops. Wine was poured into the drains rather than allow the Russians to get hold of it. They fired on bread queues and punished the area where the Kilián barracks and Corvin Alley fighters had fought so bravely by shelling the university hospitals on Ülloi ut with phosphorous shells. They used huge tanks against the citizens of Budapest, blasting buildings down, responding to small arms fire by destroying the entire house. It's how Józsi died. He and Péter and Imre and four others whose names she doesn't know, just blown into nothing, into dust and falling stone.

Nagy, who had already arranged refuge in the Yugoslav embassy, fled, while Kádár, in a Russian tank, returned to Budapest to take over the government, to dissolve all the achievements of the revolution, Kádár and his bunch of traitors, Kádár, who talked of Hungarian freedom fighters as 'fascists'. Obeying Kádár's instruction that anyone handing in weapons to a point in Rákosi Square would not be prosecuted, people took their weapons, only to be killed by Russian firing squads.

There was so much hope. And then it was over. Józsi was dead.

She was in London when, two years later, Imre Nagy was executed. Colonel Pál Maléter too, as well as 350 others, freedom fighters. Uncle Szabó from Széna Square was one of the first. Nearly a thousand people were deported and 20,000 imprisoned. People who'd been promised amnesty. She still blames Kádár.

Cardinal Mindszenty fled to the American embassy, where he'd be for the next fifteen years. Janos Kádár stayed in power until 1988.

István, who'd heard about Jószi, came to find her.

'Anci, we'll leave.'

'Where will we go?'

'I've already arranged something for you. We'll go to Vienna first, then London, Paris, anywhere. We'll get married as soon as we're somewhere else. We'll go soon.'

'When?'

'Tomorrow.'

He had it already organised. Later, in Austria, he arranged all their documents in the name of Goldmann. She remembered the odd thing he'd said at the beginning.

'We have the same name,' he said, although his name was something else then.

'That was one of the reasons I noticed you. Only one of them...'

At the time, she told herself that you couldn't rely on names. People did change their names. They'd all had noms de guerre, Sovietised names, Rákosi and Gábor Péter and Ernö Gerö, all of them but they had their own names too. She'd felt a chill, thinking of it. What was it Jószi had been going to tell her? Thinking of it now, she feels the same.

She agreed to leave because she wouldn't have wanted to stay by then. It seemed to her, rightly or wrongly, that she'd endured too much in Hungary. She was grateful to István. She hadn't had to decide, not about leaving, about marriage, the future. Docile, grieving, alone, she packed what she had and walked through the newly wrecked streets with her suitcase to meet István, the air still loud with voices,

'Help Hungary!'

She remembers that she promised to write out a translation of Kosztolányi's poem for Isabella:

> *Ezt hozta as ösz. Hüs gyümölcsöket*
> *üvegtálon. Nehéz, sötét-smaragd*
> *szölöt, hatalmas, jáspisfényü körtét,*
> *megannyi dús, tündöklö ékszerét...*

'Look at what autumn has brought us. Fruit cooling/ on glass. Heavy grapes of sombre emerald/ enormous pears of jasper-coloured light.'

Chapter 25

Glasgow, late autumn, 2001

It was December when Mark told me he was coming back. Did he tell me or did he ask? I'm still not certain. There are ways of suggesting both at the same time. It took me a moment to realise exactly what he meant, and when I did I felt only panic, then an almost irresistible desire to beg him not to. It took a while for me to feel the relief that I would eventually, knowing that at least if he was here I wouldn't have to worry about him, or not in the same way as I had done, but then, as he spoke, I was still shocked, trying to gauge what it all would mean. He was almost frighteningly open about his acceptance and his fears.

'Dan, I don't want to be here any more. I'm scared. If I have a fit and fall and end up in hospital, they'll try to operate on me again. That's what it's like here. I've told you, Jaegerson's already suggested it. They'll pull out every atom of the bloody thing, bit by bit, but it'll only grow again. It'll grow again and they'll fight me over the last fucking cell and charge me for it too. Dan, the trouble is they don't believe in death in this place – and now, I do.'

He talked for quite a long time. I didn't say anything. Every thought and fear he expressed, I'd had too in the past year. I'd imagined him every day, one small person standing amid the unforgiving speed of a vast city, the countless opportunities for falling, being trampled, for suffering and pain. About his death I'd only rarely allowed myself to think, but now I did. I didn't know what to say to him. What could I say? That I was far behind him, scared too, reluctant, living uneasily with dreams and lies?

'I don't want any of this. I don't want Jaegerson undermining my decisions, I don't want Lee nagging at me, I don't want Tam and Noah flying back and forth across the continent for months, watching me deteriorate, wondering how long it'll be before they can get back to what they need to do, despite themselves, calculating how long I'm likely to hang on.'

'Have you talked to them about it yet?'

'No. I wanted to talk to you first.'

'They aren't going to like it.'

'I know. Whatever way it happens, it's horrible, if I stay, if I don't. I'm trying to think about them too, but Dan, I'm the one who has to deal with this.'

'I know, Mark. I'm sorry to be banal, but you have to do what you want.'

'I've been feeling so positive since I decided. I'm going to try to leave all the negative stuff for a bit. By the way, I don't want you to worry. You won't have to do anything. I'll get people to look after me. I don't want you to think you'll have the burden.'

'Tell me what I can do now.'

'Let me think about it all for a few more days. I don't want to have made too many plans before I speak to the kids. It would seem sneaky.'

'I'll think about it too. When are you going to tell them?'

'At Christmas. After Christmas. '

It was all I thought about during Christmas. I spent the time waiting for the whole disassociated, unreal time of Christmas and New Year to be over so that I could begin to prepare. But how, when? I didn't even know when he was planning to arrive. I kept wondering what it was exactly had made him decide to come here. I'm still far from certain that I fully understand. The words, yes, I understood the words but what else was there that I didn't? Even now, I think I could have discouraged him from coming.

'You don't have to agree', Dalit said when I discussed it with her, but I did have to agree. As far as Noah and Tam are concerned, I'm as guilty as Mark. I accept.

They phoned me as soon as Christmas was over and they were both back home. Tam was first.

'Uncle Dan, he's spoken to you, hasn't he?'

'Yes.'

'What are we going to do?'

'What do you mean?'

'We can't let him leave.'

'Tam, I don't think you can stop him.'

'I'm not sure about that. I mean, maybe the tumour's affecting the way he makes decisions.'

'It probably is, but not in the way you think.'

'Maybe I should speak to a lawyer.'

'Tam, no, listen, he's entirely rational. You know that, you talk to him.'

'But this isn't. It's not rational to want to leave the place where you live, for God's sake, and leave your family and everything you have, your friends, your entire life.'

'I know, Tam. You might not agree, but that's different.'

'Uncle Dan, what does he want? He's prepared to go half-way across the world and just leave me and Noah, as if we're nobody to him.'

'It's not that, it really isn't. The opposite, in fact. I can't speak for him, but I think he wants to spare you what's going to happen to him. He knows enough about it, after all. I don't think you need to doubt his feelings for you.'

'Wonderful,' she said, 'so we can't even be there when our own father dies.'

Noah, when his phone call came the same evening, was brisk, trying to recruit me to their cause.

'You have to see, his treatment'll be better here. I'm sorry, Uncle Dan, but it's true.'

'Actually, Noah, I think you're wrong about that, but there's no point in arguing. Anyway, by now the quality of his treatment's immaterial. There's no treatment. You know that. He knows that. Don't you think that might be why he wants to come here?'

'I've no idea why he wants to.'

'You really don't understand?'

'No. Do you?'

'I think I do. I've just said the same to Tam. I can't speak for him. I can only say how I'd feel.'

'How would you feel?'

'That I'd hope I'd know when the time had come to accept. I'd want to do things in my own way. That it's not lack of love which is making him do this, it's a particular, thoughtful kind of love. But beyond that, I don't know, Noah. I really don't know.'

It was almost the truth. I examined my feelings closely, that mixture of slight dread, unease mixed with a certain triumph. I didn't want to feel as if I was competing with his children, as if the past was winning in an indeterminate struggle with the future. I was both scared and horrified by the thought of the unknown time ahead. For weeks, I'd wake up in the night worrying about what was going to happen, not only because of his illness. That, in a way, was the one known, pre-determined factor. I worried both for him and for me.

I waited to hear from Mark again but didn't phone him. I was scared I might interfere with the progress of his thoughts and decisions. When he phoned next, he hadn't changed his mind.

'I thought February, beginning of March. That way, I can sort everything out with work and money and so on and have everything tied up.'

He'd thought it out quite thoroughly. He'd rent a flat, get rid of most of his possessions before he left, send them to Tam and Noah. Anything he needed, he'd bring with him or buy here. He had, unsurprisingly, made a list which he e-mailed to me, with details of what he required in a flat, a proper shower, a decent kitchen, a comfortable bed. He asked questions too, about whether or not I could organise a GP for him, which hospital would see him, what he'd have to do about paying. He'd need, he said, a lawyer, a bank, a taxi company, a cleaning company.

'What am I going to need?' he'd said on the phone. Even as he said it, I laughed. It's here, all around me, what he brought and what he bought while he was here. With every item, computer, sound system, coffee machine, he said,

'After all, you can always sell it if you don't want it, afterwards...'

That day we discussed details, where he wanted to live, what type of house. It was important to him. He had, he said, no desire to live in what had been the great Jewish enclave of our childhood, the big sandstone houses, the quiet streets where hardly anybody passed on foot.

'Nearer town. You'll know best. Somewhere lively, smart. I'm too used to everything going on around me. Suburbs make me feel as if something terrible's happened to everyone and I'm the only survivor.'

He'd said he needed a flat with at least two bedrooms.

'I'll need an extra one for the time when someone has to come in to look after me.' I was surprised to feel angry, but I did; hurt, too. I resented the thought. I didn't tell him and though I had no idea of what I'd have to do, I knew that if anyone took care of him, it would be me.

In early January, once the endless tedium of New Year had subsided and shops and estate agent's were blearily open again, I started looking for a flat. The notion was too new for me to do it calmly, the language of property pages and estate agents too new, lines of photographs of buildings and rooms unlike anything I'd thought about for a long time. It was years since I had either bought or sold a house and I've never had any interest in the progress of prices or the ease with which you can buy or sell. I found it both reassuring and strange to look at the pictures of houses I knew, the ones I'd walked past in the days after Mark's diagnosis. Knowing I could live in any of them I wanted, that Mark could, seemed odd to me, as if I had the power to usurp a parent's privilege. The estate agent was amused by my ignorance of the questions to ask,

'There's heating?'

'I think you can take that as read,' he said, the snigger barely suppressed.

I began going to see flats. It felt unreal, surreal. I went round the few I saw before this one with a bewildered air, feeling as if I was cheating the polite men and women who showed me round. I said to myself often, 'What am I doing here?' in some stranger's home, casting an eye towards the beds, too inhibited to ask about them or try them out. A few places I saw were ones people had bought to rent out, pale, stark, modern, dull, not places where Mark would want to live. There were the old ones too, with stairs which made them unsuitable or long corridors or bathrooms which were inconvenient or ugly, kitchens in colours Mark would hate, with fireplaces or decor which would offend him, as they did me. Once I'd seen this place, I knew it was the only one Mark could have. It's the lower part of a large house, built no doubt by a rich Glasgow merchant, the source of whose money I'd rather not think about, a house which couldn't exist anywhere else, only here, the combination of pairs of long windows, step-corbelling and complicated roofs, a style I've never seen anywhere else. Inside, it hasn't been ruined, or if it was at one time, it's been restored to the way it should be, stairs, glass, panelling, everything. It was perfect, a magnificent grand piano in the large sitting room, the kitchen and bathroom new, well-chosen, three shallow steps to the front door. It was a bit bigger than he needed, with three bedrooms instead of two and not much furniture, which meant that I could buy new beds.

After I'd seen it I lay awake, thinking what I'd have to do to make it suitable for Mark, champing beside the phone before nine, waiting for the estate agent to open, scared that someone else would want it too. I asked about the piano.

'Oh, that comes with it.'

I wanted to ask why, but didn't. The piano made it seem natural to think about Morning. I knew she'd look wonderful flying in this room.

Mark said to me in August that I should buy this flat.

'It seems so – you. Why don't you?'

'I might. I can't really think about it now.'

'You can afford it easily enough. Sell the other one. You're never there. And there's what you'll have when I go.' We always laughed about that, about his will, the details of which he had already told me. We enjoyed swapping stories of wills, particularly of Jewish mothers and their exertion of the power of the will, and without fail we'd break into the routine about Louis who wanted to be remembered in his brother's will and was rewarded at the reading of the will by the greeting, 'Hello Louis!' and we'd laugh ridiculously.

Noah and Tam had, of course, enlisted Lee, and after initial shock she began to bombard Mark with entreaties and threats. She phoned me a few times too. They were awkward calls and during one, when I wouldn't agree with her, she ended by screaming at me that I was just as bad as my selfish brother. Noah and Tam refused, for a while at least, to give up. I think now of what Mark said once after one of their arguments. He phoned to tell me about it. He was angry.

'They're making it all so much fucking worse. I've said to them they can come over if they want. I'll pay for them to come. What's their problem?'

'I'm not taking their side, Mark, but it must be hellish for them.'

'Don't worry Dan, they like tragedy,' he said, 'they're used to it. It's learned behaviour. They learn it from every crap television drama. Look, this way, they'll have the drama without the tedium.'

I could have thought him harsh, overly cynical, but I knew that in some measure he was right. I'd seen it in my own children and their friends, the ameliorated responses, the soap-opera attitudes, even in the most intelligent and aware of them. The clichéd words, the stock reactions. The drama without the tedium. As it turned out there was a little of both for us, but that was much later. It seems now to me to be quotidian, the business of dying, both passive and active. There were days when we might have forgotten which of us it was, who was dying. After we'd been driving somewhere for a couple of hours, Mark might say, 'Are you tired, Dan? Are you okay? Would you like to rest a little?' and I could tell that really, he wished that he could be driving me and I'd feel instantly as if I was the one who was ill, the one who needed to be nurtured, protected. I felt confused because the boundaries between us were so fragile, the matter within our heads almost undifferentiated now in the ways which truly mattered. But that was later, during the spring, the lovely, soft, verdant days of summer, Mark's last.

After Mark told them he was coming here, Noah and Tam began phoning Nira and Dalit, who reported their conversations.
    'How do they seem?'
    'They're okay,' Nira said, 'just a bit shocked, I think. I told them both that they should be glad really, he's doing them a favour.'
    'What will I say to Mark?'
    'Say to him that they'll be fine.'

Mark told me about his leaving America. The evening before he left, Tamar wept on the phone and said to him, 'Dad, do you not know what this means?' and he replied that he did.
    'I only get to do this once,' he'd said.
    'So do I, Dad,' she replied. He'd wanted to say, my bit's more important than yours, but wasn't certain it was true.

What would Mark want? What would he need? For weeks, I'd waken in the night with lamps and bedlinen and bed-pans looming from the ether towards my mind. I worried for myself, too, until the moment when I yielded to the abandonment of worrying and accepted that life wasn't going to return to what I vaguely regarded as 'normal', the life before Mark's illness, before his surgery, before his decision to come here. For a time now, I'd simply have to endure. I know what's said about the death of parents, that first, open glimpse of a terrifying, unbroken horizon but this was to me far more profound, facing the death of a sibling, the mirror of my own life and death, the inevitable end of a childhood adventure.

I've come to love this house. I didn't realise until, after a few weeks
of Mark's being here, I found myself reluctant to leave in the evening
to walk or drive back to my own flat. I wanted to be with him too.
Mark would say, 'Why don't you stay?' and if I hadn't heard clearly in
his voice that he wanted me to, I wouldn't have done. There was the
day too when he referred to one of the desks as being mine. It seemed
natural after a few weeks that I should move some things in. Anyway,
it was only sensible. By that time, he was noticeably worsening.

I arranged for the lease to start the month before Mark arrived.
I enjoyed preparing, the first and indeed the only thing I'd been able
to do for him so far. I tried to be organised. The girls gave me precise
instructions, telling me that I must buy good bedlinen, towels, pillows,
anything which would make Mark comfortable. I must stock the
cupboards and fridge properly too, buy wine, champagne, check
to see that there were decent glasses. They were quite right. If I've
learned anything from Mark, it's the importance of celebration. By
the end, we were celebrating everything.

The first thing I did as soon as I got the keys was have Morning
brought round here. I decided not to put her up until Mark arrived.
Just seeing her here, in different surroundings, ones which reminded
me more of my parent's house than any other place I've lived, changed
time, István Goldmann's voice sounding to me through the years.
'Ah! Our pianist!' 'Ah, look, it's our piano angel!' I thought of things
I hadn't done for decades, the way I always felt transparent in his
presence, physically transparent, as if light could shine through me, as
if my bones and cartilage and gristle hadn't yet set into adult strength,
as if the white sun shining through the windows could illuminate all
of me, the bones of my hands on the piano keys, flesh and skin, hair
and ivory. István was quite short, a stocky, handsome man with an
abundance of dark hair which he combed back from his forehead,
like the crest of a bird, a dark-eyed, sharp-eyed bird. He must have
been in his early forties then. Philosopher, scholar, refugee. What else
was he? That, I have, until recently, never known.

1956. The reverberations from Hungary were still sounding when
Anci came to us, hundreds of thousands of Hungarians fleeing into
exile in Austria and beyond, threats of punishments and trials. For

the first few days she was with us, she stayed in her room a lot. The piano was in the room below hers, and when I practised I tried to choose things I thought might give her some comfort: Debussy, Bach, some Bartók I found in the music library. After a few days, she asked if I was the pianist and when I said I was, she thanked me.

'It was very nice, very…' she said, searching for the word, 'beautiful.'

At first, everything about Anci was as strange to me as if she'd been reincarnated from a different era, or was a sole representative from the civilisation of a distant star. Her life had made her thus, made her ask us which radio station was the party station, made her talk with a strength of hatred I'd never heard before at mention of the name 'Kádár' on the news. Her discussions with my father on politics made me feel like an over-protected child.

As I looked at Morning propped against the wall of the flat, snatches of old conversation came back, Anci pointing towards a derelict site we were passing in the car one day, asking,

'What happened to all that?'

'They bombed it.'

'Did they? Who?'

'Anci, who do you think?'

By then, we all realised that she thought our war had been trivial by comparison with hers, a view with which, however irritating, it would have been difficult to argue.

'Why are your trains always so slow?' We were on the platform, waiting for the train which would take us to Edinburgh for the day.

'To remind us of mortality.'

'What's "mortality"?'

'The state of being liable to die.'

'Oh,' she said, watching the train approaching the platform with stately, steam-driven grace, 'I tell you, you can die quicker than this.'

Almost every Saturday afternoon, she and Mark went to the art gallery to draw. She was astonishingly good, although she hadn't been studying art. She'd been studying philosophy, but when I asked her about it she claimed to know nothing.

'Philosophy? You mustn't ask me. I don't know anything. If you want to know, you must ask István.'

I'd meet her and Mark in town after my piano lesson and we'd go to a café. I liked being with her. She was little, of childlike thinness, with a lustrous beauty that made people turn to look at her, in part at least because she spoke loudly, and made points forcefully, gesturing wildly with her hands. She looked about sixteen and so it was impossible to think of her as being married. She said little about István, who phoned quite often from London or Oxford or wherever he was, and we'd listen to the odd, slightly monotonous tones of Hungarian from which we could gauge nothing.

One morning in February of 1957, she read in a newspaper that a twenty-year-old Hungarian woman had been hanged for her part in the uprising. Anci pushed the paper towards me, beginning to cry, not quite to cry, putting her head back, looking towards the ceiling, swallowing, balancing her tears.

After I got my camera, I took a lot of photographs of her. We'd go out for walks and she'd climb onto walls, or perch on the backs of park benches while I tried out what I thought were unusual angles, original views. There are a few I took of her of which I was wonderfully proud, the first ones people really praised, ones which gave me a new sense of the power of image. She'd hauled herself up onto the parapet of the empty fountain in the park and, holding on with one hand, began waving to some children who were playing on the grass. She was just high enough above me for me to be able to miss the rather dull surroundings of the park and catch her, head and raised arm dark against clouds and sky.

István arrived in late spring. He seemed more politician than philosopher. He told nothing of himself, deftly maintaining an area of safety between himself and any question asked of him, playing people one against the other with almost breathtaking skill. He was charming to Mark, engaging him in prolonged discussions about architecture, asking his opinion, deeply, earnestly, of Frank Lloyd Wright or the neo-Baroque. One day, he came into the room while I was playing the piano and stood by the window until I had finished the piece before applauding, saying 'Bravo!' in a faintly embarrassing way. I was on the point of thanking him when he frowned slightly, inclining his head.

'Really,' he said, 'one can gain so much pleasure, even from a minor talent.'

Why did Anci marry István? The question was in my mind for years. Apart from anything else, he seemed so old. I didn't even know how long they'd been married. I began to wonder if she'd discussed it with Mark. She and Mark had a jovial, quarrelsome relationship in which even I, the person least able in the world to comprehend the subtleties of feeling, could discern closeness and understanding. When I asked him if she'd ever told him anything, he said she hadn't.

'Hasn't she even said anything about István?'

'No, nothing,' but I knew instantly that he was lying. My question, and Mark's answer, or more accurately my response to his answer, suspicion, jealousy and rage, was to leave its residue of self-inflicted pain in me almost until the end of Mark's life. There was one morning shortly after Anci left when the phone rang, and on my answering it there were the usual sounds of the time, the clunks and beeps of money being put into a phone box, the pressing of buttons. I was saying 'hello' and 'who is it?' when the person on the other end hung up. I was sure it was Anci phoning for Mark, sure she'd hung up when it was I who answered.

I gave up playing the piano, at first from hurt pride, from a failure to understand that István might have been wrong, or devious, then as an act of renunciation. Anci and István left, and after that I no longer wanted to play. Playing seemed connected in more ways than I could understand to Anci.

The first time I was here in this room alone, the piano felt like a presence, a demanding one, one I tried to ignore but I knew it was challenging me, more, taunting me, inviting me with its air of smug hauteur to see what I could do. I sat awkwardly at the piano stool and opened the lid, but couldn't play. Even just sitting there returned me to a state of adolescent anxiety. I told myself that it didn't matter, but it did. Apart from anything else, Mark would expect me to play. He'd say, as soon as he saw the piano,

'Everything provided! Even the concert hall!'

That evening, I phoned round friends to ask if anyone knew of a piano teacher. Most didn't, but eventually I was given the name of an elderly lady who had been my friend's children's teacher years before.

'Let me have a look to see if I've still got her number. Yes, here it is, Miss Dalziel. God, that takes me back! Sorry, Dan, I don't even know if she's still alive. She'll be about a hundred and twenty if she is. Still, give her a try. She was very good.'

I phoned tentatively, but Miss Dalziel herself answered the phone.

'Are you a beginner?'

'Not exactly. I used to play a lot but haven't for years.'

'How many?'

'Oh, more than I like to think about. Decades.' I didn't like to say how many.

'No matter. You won't have forgotten.'

She was right. I hadn't forgotten. Not a moment of being a child, not a moment of the anticipation, the anxiety of wondering if I'd practised enough to see me through the lesson. None of it eluded me as I walked up the stairs to her flat for my first lesson. I explained to her at once that I was nervous, but for some reason it was easy to tell my story, easier still to find myself taken over by memory, as if fingers and mind could override the fear and reluctance which had prevented me form playing for so long. Miss Dalziel knew what to do, making me sit at the piano, sliding me into applying my fingers to the keys almost without my noticing as she talked about the power of memory, the indelible imprint of music on the mind. She was right. It returned, the fingering, the way my hands could move to produce the surprise, the shock of sound, even, that day, of scales, the simple exercises a child might play, and indeed, after my first lesson, I left with the feeling of a delighted five-year-old, her words of praise, 'Well done, Daniel!' directed to that same stumbling child, encouraging me to come here straight away to begin to play. I must have played for several hours, because when it began to grow dark I had to search out the unfamiliar light switches. It all returned, sight-reading, pieces I had just about mastered after weeks, months of practise years before, and most vitally, the feeling that I could: that here, at last, I was returning to something I knew. After our third lesson she asked, already knowing the answer, if now I felt more able to continue on my own. As I left, a lifetime's habit left her unable to stop herself from exhorting me still to practise.

I'm glad I did it because I played for him a lot in the last weeks. I don't know what he could still make of it, though he professed to enjoy it.

After I'd begun to play again, I felt prepared for Mark, prepared for whatever was going to happen. Thinking about the time I'd spent in London made me realise how fortuitous it was that I was here in Glasgow when Mark decided to come back. He wouldn't have wanted to be in London. Who would? He might not have come if I'd still been there.

'I feel so light, Dan, so unencumbered,' Mark said to me at the airport the morning early last spring when I went to collect him. I remember thinking, I'm sure you do, although I tried instantly to conceal any sign of it behind the airport jostle of collecting trolleys and hauling luggage. Loaded pantechnicons chugged across the face of many states. His children wallowed in suspended grief. My heart felt as if it had been replaced by lead but Mark felt light.

The weight on me that morning was a weight of years. As I drove him back here, I seemed to hear the faraway crackle of an ancient wireless giving out old news, old history, voices from other times, the slow, imponderable creak of the turning of a circle.

Chapter 26

New York, winter 2000 – 2001

Dr K. L. Jaegerson, Neurosurgeon
Specialties: Neuro-oncology, Endoscopic Neurosurgery
Suite 53
43, East Reveille Avenue
New York, NY.

To whom it may concern:

Mr Mark Blum 25th May, 1936

Dear Sir/Madam,

I enclose a full record of Mr Blum's medical history and trust that this will facilitate all further treatment which Mr Blum may require.

At present, Mr Blum is reasonably well although he has complained of mild visual disturbance, weakness in his left arm and what appear to be episodes of complex partial seizures, all attributable to the recent recurrence of his glioblastoma. Following his most recent MRI scan, I suggested further surgery as the most appropriate measure to deal with his recurrence but Mr Blum was unwilling to agree to surgery. It may be that, on reflection, and on settling in his new home, he may alter this opinion.

Throughout the duration of Mr Blum's illness, I have explained his prognosis which he appears to understand and to accept.

Yours sincerely,
K.L. Jaegerson,
Neurosurgeon.

Leaving. The word makes days and hours move faster. It makes them move slower. A parallel scale of time rushes him through the final weeks and days as it makes him wait achingly, without end, for the moment when it's done, his apartment packed and sent off, the few necessary farewells said, when he's at the airport, on the plane, away.

The weeks after making his decision are wearying. Pretending passivity, he endures Tam's suggestion that he might have lost the capacity to think for himself, Noah's attempt to be more adult than him, saying in a patronising tone,

'Now, Dad, I wonder if it might not be best to think about this sensibly,' as if the possibility exists that he hasn't done so already.

The moment for phoning Lee is one he chooses with care, on an evening when he feels calm, after a successful day.

'You're doing what, exactly?' she enunciates, not so much speaking as spitting, fury and frustration sounding from her throat until finally she croaks,

'Do you ever think about anybody but yourself?' A question which, under normal circumstances, he'd find difficult to answer.

'Look, Lee, I probably haven't got that long left. I think I'm entitled to think about myself.'

'Oh, really! Christ's sake, Mark, what about the children?

'Lee, they're not children.'

'You know what I'm saying. This is so like you, doing what you want to do, always doing what you want to do.'

'Lee, I'm leaving and I'm not going to discuss it with you again.'

'Look, I can't speak now. I'm just too distressed. I'll get back to you.'

He knows that after the call she'll be phoning Tam and Noah, thinking of tricks, plots, strategies to stop him, but nothing will, and on this particular evening he understands the deranged illusions of power behind madmen, Mussolini, Franco, the blissful freedom to say: it is as I say and I will say no more. He's been shocked by how much he's enjoyed being stubborn and unbending. Often, afterwards, as he going about his apartment, in the street, he has repeated the words exactly as he said them:

'Lee, I'm leaving and I'm not going to discuss it with you again,' thinking again of the mixed anger and aggrieved pleasure at the insult in her voice as she hung up.

'You can't go back to the past,' someone says to him, a close friend, on whom he first tries the idea. He wants to laugh, but knows that it's the stunned reaction of someone who can't think of what else to say. When he tells this to Berndt and Ali, they do laugh.

'Well, well,' Berndt says. 'Mark, are you sure you're old enough to make this decision?'

'What can I say, Mark?' Ali says, 'That we'd rather you didn't go?

But I understand. It may well be the best thing to do. In fact, I'm sure it is. Really. It makes a lot of sense. As long as you're sure.'

'I'm sure,' he says, and is.

With Kirstin, it's different. She's shocked when he tells her, but accepting as ever, finding in an instant the way to soften the harshness of his will.

'I'll be going home in the summer,' she says, 'remember? For the wedding.'

Her niece in Sweden is getting married.

'I'll come and see you then,' and he says that will be wonderful although he knows it won't be and he hopes she won't arrive, because after all, there is a finite limit to how long one can extend the grief of parting. All the same, he understands. She's always been unable to accept finality and for this he loves her, for what might be weakness or might be strength. By now he's just grateful that she at least is prepared to help him make it easy.

Over the weeks of his planning, Tam and Noah continue to hector him, to try to find new and compelling arguments for him to remain, but since there are none, their calls frequently end in petulant silence. They have, he knows, been in contact with Dan's daughters, a sensible pair who take after their mother just enough to be blunt, and after their father just enough to be kind. He complains frequently to Dan.

'I've got enough to think about without this...'

It's true. He has the rest of his life to arrange. He has to dispose of the collected goods of a lifetime. He has to organise a journey, a house-move, an ante-mortem house clearing, all in one.

Going through his clothes, his possessions, he considers each carefully. A full year's wardrobe, or not? How many shirts, how many coats? What does a dying man need, he asks himself. What, exactly? He mocks himself for this term which seems to hold too much pathos and drama to carry with him every day. He thinks of the radio discussion he heard recently on the topic of medical disclosure, a woman with an annoying voice opining,

'According to kabbalah, you and your physician must never give up hope. We have to keep reminding ourselves of the role of Ein Sof in our lives...'

He dismissed it as nonsense at the time, but now thinks the idea has some merit. Never give up hope. He's far from certain he knows what hope entails, but nonetheless he won't.

There is a stage in his leaving when the things surrounding him become affected, transfixed by a slow, plangent charm which spreads, grows like lichen over every aspect of his life. He recognises it of old. It's the phenomenon which makes things you're about to leave irrationally desirable, even if it's your own urgent, anxious choice to leave them, even if you have decided in the fullness of considered thought that you don't much like them any more. It has infested houses he has disliked when he's been about to move out of them. It has given to lovers from whom he longed and even schemed to be free, a rare and special beauty. Not that he feels anything but love for this city where he has lived for so long, but even its harsher aspect, the one which impels him to leave, seems now to have a fascination he cannot quite explain. This perversity, as everything else, must be weathered, overcome, must move with him, as it does, into a further stage, one in which he feels no longer part of what had been his life here, the stage when the loved city mysteriously closes to him, excludes him, makes him a stranger. Walking home in the evenings, he feels the streets become distant, alien. Each familiar building seems to wish to intimate to him that even if he has not progressed to the next phase of existence, the phase when he is no longer here, the unknown future, it has.

Leaving. Every day, he resists temptation. There are occasions when he happens to be in a particular restaurant or shop or bar where he knows the staff, and realises that the visit will be his last, but he carries the wealth of possible partings out with him, unsaid. What, after all, would he say?

He arranges for packers to come to take the furniture he's sending to Tam and Noah. He's been tempted briefly to feel cynical about their acceptance of the gift of the finest of his possessions but doesn't. What else are they meant to do? He understands their feeling that he's abandoning them, knowing how easy it is in painful circumstances to flip back the years, to be a child again.

'They'll be fine,' Dan says and he reminds himself of the air of confidence with which Dan said it as he packs, discards, labels items for the attention of the packers. Books, he deals with himself, sorting them into piles for Tam, Noah, Berndt and Ali. He puts aside a box for himself and Dan, ones he'll send on with the few other boxes of things he needs or wants or is going to give to Dan, a few choice things too he wishes Dan to have. In this box he puts Anci's books, still with their letters inside. He has not yet decided how to approach the discussion he must have with Dan. There is, he realises, a certain urgency to the matter. It has to be dealt with before his brain packs up, before his memory goes. He decides to write a memo in his diary to himself but can't decide on the pages of which month to write it.

Thinking of what he'll say returns the ghosts of conversations to turn in his mind, brings back the savour of the combative quality of his friendship with Anci, a memory of his method of cajoling her from sadness by goading her to anger in the form of quarrels about the war, when he'd challenge her maddening assertions about the morality of suffering, quarrels which usually degenerated into their accusing the other of childishness or ignorance.

It's always been clear to him why any man might pick Anci from a class of eager students, but his feelings for her were never sexual. He doesn't quite know why, because she held all the qualities which he would have expected to attract him most. Whatever the basis for his eventual dislike of István, it wasn't jealousy.

'Why did you marry him?' he asked her once, shortly after his arrival in Glasgow. He'd expected fury. Instead, she closed her eyes and he saw large tears swelling below her lashes as she struggled with herself to speak. She managed, eventually, to say,

'Mark, I don't know. I didn't have to decide. Stupid, so stupid. Do you think I'm stupid?'

'No, of course not.' She wept. She told him what she knew about István.

'Don't talk to anyone about it, please.'

'Anci, I won't.' He hasn't.

May. He writes it in his diary. May or before. Urgent.

In the days before he goes, he phones Lee. He leaves a message for her.

'Lee, hi, it's me. I'd like very much if you'd come out for dinner one night before I leave. Let me know if you can.'

She phones back.

'Hey, Mark. Why not?'

For him this proves, depressingly, conclusively, the power of the dictator. Their evening which he has dreaded, at a new restaurant, is

Esther Woolfson

better than he expected. They discuss Noah and Tam in proud and self-congratulatory terms. Any tendency towards sentiment is reigned in by history, although both weep a little on parting.

'We'll speak to each other lots...' she says, dabbing her eyes as she gets into a taxi, but a trail of words relating to selfishness, failure to seek a second opinion, abandonment of duty, seems to flutter lightly in the wake of her disappearing presence.

It's late winter. Over a year has passed since his surgery. He has achieved what is required of him, tied the ends of his pursuits off neatly, one by one. He feels himself slipping out of the framework of his own past life. Now, he has a journey to arrange.

Should he travel first class? He considers it. It's ridiculously expensive, but he'll only do it once. After considering it for a day or so he decides that he won't, for the same reason that he despises people who drive indecently expensive cars, spend indecent amounts on houses, clothes, jewels, because there are simply amounts one should not spend, although he knows the question to be subjective, the limits movable, aware of the hypocrisy of his setting limits in the limitless world in which he's lived for so long. He books his business class seat.

'You know, sir, it's cheaper if you purchase a return,' the young man says when he enquires about prices.

He phones Mrs Spellman at the Shoshana Blumstein Home to tell her of his new arrangements.

'I assume you're phoning to arrange a visit?'

'Yes,' Mark says, shamed into agreeing.

'If you wouldn't mind putting it off a little,' Mrs Spellman says. 'Sarah's not as well as she was. I was going to phone you in the next day or so to discuss moving her upstairs to the care ward. If you were to come, there would be no certainty that she'd even recognise you. Best wait until she's a little more settled.'

They discuss arrangements, the future.

'Don't worry, I'll keep you and your brother informed,' Mrs Spellman says.

On a final visit to collect the copy of his notes Jaegerson has promised to have ready for him, he and Dr Jaegerson shake hands, and again,

252

Mark thanks him. Jaegerson manages the smallest smile Mark has ever seen.

'Well, Mr Blum, I wish you the best in your preferred course of action,' he says from between tightly narrowed lips.

When the day arrives for him to go, he already feels distant from everything around him. All the way to the airport, he fights the word 'last'. It's not difficult to do. After all, God knows what happens in this world. He looks out of the taxi windows into other cars and for the burly black drivers or Latino families, the cheerful Haitian driving him, today might be their last day here too, who knows what might drop from the skies, might befall anyone of us in the midst of the quotidian enterprises which take our mind from the fragility of things. Things do change. Hearts stop suddenly on football fields. Buildings fall down. The earth, having bided its time, in a furious moment of subterranean rage, stamps and shakes and splits.

Two encounters alter his mood, tilt him from the entirely reasonable tendency to melancholy towards relief and pleasure. The first is as he's pouring himself a drink in the business class lounge, hearing a voice behind him say his name, turning to the unwelcome sight of one of his least favourite clients, a woman who, during the course of extensive building work on her house, would phone regularly at midnight to discuss or to complain.

'Mark, good to see you! My, you're looking so well!' she says.

'How kind, thank you.'

'And where are you going?'

'To visit my brother in Scotland.'

'Scotland!'

There is a brief discussion about the abundant charms of Edinburgh. More important than that, she's been meaning to call him to discuss possible work on a house her son has bought. He must promise to phone as soon as he gets back. Will he? He will, assuredly. He promises. The minute he gets back.

The next occurs on the plane. He's childish enough to love being upstairs in a plane. He hands over his coat for the stewardess to hang in the closet and begins to settle himself with the usual pleasure he feels in travelling, taking out the magazine from the pocket in front of him, arranging his books and bags when a woman is shown to the seat next to him. She's young, or young in his terms, forty perhaps, elegant and pretty. She smiles at him and as soon as the plane has accomplished its thrilling manoeuvre of speed and flight, with an air of practise and experience she sets about preparing herself for sleep, taking off her boots, putting on the slippers the airline has provided, stretching finely stockinged legs in front of her. She shakes loose her dark red hair, arranges the plane pillow and 'do not disturb sign' precisely, and wraps herself in a blanket. Poised before putting on her black satin eyeshade, she smiles dazzlingly at Mark. 'Goodnight,' she says and as he watches her settle for sleep, he remembers a Gabriel Garcia Marquez story he read in a *New Yorker* many years ago, of just this, a beautiful woman who sleeps beside him on the long flight from Paris to South America, a wonderful story which, he remembers, captured the marvellous intimacy and strangeness of journeys. The memory of it, the experience which now overlaps it with such muted, erotic charge delights him. Perverse enough to love plane food, he accepts his tray, handed over the sleeping form of the woman beside him and he drinks the free champagne, thinking not of the plane gliding over his former home but of this unexpected proximity, this secret pleasure. The country moves away below him, the line of coast, the lights of America but he doesn't look down. He looks instead at the line of the woman's arm, her body under the plane blanket, colours mingling in the sheen of her hair and as the plane lights are dimmed, as they move out over the fathomless ocean, he too sleeps, and dreams.

Chapter 27

London, late autumn 2001

She has just finished writing out the poem when she hears Isabella open the door of István's room above her, then the sound of her footsteps on the stairs before the tentative knock at the study door.

'Anci, can I come in? Can I look at what you're doing?'

'Of course, come in. It's just ideas so far. Look, these ones are for *The Marsh King's Daughter,* and these are for *The Ice Maiden*.'

Flatteringly enough, Isabella gasps.

'Anci, they're so lovely!' she says. 'Look at your gorgeous toads!'

'Nice toad and nasty toad. He's the one I'm going to use, nice toad. Have you ever read the story? I just wondered if you think he looks sweet enough.'

In the kitchen, over coffee, Isabella produces her little notebook, the one which Anci slightly dreads, the one with questions, the one in which Isabella writes her answers.

'I've got another list of things to ask. I hope you don't mind.'

'Not in the least.'

The questions this time are mainly to do with names, with books written by people István worked with at one time or another. Anci tells her everything she knows about each.

'Oh yes, the other thing I wanted to ask. Have you any early photographs?'

'No.'

'None at all?'

'None. Neither of us had any.'

'That's really sad.'

Anci raises an eyebrow,

'I suppose it is,' she says.

'I wish I'd known István,' Isabella says. It seems to Anci that her voice is wistful.

'Do you really?' she says.

As she resumes her work she knows that, in fact, there are one or two photographs of István somewhere in a drawer that she's not going to seek out for Isabella, the usual ones of the time, an anonymous-looking infant on the knee of an imposing Jewish matriarch in a high-collared dress. The first ones of herself are those Dan took, the photo on the stairs. There are none of her before that, not even of her wedding. Someone, a paid photographer at the City Hall in Vienna, had tried to step in front of them to take one but she put her hand across her face. Days away from Hungary, days away from Józsi's death.

'We'll leave,' István said and she'd been like one of the dolls in the toy box at the orphanage. She thinks of Mark, asking her about it after István arrived, thinks of herself crying, wanting to know if he thought she was stupid.

In Glasgow for those few months she hadn't had to think of it. She could pretend to herself it hadn't happened, that she was the same, single, free. She'd almost hoped István wouldn't come for her, that he'd forget about her, find someone else. She pretended until the day István arrived, and faced what she had done only when Mark asked her.

The beginning was difficult, those first days, lying on her bed in her room in the Blum's house, listening to the sound of the piano downstairs, the uprising still unfinished in her, still buzzing, insistent, still livid inside with the unperformed obsequies for Józsi's death, only the example of the past making her do what she'd always done, continue. Later, she'd marvel at some of her swimming companions for their dogged ability to do just the same.

She liked Glasgow. It was easy to lose herself in a place she'd never before even imagined, an island of rain and grey and fog, to lose herself in the warmth of attention, of people trying to help her, teach her, ease her from pain.

Mark is dead and now, suddenly, each argument they had rises to her mind, but she can neither laugh nor cry for her obstinacy, or for his relentless goading, or for the fact that she never told him, even years later, that he'd been right. Their afternoons, too, beyond expression of gratitude, the ones when they went to the art gallery to draw, when his refusal to allow her any self-doubt sowed the seed of the confidence with which helped her re-make her life. She thinks of his endless comforting.

'Do you think I'm stupid?'

'No, of course not. Anci, tell me about it. Tell me about István.'

For weeks, months, there were reports about Hungary on the news, Kádár's government, Kádár's repressions, the eventual executions. Jean Paul Sartre and Albert Camus both wrote of their admiration for the revolutionaries of Hungary. 'Budapest gave the same lesson to humanity that Spain did 20 years before…' Camus wrote.

Hearing the names of her homeland in another place gave her the first, chill glimpse of the magnitude of exile, forcing her to accept that there was no possibility of return. In February 1957, when she read in one of the papers that a twenty-year-old had been hanged for her part in the uprising, she wept, feeling that leaving Hungary had been a terrible betrayal. Dan was with her when she read it. He held her hand, telling her gently how glad he was that she was there, and safe, and couldn't have known how much she'd wished she'd stayed, that she'd been with Józsi in the path of that Soviet shell.

She thinks of the girl on the stairs. Dan took the photo in a park in Glasgow, one of many he took while he was experimenting with his new camera. She'd climbed up onto an empty fountain and balanced there while he took shot after shot, kneeling or crouching on the grass. She thought of it when she was at his exhibition, wondering if she could have realised then what he might become. At the time, she thought he was going to be a pianist. She doesn't know why he changed his mind. He was wonderfully gifted. He played for her when she first arrived, Bartók, Bach, pieces she understood he had chosen specially for her.

She and István left Glasgow in the spring of 1957 and came to London. István began work immediately. She'd felt unbearably alone. She missed Glasgow and the Blums, Eve's English lessons, discussing politics with Dr Blum. She missed Mark, their afternoons drawing at the art gallery, his constant, no doubt exaggerated expressions of envy at her talent. She missed hurrying with him through the dark, busy streets, loud with the noise of starlings, to meet Dan who'd been at piano lessons, the little Italian café in Sauchiehall Street, the mugs of hot chocolate, the tram ride home when the three of them would sit upstairs at the front, crammed into the little glassed in compartment, watching the lights on the Clyde. She missed Dan.

Even phoning then was difficult. It's hard to imagine now the whole burdensome procedure of stuffing coins into a black box in a kiosk, pressing buttons, button A and button B, before the money almost inevitably disappeared with a clatter while the familiar, longed-for voice on the other end of the line dropped into silence. She phoned the Blums once or twice in desperation, to speak to anyone who answered. Once Dan did, but the phone box stole her money, leaving her frantically pressing buttons as his voice retreated beyond reach. She had no money to phone back.

Dan had seemed inexplicably distant when she left, almost angry. There had been no opportunity to ask him why.

What was it Joe said the other night?

'Why don't you get in touch? A letter of condolence or something?'

She wonders if he'd think it strange.

In London, within a very short time, István began to prosper. He was a popular teacher, interesting and funny. He pursued his research with vigour, travelling a great deal, his life apart from hers, in lecture rooms and libraries and fellows' dining-rooms, the inner spaces of institutions men like István, from habit and a perception of right, inhabit. He was pleased with his career, ambitious.

She was alone, and after she discovered the Highgate ponds she began to go daily in good weather, in the creeping chill of autumn too, unwilling to let go of necessary routine, the walks there and back, the changing, swimming in the duck-floating water. Swimming. Freud, no doubt, would have had something to say on the matter. In a way he'd have been right, the womb-like comfort of water, a place of succour, with other women, ones who would show her what was possible, that one could both suffer and progress, maintain, through every experience, the ability to live, to go into shops and buy fish and milk and magazines, put on flowered swimsuits and swim. They've died in the past few years, lots of her early swimming friends, Dolly, Helga's mother at ninety, just a couple of years ago, more of them, women she loved, Maud, Dorrie, Flo, friends, people to whom she owed debts of gratitude, Margaret Braithwaite too, four or five years ago. She's been to more funerals than she can count, more orations for brave, indomitable women, the ones who, with Mark, Daniel, Helga, made her begin again.

She hears Mark now: 'You can, Anci, you can,' although she doesn't know what had made her believe him, because he couldn't possibly have known.

Exile, a word which can't capture the bleakness of the reality of relinquishing your life, the past, your language, everything you've known. There are moments still when she thinks of her last day in Hungary, how she lived through it not knowing it was the last.

What did she imagine her life would be? She can't remember or didn't know. Nothing, or what she'd agreed to in the very moment when she wasn't capable of deciding. Marriage, children perhaps. When she thought of children she was made eager by the prospect, but it didn't happen. She didn't conceive. The memory of years of childlessness will never go away, years she had to fill with effort, tormenting herself with Eve's word, *troubled*. What stopped her from conceiving? Was it something which froze the insides, killed the sparking mechanisms of the body's desire to reproduce? Was it a deep knowledge of the nature of the world which damped the body's exuberance? Was it semi-starvation during her formative years? The haphazard nature of her menstruation? Something wrong or blocked or missing?

'All of them possibly, or none,' Margaret Braithwaite said, Margaret, fellow morning-swimmer, obstetrician, to whom she spoke diffidently one day, who briskly arranged tests and examinations and all the horrid things which had to be done. Nothing to explain it had been found.

'All looks as it should to me but, my dear, there's so much more than one knows about when it comes to reproduction. Most things in medicine, in fact. You won't like my advice, but it's all I've got. Take your mind off it. Do something else. Be busy. Don't hope and don't give up. One never knows.'

She hadn't minded the advice in the absence of anything better. She did as she was told. She drew and swam and began to make the garden from the ruins.

For years, every day was blanketed in a waking fog of anxious fear. Now there would be names for it, acronyms, tablets. Then, there was the slow living out of days, the repetition of the years of childhood, dreading morning, dreading evening, lightening sometimes but never going away. From here, the distance of the years, she's glad that she was sad in a time when sadness was still allowed, when to feel grief was natural, when no-one tried to drug her or make her describe the way she felt, when she could turn her sadness among the rotting leaves under her spade, delve her hands deep into earth to spread roots and firm down soil, when she could make herself work, teach herself what she must do to live. She swam, and for years she did as Margaret had told her to do, didn't allow herself to weep for what she thought was the death of her genes, her family withering within her. She dug the garden and hauled away the bricks and inside, carried Józsi, like the pregnancy she was denied. During the years she had to fill, she could reflect at will on the nature of time, which seems so long but is so short.

It was on her walks to and from the ponds that she began to pick up conkers and leaves and take them home to draw. She bought paper and pencils and inks and began teaching herself about small creatures, picking up dead birds in gloved hands, often to the consternation of passers-by, putting them into plastic bags to carry home. She spent days watching magpies and crows, in summer, sitting by the pond in her swimsuit drawing ducks and moorhens. She took books from the library, studied anatomy from the works of artists and from plates in anatomy books. István noticed and suggested the names of publishers.

The day her first illustrations were accepted, she phoned Mark in New York. He was as pleased, as excited as she, shouting 'I'm so proud of you!' through the fog of distance. Those were illustrations of a story about a small girl and a mouse. Now, across her page, a series of courtiers and rogues, smirking and fawning, process towards the corner where a small, fat man stands naked, holding aloft an invisible garment between his two, plump hands.

She was over forty when she conceived. She'd had no idea she was pregnant. Margaret, near retiring by then, noticed before she did, looking at her with a critical gaze one early morning at the pond.

'You're very pale, Anci. Why?'

Next day, she carried a urine sample in her swimming bag to hand over. She still didn't believe it could be possible when Margaret phoned.

'My dear,' she said, 'I think you're going to be pleased...'

She even swam during pregnancy, Helga and Dorrie and Maud and all the others taking a brisk interest in her progress, spoiling her, bringing her healthy things they'd cooked or baked or grown, books and papers they'd written on relevant subjects, baby clothes they'd made specially for her.

Sometimes now when she's swimming, she believes that the years of her life were in that water, years of emptiness and pain. She dissolved the past into those ponds and when, a few years ago, they drained the ponds and scooped out tons of mud from the bottom, she felt they were carrying away her history and was glad. By then, her children were growing, like the trees in the garden she planted in the days after she returned from hospital with each of her sons. Helga questioned the wisdom of her digging so soon after giving birth.

'Anci, are you sure you should be doing that?'

She'd just laughed. Now, she'd thought, she could do anything.

István refused to be present when the boys were born.

'I'd rather be in the cave with Cyclops,' he said, and she was relieved because she knew she'd rather he was, too, than to have had him there. He was, even more than she, from a different generation, a good, devoted father who never allowed his sons' ages to protect them from his expectations, throwing them esoterica as he'd have thrown a stick to a dog. Their cheerful resistance never failed to delight her.

Why did she stay with István? Because it never occurred to her to do anything else. Hers has been a life without design, clinging to the continuity to be found in fortitude, endurance. Unfashionable now, she knows, probably justifiably so. If they'd parted, at the very least, she'd have lost half her memory.

István's fame and success never surprised her. She looked with equanimity on his regular appearances on television and radio, the reverential praise which greeted each successive book. They even had to remove their name from the phone book to avoid the unwelcome attention of admirers, students, often women, who'd phone to ask for him, their tone uncertain when they heard her voice. She thinks of an evening some years ago, herself, Helga, a few other female friends in the kitchen, cooking, drinking wine, hearing István's voice suddenly issue from the radio, talking portentously, with many classical references, on the subject of love and lovers. One of her friends had glanced towards her, it seemed anxiously in the second before she, and the others had begun to laugh. They'd laughed until the tears dripped, laughter, which like fire, erupted in snatches all evening, an evening which for all of them after that, felt light, touched with their own power.

István died within three days, after a succession of strokes. At his bedside, she remembered conversations they'd had over years.

'I'd better go quickly when I do,' he'd say. 'You wouldn't have much patience with a lingerer.'

'What nonsense, darling,' she always said, knowing he was right.

She thinks of what she didn't know of István, or what she may have known really, in that space inside oneself where knowledge of the truth resides. She wonders if she's always known quite well what Józsi was about to tell her.

The only person she's ever told was Mark.

'Mark, please, don't tell anyone,' she'd said.

'Anci, I won't.'

And now Mark is dead. She thinks of the notice in the newspaper. 'Looked after with devotion.' She thinks of how Dan must be feeling now. They were close, Mark and Dan. He was kind to her, more than kind. She thinks of his playing the piano for her, his sweetness, his smile, lovely Dan.

'Why don't you get in touch? A letter of condolence or something?' Joe said. She'd said she couldn't but perhaps she can. A letter.

The heap of Michael's possessions lies in the hall, waiting to be packaged and sent. It's afternoon by the time she feels that she's done enough work to justify a break. She rummages a box from the hall cupboard and dumps everything in.

Late afternoons are fragile at this time of year, about to be taken over by the clock and by darkness but today, it's still bright. Carrying the box in her arms, she goes into a shop on the way to the post office and buys marshmallows and a couple of tins of cocoa for Michael and, at the counter, adds some small Hallowe'en things, a small stuffed bat with a red satin cape, a bean bag witch, a large, revolting hairy hand made of rubber. He'll be delighted, such a child still, loving Hallowe'en as he did when he was little and as she walks on, she sees it all, these occasions, her life, her small happinesses, her children, the way in which women endure for the recompense of ephemeral things, the light in the garden, the brief admiration of other men, the kaleidoscope of fragments.

She will, she decides emphatically, phone Dan. There's a debt she owes him. Repayment in kind is the very least she can do. Definitely. She'll phone.

Chapter 28

Glasgow, late autumn 2001

The months Mark and I spent together here seem now so brief, the life we created for that short time, time which, shamefully, I'd dreaded for being open-ended, an eternity of questions with no answers. Even driving Mark back here from the airport, I felt that weight of gloom, a sense of the inexorable hanging over me, the inescapable knowledge of the beginning and the ending, all that his arrival would mean. It was only when he saw Morning and cried, exclaiming with joy, planning straight away where we'd hang her, where she'd look best, that I felt the weight of lead I'd carried in my heart lighten and lift and I knew that it was a result of Mark's courage and not of mine, that it would always be this way because he was brave and I was not.

As I'd expected, there was the initial unease of beginnings. For the first few days we tested, measured one another, learned what to do and what not to do, circling, establishing territory and rights like a pair of elderly bulldogs. We were ridiculously polite, constantly asking the other if what we were doing was really what the other wanted to be doing. As it was, I don't think either of us cared, we were both relieved to be together at the end of what, for Mark, must have been wrenching process, leaving a place he loved, where he had lived for most of his life. What amazed me was that he seemed so instantaneously easy here, amused or thrilled in turns by everything, people, the flat, the city, the preparations I'd made with such anxiety and consternation, fussing as I had done over every packet of oatcakes or jar of marmalade, wondering if he'd like them. He did like them. He liked everything. His enthusiasm shamed me.

'Where did you find this!' 'Wow, look at this!' 'Hey, Dan, this is fabulous!'

The first thing we did together, a couple of days after Mark arrived, was to hang Morning. I wouldn't let him help me lift her, but he directed operations, yelling, 'A little more to the right, no, not quite,' both of us convulsed with laughter until she was in place, where she is now, flying in serenity. As we switched the lamps on that evening,

I thought of her counterpart, Night. Night, with her children, Sleep and Death.

As I'd anticipated, he was delighted by the piano, too. On his first evening, he insisted I play after dinner. I did, some Chopin nocturnes.

'My God, Dan! Every bit as good as you were,' he said.

It was on the first days that we developed the habits we'd maintain until the end of his life, eating well, celebrating for no reason, going out for evening walks. That we did on many evenings, in all weather, with conspiratorial delight. We went out after dark, or later, after the clocks went forward, at dusk so that we could peer through the lit windows of other people's houses. It had a feeling of the clandestine, both of us setting off knowing that it was with the aim of gaining glimpses into other people's lives.

'Look, Dan, the witching hour,' Mark would say, 'the hour when nosy buggers go about.'

'If they're not pouring their first gin of the day,' I'd reply and we'd set out at first, in March and April, in our long dark coats, like burglars, rejoicing in the notion that we were stealing from hapless householders, dragging beauty out through their magnificent windows, cataloguing their possessions, coveting at will. It was a time of day we loved. By late summer, our walks had become circumscribed. We still went, but our routes were shorter, our pace slower.

At first, it was almost difficult to remember why Mark was here. For those first few weeks he marched about Glasgow, renewing his acquaintance with the city, visiting places he'd wanted to see, our old school for some reason I couldn't quite understand, the Art School, the Art Gallery, the Burrell. He busied himself buying things to replace ones he'd left behind, a computer, his precious coffee machine. He'd report to me on his daily adventures, what he'd seen and where he'd been. One of his the first things he did was go to see the GP I'd arranged for him. Even that pleased him.

'Dan, it was incredible! Such a nice guy! He took me through everything and when I asked him about payment, he said, "Payment? What payment?" Can you imagine!'

The 'everything' the GP discussed was what would be done, or available in the months to come, pain relief, nursing care. 'We'll always be here,' he'd said and Mark was reassured. He seemed unexpectedly happy, and well, so well that there were even times in the first two or three weeks when I wondered if the tumour really had recurred. It had. I accepted that one day in early April. Mark was standing his kitchen with a carton of milk in his hand. I saw him turn in the middle of the floor, trying to locate the fridge.

The moment was symbolic, when I began to see how it would be, a process speeding through April, May. Pesach was in April. Nira and Dalit both came up from London for the first Seder. I cooked and Mark made his famous *charoseth*. I watched him, the odd way he held his left hand, adjusting the knife, moving the apple uncertainly on the chopping board.

Even at the end of April I was still working, spending most of the day in my own flat, but with only half my usual concentration. I'd phone him every morning.

'Any plans for the day?'

'I need some things for the computer. I'll have a walk into town.'

I'd think about him all day, and in the evening he'd show me what he'd bought. I began to feel reluctant to go home in the evenings, but I did.

One day we went to Edinburgh and, walking up the Mound towards Chambers Street, I thought I saw a change in his gait, a slight difference in the way he walked, although I could neither have described it nor been sure that it was there.

By early May, I thought I noticed a tremor in his left hand.

'Hey, Dan, can you see anything odd?' he said, holding out his hand. I told him that I couldn't.

I began to worry. I spent more time here, arriving in the middle of the morning when sometimes he was still in bed. For the first time, he admitted that he felt tired. Every morning I'd take the leather rucksack he sent me as a birthday present a few years ago, and on the walk over here I'd cram it with magazines and newspapers and cartons of milk and food from the deli for lunch. Packing the bag reminded me, for some reason, of when the girls were small, the rituals of nappies and dummies and bottles, things which had to be carried, imperatives which felt permanent but weren't, which, in truth, were momentary and transient, whose preciousness one realised only after the need for them had gone. When I thought of it, both of them and Mark, I'd feel my heart turn and roll with love and anxiety and fear.

In early May I noticed a change in the way he turned his head, moved his arm. Reading, he held his head at an angle, looking puzzled. It was as I'd imagined during my swim in New York, the knocking over of things on his left side, an imbalance in him which made me anxious for his every move. He said to me one day about then,

'I've left an article about Christian Boltanski on your desk for you,' and I took it as a signal that my place was there. I asked him if I would like me to move in, and he said,

'Oh, Dan, yes. I haven't liked to suggest it.'

It was easier being there. At first, I didn't have to do very much, just be vigilant, just catalogue, one by one, his losses.

In late May, Mark talked to me about Anci. From the way he did, I could tell that he was anxious to have things said, as if, by delaying, he might miss the chance to say them. I could almost imagine a diary entry saying 'Discuss Anci!' We were sitting outside on the steps on a mild evening, with a before-dinner drink.

'Dan, we've got to talk about Anci,' he said.

For a moment, I thought of saying, 'Why?' Trying to deflect him, to deflect pain or sadness, feeling my breath stolen, a simultaneous slick of chill and warmth down the length of my back.

'I know we do.'

'You know that I kept in touch with her?'

'Yes. I always wondered. Then I saw her books in your bookcase.'

'Did you look at the letters?'

'No.'

'Why not?'

'Because I was afraid of what they'd say.'

'Silly bugger,' he said, 'I wish you had.'

What he told me that evening changed both past and present. I've had months to think about it, but still I can't believe my blindness, still can't accept my capacity for rancour. Would I have acted differently towards both Mark and Anci if I'd known what it was she told him? Most definitely, I would. I'd have known of her unhappiness, that she'd been married to István for only days before she came to us, that she'd had to decide to stay or leave while Soviet tanks were still shelling Budapest, the day after her brother was killed. I'd have known that her brother had been about to tell her what she already thought anyway, which was that István was some kind of high-ranking officer in the secret police or in the government department which controlled them.

'What made her think that?'

'Everything, she said. He had lots of money, apparently a pretty rare phenomenon at the time. He'd spent time in Moscow when all the people who eventually took over Hungary were there. He was never straight with a story. He wasn't to be seen during the uprising, then came back and rushed her away. She said that all the signs were there, once she saw them. He arranged their documents in her name.'

'He wasn't Goldmann?'

'He said he was. Apparently he'd always told her that but she'd never quite believed him.'

'How in hell did she ever have anything to do with him?'

'Come on, he was her teacher at university. She was eighteen, straight out of some fucking orphanage. He wooed her. I never saw the attraction, but I could imagine how she did. She was trying to find ways of ending their relationship when the uprising began. She'd begun to realise what he was.'

'Did she love him?

'Of course not. And she didn't love me, either. There was only one person she did love.'

'Who?'

'Oh Jesus, Dan, you are as stupid as I thought.'

Then June, July, August. We spent the summer, on the days when he felt well enough, driving to places he'd picked from books he'd bought in New York, castles, gardens, some I'd been to before and some I hadn't. I avoided gardens with steep paths and precipices but plenty were walled, with flat flagstones, wide steps, stone benches and ponds, his favourites. I was always terrified in those steep, circular castle stairwells when I had to manoeuvre myself to be behind him as he walked up, in front as he walked down. The ladies with the tartan sashes who showed visitors round assumed from his accent that he was a tourist. He'd engage them in conversation, with his usual charm and when I'd hear him say, 'I've come back here to live,' always, I'd hear a different ending.

Wandering through the rose gardens, past yew hedges, clipped box giving off the scent which for me is the scent of history, and Scotland, I'd think how at one we must have seemed. I imagine some people would have thought us a gay couple, had we not so obviously have been brothers. Even then I wondered. Mark's face was becoming rounder, with that characteristic steroid look. I was grateful for the steroids. Dexamethasone kept him high and singing.

The evening Mark first mentioned Anci, we continued our conversation after we'd gone back inside. He had champagne in the fridge. I lit candles and we sat over dinner and raised our glasses to one another.

'When did you speak to her last?'

'Three years ago, maybe. A bit less. After Tal left, certainly.'

'Did you tell her?'

'I did.'

'You didn't contact her after István died?'

'I thought about it but what was I going to say? I'm sorry István's died? Anyway, I knew I was ill by then. I couldn't not have told her that.'

'Mark, why did she stay with him for so long?'

'Christ knows. A different generation. Everything that had happened to her. I don't know. She was miserable for years and then she had her sons. She's made a life.'

Noah and Tam phoned Mark often, and in late June came to see him for a few days. I moved back to my own flat while they were there but was fearful every moment that they wouldn't be vigilant when they were crossing roads with him, that they wouldn't check the temperature of water for his shower, that they'd leave him alone with the kettle, expect him to plug things in, take glasses out of the cupboard, open bottles. When they left I was worried he'd be upset, but he was calm.

'Great to see them,' he said, apparently unconcerned. They too seemed to have come to some kind of acceptance, seeing, I suppose, how the next few months would be.

After we talked, Mark told me there was letter he'd written to Anci in his desk.

'I want you to give it to her. Dan, phone her first.'

'I couldn't'.

'Jesus Christ, Dan, you sound like a twelve-year-old.'

'That's what I am. A twelve-year-old in a wrinkly hide. You've discovered.'

'Fuck it, I've always known it. But Dan, listen to me, you've only got one chance of anything. Do what I say.'

About the same time, I got a phone call from the estate agent, asking if we'd thought any more about buying the flat. It didn't matter because we still had months of the lease left. All the same, I wanted to think more about it. I hesitated for a second before telling him that my brother was very ill. I said that we'd decide at a later date.

'I hope he'll be better soon, sir,' the lad said.

'Thank you,' I replied to him, wondering afterwards why I didn't leave it at that, why I said, 'I'm afraid its not really that kind of illness.' Was it to hear the start, the hesitation? Was it to shock him into leaving us alone a little longer?

'Oh, I'm sorry.' I heard an unspoken anxiety in the estate agent's voice. The words there behind his hesitation, the words, 'Oh, I'm sorry, sir, I almost don't like to mention it. It's one of our rules. Tenants are not allowed to die in our flats.'

But they are. They can do whatever they like as long as it's legal. As long as it's quiet, does not damage the fine hardwood fittings, the Arts and Crafts features, the stained glass windows, as long as it does not constitute a hazard to the other occupants of the building, as long as there is no trace of its ever having happened.

He began to get headaches. He was given painkillers but there was a residue of pain, something left, was how he described it. I'd stroke his forehead or massage his neck in a way that once, I could never have imagined. In a way, touching him comforted me. The closeness of him almost took away my fear of the time ahead.

Chapter 29

Glasgow, spring, summer, 2001

There's no doubt. He was right. Mark feels no regret. From the moment of raising the plane's blind to the glow of red winter sunrise, to the abrupt alteration from metallic, wrinkled sea to green, brown, rain-glistening land, he has known.

His rightness has manifested itself in everything, his pleasure in seeing Dan, in the streets, changed but still familiar, in the flat, Morning, waiting against her wall. Dan, he thinks, has provided wonderfully for him, the flat, the building, his thoughtful preparations. On the first evening, after Dan has gone home, he unpacks, tidies away his clothes, arranges his pens and papers on his desk. In bed, he listens to the night sounds of another country, dissonant engines on the roads, the occasional plane overhead. Even the air feels different. He touches the scar on his head. He has brought his dangerous companion home.

It's tricky at first, negotiating his way in someone else's life, someone to whom he has said so emphatically that he will not be a burden or a nuisance. He and Dan, after a few days of shadow-boxing, of being too eager and too polite, relax. Dan goes back to his flat to work, while for him, there's a city to be regained. For the first few days, he's busy with tasks, buying what he needs, walking round shops with the pleasurable air of being on holiday, in a place where he now lives. The concept's odd. He wonders how long it would take him to feel properly that he lives here. Now, he supposes, he never will.

He goes to visit the GP Dan has arranged for him. The premises are shabby, some of the clientele equally so, a pale, wizened, coughing bunch in the waiting room, but when he thinks of Jaegerson's office, the maze of corridors, of Jaegerson himself, it's without nostalgia. The doctor, a young man, Dr Bruce, like the junior staff in the hospital in New York, a teenager in an adult's guise, is good-humoured and efficient. He looks at Mark's notes.

'Excellent decision,' he says.

'Which?'

'To come back here.'

The future is discussed but Dr Bruce is reassuring; care, nurses, pain-relief, he deals with it all. Mark asks about payment. To his amazement, Dr Bruce waves away the question with his hand.

On most evenings, he and Dan go for walks. Their delight is to look in through other people's windows. They're huge windows, unlike New York, not halfway to the sky. He likes being a voyeur. It suits his situation. Every day he is more conscious of being slightly on the edge, moving outside the rest of life. It may, he thinks, be the return of the complex partial seizures, the 'strangeness', but it hardly matters because now everything is strange.

Walking in the streets of Glasgow, Mark notices that something is gone, the starlings, their wonderful, crazy evening singing. He's disappointed. He thought they'd still be here.

Now more than ever, Mark is glad of his lists. He has to refer to them often. He has to visit all the places on them, ones which he has already decided, with only minor retrospection, that he will, his school, the synagogue, the Art Gallery. He walks past his and Dan's old school which has been converted into flats, ugly ones. It seems oddly suitable.

In the synagogue which, on the morning he goes, a weekday, is empty, he sits for a moment, having been let in by the caretaker, on one of the rows of empty seats. He opens the prayer book in front of him. The text, blackly, whitely arranged, squarish letters stopping, stolid on the line, underhung by dots and lines of vowels, is where it should be but it moves slightly, sideways, sliding, switching briefly, on and off. He has to shift his head to read a few words, *melech, yom, baruch,* king, day, blessed. He takes his glasses off, to be lost for a moment in deep, dark space.

The Art Gallery is unchanged, the scent, the rooms of trains and animals and costumes, all the same. Upstairs, in the stained glass cloisters, he places Anci at the end, sitting on the floor with her drawing board, sketching the marble statue of a girl. The stairs are broad. On the way down, with his right hand, he holds the wide stone balustrade. It's one of the things he loves here, the sensation of sandstone under his hand, the look of light on slate, the feeling that he has come back to what he knows.

For the first weeks he's here Dan is still working, which allows

Mark to be alone. Their evenings together, after their walks, are companionable. One or other of them cooks, or they go out for meals. He lights candles always, and insists on celebration. It's important, he thinks, to celebrate. The days and evenings are pleasant, but make him lazy. He sleeps for too long, feels guilty when he wakens. Perhaps, he tells himself, it's only because he's free of the demands of a structured life. It's not the only thing he feels guilty about. He's allowed himself to put on weight.

'God, I'm fat!' he says to Dan, pinching at himself.

'Nonsense. A little portly, maybe.'

Dan's like that. He lies from kindness, claims he doesn't notice the tremor which has begun in Mark's hand when actually, he does.

At Pesach in April, he phones Noah and Tam and Berndt and Ali to wish them a good Seder. He thinks of last year's Seder, of Lisa's singing. This year, Dan's girls come up from London and the evening's lovely, this joyful, easy Seder, his last.

Time, for Mark, begins to feel strange. It's as if he's losing time. He's losing space too, losing himself in space. One day it starts. He turns, doesn't know exactly where he is. It's the beginning. It happens often, he's lost in the kitchen, in the corridors of the flat. When Dan moves in, he's glad. He's no longer certain on his own.

The seasons change, but here they seem to change imperceptibly. He'd forgotten. Early summer is little different from spring, late summer only a little brighter. In June, when Noah and Tam come to visit, Dan moves back to his own flat. Mark loves seeing his children but misses Dan. It's only for a few days, but there are things he's afraid of without Dan. He's afraid of roads. He's afraid of water. He's afraid of everything on his left. Space seems to have disappeared. Often, now, he turns to nothing, turns and turns and turns.

It's like this over the months, logging each loss, each failing, like doorways; through this one, there may be something, which will trip him, or will fail to open for him, something which will lead him to the edge of a dark stretch of water with no barrier and no sound to warn him.

There's no pattern, nothing to predict and so, when he talks to Dan about Anci and István, he feels it's none too soon. The relief of having done it overwhelms him. He might have died without Dan knowing, and now he won't. He's told Dan where the letter for Anci is. 'Give it to her,' he says, 'will you promise me?' and he thinks Dan will. When it comes to the telling, he tells Dan everything he knows. He wonders why he worried about secrets. What can be a secret now? Specially since it's such a pleasure to watch the moments of happiness cross Dan's face.

In summer, he and Dan go on journeys together. They drive and walk, sit in shade in lovely gardens. They walk but his walking is failing, his left leg forcing him to an uneven shuffle. Dan buys him a stick which he doesn't want to use. Dan uses it instead.

'Aren't you ashamed of yourself,' he says to Dan. 'People will see and know you've stolen it from a poor old limping man.'

Often, when they're out for the day, he snoozes in the car, wakens to rain, to Dan's music playing, evening sunshine. He worries that Dan is getting tired. He looks thin.

'Are you okay, Dan?' he asks. 'Would you like to rest?' but Dan just laughs.

Every morning he says, 'Dan, check the calendar. What's today?'

Every day is new moon, full moon, a saint's day for an unknown saint, a poet's birthday.

Time is too fast. There's a tingling in his hand and arm, and one day Dan has to take a plug from his hand after he's spent a long time trying to fit it into a socket.

'Damnable European plugs,' he says, 'don't any of them work?'

Rosh Hashanah, he sees from the calendar, is in September, the middle. He'd like to see it. He will feel complete. September. That's soon. It's soon.

At night, he sleeps and doesn't sleep. Nights are long. Sleep is like a waking dream, a sleeping dream. He wakens to darkness. Dan is there, saying,

'Shall I read to you?' Mark asks for the Psalms in Scots. Often, not always. Dan complains,

'Christ, Mark, must I? It reminds me of Burns competitions at school.'

'Just read it!' he says and Dan does. Sometimes, it's poetry. Dan falls asleep in the middle of reading.

Sarah. He remembers Sarah.

'Dan, have you spoken to Mrs Spellman recently?'

'Yup. The other day.'

'How's Sarah?'

'The same. Doesn't know what's going on.'

'Like me.'

'Idiot.'

Autumn. Early. A girl comes in now every day. She's pretty and serious and is called Angela. She's a nurse. She does things for him he wouldn't want Dan to have to do.

'Sorry,' she says, 'I know it's undignified.'

'Don't worry,' he says, 'I don't think that's where my dignity lives.'

Dan plays the piano for him. It's wonderful to hear it from the other room, to waken to the sound. There's his television, which he sees but doesn't watch. It flickers past, an eternity of nonsense. One day it isn't there. It doesn't matter. The light hurts his eyes.

'Where's the television?'

Dan says something he can't remember. The display on his clock shows the days in green. It is September.

September. Autumn now. Leaves scud past the window on the sunlight. There is sun in the morning. When it's winter, the afternoons will be like a sad guillotine. He will not be here in winter. It's as well when there is darkness. Light is a signal of the mind's beginning. When you close your eyes, there's still light, patterns of it, broken with the darkness. We're the same as all things, as plants, as doves on roofs, we incline towards the light. He thinks of consciousness. We're conscious too, until we sleep.

Angela is here often. She and Dan help him drink water. His mouth is dry. He would, if he could, lift his own glass to his lips. In the evenings, Dan helps him drink sips of wine, champagne.

'*L'chaim!*' he says without fail. Oddly, he's no longer hungry.

One evening, Dan lights candles and says that it's Rosh Hashanah tomorrow. He recites the *shechayiyonu*. Mark thinks of the words in

English, 'Who hast kept us in life, and hast preserved us, and enabled us to reach this season.' It's Erev Rosh Hashanah, and they both say 'Good *Yomtov*!' and hug one another. Mark's hug is lop-sided. He apologises.

'It's not half-hearted,' he says.

In the night, he thinks of the psalm, *Man, as he stans, his days are like gerss, like a flowir o' the field he grows...* is there anything more beautiful? He thinks of the angel. Morning. There's Night, too, somewhere. Dan has told him. Night with her children, Sleep and Death. His books on the brain describe sleep as 'the little death.' That is beautiful too.

The girl is here again. She smiles.

'Hi Mark,' she says.

The cornice is white. It's curled with acanthus leaves, heavy with grapes. Outside, there are clouds. Grey and ochre, and purple. He can see doorways and hydrangeas. Lime trees in whose sticky emanations insects catch and drown. This is the only world. This is a house of treasures.

It ebbs and ebbs and ebbs. He listens to his breathing and it is as if he is a sound in his own ears. He sees the rising of his chest. He looks out and the sky fills the window.

Chapter 30

Glasgow, late autumn, 2001

It happened so easily and with such difficulty, Mark's death. After the summer, it was as if there was a response in him to autumn approaching, to winter, as if his disease listened to the seasons, closed up against the darkness. Neither of us knew what to do. We had to steer our way as we did as children, riding one bicycle together, uncertainly, dangerously through the twilight.

Slow during spring, Mark's disease progressed through the summer, gaining speed. The tremor in his hands grew worse.

'Look! You must be able to see it now!' he said, almost in triumph. That time, I admitted that I could. The hesitation in his gait I'd seen in Edinburgh grew more marked, grew to a shuffle, a limp as he tried to find a way to disguise it.

He still loved to eat and drink well. He looked forward to going to the supermarket, stumbling out of the door shouting,

'Dan, have you got the list?' Cooking, as an activity, was wonderful. It took up time. He'd sit and talk to me in the kitchen as I cooked. It was lovely, companionable. We were both scared of empty time, of boredom.

Everything in me watched, noticed. He had to look momentarily for his cutlery before eating. He couldn't read a page without half of it disappearing. I helped him dress, otherwise he buttoned everything awry. I had to open his bottle of scent.

'Here, here, and here,' he'd say, pointing imperiously as I dabbed it on.

I watched and watched. I watched through days and nights. I watched in the spring light, through the summer and its fading. I watched as I had every moment with him since I knew of his illness, during the time we had spent since our meeting in New York, watching. His very substance changed in a way which frightened me, made me cherish him but I was scared, not of Mark but of that which interposed itself silently and perpetually between us.

We'd had a good summer. After it, Mark looked tanned.

'I don't look bad today, do I?' he'd say, peering into the mirror, amazing me yet again with his capacity for snatching moments of normality. 'Fat, though!'

Each one was a kind of victory. He set dates, rejoiced if they passed. I found it profoundly painful. He wanted to see in Rosh Hashanah.

I have a small file of Noah's letters on my desk, no longer hidden away.

'Dear Uncle Dan,' he wrote in his impressive writing, writing which looks as if he delegates one of his crows to write for him, black and organic, angled lines of trees and beaks and claws, at variance with the words, the gentleness of Noah, the sorrow, the care expressed in the sharpened lines. 'The crows are beginning to settle for winter. They find mates early in the year and by now have begun to prepare and store and consider winter. Their plumage is back to perfection again, they look like they've all been and bought heavy new winter coats. Winter's the time when we tie up what we've been working on all summer. It's good to have such a goal in front of me at this time.'

I spoke to him quite often too, and to Tamar. Their phone calls became routine, more like waiting than enquiring.

Even when he was fading fast, we drank together in the evenings. We lit candles. From the first, we celebrated everything. We celebrated Mondays. We celebrated the first day of a month, the last. We celebrated Baudelaire's birthday, the solstices, Rosh Chodesh, anything on the calendar, and when a friend gave us a French calendar we celebrated saints, good Jews as we are. Were. Mark became obsessed by saints. He found a saint for internet users, 'My patron saint, St Isidore!' I was glad of our celebrations. Mark lit candles and our lives blazed small and bright there, an evening before darkness.

Late summer was hard, the decreasing light seemed to mirror every loss.

Then there was that terrible day, September 11th. In the morning I was in the kitchen reading the newspaper when I heard the first news flashes. Mark, fortunately, was sleeping. My first thought was to move his television, which I did, wheeling it out as quietly as I could.

Waking later, he said,

'Where's the TV?'

'Oh, it's gone,' I said, 'to be serviced.'

'Serviced?'

'Yes, it has to be serviced every year. It's the law here.'

'Really? You're kidding. Weird,' he said, laughing before he fell asleep.

Of course, I watched the television obsessively in my room during the nights that followed. It felt duplicitous, but I thought of him searching in his failing brain for names. Worse, finding some. He never knew. He asked for the radio but I put on music for him instead. He didn't complain. Latterly, putting the earphones from the stereo over Mark's ears, my hands trembled at the mere knowledge of the fragility of the systems which lay inside that hood of bone. I bought earphones which I thought would be comfortable for him and eased them wide over his head, levering the pads of foam against his skin, afraid of the pressure from without as from the pressure within.

At night, when he couldn't sleep, I read to him. He always insisted first on the bloody Psalms in Scots. He had a *New Yorker Book of Poems,* too, a huge thing and I picked from that at random, falling asleep over Elizabeth Bishop and Anne Sexton.

'You fell asleep,' he'd say accusingly when I woke suddenly in that horrible chill of night.

They were quick, the last few weeks, the last few days. By then the nurse came in several times a day, calm and undemonstrative, a girl with straight dark hair, who conveyed in a way I found uncanny the sense that nothing much was happening. She taught me the everyday nature of death, made it ordinary. Angela, her name. She was there, took over, banished me, sent me to make coffee, to buy her newspaper, Angela who, after it was over, after Mark had, with effort, ceased to breathe, came in quietly through the front door as if she already knew.

In the last days, often, he smiled. He looked at me. I wasn't sure that he could even see me. During those days I felt guilty eating or drinking. I'd go into the kitchen and pour myself a glass of wine, almost furtively, and the acuteness of my knowledge that I would never drink with Mark again would flood me with a sensation which seemed to replace my blood with ice. I knew he wouldn't hear, but I closed the fridge door with a passionate care of quietness. I laid my glass down in utter silence. I heard my own swallowing resounding through the rooms.

Erev Rosh Hashanah, I lit the candles for Mark in his room. I said the *shechayiyonu*. We hugged each other, wished each other 'Good *Yomtov*.'

He said, more times than I can remember,
  'Phone her. You're going to, aren't you? Promise?'
  'Yes. I told you. Now shut up.'
  I think they were his last words to me.
  I will. I promise.

Dark now, completely dark. I can't stop myself from opening the bottle of scent. Such a sorry thing to do, but I do it nonetheless. I open it and sniff and we're driving, Mark and I, or rather I'm driving with Mark beside me, on the one of the steep, dark green roads between Arbuthnott and Fettercairn. It's quite early in summer and the north-east light and darkness are peerless, weighty black rain clouds leaking brilliance at their edges, the earth the deep, gashed red of the Mearns. We've left the tiny church at Arbuthnott and climbed back up the hill to the car. Mark walks less well these days, but refuses to use the stick I've bought for him, which I use instead. Walking takes a long time but he's alight with his admiration of the church. The graveyard is where Lewis Grassic Gibbon is buried. We talk a bit about his books, about *Sunset Song*, the wonderful Chris Guthrie about whom men could dream. The sky is dark and slate, nearing navy. We're just driving away when the rain begins, magnificent, battering summer rain. It becomes impossible to see through the windscreen, the wipers, even at their fastest, ploughing water vainly across the glass. We stop. The road is narrow, edged with flowers, cow-parsley, daisies, buttercups. It's chilly so I leave the engine running. I do what I've learned to do, look critically at my brother to decide if he is weary, in need or in pain but on this occasion, he seems to be none of those. We smile at one another. We can maintain the illusion that all is well. With his right hand, Mark presses the button and lowers his window and, with some effort, extends his left hand out of the window. We watch, laughing, both of us for no reason, laughing as the water soaks his outstretched hand, the sleeve of his shirt, as with his useless hand, he tries to catch the rain.

Fiction from Two Ravens Press

Love Letters from my Death-bed: by Cynthia Rogerson
£8.99. ISBN 978-1-906120-00-9. Published April 2007

Nightingale: by Peter Dorward
£9.99. ISBN 978-1-906120-09-2. Published September 2007

Parties: by Tom Lappin
£9.99. ISBN 978-1-906120-11-5. Published October 2007

Prince Rupert's Teardrop: by Lisa Glass
£9.99. ISBN 978-1-906120-15-3. Published November 2007

The Most Glorified Strip of Bunting: by John McGill
£9.99. ISBN 978-1-906120-12-2. Published November 2007

One True Void: by Dexter Petley
£8.99. ISBN 978-1-906120-13-9. Published January 2008

Auschwitz: by Angela Morgan Cutler
£9.99. ISBN 978-1-906120-18-4. Published February 2008

The Long Delirious Burning Blue: by Sharon Blackie
£8.99. ISBN 978-1-906120-17-7. Published February 2008

The Last Bear: by Mandy Haggith
£8.99. ISBN 978-1-906120-16-0. Published March 2008

Double or Nothing: by Raymond Federman
£9.99. ISBN 978-1-906120-20-7. Published March 2008

The Falconer: by Alice Thompson
£8.99. ISBN 978-1-906120-23-8. Published April 2008

The Credit Draper: by J. David Simons
£9.99. ISBN 978-1-906120-25-2. Published May 2008

Vanessa and Virginia: by Susan Sellers
£8.99. ISBN 978-1-906120-27-6. Published June 2008

Senseless: by Stona Fitch
£8.99. ISBN 978-1-906120-31-3. Published August 2008

Glenfarron: by Jonathan Falla
£9.99. ISBN 978-1-906120-33-7. Published September 2008

Short Fiction & Anthologies

Riptide: New Writing from the Highlands & Islands: Sharon Blackie & David Knowles (eds)
£8.99. ISBN 978-1-906120-02-3. Published April 2007

Types of Everlasting Rest: by Clio Gray
£8.99. ISBN 978-1-906120-04-7. Published July 2007

The Perfect Loaf: by Angus Dunn
£8.99. ISBN 978-1-906120-10-8. Published February 2008

Cleave: New Writing by Women in Scotland. Edited by Sharon Blackie
£8.99. ISBN 978-1-906120-28-3. Published June 2008

Poetry

Castings: by Mandy Haggith
£8.99. ISBN 978-1-906120-01-6. Published February 2007

Leaving the Nest: by Dorothy Baird
£8.99. ISBN 978-1-906120-06-1. Published July 2007

The Zig Zag Woman: by Maggie Sawkins
£8.99. ISBN 978-1-906120-08-5. Published September 2007

In a Room Darkened: by Kevin Williamson
£8.99. ISBN 978-1-906120-07-8. Published October 2007

Running with a Snow Leopard: by Pamela Beasant
£8.99. ISBN 978-1-906120-14-6. Published January 2008

In the Hanging Valley: by Yvonne Gray
£8.99. ISBN 978-1-906120-19-1. Published March 2008

The Atlantic Forest: by George Gunn
£8.99. ISBN 978-1-906120-26-9. Published April 2008

Butterfly Bones: by Larry Butler
£8.99. ISBN 978-1-906120-24-5. Published May 2008

Meeting the Jet-Man: by David Knowles
£8.99. ISBN 978-1-906120-30-6. Published October 2008

Visit our website for comprehensive information on all of our books and authors – and for much more:

- browse all Two Ravens Press books by category or by author, and purchase them online, post & packing-free (in the UK, and for a small fee overseas)

- there is a separate page for each book, including summaries, extracts and reviews, and author interviews, biographies and photographs

- read our daily blog about life as a small literary publisher in the middle of nowhere – or the centre of the universe, depending on your perspective – with a few anecdotes about life down on the croft thrown in. Includes regular and irregular columns by guest writers – Two Ravens Press authors and others

- visit our online literary magazine, CORVACEOUS. Each monthly issue brings interviews, articles, criticism, and new works of prose and poetry by a variety of authors, both new and established

www.tworavenspress.com